BIG
NAME
FAN

BIG NAME FAN

RUTHIE KNOX
ANNIE MARE

KENSINGTON
PUBLISHING CORP.
kensingtonbooks.com

In honor of all the ships we needed and never got.

*For the fanfiction writers who saved us
when no one else would.*

Cast List

Bexley Simon (Bex)	PI Cora Banks on *Craven's Daughter*
Franklynn Simon (Frankie)	Cineline Studios production assistant and sister of Bex and Vic Simon
Samantha Farmer (Sam)	Former FBI agent Henri Shannon on *Craven's Daughter*
Jen Arnot	Makeup and FX artist for *Craven's Daughter* (deceased)
Luciana de León	Celebrity guest star on *Craven's Daughter*
Amethyst Van Runkel	Producer of Cineline podcast *Craven's Daughter: Cold Case*
Niels Shaughnessy	Head of Cineline Studios
Victoria Simon (Vic)	UC–Davis student and sister of Bex and Frankie Simon
Carl Moreland	Camera One for *Craven's Daughter*
Toni Arnot	Jen Arnot's mother
Bette Holloway	Writer of *Craven's Daughter*; Aaron Gorman's stepdaughter

Georgie Hayworth	Former Chicago detective; script consultant, *Craven's Daughter*
Chaz Morgenstern	Rose, the receptionist on *Craven's Daughter*
Aaron Gorman	Showrunner of *Craven's Daughter*
Josh Miller	Set designer/head of art direction for *Craven's Daughter*
Kim Ryerson	Prop master for *Craven's Daughter*
Marilee Plungkhen	Actor on *Charles Salt*
Dajahne Hammon	Former child guest actor on *Craven's Daughter*
Cicely and Eleanor Greene	Current owners of Chicago apartment used on location
Johnny Kerr	Mike, the building super on *Craven's Daughter*
Saanvi Kaur	Head of United Broadcast Corporation (UBC)
Juan Ramon	Cineline Studios senior stage manager
Judy Lawson	Los Angeles Police Department detective
Haris Ahmadi	Cineline Studios production assistant

BIG
NAME
FAN

Stage 46

There was the infamous balcony.

The first time Bexley Simon stood on it, lit from every direction, her palms damp as she clutched its faux wrought-iron railing in both hands, she'd had one chance left to fake it till she made it. She'd thought her heart might burst from worrying that everyone on this soundstage could tell.

Her footsteps echoed in the empty television studio. Someone had turned on a few can lights. They cast dim pools of yellowish illumination on the cramped spaces of the *Craven's Daughter* set, which had been pulled from the metaphoric mothballs of Cineline Studios on the whim of men in suits who felt that five years off the air was a milestone worthy of a cheesy reunion special.

There was the hallway with its rows of false doors.

Here was the wood-paneled office of PI Cora Banks, a woman Bex hadn't been since the show wrapped.

She turned in a slow circle, finally resting her eyes on the desk with its green banker's lamp discreetly bolted to the scarred wood surface. She knew just where there was a nick in the heavy brass base of that lamp that could catch a thread in her costume and rip it if she wasn't careful.

She rubbed the nick with her finger.

"I can see now why you didn't consider yourself father material." Bex spoke the opening line of the pilot aloud, remembering how the desk had been dressed for the episode with teetering stacks of paper, knocked-over coffee cups, and crushed fast-food contain-ers. She could still feel the bite at her waist where the sound tech had shoved a microphone's battery pack between her skin and the extremely tight waistband of her flippy pink skirt.

For six years, Bex had played sunny former kindergarten teacher Cora Banks, who tracked down her absent father, Joe Craven, with a DNA test just in time to learn he'd died—but he'd left her his detective agency. Naturally, the cause of his death was the first mys-tery tackled by *Craven's Daughter*'s newly minted investigator.

That was eleven years ago now. Bex had been as young and green as the kindergarten teacher she played. Her bright red curls and fresh face had hardly needed to be touched by hair and makeup.

A loud, hollow knock made her jump and whip around. The older of Bex's two younger sisters gave her a tiny wave. "Isn't it the most haunting thing ever to see it resurrected like this?" Frankie wore her preferred all-black uniform of jeans, long-sleeved T-shirt, and boots, with the addition of a headset flattening the halo of short brown curls that always reminded Bex painfully of their late mother. The show Frankie worked for as a production assistant, *Timber Creek Farm*, filmed in a soundstage just down the hall in the same wing of the Cineline studio building. It was likely she had dropped by Stage 46 to see if Bex would really show up for the meeting that studio head Niels Shaughnessy had arranged for her in this oppressively nostalgic setting.

"Haunting?" Bex asked.

"It's so dim and cramped. Full of dark corners. But maybe it just feels that way because I've spent two years on *Timber Creek Farm* with the key light cranked all the way up."

"It's dim, I'll give you that, but I don't know if it's haunted." As Bex said this, she caught a glimpse of the pebbled glass door panel, with its chipped gold-and-red letters reading CRAVEN INVESTIGA-TIONS, and got goosebumps from her scalp to the soles of her feet.

Maybe it was a *little* haunted.

"Some of us came to take a look yesterday," Frankie said. "We heard they'd pulled the set out of storage to get ready for the reunion. Did you know none of the pieces has ever been recycled for other sets? They must've archived it all for an installation or studio tour at some point."

"No doubt."

Frankie sank into one of the leather-padded metal chairs. "It wasn't my idea to sneak in here, but a bunch of the crew are part of your delirious fandom. I showed everyone where I'd carved my initials into the baseboard of the hallway set and told them stories about you and Sam that led to rounds of free beers and tacos, so thank you for that."

Bex laughed. "One of the many perks of being my sister, I'm sure."

"I don't know about perks. Vic says ever since that last syndication deal with yet another streamer, everybody on campus has started wearing those faux-vintage *Craven* T-shirts. Now your face is everywhere she goes."

"And here she thought she'd finally escaped us." Bex and Frankie's younger sister, Vic, was in her second year at UC–Davis.

Bex had seen the T-shirts. There were so, so many with Cora and her partner, Henri. Bex and Sam. She'd lost track of the licensing deals long ago, and it didn't surprise her anymore when she ran across a mug with a *Craven's Daughter* catchphrase on it or a beach towel with Henri and Cora standing under the show's titling. "Vic should be grateful. That syndication bonus is going to pay for her to go to vet school in a few years, and probably open her first clinic."

"Sure, but she can be grateful at the same time she's annoyed at being stalked by your visage. They're not mutually exclusive." Frankie leaned forward. "Speaking of your visage, you know what I saw the other day? One of those BEFORE THEY WERE FAMOUS lists on the Internet. There was a picture of you after you won your first

Tony, crowded into a pizza place in Manhattan with a bunch of other people in evening gowns. You were pretending to bite into the award."

Bex did the mental math. She'd been barely older than Frankie. That night in New York was the culmination of three heady years of lucky breaks and two long-running shows, the second on Broadway. Bex's life was *tops*. Every moment felt like a solo belted out under a spotlight right before intermission.

But then she'd gotten a middle-of-the-night phone call that dropped the curtains and trapped her in a suffocating darkness.

Her parents were suddenly, cruelly gone, wiped from existence by a traffic accident on Highway 270. They'd been on their way home to the Dutch Colonial in Columbus, Ohio, where they lived with Bex's two much-younger sisters—Victoria only five years old, and Franklynn just turned ten.

Bex adored her sisters, and because she couldn't imagine abandoning them to spend the rest of their childhoods subject to the less-than-tender ministrations of the indifferent alcoholic aunt who was the only other candidate to be their guardian, she had stepped into the role. She'd moved Frankie and Vic to Los Angeles, where she leveraged her Tony so hard, she was surprised the metal didn't crack. She got herself a fancy Hollywood agent and manager and told them she wanted the lead on a sitcom or weekly drama. She would settle for nothing less than an everyday acting job with a regular paycheck and a scheduled seasonal hiatus.

There wasn't a bottomless amount of money from the estate and the life insurance payout, but there was enough for two years' bills and groceries. Bex auditioned and studied and networked and auditioned some more. Anytime there was a lull, she called her agent and begged. After two failed pilots, the third one brought her lucky streak back.

She could admit she'd been typecast for the part of Cora Banks. The casting call described Cora as *irrepressible and tireless, the unjaded girl next door whose youth means she's constantly under-estimated.* That was Bex.

At least, it had been.

"I've never seen that picture before," she told Frankie. "Did my skin look as good as yours? Because I honestly can't remember what that's like."

"Sam was on the list, too. From when she was at Yale Drama, a production of *Hamlet*. I linked it to her, and then she texted me a whole bunch of her own pictures from that show. So many." Frankie pulled her giant phone out of one of her pockets. "Want me to show you?"

"Those, I've seen." Bex had looked at them years ago, sitting on the floor of Sam's living room, sharing a pour of whiskey in a crystal highball glass, comparing their early show business stories and pretending they didn't want to taste whiskey from each other's mouths.

Frankie pulled her boots up onto the seat of the chair and wrapped her arms around her knees. "In case you're wondering why I'm bringing up your libertine Broadway era, it's because of this." She flicked a finger toward the PI desk. "Because, in my opinion, you'd be smart to think long and hard about the choices you were making back when you still *made* choices, before Hollywood got its hooks in you. Is this really what you want to be doing?"

Well, shit. Bex's sister had shown up with an agenda. One might call it an *irrepressible, tireless, unjaded* agenda.

Frankie was her housemate. They'd already had half a dozen different versions of this conversation in the days since Bex told her sister she was being considered for the lead role in a new Cineline ensemble medical drama called *Venice Memorial*.

After *Craven's Daughter*, Bex had sworn off TV serials in favor of returning to singing and dancing on Broadway, as well as taking a few thought-provoking roles in the kinds of films that premiered at Sundance. Bex *loved* theater and movies. They felt big enough to contain her. She'd thought it was *her* time, finally, to get back to the life she'd just started to claim when her parents died.

Her plan was a good one, too. It brought her critical acclaim, awards, money. She'd earned the elusive higher echelon of fame and the respect that came with it.

The trouble was that ever since Bex lost *Craven's Daughter*, every part of her life *but* her career had gone off the rails. She missed the show that had given her and her sisters a predictable routine, people they loved, life-changing paychecks, and the closest thing Hollywood offered to stability. A home, almost. She missed the easy connection she used to feel to her sisters, even as they bickered and bitched and yelled and cried their way through the tribulations of Simon adolescence. She missed feeling like a family, one that wasn't scattered to four corners with nothing but a group chat to see them through.

And Sam, the part of her that wasn't about stability, plans, lists, and family responsibility whispered, furiously. *Sam, Sam, Sam*.

"No comment," she told Frankie. Because she couldn't tell her, *It's too late for me to get anything I really want.*

"To be clear," Frankie said, "I think you're making a colossal mistake. Not so much because you agreed to do the reunion special, but because you agreed to Niels Shaughnessy's plan to get *Sam* to do the reunion special when you and I both know she doesn't want to."

She and Frankie hadn't seen a lot of each other recently. They didn't talk as much as they used to before Vic went away to college, much less confide in each other. The longer stretches of silence and the uptick in small arguments had been getting uncomfortable.

"Again, I don't care to—"

"Why would she want to?" Frankie interrupted. "Why? *Why?* Sam is literally printing money at this point, taking juicy parts other actors would kill for. She walked off this set at the end of season six without telling anyone she wasn't ever coming back, without doing a series finale if there even was a script written—which, let me tell you, a lot of the water-cooler gossip around here has been obsessed with the mystery of the missing script the past couple weeks, oh my God—"

"Frankie!" Bex knew where this rant was headed, and she didn't want to hear it.

"—but what *I'm* actually hung up on is everything *you're* willing to give up to someone like Shaughnessy. You know your situation isn't the same as when you got hired on *Craven's Daughter* with no acting credits and he was the man upstairs, right? He would be a fool not to cast you as the lead in *Venice Memorial*. But instead of telling him to sign whatever contract your people write or kiss your ass goodbye, you're giving him the *Craven* reunion special he wants. *And* you're agreeing to host a six-episode rewatch podcast before the special in order to build up enthusiasm for the reunion. *And* you're giving him Sam's cooperation, which he can't possibly get except through you, even though you and Sam are estranged—"

"Not *estranged*." Bex's stomach flipped over the word.

"—just so Shaughnessy can feel like a big man who gets to audit you all over again and decide if you're good enough for him to put back on TV. I know why *he* wants it. He wants his ratings, and he wants to feel like he's God on a cloud, poking out his finger to bring those ratings to life." Frankie's color was high, her eyes burning with the injustice of what Bex was permitting to happen. "But you agreed to come on this set and take a meeting that could be an email with *Sam Farmer*, who you miss desperately but haven't really talked to in years, to convince her to do this reunion, just so a network asshole can see if you'll still dance when he hits a drum. And you will. You always do, Bex. I just want to know why."

For you. For you. Bex's hands were in fists. *Remember when there were family dinners every night? I don't want to sing a farewell review on Broadway when I'm ninety and my sisters aren't in the audience because I abandoned them the moment they didn't need me to sign school permission slips anymore.*

But she didn't say any of that. The one time she'd tried, it had precipitated a fight in which Frankie told her, with an ice-cold blade in her voice, *Lie to yourself about what you want, but don't pretend it's my fault.*

Bex took a deep breath of Stage 46. It smelled the same, like the cloudy pink cleaner they used on the floors and burned coffee from the craft services table. Of course it was the same, in every way that counted. This was the world where Frankie had grown up. She'd done an internship on this very soundstage. Frankie understood the situation as well as Bex did. Probably better.

But Bex had a plan. It was the only plan she'd been able to think of that would fix the parts of her life that felt like they'd spun out of control, and therefore it was the best plan.

"Bex."

"Stop."

"Sam is going to be here any minute. It's hard for me to believe she would even agree to come to this dusty soundstage to have a business meeting when she knows what Cineline wants as well as we do. Which means she's willing to do something genuinely gruesome in order to talk to you. Really, really talk to you. I don't want to believe you're going to use this opportunity just to feed her lines from the suits upstairs."

Bex didn't want to believe that, either.

Technically, she and Sam were *not* estranged. The last season of *Craven's Daughter* had been incredibly hard to trudge through for everyone. She and Sam had both worked nonstop since the end of the show, and they were frequently out of town for long periods, but they exchanged the occasional greeting over text. There had been a few brief and awkward phone calls. Christmas cards. Sam had maintained friendships with Frankie and Vic, which meant Bex heard things from her sisters about how Sam was doing and, she assumed, vice versa. If she and Sam were to run into each other at the Culver City Whole Foods, Bex was certain they would say hello. Sam would probably point out a quiet corner to talk for a few minutes where they would be less likely to cause an international incident for the very fact of standing next to each other.

But they weren't Sam and Bex anymore. Whatever "Sam and Bex" had ever been. And wasn't that lack of definition their whole problem?

Bex looked past the desk to the big window that opened onto the balcony. "The truth, Frankie? I'm afraid." She started to say something else, but her throat caught, making her eyes water. "Maybe you're right about all of it, but I'm mostly afraid because I loved *Craven's Daughter* so much, and the way things ended was awful."

Her sister followed the direction of Bex's gaze, and the frown between her eyebrows deepened. "Jen, you mean."

They'd lost their parents, and then after they'd finally gotten settled in their new lives after five steady, predictable seasons of *Craven's Daughter*, another sudden loss had befallen them—this time of Jen Arnot, the makeup artist who'd been the girls' favorite crew member and Bex and Sam's friend—everyone's friend—who fell to her death from the real-life Chicago balcony that existed in replica on the *Craven's Daughter* set.

"When I came over here with my work friends to look at the set, they took pictures on the balcony," Frankie said. "That was rough."

"I'm sorry."

The words fell flat in the empty space between them. Bex wished she had something better to tell her sister, but *I'm sorry* was all she had. *I'm sorry Mom isn't here. I'm sorry Dad couldn't see this. I'm sorry Jen's gone. I'm sorry Sam doesn't come around like she used to, but you go ahead and have dinner with her. I'm sorry.*

"I know." Frankie blinked and ran her fingers through her curls. "But you did say yes to the network. To Shaughnessy. Without consulting or informing me and Vic. You want to do something for us? With us? Then *include* us."

Bex willed the heat in her cheeks away. She didn't want to talk to Sam on the heels of another fight with Frankie. "I know you snuck out to see me because you care, but you must need to go back to work."

"I do." Frankie dropped her legs to the ground and sat up, directing her intensity at Bex. It was a lot of intensity. She and Frankie were alike in this, with the difference that Frankie had never worried about pleasing people, which made her a great deal scarier than Bex could hope to be. "Tell me, though. You're here, completely alone." Frankie gestured at the expanse of empty soundstage beyond them. "It's dark past the edge of the set. Say I never appeared. It's just you, waiting. Until Sam comes in. Sam. In one of her *outfits*. Right there." Frankie pointed at the open doorway. "What happens next? What exactly are you anticipating?"

Bex searched for an answer. In the time since she'd agreed to Niels's terms, she'd avoided thinking about everything Frankie had hit her with by focusing on the *Craven's Daughter* fans, who had been clamoring for a reunion almost since the show came to an end. These were people who had shipped PI Cora Banks and Agent Henri Shannon hard without getting to see that ship sail. Even though they never would be able to watch their finale or find out the secret reason Henri left the FBI in a cloud of disgrace, at least they could see the cast reunited against the backdrop of the set, answering questions posed by the show's most celebrated guest stars.

But the fans weren't why she'd agreed to come, and now Sam could hit her with all the same arguments Frankie had, plus introduce all the complications of the *other* ship that never sailed.

Sam and Bex.

She spun the gold stud in her earlobe until she noticed her sister watching. The earrings had belonged to their mother. Bex wore them for good luck and touched them too much when she felt anxious. Frankie knew this, damn it.

"I don't have a plan for Sam," she admitted.

Frankie gasped and put both palms on her cheeks.

That was fair. Bex was a planner. She had plans for everything. Frankie knew this, too.

When Frankie spoke again, her voice was thick. "It'll be okay in the end. If it's not, it's not the end."

That was what Bex had told her sisters, over and over again through their years together.

Frankie stood and gave Bex an unexpected hug, and standing in the embrace of her wiry arms, Bex almost said that they should leave together. She would follow Frankie to the soundstage where she worked and hide in bright and sunny and soothingly imaginary Timber Creek, California. Do a guest spot. Anything.

But then she heard high heels clicking against the 1950s-era linoleum in the hallway outside the studio.

Frankie's brown eyes went comically round. "I've got to go."

"Wait!" Bex whispered as the heels came closer. "You're not going to stay and say hi?"

"Fuck, no!" She was already clear of the set, looking back over her shoulder as she hustled through the empty fourth wall and off toward the dressing rooms. Exiting that way, she wouldn't encounter Sam. "I don't handle palpable discomfort well. It's like when I have dairy. Call me later! Break a leg!"

"Jesus," Bex said to herself. The tapping of the heels was louder now. It had to be Sam. No one else walked like that.

Bex tried to find a natural way to hold her body. She pulled her hair over one shoulder, then the other. Then she sat on the desk again and crossed her ankles. Why had she worn this stupid jumpsuit? No one who was five foot two in heels should wear a jumpsuit, even setting aside the fact that wearing a jumpsuit meant that every time you peed, you had to practically strip naked. She'd only put it on because she'd already spent way too long trying to decide what to wear, and the jumpsuit—black, shiny, real fashion in every way, complete with a gold zipper—was the least Bex-like outfit in her closet.

For some reason, she hadn't wanted to be too Bex-like around Sam. If she imagined showing up in Capezio ultrasoft dance tights and one of her stepdad's decades-old OSU sweatshirts with the neckline cut out of it, it felt too much like being naked.

Not that she was trying to avoid being naked with Sam. That wasn't what she was thinking either.

Bex sucked in a breath and put her finger through the gold ring on the zipper of her jumpsuit, fiddling nervously as the heels made their way across the studio floor.

Which was how she ended up with the end of her index finger extremely stuck in the gold ring and—in the panic of trying to yank it out—accidentally unzipping herself halfway to her navel just as Sam entered the office segment of the set.

Too Late to Make a Plan

"**Y**ikes." Sam stopped in the doorway.

Bex yanked up the zipper and freed her finger, catching a lock of the hair she'd draped over her shoulder and ripping it out in the process. "Fuck!"

"Do you need a minute?" Sam smiled the way she always had, like a smile took twenty years to fully develop on a person's face. She crossed her arms and leaned in the doorway, making various expensive suit fabrics and thin gold bangles attractively drape and clink.

"I was checking a rash," Bex said, and then actually died. Her heart stopped, she took her last breath, and she watched her body sink to the floor from above, where she was floating toward the light.

She consoled herself that she had been spared an awkward first meeting with Sam by instead crashing right into a humiliating one.

Sam did not seem to notice Bex's death, so Bex had to come up with more words. "I was not. Doing that. I don't have a rash. I don't know if I have ever had a rash." She wasn't breathing, she realized. "Anywhere."

Sam's high-waisted black suit pants were embroidered with red poppies the size of dinner plates. She didn't have a shirt on, just a bra under the jacket. Her honey blond hair wound around her head in an intricate crown of braids. It was two o'clock in the afternoon on a Wednesday.

Sam was still Sam.

"I believe you. I can't imagine Bexley Simon getting so much as a hive. Where would something like that go in your day planner?" One of Sam's beautiful caramel eyebrows lifted.

No matter how Bex tried, she could not lift just one of her eyebrows like that, but she knew there had been a time where she answered what Sam was asking with all the same coolness Sam brought to her doorstep.

"So." Bex held Sam's eye contact and mimicked her posture, even though Sam was standing in pointy heels, whereas Bex was perched on the desk. She had learned in an acting class at conservatory a hundred years ago that mimicking someone's posture was a surefire way to establish dominance over the interaction. "You're here."

Sam cocked a hip out.

Bex did her best to *lean* in a manner that achieved the same laconic, cowboy-like insouciance Sam exuded.

Sam put her hand over her mouth to cover her smile, which didn't work because Bex could see it in her cheeks and her eyes and a telltale wrinkle across the bridge of her nose. "I am."

Bex put her hand over her own mouth, raising her eyebrows to dare Sam to call her out. "I see."

That was when Sam started laughing. Really, genuinely laughing. It had been a very long time since Sam Farmer laughed in Bex's presence, but nothing had changed about the way it made her feel. For a while, in the beginning, Sam was the only one who could make her laugh.

"I'll let you pick." Sam put her fingertips to her flushed cheek. "I can either walk out and come in again, or I can concede defeat."

"Well." Bex started sliding off the desk. "I have never fucking figured out how to grab the upper hand in that exercise.

Effective dominance would have more . . . just *more*. I would feel I had gotten more-ish."

"I wouldn't say you're not effective. And, mirroring or not, we both know who has the upper hand. You always do."

Bex sighed. Had the floor always been so far away? She scooted the rest of the way to the edge of the desk, feeling for the ground with the tip of her shoe. "I told myself I wouldn't *Bex* this meeting quite so hard, but honestly—*motherfucker*." She whipped around at the unmistakable sound of tearing fabric, then goggled in dismay. That goddamn fucking nick in the brass had got her *again*. She yanked the shredded fabric out of the catch in the lamp and pulled it over her backside, recalling too late that she had put on a thong this morning. *Why?* She'd wanted to have a clean line under her jumpsuit! In case Sam looked and judged her for *not* having a clean line. *Good God.*

"Maybe it's only a tiny hole." Sam stepped forward as though to help, but Bex held up a hand. This lamp never took a minor fabric sacrifice, which meant her thong-wearing had come into play here. She reached back to confirm the worst. Her entire hand met her very bare ass.

She clamped her lips so she wouldn't scream.

"Problem?"

"That depends," Bex said. "On so many factors."

"Tell you what." Sam did a rapid visual survey of the set before her gaze settled on the same padded chair by the desk that Frankie had just vacated. "Let's arrange ourselves more comfortably in the middle of this dark and not-at-all-creepy set. We can recenter and see how we feel." She dropped into the chair and put her feet up on the oak desk, stacking her ankles so both of her heels pointed straight at Bex.

It was a punch in the gut. That was Sam's chair. That was how Sam's character, former FBI agent Henri Shannon, would occupy it when giving a signature cantankerous dressing-down to PI Cora Banks. *Tell you what, Cora. Tell you what.*

But, despite the pose, Sam didn't look like Henri at the moment. She wasn't a tortured, closed-off lone wolf who wore the same dark slacks and white Oxford in nearly every episode for six seasons. Sam was bedecked and adorned. She took full advantage of her long legs and easy charm. And Bex knew that all Sam's charm and fashion and flirtatiousness hid a heart so soft, it was easy to hurt her.

She knew that because she'd likely hurt Sam more than anyone.

One of the can lights caught the little curls and wisps from Sam's effortlessly deep blond braids—effortless because Sam's "money"-blond was natural, and sure, yes, Bex was similarly a "natural" redhead, but she had to have her color "enhanced" every four weeks so that it "read" for the cameras.

The network had never needed to enhance anything about Sam. Mostly, they'd tried to tone her down enough to be believable. Sam had once confided to Bex that she'd expected, after she finished drama school, to spend years in fringe theater, picking up bit parts. Instead she'd landed the first TV role she tried for, a new principal in a long-running sci-fi serial that America had binged solely for the riveting, singular spectacle of twenty-two-year-old Samantha Ellen Farmer's charismatic beauty.

Bex had been one of those Americans.

Her eyes had begun to burn threateningly. She swallowed. "Thanks for coming here."

Sam's expression softened. "You know, it occurred to me on my way over how completely ridiculous Aaron Gorman's ideas were." She said this as though she hadn't noticed Bex getting emotional. More likely she had noticed and had decided to extend Bex the grace of not mentioning it, which meant that now Bex was missing Sam's laughter *and* her decency, and what could Sam have missed about Bex, exactly? Her tendency toward clumsiness unless she was dancing or in character? Her compulsion toward bossiness and control?

"*See You Never*, for example," Sam said. "A classic Gorman."

Aaron Gorman had been *Craven Daughter*'s showrunner, though the bombastic Hollywood veteran pushed the writing and a great deal of the show's arc off on his ex-stepdaughter, Bette Holloway, so he could focus on his role as director.

Sam picked an invisible bit of lint off her blazer, the corners of her mouth revealing just a hint of disdain to be speaking of Aaron and his first hit television show. "I watched *See You Never* obsessively, as you know, because I was legally obligated to as a young and shiny queerlet in Oakland, and even if I hadn't been gay as a maypole, who could look away from the spectacular cleavage of Luciana de León? Not me. But tell me, Bex, did it make any actual sense? Four beautiful people in their twenties who had just been released from prison, all of them having committed crimes that put them away long enough to serve drama but not bad enough to worry the audience, and these four can somehow rent a loft on the Lower East Side together? This show captured Americans' imagination. America related to these characters."

As Sam came to the end of these remarks, Bex noticed how her forefinger worried the arm of the chair. Aaron Gorman was a subject they'd learned to avoid in the past, skirting disagreement. Bex hadn't dared criticize the man whose approval meant her paychecks got signed, while Sam challenged him at every turn, criticizing him for queerbaiting fans with Cora and Henri's romantic-but-unrequited tension and pushing him to get a handle on some of the more outrageous personalities on the show, like the set designer, Josh Miller, who frequently held up shoots with his beefs and perfectionism.

But that was years ago. Bex's sisters were safe, so her survival didn't depend on her acquiescence. Things could be different this time, even if she still had to make compromises to do what was best for everyone long-term.

"Wait, I'm sorry," she said, feigning confusion as she picked up Sam's cue to lighten the mood. "You're saying that primary school teacher Cora Banks could *not* have inherited her dead deadbeat dad's Chicago investigation agency and run to ground a disgraced FBI agent who happened to need a job because no one else would take her?"

Sam laughed again, killing Bex. "Is it like a naked emperor thing? We're standing around admiring Aaron's clothes while his pasty self is out in the breeze?"

Bex felt her throat go hot, a sure sign she shouldn't open her mouth. "There's nothing that can't work in Hollywood if the chemistry's good enough. Or if the man making it is white enough."

"Well, Bexley Simon! Letting loose at last."

She cast her eyes to the ceiling, mostly so she didn't have to bear Sam's grin. It changed the shape of her face, turning classy, urbane Sam into someone so unguarded, Bex heard her heart whisper *mine*. "Don't."

"Don't what? Don't say the chemistry was good enough? It was more than good enough."

"Don't tease. Not yet. Do small talk. Ease us in."

Sam drummed her fingers on the arm of her chair. "Small talk. Okay. You got me here, Bex. In the studio. We're talking. Shaughnessy wants this reunion special. You've agreed to do it. It's not really a reunion if I won't do it, too, but I flounced the show at the end of the last season, so no one knows if I'm game. They're hoping you can convince me. Is that about the shape of it? Although"—Sam looked around at the set—"I have to guess Shaughnessy also wanted to see if you, and by extension you and I, would agree to talk about it here, on old Stage 46, which is the kind of game he likes to play. It tells me he wants something from you that's more than the reunion. Probably he wants to take the temperature of how much power he's still got over you."

Bex had to shake out the fists her hands had curled themselves into. "That's not small talk."

"We're not small people. In personality. In Hollywood. You are a small person *technically*, but your hair's as big as ever, and your voice isn't small. Not even your stage whisper. I could hear you trying to make Frankie get you out of this from the other end of the hall."

Bex stopped herself from reaching up to touch her earring. She was starting to feel the consequences of coming to a meeting with Sam Farmer without a solid plan. She could at least employ some strategy. She needed to keep the focus off her own reasons for being here and squarely on Sam's. "Are you going to do it?"

"I am."

Sam restacked her feet on the desk as Bex adjusted to this unexpected news.

"Or, I should say, I'm going to give them the reunion special," Sam corrected. "I don't love it, but the ask came to me after it had made the rounds to everyone else, and I could see very plainly that it would mean paychecks for everyone. That's the kind of lower-circle-of-hell move Shaughnessy likes to pull on *me*. But the podcast sounds like torture."

Well, that stung a little. The network had decided to lead up to the reunion two months from now with six episodes of a weekly podcast called *Craven's Daughter: Cold Case*. The idea was that the podcast's hosts would discuss the fan-voted favorite episodes of the series, playing video clips and collegially trading memories, anecdotes, and analyses of the show. Every episode would include interviews with cast and crew who'd contributed to making it a favorite. Niels wanted the hosts to be Sam and Bex.

Of course, of course, because Sam and Bex were the show's leads. But also because the first episode of *Craven's Daughter* to follow the pilot, "Everything I Know I Learned in Kindergarten," had kindled what would grow into one of the biggest will-they-or-won't-they wildfires in television history.

Bex's capitulation to the podcast had been bundled in with her agreement to do the reunion special—part of what she'd thought of as "pacifying Niels"—but she actually liked the idea of spending a few hours a week in a recording studio with Sam. It sounded like such a measured, careful way for them to revisit the past and, if things went well, dip their toes into the possibility of friendship again.

"Did you actually say no to the podcast already?" she asked.

"Yeah. And yet here we are. I'm still waiting for you to tell me why you're here. Why we're *here*. Why this set's been dragged out of the darkness early to accommodate our meetup."

"You know how network men are. They love drama more than they love prime rib buffets. Network men do things like this because they think it will work better than, I don't know, something normal."

Sam let her arms drop to her sides. "See, what I think would be normal is *we* talk about it."

Include us, Frankie had said. Bex gritted her teeth and gestured between the two of them, possibly with a little bit of heat. "That is what we're doing."

"On their terms, we are."

"Ugh!" Bex crossed her arms. She wanted to stomp her foot, but the floor was too far away. "Okay." She took in a breath. Professional. Extremely, very. "Why don't you want to do the podcast?"

Sam kept her eyes steady on Bex. The youngest of five close-in-age siblings and the only girl, Sam had been raised by a single periodontist dad in Oakland who believed in straight As, four-season sports, and camping. At eight years old, on a Saturday morning in June, Sam had come out to her father as a lesbian and then demanded he drive her to the Pride parade that started in an hour. As a rule, Sam did not prevaricate or perseverate. Bex braced herself.

"We have to back up," Sam said. "I have some preamble-type thoughts."

"Please. Share your preamble with me." Bex spun her hand at Sam, aware that there was something very Cora-and-Henri about this conversation, as though their presence together in the studio really might be summoning old ghosts.

Which was what the network men wanted. And that meant Sam was right to question the whole thing. Again, *ugh.*

"Thank you, Bexley. As you know, our characters, Cora and Henri, were conceived as friends. Aaron has said on numerous occasions that he didn't care if my character was 'Henry-Henry or Henri-Henrietta.' He cast us because Penny Boucher told him to, and she told him to because our chemistry read together—the first time you and I met in person—set a small fire in that grubby room where they had us audition, and Penny had to use the fire extinguisher to hose us off."

Sam shot her a fast, wicked smile that Bex was in no way prepared for.

She wished she could say she hadn't thought of their chemistry read in ages, but in actual fact she thought of it at least once a week. Bex hadn't had a date or a kiss or a sexual encounter as hot as that chemistry read in all the years since.

No. Not part of her plan. Not what this was about. She'd somehow forgotten what an unrepentant flirt Sam was. She gave her what she hoped was a quelling look.

"But Aaron not caring what our gender was had nothing to do with his fervent belief in the equality of all," Sam continued, unquelled. "It was because he thought the most compelling part of *Craven's Daughter* was his concept for the show."

"His concept being a detective procedural that paired a bleeding-heart Goody Two-Shoes with a grumpy know-it-all who's keeping shadowy secrets," Bex clarified.

"An odd couple, yes. As far as Aaron's concerned, it had never been done before in God's own Hollywood. And with a murdered celebrity guest star every week? Fucking call it, it's an original!" Sam's sarcastic declaration punched through the empty space of the abandoned soundstage. When she spoke again, the hard edge had left her voice. "We both know that when the ratings for *Craven* slayed right off the bat, it wasn't because of Aaron's concept. All of America knows. Our global partners in syndication know, including that bizarre animated version of the show that's so hot in New Zealand. But Aaron's mediocrity isn't my point. My point is that there wasn't supposed to be a romantic arc on *Craven*, chemistry or no chemistry."

The chemistry would never have happened if they'd cast a *Henry*, Bex was certain—especially one old enough to be a disgraced former FBI agent. But with Sam, it had happened and happened, to the tune of six ratings-busting seasons, millions of words of Cora + Henri fanfic, and Mystery Con cosplay that made the back of Bex's neck hot. They'd even been immortalized in an *SNL* skit in which their characters had very much been . . . not coy.

Bex hadn't ventured too far into the world the fans made. She'd worried it would color her perception of Cora, and she understood the fandom as something that was for the fans, not for her, and not even *about* her, really, so much as it was about how *Craven's Daughter* made the people feel who watched it avidly, week after week, year after year.

Keeping herself outside of fan spaces also meant that Bex didn't have to witness their disappointment in the show's direction when Aaron refused to make the romance canon. He permitted and even encouraged the direction Bette's scripts increasingly took into the realm of queerbaiting, but when Sam said Aaron needed to give the audience confirmation of Cora and Henri's romantic feelings, he'd shot back that it would be "a distraction." *Craven* was a detective show. It was not a love story. And so he directed Bex and Sam to never speak of their characters' feelings about each other in a public setting unless they wanted to be fired. Niels Shaughnessy had backed him up.

"It was wrong what they did with our characters," Bex said. "It hurt so many people."

It had hurt Sam most, because she was both out in Hollywood and a visible LGBTQ activist, much more visible than Bex was. Bex had the artistic pansexual reputation many Broadway babies shared, but she was too busy with her sisters for dating or activism—and then too caught up in her feelings about Sam to be able to say anything publicly at all. At her manager's advice, she avoided talking about love, sex, and relationships in interviews, which gave Bex's personal life an aura of mystery it didn't deserve. It had become one of those rumors everyone acknowledged as fact that Bexley Simon kept her personal liaisons very private. In fact, though she'd taken a few haphazard stabs at dating in the past five years, she hadn't had any liaisons worth calling "personal."

Sam was different. Before *Craven's Daughter* and in the years since, her dating life had been the subject of intense speculation and gossip. Bex couldn't keep count of how many women and nonbinary people Sam had been rumored to be seeing since *Craven* wrapped. She didn't *think* many of those relationships had been serious, but that didn't mean they weren't important to Sam.

As a rule, Sam didn't ruminate or worry, but when she made up her mind about something, she acted. After it became clear that *Craven's Daughter* was not addressing the queer elephant in the room, Sam had dived into many conversations about it. With Bex beside her, she'd talked to the network head and tried her best to work with Aaron and with Bette, but she never got anywhere, until finally Sam wanted to be anywhere but there. Especially after Jen died.

Bex suspected the only reason Sam stayed on as long as she did was to make sure Bex and her sisters got the syndication residuals, streamer deals, and bonuses that came with a hundred-episode run.

"I'm sorry," she said. It seemed like the only thing she could say today.

Sam sighed. "Yeah, so. It was wrong. It did hurt people. That makes it fucking complicated for me, politically and personally, that the network has chosen the episodes for the rewatch podcast based on fan votes, and the fans, enthusiastically and overwhelmingly, have voted for *those* episodes."

Bex nodded, biting her lip.

"I have done a lot of work in my community to make up for my silence," Sam said. "But if we host the podcast rewatch and I have to sit with a microphone in front of my face and watch clips of us gazing at each other longingly while exchanging don't-say-it banter, I might actually be the first victim of the show who dies in real life. I can't put myself through that."

Bex understood. *Haunting*, Frankie had called it, and Bex's body knew what she meant. Her body remembered the hard work, the precision it had demanded, the exhaustion. Her heart and her throat recalled the grief of Jen's passing and, not even a year later, the confusion of the day they'd finished filming and Bex's agent had called to tell her that Sam was out, and the series would abruptly terminate with the episode they'd just wrapped.

Bex had known *Craven's Daughter* was nearing the end of its run. Sam's negotiations over her contract renewal had stalled and turned bitter. Her relationship with Bex had gone spectacularly wrong with one calamitous and heartbreaking conversation that Bex could not repair.

What she hadn't expected was to be told that the series would end where they'd left it, on the twenty-second episode of its sixth season, and fade to black without resolution. Not for the characters. Not for the fans. Not for Bex and Sam.

But maybe this didn't have to be about them.

"You know what?" she asked. "You're right to think of the fans. For nearly five years, I've been watching our fans do everything they can to find closure. Even though I've gone back to Broadway and done a bunch of other projects, I'm still asked what happened. I'm sure you are, too. And what our fans want to know isn't what happened to Aaron's genius show, why it got canceled without so much as a finale. They're asking, 'Do *you* know? Do *you*, Bexley Simon or Sam Farmer, know what happened to Henri and Cora?'"

Her voice had gotten louder. Bex could feel it reverberate through the studio the same way it always had when she stood in this spot playing Cora fighting with Henri. *Tell you what*, Henri would say, and Cora would cross her arms, straighten her posture, and let her clear, sweet voice ring out.

"They tell me, 'I couldn't help but hope that in the end, whatever had been holding Cora and Henri back would be explained,'" she said. "They tell me, 'So many times, I felt like it was silly to want Cora and Henri together, but I wanted it so bad anyway. I *wanted* it. It meant something to me. I hoped that in the finale, maybe something would happen that would tell us we were right, and there was something there between them that was more.'" Bex felt the little muscles in her chest relax. "You and me, Sam— we've had so many opportunities. We've moved on. We—" But then her throat caught, and she couldn't continue.

We've moved on. What a thing to say, when she still eavesdropped anytime she heard Frankie and Vic talking about Sam. When she hadn't stopped asking them questions, trying to sound casual, never sure what casual was supposed to sound like.

Her sisters were merciful. They told her whenever Sam was traveling for work. If Sam left the country. If they'd heard Sam had landed a big role.

That was what moving on looked like for Bex.

She didn't know what it looked like for Sam. She wasn't even sure if Sam was seeing someone at the moment. There'd been rumors she was in a relationship with her costar from her last film project, but Vic wasn't at home to confirm or deny those rumors for Bex, and lately Frankie had been hard to pin down on the subject of Sam.

Whoever Sam was seeing or not seeing, it wasn't Bex's business. She made herself focus on what mattered: securing Sam's cooperation.

"An unbelievable number of our viewers still care, right?" Bex asked. "And that's a miracle. To have made something that so many people care about. So I'm not going to ask you to do this podcast because the network wants you to." She wrinkled her nose. "Definitely not. But what if we have a chance to make it up to all of them"—she gestured in the direction of the fourth wall—"and tell them what the fuck happened to Henri and Cora?"

"Nothing happened, though," Sam said. "There's no ending. If the rumors are true and Bette really did write a script for a finale, nobody ever showed it to me. I agree with you that the fans deserve better, but I can't give it to them." She crossed her arms. "That's my point, which you're missing. Aaron could have given it to them, but he wouldn't. Niels could give them whatever he wants, but he won't. *I* can't give them anything of value. Not anymore."

Bex put her hands on her hips. "Maybe we can't film the episode they never got, but the fans are already out there writing stories and publishing them on the Internet to give us a thousand different happy endings. They don't need *us* to tell them what that looks like. They need us to talk about it. Just *talk* about it, finally, and say the things that Aaron and the network wouldn't let us. Say that Cora loved Henri. Say that Henri loved Cora. Wouldn't that be worth something? Wouldn't it actually be worth a *lot*?"

Her ears were too hot, and Bex's confidence eroded a bit under Sam's scrutiny. She sometimes—maybe more than sometimes—had been known to avoid Sam's scrutiny. But this time, she took the moment to reacquaint herself with Sam.

There was the almost-heart-shaped mole on her jaw. There was the speck of green, bright against the blue of her left eye. There was the place along her hairline where Sam had a cowlick and disguised it with styling—the one imperfect thing about her that somehow made her more perfect. Bex hadn't forgotten. She knew Sam Farmer with her whole body, just as well as she knew Stage 46.

Better.

"The other thing is, I've missed you," she added, before Sam could speak.

"Good *night*, Bexley." Sam looked upward, as if seeking help from a divine source.

"Well, I have."

"I've been around. Very obviously around."

"So have I!" Bex protested. "Why was I supposed to be the one to send an engraved invitation?"

Sam leaned all the way forward. "I don't know, Bex. Why would I be waiting for an invitation from you that never came?"

The question stung, but it was better to have it out in the open, acknowledged between them—that Sam had taken her shot.

Mostly, Bex didn't let herself think about that moment in her dressing room before they filmed what would turn out to be the final scene of the last episode of *Craven's Daughter*. She didn't let herself remember anything from that morning—not the frustration, still in her chest after getting off the phone with Vic's babysitter, who was quitting. Not her simmering rage over the paparazzi shot her manager had emailed her the night before, reporting that everyone thought Bex's end-of-season extra five pounds made her look like she was pregnant. If Bex remembered those feelings, or the lemon-glazed poppy seed muffin she'd been eating for breakfast, or the pale mint color of the ruffled blouse the costumer had put her in for the episode, then she would remember what happened next.

When Sam knocked on her door and slipped into her dressing room, it was the first time they'd been alone in a series of weeks in which the tension between them had been one heartsick fever after another. She *knew* Sam was finally going to say something, and she wasn't ready, not yet. Or she was, and didn't understand her own heart underneath the layers of duty and obligation and fear.

Either way, she'd said Sam's name, and she really didn't like remembering how Sam said hers back. Like she already knew Bex wouldn't say yes. Like she was resigned to the fact that Bex would never admit what was plainly happening between them, *had* been happening for so long, because Bex was just as silent as the network about Henri and Cora, and one hundred times more hurtful.

Bex didn't like to remember how she said, *I want*— and then stopped, cutting off the end of her sentence with a muscled squeeze of her heart. How she shook her head back and forth.

She hated when she woke up from a dream with Sam's sad voice in her ear—*Let me know when you figure out what you want*—and the sound of her dressing-room door shutting. She had dry-sobbed behind that closed door, without sound or tears, and wanted to throw something so hard that it broke the world.

That was where Bex had left things with Sam. For not-quite-five cowardly years.

And she hadn't figured out what she wanted. She'd tried, but the only thing her trying amounted to was Bex's recognition that there was no way to get back the life she'd lost when she lost her parents—and in the demanding travel, the back-and-forth-from-New-York life, uprooting Vic at the end of high school for a year, she'd lost too much of her closeness with her sisters.

The only thing she wanted now was to fix what was broken so she could feel like she had a home again. *Venice Memorial* would give her that, even if she had to give up other things to get it. Like a small portion of her integrity.

"That is a fair callout," Bex said. She wished she had a pen and a notebook and five minutes of silence. She needed to regroup and make a new plan for this conversation with Sam, whose objection to the podcast was perfectly reasonable but also unacceptable.

Just when Bex had started looking around for where she left her bag—was it in her car?—Sam said, "Okay."

"Okay what?"

"I'll do the podcast with you. Of course I will. You're already casting about for one of your journals, and once you've made a list, I'm doomed. But also because you're right." Sam reached out and tapped her finger on top of the desk, twice, hard. "Our fans deserve the truth. I can give them that, at least." Sam shook her head, but she was smiling rather gloriously. "However. I'm not going to be a good girl for the network anymore. If they don't like it, they can take it up with my management. I'll speak my mind. Not just about Henri and Cora, but about everything. About why I left. About Jen."

Jen Arnot's death in Chicago had brought Bex and Sam low with grief and complicated what was already difficult between them. The network's handling of the tragedy, with smothering mandatory silence piled on top of the screaming silence about Cora and Henri's attraction to each other, had spelled the end of *Craven's Daughter*. "I want to talk about Jen," Bex agreed.

Sam's mouth softened. "All right."

"All right." Bex put a period on their understanding of each other. "This podcast will be our podcast. We talk about what we want."

She would worry about how Niels Shaughnessy felt about their decision at a later date.

Sam leaned back. Everything about how she held and moved her body was looser, though Bex knew Sam well enough to know that she should stop now. Offering any more points to consider or speeches and concessions risked shutting Sam down.

Bex didn't want to shut Sam down. She wanted to find a way to fix what she'd destroyed so she could have her back. Not in the way they'd both wanted, once—she had ruined that. But there had been a time when Sam's friendship meant everything to Bex, and she seemed to be the only person in Hollywood who could handle the package deal that was the three Simon sisters. Losing her had been like losing a limb. Even now, with just this one tentative thread of reconnection between them, Bex found herself imagining how good it would be to tell Sam every single thing on her mind.

If they made it that far.

Pushing her shoulders back, she summoned a little bossy brightness. "Let's get out of here. It's too weird. We can stop by Frankie's studio and say hi. Feed the rumors something healthy to eat." Unwilling to wait on an answer, Bex grabbed her bag and started to walk off the studio floor toward the dressing rooms. She heard Sam's throat clear behind her.

"What?" she turned around.

Sam had her hand over her mouth again, presumably to hold in check the very big grin behind it and keep herself from breaking into laughter. "Um. There's— Well, Bex, there's your ass. Half of it. But all of it." She made a gesture in the direction of the missing part of Bex's jumpsuit.

Right. Sure. Yes.

"So I would appreciate it," Bex said, "if you would walk closely behind me to the parking lot. I think we'll skip Frankie for now."

Sam unbuttoned the button on her blazer.

"Um." Bex blinked. "No."

Sam shrugged out of it. Her bra matched her pants, with two big peonies embroidered onto the most important areas of black mesh. "Turn around. I won't look."

"You don't have to do this." But Bex turned, holding together the rip as best she could, and then Sam was easing her into the red silk lining of the blazer, and Bex was surrounded by Sam's sugar-and-musk perfume.

Possibly spending a few hours a week closed up in a podcasting studio with Sam was not the brightest idea Bex had ever had. She took a long time to roll up the sleeves before she turned around.

"Thanks." The blazer was more than long enough to cover her bottom but too slim-cut to accommodate her other assets. "It won't button, though."

"Rub it in."

"And you're going to go out there like that?"

Sam looked down at herself. "I only put the blazer on this outfit for you. I'm aware of your sensibilities."

"When it's convenient, you are." Bex started toward the exit.

Sam got to the door first. She held it open for Bex. "Do you want to talk about what we're aware of only when it's convenient, or should we save it for the first podcast?"

Bex tried very hard not to blush, but that never worked. When she turned, she caught Sam smiling, looking so *Sam*. "Walk me to my car, and I'll give you back your jacket."

"Keep it." Sam reached out and popped the collar on it. "Looks cool with the jumpsuit."

Bex wondered if it was too late to make a better plan.

A Real, True Fan

Luciana de León pulled her shock-mounted microphone toward her perfect red lip. A waterfall of wavy, dark hair cascaded over her champagne silk blouse as she continued to run the interview Bex and Sam had been trying to conduct for their podcast like it was one of the slick limited-series dramas she produced for her multimillion-dollar studio—uncompromisingly and with plenty of shocking revelations.

"*Craven's Daughter* was a Hail Mary for Aaron Gorman. I'm not supposed to say that."

Bex glanced toward the booth at the back of the recording studio. Amethyst Van Runkel, the producer Cineline had assigned to the series, stood frowning behind the glass, a clipboard clutched to her chest. Her dark flyaway hair looked like she'd been running her hands through it repeatedly, but she gave Bex a doomed smile and a thumbs up.

Amethyst didn't have the firepower to control this recording session. To her credit, she seemed to know it.

"But it's true," Luciana added. "He was fucked."

Until twenty-five minutes ago, Bex hadn't remembered what it was like to be around Luciana de León. Then Luciana had flung open the door of this shabby room in the basement of Cineline's second-tier Inglewood production facility wearing white-on-white, collar-to-heel silk that matched the sparkle of her suite of massive diamonds, and a whole bunch of memories hit Bex at once.

She'd been twenty-six years old, on the set of her first television show, with no relevant experience besides two failed pilots and her third, successful pilot for *Craven's Daughter*. Luciana was unequivocally famous, not just because she'd made the character of Maria Paz on *See You Never* one of the most memorable love-to-hate-her women on television, but also because she continued to have both a dizzyingly powerful career and a media storm of a personal life.

Sam didn't seem nearly as bowled over as Bex. She had her embroidered cowboy boots propped on the surface of the shiny round conference table they were seated around in ergonomic chairs, with the result that the hem of her illegally near-invisible slip dress had drifted halfway up her thighs. "You can say whatever you want." She winked at Luciana. "I'm certainly going to."

Bex could not bring herself to make eye contact with either one of these women, for very different reasons. Luciana was difficult to take in because that was her actual look—distract, dazzle, conquer. With Sam, it was personal, obviously. But also *personal*, if she was being honest with herself about how she was responding to Sam's legs. However, she didn't have any kind of go-ahead to be honest about Sam's legs, did she? They hadn't had the chance to really get into it that day on the old set when Bex had come superearly, worn fashion when she knew fashion was not her calling in this life, and drunk in Sam like she was the last glass of water on earth. In the two weeks since, Frankie and Vic had been waiting for Bex to talk about all the things she and Sam hadn't gotten into, but Bex had been acutely busy eliminating items on a three page to-do list she had written precisely to avoid anything *personal*.

She adjusted her ceiling-mounted microphone in front of her face. Thankfully, it was big enough to conceal her expression when she had to avert her eyes from the strap of Sam's dress sliding down her shoulder.

Friendship. That was what she was doing. Dipping her toes into the possibility.

Luciana winked back at Sam, making her smile. "Good. It's best when I can say whatever I want, Sam Farmer."

Bex felt no jealousy. She was a professional spending time with old friends. Possibly reining them in a titch when they stepped over the line.

"Let's start with how this episode even happened." Luciana spoke into her own microphone now. "Your showrunner and director. My first director, the man who gave me my breakout role, but that was years and years ago by the time I walked onto the *Craven's Daughter* set. Aaron had run through a string of failures. His ex-wife's brother was in the C-Suite at Cineline— Jeff Gantry—so Aaron had the good fortune to nepotism his way into one more chance. This is how white men fail up. 'He's lost his touch,' everyone says. 'Let's give him one last network serial that's certain to tank!' Yes, that sounds correct. They're throwing money at him, and he's pulling in favors to gather as much talent in his corner as he possibly can. He starts calling, leaving me messages, has the script for the pilot couriered over so I can get a feel for the show. When I first read it, I turned up my nose. Not impressed."

"So why'd you do the guest spot?" Bex was genuinely interested now. Her agent at the time had been nothing but superlative about Aaron and the script, insistent that Bex was being offered the chance of a lifetime. Bex had read the script for the pilot and realized that her agent's confidence in her talent extended exactly as far as the circumstances of her last failure. She'd put the script down on her kitchen table, looked at her Tony, and apologized to it for how low she was willing to go for her sisters.

"I grew up Catholic. Can't resist a good Hail Mary." Luciana laughed, a glittering, infectious sound. "I'm kidding. Actually, I did say no. A real no, not a Hollywood no that's just an opening for more negotiations. Then he reminded me that he gave me the job on *See You Never* when I was just a daytime soaps baby with plastic hair extensions, and I folded." She laughed again.

"But you were in the first episode," Bex said. "Aaron didn't write that one. He only wrote the pilot, and then Bette Holloway took over from season one, episode one. I seem to remember you and Bette spending a lot of time with your heads together on set, editing. What can you tell us about that?"

"What I remembered, watching the credits roll by for the episode after I chose my clips for this podcast, was just how many people Aaron strong-armed into working on his show." Luciana seemed to have no intention of answering Bex's question. "The casting director, Penny Boucher? She was someone he'd come up with from grade school. He'd worked with your set designer, Josh Miller, on that big-budget flop, the murder mystery film set in postwar Philadelphia. Gloomy interiors and an impenetrable plot, completely unwatchable, but gorgeous to look at."

"Also the most *involved* set designer I have ever dealt with on a shoot?" Sam lifted an eyebrow at Luciana, who laughed in response.

"Yes. This is me rolling my eyes for our listening audience. Josh Miller is one of those geniuses who can't stay in his lane. It never occurred to him that because he was good at one thing, he might not be good at everything, and heaven forbid Aaron should tell him. But just to give our audience a crystalline picture, I should say that for a Cineline show, the set designer *does* create the entire mood, the look, the colors. They oversee design and construction. If the angles matter to a scene's artistic interpretation, set design might even be involved in some of the elements of blocking and choreography. But they don't typically lurk around set day after day snarling at cast and crew."

"He is . . . passionate," Bex said diplomatically.

"Indeed. And so was your makeup artist, Jen Arnot, may she rest in peace, who had done *Bloodright* with Aaron—"

Bex couldn't help it, she flinched at hearing Jen's name spoken into the microphone. She glanced at Sam, who was listening to Luciana with a serious expression that matched a new tightness in her shoulders.

"—and then won an Oscar for her work, which he hated. That didn't stop him from hiring her for *Charles Salt*. Once again, Jen's groundbreaking prosthetic effects stole his limelight, but he still invited her to do makeup for *Craven's Daughter*. Keep in mind, this wasn't about Aaron finding people he liked. Aaron knew who was *good*. Failure was not an option." Luciana looked from Sam to Bex. "The only people in that studio who didn't know Aaron from way back when were the two of you. You were just *infants*. But the one thing Penny Boucher could do was make a match. You want to cast a couple who seem authentically like they can't keep from ripping each other's clothes off? Hire Penny. She'll get the job done."

Bex met Luciana's smile with one of her own, calibrated to convey enough warmth to match Luciana's possessive, slightly condescending friendliness, but her ears were burning. How many times had Bex stayed calm while someone teased her about her chemistry with Sam? Many times. So many. This time was no different. That it *felt* different, she chalked up to how long it had been since she and Sam did this kind of thing together.

And a little bit, also, to Sam's just-on-the-verge-of-see-through slip dress.

"But Bex and I were talking recently about how Aaron didn't want a romantic arc." Sam pulled her boots from the table. She leaned forward, drooping the neckline of her dress in a way that threatened to expose her from throat to navel. "Even after it started happening."

"These people I've mentioned weren't just talented." Luciana folded her arms, looking every inch a Hollywood dream-maker who knew what she was talking about. "They didn't *just* owe Aaron or think they did. They were people with pride who weren't going to let Aaron fuck up." She tilted her head. "Your iconic chemistry, and the obvious romance of that show, was Penny Boucher deciding to rescue a tired premise by giving it a spicy twist."

Bex kept her expression neutral while she received this earth-shattering perspective. No one had ever suggested *Craven's Daughter*'s "obvious romance" was the result of the casting director's independent decision to rescue Aaron.

If it *was* what had happened, it had sure as hell worked.

"Aaron had no objections," Luciana was saying. "He knew how to surround himself with talent. He just took it in stride, feeding everyone his 'I don't care if it's Henry or Henrietta' line."

Sam laughed. "He did love to say that."

"There was also his willingness to make naked bids to the American public," Luciana continued, "by conceiving a show where the weekly guest star, the murder victim, was so famous that the people would suffer serious FOMO if they didn't watch."

"The guest stars, more than anything else, were how I learned to act in Hollywood." Bex was grateful to have an ordinary response available to steer the conversation back to safer territory.

"Nothing like spending your early twenties as a nobody in America's living rooms playing opposite literal legends," Sam said.

"Thank you. I am legend. And because both of you rose to the challenge, you are, too. It all worked. Even though Aaron wrote that stinking pilot, he had the vision to pull in Marty van Houser to play the dead dad. I have to slow-clap. That captured the attention of every Boomer who'd ever watched *American Glory*, which was all of them. Then me in the first episode, when I was at the height of my post–*See You Never* popularity and right in the middle of an ugly divorce from a husband who'd slept with his younger, blonder, white costar? That captured everyone else. *That's* why I pushed Bette on the script."

"You're talking about Bette Holloway, our writer," Bex interjected, conscious of Amethyst's instruction that she and Sam should clarify context for the listeners. "She was Aaron's stepdaughter, but he'd divorced Bette's mother by the time we were broadcasting. *Craven* was Bette's first writing job."

Luciana tossed her hair behind her shoulder. "I'd heard she had raw talent, but she hated Aaron, even as he was giving her a huge break. Aaron was notorious for insisting on collaborating with *one* writer. A lot of eyebrows went up when he tapped Bette for this job. I wanted to help her understand what *she* could do. How to make her ambition bigger than her feelings about her ex-stepfather."

Sam shook her head. "If I could time-travel, I'd hand-deliver this interview to myself. That way, I could show up on set already knowing I was walking into a pressure cooker."

Luciana's smile was the smile of a mountain lion contemplating a slow hiker. "I'm so glad you say that, Sam. Because, *because*"—she tapped her lush top lip with one beautifully manicured fingernail—"there is something interesting about your pressure cooker that I have discovered. First, though, let me tell you what I haven't said yet about *Craven's Daughter*." Luciana looked from Bex to Sam. "It's a confession. My confession to you both."

"Say it." Bex couldn't keep the intense curiosity out of her voice.

Luciana crossed both hands over her heart. "I'm a huge fan. I like to think I am the very hugest fan of *Craven's Daughter*, because I am, of course, huge."

"No," Sam laughed.

"Yes! No one even asked me to be on this podcast. When I heard it was happening, I gave Niels a call. I was always and ever a real, true fan."

"Really!" Sam was grinning her unguarded grin at Luciana. "Always?"

"How could I not be? Bexley's Cora is so down-to-earth, grounded but hopeful in a way that inspires, and you played Henri as the partner we've all been looking for—steady, smart, always paying attention and catching things the rest of us miss. It was such a beautiful relationship to *live* in for the span of an episode. I was devastated when it ended. And, as I hinted, I have an ulterior motive for coming here today. One that confirms these dramas behind the drama."

Sam was now on the edge of her seat. "Which is?"

"First, have either one of you read *Craven's Daughter* fanfiction?"

"No," Bex said, with a shake of her head.

It took her a moment to realize Sam had answered, too. "Some," she'd said.

Bex turned to her. "Really? During the run of the show?"

"Toward the end, when I was having a harder time with the direction they wouldn't take our characters in. I think I was trying to reassure myself the romance was there. Our fans saw it and wanted it, and it was important to them for the same reasons it was important to me."

"Oh." Luciana sighed. "Yes. Queer viewers, Black viewers, brown viewers, all of us have been waiting for these white men in Hollywood to catch the fuck up for so long. I hear that. And I'm sorry." Luciana nudged Sam with her knee. "Did you ever read the fic by someone who wrote under the name CravingCraven?"

"Maybe?"

Luciana shook her head. "You would know if you had. They're a Big Name Fan."

"Ah." Sam nodded. "I didn't read enough to pick up that kind of thing."

"Catch me up, cool girls," Bex said. "A Big Name Fan?"

Of course Bex was aware there was a library's worth of *Craven's Daughter* fanfic in the world. She'd guested on fandom podcasts where she'd been asked about it. During the show's run, she and Sam had done a couple of fan cons and had listened to their viewers' breathless recounting of how the show had inspired them to write when they had never been writers before, or how their Alternative Universe *Craven's Daughter* fic where they'd written

Henri as a sea monster had inspired them to pen their first fantasy novel. Sometimes, written profiles of Bex or Sam opened with a discussion of the fic as a way to discuss the famous chemistry, given how many of the stories "fixed" the unwillingness of the show to get their characters together. There were thousands of Cora and Henri fanfic romances containing every possible trope, so much so that fans considered the relationship "head canon"—in other words, an established fact, true in the fans' imagination.

But the idea of Luciana de León curled up in an expensive ergonomic chair in front of her sleek computer scrolling through fic was difficult to summon, even as Bex tried. Was this flattering? Shocking? She had no idea.

"Your Big Name Fan is someone who just about everyone in the fandom knows about," Sam said. "Sometimes the term has a bad connotation, like the fan's gotten too big with themself, but usually it's someone who brings the fans together. Maybe they organize the con or run the forum, or maybe they write the best fic."

"That." Luciana tapped the *t* sound at the end of the word, making it land decisively. "The very, very best *Craven* fic. So my first goal, today, is to find out if one of you two is CravingCraven, and if not, then who on that soundstage was."

"What?" Bex laughed, though she could tell Luciana was serious. "Why would you . . . ?"

Luciana smiled coyly at Bex. "That's just the kind of *Who, me?* I would expect from CravingCraven, trying to stop someone from unmasking them."

Bex looked for help to Sam, who only shrugged. "We both know I don't know everything about you, Bex. Even if there are those who wish I did."

"Holy cow," Bex whispered, forgetting about the mic. "I promise I'm not CravingCraven. I'm good at telling stories but not writing them."

Luciana stared at her for a long moment of dead air. "I believe you."

"It's not me, either." Sam drummed her finger against her bare forearm. "But I'd love to hear why you thought it might be."

"Let me demonstrate why, instead." She turned toward the sound booth, where Amethyst was goggling at them, probably wondering how she could edit this episode without getting fired. "Run my clip, darling?"

Nervous, Bex pulled her microphone closer. "Just to set the stage for our listeners, we're about to view a video clip that Luciana's selected from her appearance on *Craven's Daughter*. Sam and I don't know what clip she's chosen. We'll be surprised, too. You guys will be able to hear the audio of the clip, so you can follow along. If you want to see the video, the clips will be posted in full on the podcast's website."

As Bex finished this explanation, the big projection screen against the wall lit up, and Luciana's video started to play. The sound was too loud in the small studio, so loud that Bex could hear the intermingled rapid breathing of both characters and the scrape of someone's shoe against the floor of the set.

"Are you okay?" Cora Banks crouches underneath the big wooden desk on the office set, glass scattered on the floor around her from gunshot, the Peter Pan collar of her flowered blouse dotted with blood. Her eyes are huge. She's whispering, but with a thread of tears.

Henri's flushed face is smeared with blood. Her ponytail is coming apart, and she has a gun holster cinched tight across her chest. She searches Cora's expression. "Why wouldn't I be?" Her voice breaks, sheared off, the last vowel crashing over the cliff of how she's looking at Cora.

Cora shakes her head. She reaches out in the tiny space under the desk with a trembling hand and gently pushes a lock of hair off Henri's forehead, touching a bullet graze that Jen had expertly applied with scar wax and stage blood. Henri hisses and flinches at the contact with the wound, and Cora's fingertip comes away red.

"You're not," Cora says. "It's okay if you're not okay. That's what I tell my students. There's a lot you could learn from a kindergarten teacher, Agent Shannon."

Bette, who wrote the episode, had meant the line to be a quip at the end of the scene, but Bexley's voice had gone hoarse delivering it. The way Sam was looking at her hadn't allowed for a quip.

Even on the big screen, all these years later, Bex couldn't tell who leaned in first.

They didn't kiss. Their lips didn't touch. Nothing happened.

That was what she'd told herself afterward in her dressing room, when she had to tell herself something to make her hands stop shaking so she could unbutton the tiny buttons on the blouse of her costume and change into her real clothes. *Nothing happened.*

But what had *almost* happened was undeniable.

Aaron never mentioned it. Nor did he cut it from the episode. An interruption to their *almost* was filmed later and edited into the scene, with the receptionist character, Rose, walking in on the carnage of the office and calling out to Henri and Cora.

Moments like the *almost*, combined with the way the ambiguous direction in the show's scripts seemed to keep making room for them to happen, were why Sam and Bex had thought they had an ally in Aaron when they first went to him about Cora and Henri's arc. They were wrong.

Bex inhaled to chase away the memories. She looked to Sam, hoping she would start talking about the scene, what it had been like to shoot it, *anything*, but Sam was gazing at the blank white projection screen, preoccupied with her own thoughts.

"Well." Luciana leaned into the mic again. "I have so many

questions for the both of you, but first, I've prepared a dramatic reading."

She got out her phone and tapped and scrolled. Bex felt a little short of breath at their departure from format—Amethyst had made it clear they were supposed to discuss the clips at some length—but she supposed they'd just have to record and edit in a conversation later. Luciana had abandoned the script, and there was nothing for Bex to do but improvise.

"Here we are. An excerpt from 'It's Okay If You're Not Okay,' an in-canon, one-shot short by CravingCraven. For our listeners who don't read fanfiction, you should. It's everything. 'In-canon' refers to a story that follows the same plot line as the fiction that inspired it, but in this case it supplies all the emotions and internal thoughts the viewer can't have access to. 'One-shot' just means it's not part of a longer piece. It's a one-off short story. Rated M for Mature."

She flashed Sam a smile and began to read.

> Cora couldn't feel where the glass had cut her knee, or smell the gun smoke, or hear how silent the office had gone in the wake of the gunshot after Henri had grabbed her by the waist and pushed her under the desk before firing off two shots down the hallway. When she'd met Henri, her holster marked the closest Cora had ever come to a gun, and right this moment was the first time she'd ever heard one fire. Henri's graze on her forehead was the first gunshot wound she'd seen.
>
> Why didn't that matter?
>
> Why was it that all she could feel was Henri's breath against her mouth? All she could smell was her wintergreen Altoids? And all she heard was how fast her own heart was beating?
>
> And then, all she could feel was Henri's hand

cradling her jaw and how it sent a wash of goosebumps under the collar of her dress.

"I'm okay," Henri whispered.

"You are?" Cora didn't say this out loud,
because Henri's mouth had met hers—or she
did, and her words were lost in a kiss that sent her
racing heart into an insistent pulse in the secret
places of her body and made her reach for something to hang on to. What she found was the front
of Henri's shirt, bisected by the leather strap of her
holster, and Cora grabbed on to that strap and
pulled Henri close so she knew that Cora wanted
this. Wanted her.

Luciana set her phone down and fanned herself. "So fucking
good, right?"

"Um," Bex started, but nothing else came after. She couldn't
think past the kaleidoscope of feelings and memories the story
had dragged out of her. The wintergreen smell of Sam's breath.
The way Sam's hand had felt, hot against her jawbone, making her
body heavy, drugging her with every heartbeat until she'd closed
her eyes in anticipation of that kiss that never came.

Sam reached slowly up for her microphone. Bex watched the
strap of her slip dress slide down her golden shoulder, then realized
she was staring but couldn't do anything about it because the fanfic scene was burning through her brain like dry kindling on fire.

So of course Sam caught her staring, and all Bex could do was
plead helplessly, silently, for her to make it stop.

"Let's give Bexley a moment," Sam said, which made Bex's
cheeks glow even hotter. She leaned back in her chair, towing the
microphone to the farthest reach of its ceiling mount, and crossed
her legs as though she were completely unaffected.

It was what Sam did when she was completely unaffected.
But it was *also* what Sam did when she was worked up, flustered,

or upset and didn't want anyone to be able to tell—because, she'd once explained to Bex, she grew up in a house with four older brothers and was forced to learn very young how to protect herself.

Sam wasn't upset. She was *excited*, and trying hard not to show it.

What had Sam seen in the clip?

"While our Bexley is recovering, I'm happy to address the elephant in the room," Sam said. "In the clip, on the show, there's no kiss. The fic drives right at that and gives the fans what they want. But that's not the only thing Luciana noticed. She must have spotted a few other things that our listening audience, even the die-hard *Craven* fans, couldn't have."

"This is delicious," Luciana said. "I am living for it. Tell them what you heard, Samantha. I want to hear what shocked and surprised you."

"Number one, in the fic, Cora cuts her knee. That happened for real."

Bex let out an involuntary noise of surprise, beginning to understand what Sam was excited about. "It did! I had to get stitches! But you can't see it in the film, can you?" She glanced toward the booth, wondering if she should ask Amethyst to play it back for confirmation.

"No, you can't," Sam said. "Our knees aren't in the frame after we stand up, and even *you* didn't notice your knee was bleeding, Bex, until later, when you changed out of your costume."

"That's right." She remembered returning to the set in search of a first-aid kit, the crepe dress pants she'd worn for her first real day of work rolled up to her thigh. She'd smeared blood all over her leg when she pulled the pants on, ruining the lining. She'd been so embarrassed.

"Everyone was surprised she could have been cut so deep by breakaway glass," Sam said to Luciana. "It's made of sugar. It's not supposed to be able to do that. I went to look at the shards left on the set, but someone had already swept them up. I wanted to see how sugar glass could've cut Bex."

"If it really was sugar glass," Luciana said. They were leaning toward each other, speaking crisply and fluently into their mikes. Bex felt like she was hearing every other word as she scrambled to keep up. "What else did you see?"

"This one's kind of throwing me for a loop. It's the dialogue in the fic. I say, 'I'm okay,' and Cora says, 'You are?' Those lines aren't in the episode that aired."

"Oh, whoa." The realization hit Bex as a wash of cold from the nape of her neck to the base of her spine. "Those were the lines in the original script, but we didn't say them on TV."

Bex had memorized every word of the episode's script, obsessively preparing for her first real day of filming—not a rehearsal, not a pilot, but a network show with a shot at the career she'd strived for. After Aaron called *cut* on the last scene, freezing on Bex staring at Sam in a hazy, lust-drunk fog, she had been humiliated to realize they'd dropped lines. She and Sam had talked about it afterward, and Sam—who had more experience of television from her seasons on *Utopia*—had reassured her it wasn't an issue.

Bex looked at Luciana. "You remembered that, too. How?"

Luciana tapped her temple. "I was elbows-deep in that script with Bette, as you said. *I* remember you were cut and needed stitches. *I* remember Sam's mints. I was there. But who could have written this story? Only someone who was also there. No one else. This story made me go back and reread all the CravingCraven fic I could find. What I am telling you is those fics are brimming with insider information. *Knowledgeable* details." She settled her chin in her hand. "So CravingCraven really isn't one of you?"

"No," Sam said.

Bex shook her head, her thoughts scattered, but then remembered there were no cameras. "Not me."

"Well." Luciana leaned back. "Then let this episode be a flag waving in front of your fans. Someone in Wisconsin will have made a complete codex within the week, cross-referencing six seasons with CravingCraven's entire catalog."

"So, hypothetically, there could be behind-the-scenes drama in the fic, maybe even things Bex and I didn't know about," Sam said. "Is that possible?"

"It's more than possible," Luciana said. "It's for real."

Bex had never imagined the fanfic as more than a kind of echo, a response to what she and Sam were doing on *Craven's Daughter*, but what Luciana was describing was something different—a separate fictional world, brimming with details and emotion, whose most celebrated writer had a real-life link to their show and a fresh perspective on it.

"That's fascinating," Sam said. "What a mystery."

"Someone who remembers what we remember but from a different viewpoint," Bex said. "Someone who wrote everything down when they were seeing it, with all the feelings, the conflicts—"

"There could be answers there," Sam said.

Luciana leaned forward, her eyes wide. "Answers to what kinds of questions, Samantha?"

"Why the fans never got what they wanted for Henri and Cora," Sam replied. "For starters."

"The machinations and secrets of the cast and crew. The silence of the network. And the good news is that you have a platform now"—Luciana gestured at the podcast studio—"tailor-made to get to the bottom of things that never got the full explanation they deserved."

"That's why I'm here." Sam's voice had risen to a higher pitch, genuinely excited. "To talk about what the media never got to the bottom of, what we weren't allowed to talk about. What the police never got to the bottom of. Cineline even titled this podcast to help a girl out. *Craven's Daughter: Cold Case.*"

All at once, Bex fully understood the source of Sam's excitement. "You mean Jen."

Sam's mouth firmed. "I do. I'd love to make what happened to her make sense."

"Yesss." Luciana's her eyes were shiny, her hands over her heart.

Again, Bex remembered their audience. "Jen Arnot, for those who didn't follow or didn't know about our tragedy, was the makeup artist for *Craven's Daughter* and a dear friend of mine and Sam's. Most of her career, she did FX makeup, and she was famous in her own right. But her health suffered, she believed from sensitivity to the solvents and specialized chemicals FX artists use in their work, and she'd had to step back from the full-time FX work that had made her famous. *Craven's Daughter* was lucky to have her. I don't know that there's ever been a procedural on television with more realistic wounds, corpses, and blood. Unfortunately, Jen died in an awful accident when we were on location in Chicago getting exteriors—"

"Outdoor scenes," Sam cut in.

"Yes. We went to Chicago to film exteriors every year."

"You and I were out the night before." Sam had her elbows on the table, her attention on Bex. "We went to that standup comedy show."

Bex shivered in the warm studio. "We'd wrapped our big scene on the balcony that night."

"Tell us about the balcony." Luciana's voice was a low purr. "I think of it almost as a character on the show, it's so familiar."

It was her smooth delivery of this imperative that shook Bex out of the moment enough to recognize they'd veered far from the promised format. Alarmed, Bex looked over at Amethyst in the glass booth.

Amethyst pointed at her tablet, indicating that Bex should look at her own, set up at the center of the table so Amethyst could silently communicate with them as they recorded.

It's sensitive, but we'll edit for issues of slander
or defamation. Stick to what's true to your
experience.

Sam clocked the message on her own tablet's screen and gave
Amethyst a thumbs up. "This happened before I was cast, but I
was told the network hired and fired three location scouts trying
to find the balcony Josh wanted."

"Josh Miller, our set designer," Bex reminded the audience.

"Yeah," Sam confirmed. "They knew they wanted to build a
Chicago set in L.A., but Josh insisted there had to be a real building, a real balcony for exteriors, or it wouldn't feel right. Eventually, they found it on the third story of a building on the Near
North Side. We had a replica on set, but it was only for close shots.
We filmed the season finales and major turning points on the Chicago balcony, because that made it possible to do the wide shots,
pulling away, showing street life with background actors."

"Bette always said the balcony was the heart of *Craven's
Daughter*," Bex remembered. "If she put a scene on the balcony, it
was because she wanted it to really slay."

Poor choice of words. Her hands were trembling.

"Tell us what happened," Luciana said.

"I woke up to someone pounding on the door of my hotel
room," Bex remembered. "There were a dozen texts on my phone.
It was about Jen. She'd been found in the alley. No one knew why
she was there. We'd wrapped the shoot the day before. It was confusing. My agent and manager kept calling me, and I kept asking
what to do, and then finally, around midnight, we were told the
network wanted everyone to return to L.A."

In California, Jen's dying had felt like it happened in another
world. Bex crossed her arms, chilled by leftover grief. She stood,
pointing her body toward Amethyst, and sliced a finger across
her throat.

Luciana and Sam took off their headsets at the tone that meant Amethyst had stopped recording.

"I just wanted to steal a minute. I don't think we shouldn't talk about it, but I don't want to be recording and crying at the same time. I want to keep it . . ." Bex looked at Sam.

"Respectful," Sam filled in. "Not salacious. A part of what happened to us."

"Yeah."

Sam stood up and retrieved seltzers for everyone from a small fridge outside the studio doors. Luciana made a call in the hallway. It was what Bex needed. Just to breathe.

When they pulled their headsets back on and Amethyst started recording, Bex felt a little stronger.

"Everyone called it 'the accident.'" Sam's voice had gravel in it. "We had all these theories. Jen jumped. Someone pushed her. She was attacked. There would be security footage. The police would find witnesses. The network told us nothing but what we shouldn't do. 'Don't talk to the press. Don't talk to police without a network representative present.' We never got answers. Not *one* answer, anyway, just a lot of little pieces of an answer that were hard to put together. Jen was alone when she fell. They were pretty clear about that."

"I tried to block out the speculation and the gossip," Bex admitted. "My sisters thought of Jen like an auntie. I focused on helping them cope. And the show had to go on. What I did hear was that Jen stayed behind that night. She was sleeping off a migraine. Her migraines were terrible. She had a medicine that helped, but it made her feel shaky, so she'd sometimes grab a nap after she took it. When she woke up that night, she went out to the balcony for fresh air, but she would have been unsteady on her feet. She was likely confused."

Bex found that she couldn't continue. Sam picked up where she'd left off. "The balcony we had on set here in California was almost an exact replica. It would be easy to get confused.

Sometimes when we were filming in Chicago, I got a little disoriented and had to remind myself, *Hey, there's a thirty-foot drop right there*. Because on set, our balcony was only a couple feet off the ground. People sat on the railing. Hopped off." Sam had her hand over her heart. "I hated losing Jen," she said, with raw emotion. "I hated the way the network and our cast and crew handled it. Everything about it. Everything."

"It was never the same after that," Bex said.

It was never the same after that. It felt like a revelation, making Bex wonder why she hadn't paid more attention to the ways that Jen's death had changed her life. Maybe it would have felt selfish to acknowledge it, since she had the great fortune of still being alive. But *wasn't* it true? Jen died, and Bex changed. Sam changed. Frankie and Vic changed. *Craven's Daughter* changed. Bex messed up with Sam, and Sam abandoned her. She had to find a new job. She was afraid again.

Jen died, and her death unpicked a stitch that had held Bex's life together.

"Back then, we couldn't make sense of so many things," Sam said softly. "But now maybe we can. We have this loss. We have this fic that someone was writing from inside our own show, someone who took our side against a studio that decided advertisers wouldn't buy time on a ratings-busting series if the two women on it loved each other."

"But that was then," Luciana said. "This is now. Now it's you and the fans against the whole world. Like you said, Sam. It's *your* cold case. You can find out the things you need to know. Answer your questions and put them to bed."

"I have a lot of questions." Sam looked at Bex. "I'm going to ask *you* again—"

"You don't have to." Bex jutted her chin at Sam. "I'm in."

Even though there was so much she needed to think about, the words Luciana had just said were clanging in Bex's head, drowning out everything else.

You can find out the things you need to know.

Bex had spent her whole adult life telling other people's stories for her job. But this story, her story—her and Sam's story—she'd never been able to tell, because she'd been hostage to the threat Sam put into plain language for their listeners.

The threat of two women loving each other.

Just that. The idea that if Cora and Henri loved each other, advertisers would step back. The network would lose confidence. Aaron would storm out, and without him, the show would falter. Bex would lose her job—the one way she knew how to keep the world together.

But what if they *had* loved each other?

That would be a story worth telling, even if they only told it to their fans. Even if it was a story Bex only needed to tell herself.

Even if she wasn't sure whether the two women she was thinking about were Cora and Henri or Bex and Sam.

Luciana stood up, silk shimmering. "My work here is done. I'm adding you both to a group chat. Keep me posted."

I Played a Detective on TV

"**O**h! You know what I would love so, so much?" The photographer from Cineline's media services and publicity department put her hand on her hip with a saucy smile at Bex and Sam. "Let's get a few shots of you two under the desk!"

Bex smiled back in a way she hoped was not pained. She reached under the bustline of the daisy-printed, flare-skirted dress she wore and attempted to adjust her bra, which had the gravity-defying architecture necessary to pull off the dress's shape but itched like an actual plague. There was also a white patent belt. Pink patent shoes. Her hair was big, her lashes long. She was the sexy version of Cora Banks. This was a favorite publicity photo choice for *Craven's Daughter*, one she'd hoped never to revisit.

Sam didn't seem any more comfortable playing the sexy version of Henri. Her dark slacks were so tight, Bex thought she'd better steer clear of the lamp on the PI desk. One tiny rip would have those pants bursting into shards, leaving Sam wearing nothing but an Oxford unbuttoned to her navel and a gun holster that looked like something you'd buy at a shop in the Valley off a big-busted mannequin in a red-neon-lit window.

They'd slicked her hair back, too. Media people cherished a collective fetish for slicked-back-hair Sam. Something about her California tan, broad cheekbones, and full mouth made every stylist who'd ever met her want to throw her in a white tank top and spray her with water.

Understandable, but unfair to Sam.

Bex sized up the area under the desk. It hadn't gotten any larger in the past five years. If she crawled under there, her boobs would be holding up her chin. "That space is small, and my heels are high," Bex told the photographer.

"Kick them off! I'll arrange them in front of you, maybe in a little tableau with Henri's holster. Like a visual wink!"

The photographer's assistant came jogging up, presumably to take Bex's shoes and Sam's holster.

"No," Sam said.

"Absolutely not." Bex stepped away from the assistant, who had already knelt down in front of her to retrieve the shoes.

The photographer bit her lip, genuinely confused. Bex empathized. She was confused, too. Every bit of the costume was pinching, chafing, and hot. Her fake lashes were sticky. Her lips had been overlined, making her mouth feel like a big red smear across her face.

She stepped out of the shoes herself, not so she could crawl under the desk, but because her arms and legs had gone numb. She reached up and clawed at the bustline of the dress, trying to find something to loosen, but couldn't. She was trapped.

She backed up, leaned against the desk, bent at the waist, trying to breathe.

"Hey." Sam crouched in front of her, looking into her eyes.

"Yeah. I'm not doing this. I can't do this, I don't think."

Sam gripped her elbow. "It's okay. We can—"

"So the rumors are true!" A man's voice rang across the soundstage, the vowels cinched by an early life in Queens and an adulthood with too much money. "Love to see it!"

Niels Shaughnessy's leather-soled wingtips tapped onto the *Craven* set. He wore a ten-thousand-dollar suit without a tie, a look he often sported when he came down from his penthouse office to check on his subjects. Sam said he took off his tie because he aspired to look like one of the sun-kissed Robert Redford candids he'd framed on his office wall, and he did, kind of. A craggier, late-middle-aged version with veneers and an artificially low hairline he'd purchased in Turkey sometime in the break between *Craven*'s second and third seasons.

Bex stood and turned fully to face him, and for the first time, she didn't automatically smile when he grinned at her. She didn't laugh. She didn't arrange herself to display her best angle. She just stared at him and thought of what Frankie had said about the *Craven's Daughter* set.

Isn't it the most haunting thing ever to see it resurrected like this?

Not ghosts. Guys in suits who reminded Bex she had been here to feed two children and live in a good school district and never, ever fuck up. That was what had been haunting Bex for years. Niels Shaughnessy. Men like Niels Shaughnessy. She pushed her palm against her heart. Maybe it was going so fast because it wanted her to run away from this specter.

"Niels." Sam's tone was the perfect marriage of a question and a dismissal. Bex would have to practice that tone in the mirror. It must be so useful.

"I couldn't stay away. You know what you should do?" He looked toward the photographer. "Get some pictures with them under the desk."

"Not doing that," Bex said before Sam could respond. Her voice had zero tone. It could've been a robot voice on an automated phone system. Nevertheless, her refusal smacked against Niels's face, drooping his distinguished creases into an ugly frown.

"The team was looking at the old marketing portfolio to pass on to production for promos. We remembered what we loved about the show."

What you loved about the show gives me hives, Bex thought.

That was when her brain came completely back online, because it was a new kind of thought. It turned her *run away* heart rate into an *I think I'm pissed* heart rate and warmed up her muscles. "That's why this isn't working." Bex gestured at herself, girdled into the dress. She searched for her next line in her head and couldn't find it, so she said her first line again, louder. "That's why this isn't working. This." She grabbed the skirt of her dress. "And this." She pointed at Sam's hair like a wet helmet.

Niels's frown deepened. He didn't understand. She knew she should care, but she couldn't, somehow, with Sam here. She wasn't going to get on the floor and cram herself under the desk with their mouths almost touching and inches of cleavage that would be airbrushed to remove her freckles until she looked like a powdered doll.

"It's boring," Sam said, unbuckling her holster. "No offense, but the fans have seen it. The poster's still tacked up in their office cubicles. We need to show them Cora and Henri like they haven't seen us before."

The network head rubbed his hands together. Bex could visibly see him switching gears in order to regain his hold on the scepter of power, which reminded her she was supposed to be letting him have it so he would give her what *she* wanted.

Her stomach twisted under her tight clothes as if it were trying to tell her something.

"Gotcha," Niels said. "Smart." The photographer had already sprung to a rack of clothes and started flipping through them, hissing directions at her assistant. "Come up with something better," he told them both. "Nostalgic but fresh, and kind of sexy, but classy-sexy. And young. Definitely young. But more sophisticated."

"Nah, let's circle back another time. I don't feel like the energy's where we need it today." Sam dropped the holster on the floor. "Take five to change and meet me at our old spot?" she asked Bex.

"Yes."

Saying yes to Sam was the easiest thing that had happened in the past hour. Bex didn't look at Niels when she walked off the set.

Her brain was too busy, trying to identify the words that would match her feelings. So far, all she had was anger.

She discarded the costume in her old dressing room without bothering to hang it up. She left makeup remover wipes on the vanity, the lashes sticking to them like spiders. She always cared for her costumes. *They belonged to the studio.* She never left any kind of mess behind. *She had a reputation.*

She didn't say no. *She was lucky to have the work.*

Bex learned her lines, stayed as late as they wanted, gave them as many takes as they requested, took direction, tried and tried again and sent thank-you notes and gifts after the season wrapped, because she was a professional. The most professional.

Her mother had been a classically trained pianist. She'd worn gold earrings every day while teaching music lessons to children who would never have to worry about making bills. Theresa Cunningham, single mom, was the kind of woman who checked her lipstick in the mirror and stayed up late to iron a crisp pleat into her silky trousers. Even when she and Bex had to move from the apartment with the scary landlord to a different one where they shared a bed, the stubborn lift to her mother's chin made Bex's heart burst with everything she wanted her to have.

Her mother had met Avery Simon after a day of back-to-back piano and voice lessons. She'd been fighting a cold, locking up the exterior door of a church that had let her use its space to teach her students. He was chasing a stack of papers that had fallen out of a folder and blown across the church lawn as he made his way to a client's office down the street. It would have been a classic meet-cute, except the papers were wealth management documents, the client down the street was the father of two of Theresa's most entitled, least well-behaved piano students, and Avery's client had fallen two months behind paying for his children's lessons.

Most times, Theresa would have kindly helped pick up the papers, making witty small talk. But this time she broke. Avery Simon got a searing earful about rich men who didn't pay and the women who propped them and their children up, and then Theresa let Avery take her to dinner because he'd accepted her screed with humility.

Bex was starting to understand what kinds of feelings had led up to her mom losing her shit on a church lawn with a stranger.

She exited out a door at the back of Stage 46 and traveled through the maze of exterior sets on the studio's lot. It was windy. If she'd still lived in Ohio, the weather would've made Bex think a storm was coming, but this was Los Angeles. Despite the strong top note of smoke in the air, the sun was shining, the cloudless sky a muted duck's-egg blue.

Rounding a corner, she spotted a familiar false brick wall and stopped, surprised it was still here.

There was Sam, sitting on the disused and abandoned New York City brownstone stoop of, ironically, the loft apartment set from *See You Never*, the show that had made both Luciana de León and Aaron Gorman famous. Decades ago, this set had been part of the studio tour, but it was decommissioned in the second season of *Craven's Daughter* and moved to this lonely dead zone on the lot, crammed in beside carnival equipment and the oversized props for a Chinese New Year parade scene. The stoop became a favorite hangout spot for Bex and Sam, a home away from home where they could steal fifteen minutes of privacy together.

Their spot.

Sam had her legs stretched out on the stairs and her back against the fake brick side of the stoop, a knee up, her wrist draped casually over it. She'd brushed the gel out of her hair and changed into an old Yale Drama sweatshirt and ripped jeans, her Oakland A's ball cap sitting on her knee. She looked so painfully familiar, like how Bex used to see her every day, it was difficult to believe the years they'd lost each other had actually turned the earth and taken it around the sun.

"Hey," Sam said.

"Hey to you." Bex dropped her big bag and sat down on the

step across from Sam, leaning her back against the facing false bricks. Their assigned seats. She sighed. "That was a shitshow."

"I only wish I had a picture of Niels Shaughnessy's face when you checked him. I think that's the first time I've ever seen you do that. If I *did* have a picture, I would blow it up and hang it over my bed before I filled the water glass on my nightstand with his tears."

"I don't even know *why* I did that." Bex's skin still felt too tight, her clothes overwarm despite the breeze. She'd banged into a countertop on the way out of her dressing room, and her hip ached where a bruise would inevitably form.

"Don't you?" Sam cocked her head, studying Bex. "Guess."

Bex stretched her legs. "I put on that dress and those heels like I owed someone something," she said. "And then I'm being told to crawl under a desk with you, and I can't breathe, and my heart's exploding. Oh, and here comes Niels, wanting more of what I don't have to give."

He wanted to know he had power over Bex. That's what Frankie had said, and even Sam had implied that it was obvious. Bex had thought she was fine with that exchange. After all, giving Niels the upper hand so she could have the part she wanted was *her plan.*

Maybe she'd been away from network TV and its power games for too long.

"Did I have it back then, Sam? Whatever he wanted?"

Sam played with the ends of her hair, looking at Bex steadily like she was seriously considering every part of Bex's question. Her face, her focus, her entire energy paid attention to Bex like no one else ever had. "The nastiest fear of this business is scarcity," she said. "That there isn't enough. There isn't enough work for a gay woman to consistently be cast, or there's only enough for her to have one part a year. There isn't enough for a Black actor, especially if the studio 'already made' a film with a Black cast. There's less and less, the older we get. Meanwhile, we're asked to pretend like we have so much to offer. We're so beautiful, so young, so sexy, so interesting, so white, that whoever hires us never needs to fear scarcity again. Behold"—Sam lifted her hands in the air—"I am the fatted calf you have waited for. I will feed you and your children generously, and their children after them."

Bex laughed, shaking her head. "God."

"And that's what we internalized! We took in that there's basically no work for anyone, ever, and if we get lucky enough to work, we have to be more, no, more than that. So my answer, Bex, is that this is a business that behaves as though it's starving even while a human as glorious as Viola Davis exists. It's a business that's constantly on the hunt for the next nineteen-year-old cis, straight, white actor while there's experienced, singular talent that's being left on the shelf or, worse, used once and thrown away. None of us are what any of them want."

Bex recognized the truth when she heard it. "So then what do you do?"

"Fuck 'em," Sam said. "And repeat yourself. You know how many times I've had to remind my agent she can't ask me if I'm going to talk about my girlfriend on a press junket just because she got a worried call from an executive producer who's hoping maybe I'll be more straight on this one?"

Girlfriend. Not the point of Sam's righteous tirade, but Bex wished she could ask for a clarifying footnote, like, *And do you have one of these "girlfriends" at the moment?*

"A lot of times?"

"All of the times, Bex. All of them. At the end of the day, no fucks means I can close my eyes and fall asleep knowing that whatever it is I have is what they have wanted to give *me*. Me. As I am. And anything I didn't have that I lost out on or was never offered was going to be something that hurt too much to feel sad about."

Bex had met Sam's dad a few times. He was a jovial, mildly clueless man who'd fathered his five children with four different women and didn't seem bothered that he'd ended up with a mishmash of partial and full custody of the whole lot of them. Sam's mom hadn't been sure about having a kid when she found herself pregnant. She'd tried, but she couldn't stick it out. Sam saw her every few years for an hour or two and seemed content with this arrangement.

Bex had always thought Sam had a gift for being content. Now she thought maybe Sam had a gift for deciding what was worth fighting about. Like Bex's mom.

"I like it," she said. "You have to help me, though. I'm willing, but I'm brand-new to figuring out how not to hand over any fucks."

"I can do that," Sam said. "That is something I *can* do, when it comes to you, Bex."

"Right." Bex had let the stoop go to her head.

"Because it's been longer than a long time." Sam met her eyes. "Offering you a little help keeping hold of your fucks is easy. I think, though, more than that would be too hard for me when I already got my answer about us five years ago."

She nodded her acknowledgment of Sam's gentle boundary. She *had* hurt Sam. That was what Sam meant. But Bex had known that already. The way Sam left *Craven's Daughter*—left the set, then left the show, then left L.A. and didn't come back except to breeze in and out between projects for the next few years—was all the confirmation Bex had needed.

Will they or won't they? It was the worst-best trope in the world for a reason.

"Serious question," Sam said after they'd sat in the breeze for a while, listening to the far-off sound of the backup alarm on a studio truck while Bex thumbed through her mental notebook of regrets. "Have you been reading the fanfic all week like I have? Because I've got to say, I've run across some flattering descriptions of myself. I read one last night that said I had eyes like the sky. Do I have eyes like the sky, Bexley?"

"Yes." Bex was grateful for the olive branch of humor. "Every project you've ever done has been lit, in part, to make your eyes so blue, they don't look real. As you well know."

"Like that. I was reading a lot of things like that, but I enjoy it more from you. Now tell me about my legs."

Sam was teasing her, letting her know she'd noticed Bex's attention in the podcast recording studio, but Sam teased and flirted with a lot of women. Bex resolved not to let it go far enough that she'd get confused and hurt herself and Sam all over again.

"Once I figured out that 'AU' meant 'alternative universe,' and what a one-shot was, versus canon, versus fluff, versus angst, et cetera"—Bex made a dramatic gesture—"I was most interested in how many times the words *lush, expressive, fiery-haired,* and, let's just get it out there, *edible* came up in descriptions of me."

Sam let out a surprised laugh. "So we're obviously hot." She tapped her lip. "Why is it that being told I'm such a hottie in these fanfics is better than any media write-up? My ego is enormous, I don't mind telling you. It has been stroked into a truly terrifying size."

"Gross." Bex dug in her bag for her water and took a drink. "But I know what you mean. I think it's because they're not telling *you.* Or me. They're telling themselves and each other. Even when what they write isn't flattering, instead of feeling like a pan in a review, it only feels interesting because you can see so much care and love and attention in there."

"They're making something with what we made. Always more interesting than getting someone's opinion. Speaking of people making something with what we made, I saw you jumping in the comments on that explainer TikTok that's making the rounds."

"I only left a heart."

Sam laughed. "'I only left a heart,' she says. There are hundreds of videos and three Buzzfeed stories about that heart already."

She was exaggerating, but it had certainly been a strong week for media coverage. Their podcast with Luciana had hit the top spot in the rankings within twenty-four hours and held there. "It was a good explainer."

"Yeah." Sam folded herself into crisscross applesauce and tapped her ball cap against her knee. "Luciana wasn't wrong about the podcast waving a flag in front of the fans. I'm in awe of how well these people drive the Internet. Did you see that crowd-sourced list that had every person in the credits of every episode, what episodes each person worked on, number of episodes, codes for episodes that line up with the romantic arc, and a separate tab for who was consistent on set for each of *those* episodes? Or the script deep-dives, serving the kind of textual analysis you only find in Taylor Swift lyrics breakdowns to get to how much they think was written to be romantic and how much we brought to it. Who was involved. Everything."

"Everything," Bex agreed. "Including everything about Jen."

That had been difficult at first, seeing Jen's accident and its aftermath through so many third-party perspectives. Some were breathless with conspiracy, others so dry and calculating it was all Bex could do not to get angry. She found herself circling like a restless shark, moving from fanfic to social media posts, from CravingCraven stories to anything else. And remembering Jen. Remembering what it had been like after losing Jen.

Sam cleared her throat. "Validating."

Yes. Remembering that, too—that when Jen died, there had been a lot of pressure not to talk about it. The studio had instructed them not to speak in public about Jen, and that silence had extended to private conversations on set as everyone, together, enforced the unspoken rule that they were supposed to put Jen's death behind them as an unfortunate accident, best forgotten.

Sam must have felt the same pressure, but she hadn't succumbed to it. She'd stopped table reads to ask questions. On set between takes, she would interrogate crew about what they thought might have happened, how they felt about the investigation or the official conclusion that Jen's death was an accident. Sam kept trying until Bex could feel her frustration like a heartbeat.

"I'm glad," she said. "You've been owed that validation for a long time."

Sam slid her ball cap onto her head as the sun changed its angle, throwing her eyes into shadow. "I don't know how deep you got into the fan analysis of CravingCraven's fic."

"Not super-deep. I did see one person asking who one of the pirate characters was supposed to be in the CravingCraven AU with the pirates, and I thought it was so funny, because when *I* read it, I was just, like—"

"That's a gender-flipped Alicia! Our script supervisor is the pirate!"

"Exactly." She held her water bottle out to Sam, who accepted it and took a long drink. "Because of the thing with the bangles and how the pirate smelled like he'd just peeled an orange. Our fans got it right that the pirate was crew, not cast, but they can't see the things we can see right away. It made me want to help them. That's why I left that heart."

"You know what makes me really angry?"

"So many things."

Sam laughed. "Less than you think. But what makes me angry about this, specifically, is these fans were always there, rooting for us." Sam's eyes found Bex's. "Back then, it would have been nice to have solidarity like what I've felt in the last few days."

"We were facing so much denial."

"I felt like no one cared about Jen." Sam's voice was a little thick. "And definitely, for sure, no one wanted to consider the possibility that maybe Jen's accident wasn't an accident."

Bex took a deep breath to thaw the ice that had climbed into her chest. "I always thought, you know, the investigation had to rule out murder. Murder was *ruled out*. That means if Jen really was killed, there was a conspiracy. The kind where you make a murder look like something else. I know we just played detectives on TV, but we did learn some real detective things. Remember Georgie Hayworth, the retired Chicago detective who came on as our script consultant expert?"

Sam nodded.

"Georgie told us that conspiracy to murder and staged scenes are exceedingly rare in real life. Or they're really badly done in the heat of the moment."

"You mean like putting the gun in the victim's hand to make it look like suicide."

"Right. But they put the gun in the victim's nondominant hand, or the wrong way, or it's the wrong injury for that. The police in Chicago were convinced that Jen fell."

According to the fans, it was simple. Either Jen had fallen or someone had killed her. If she'd fallen, there should be a way to know why and how it had happened. If someone had killed her, then who had done it, and what was their motive?

They were questions Sam had tried to get answers to, but no one had wanted to help. Bex had been afraid even to ask them.

"I know I'm biased by the feeling of solidarity with these fans. That's huge." Sam ran her hands over her knees, restless. "But I don't like that they've only got scraps to work with. You're right that we know things they can't know. We were there. And now, because of this podcast and reunion special, we have access to everybody from the *Craven* cast and crew, so we can find out what *they* know."

Sam handed Bex's water bottle back to her, empty now. She'd spoken so casually, Bex might easily have been fooled into thinking what she'd said was the only logical conclusion.

It had been a long time since Bex sat on this stoop with Sam, but not so long that she could be tricked by Sam's casual tone into missing her meaning. "Sam."

"What?"

"You know TV detectives aren't real detectives."

Sam crossed her arms. "I said nothing about playing detective."

Bex crossed her own arms in an attempt to keep up. "You didn't have to. You're suggesting we do more than try to get some of our questions answered in the natural course of doing the podcast. You're suggesting we *investigate* this. In front of our fans. *With* our fans. That we use Cineline's podcast—"

"Our podcast. We agreed."

"—to drag out the studio's dirty laundry about a person's death. An actual real person who we both loved." Bex thought fleetingly of Jen's mother, Toni, a wonderful woman who Bex still kept in touch with. Bex needed to call her. She should have called her already.

"Don't forget the dirty laundry about not letting Cora and Henri get together," Sam said. "So far, I'm finding the airing of that particular laundry a good thing."

Bex was, too. "I don't want to get anyone fired."

Sam narrowed her eyes. "You used to keep a burn list on a Post-It in your purse with an ever-changing roster of people who you wanted to get fired."

Bex still did that. "I mean, like, Amethyst, specifically. Our podcast producer? I don't want to get her fired. Frankie told me she's a friend."

Sam shrugged. "I covered that."

"Oh, I didn't realize. Congratulations, new Cineline network executive Sam Farmer."

Sam made an exasperated growl in her throat that Bex knew wasn't really exasperated, just Sam not giving her the laugh. "What I'm saying is that I got us made producers of the podcast. You have the paperwork waiting with your agent, probably, by now. I didn't get it inked until this morning."

"How on earth did you make that happen?"

Sam tossed her hat a few feet in the air, then caught it. "I don't think anyone upstairs has put any stock in the fandom buzz about the episode. They always assume it's the star that makes something big, not the content. You think Niels reads fanfiction? Of course not. He thinks like Aaron did—if someone as big as Luciana is on, plus me, plus you, then of course the podcast is going to do big numbers. The only thing he cares about is that the numbers on that episode mean the studio can charge more for ad time. So I just had to tell them I didn't want to be outshone like that again on the podcast or I would walk . . . unless, of course, I was a producer. And they're like, *Chrissakes, Farmer, is that all you want?*"

"Yikes. You are scary."

"I'm a survivor. So are you."

Bex wasn't sure it was supposed to be a compliment, but it landed like one. "Professionally, maybe."

Sam pushed off her ball cap and widened her legs so she could lean closer, peering at Bex, who didn't do anything to deflect Sam's inspection. The light was golden hour, the wind had dropped off to a sweet breeze, and her heart felt like something torn out of an old scrapbook. She let Sam see her, sitting in their spot in the studio parking lot, talking about things she'd thought she left safely in the past.

"I meant it, you know," Sam said. "When I said I was always right there."

"I know you were." Bex wrapped her hands around her elbows. She looked up to see Sam still watching her. Her eyes really were the same blue as the sky. The ache of emotion tasted like wildfire smoke in Bex's throat, and her heart fluttered in the California breeze—a useless scrap of paper.

"I was afraid," she confessed. "Back then, in season six, when you were ready to talk about the things we'd never talked about, I wasn't. Not yet. It's not that I didn't feel what you did. I didn't think I could have it. And then you left." There was more Bex could say about that—about how much it hurt her the way Sam left. But she wasn't ready to get into any of that. "So I avoided you and skulked around the margins when you hung out with my sisters, like some kind of ridiculous ghoul hoping you would take mercy on me, and that wasn't fair."

Sam laughed, a real laugh. "You did skulk."

"I did. Textbook skulking. Wandering past the windows while you were by the pool with Frankie. Hiding behind friends at Vic's high school graduation. Shameful."

"Keep talking."

"And I *never* read about your date at a red-carpet event and then casually asked Frankie at dinner how you were doing in a very odd tone of voice. That would be ghoulish. And I for sure, for *sure*, didn't wear a fucking jumpsuit to the meeting where I would talk directly to you for the first time in ages, even though what you have seen me wear ninety percent of the time you've known me are my dance tights and a sweatshirt so ancient that it would be easily mistaken for a rag." She took a deep breath, then forced herself to say the thing she really needed to say. "I'm sorry, Sam."

For a long moment, Sam looked at her, her eyes soft, and it wasn't horrible. "Okay. That's enough. We're good."

"Just like that." Bex felt a dimple sinking into her cheek as a cautious smile broke out.

"Only took five years."

"Not quite five." Bex bit her tongue to keep herself from adding something more, like, *I'm glad we're friends, it's good to be friends again, let's shake on our new friendship.* Because there was a part of her that wanted to smooth the situation over with those kinds of platitudes and construct a new barrier, a backstop against what she actually felt.

What she felt, authentically, was that she and Sam had never been friends.

That they *couldn't* be.

It was possible for Bex and Sam to pretend to be friends. They'd done a great deal of that once upon a time. Sam's house was only a ten-minute walk on a trail in the Hollywood Hills to Bex's backyard, and they'd worn it smooth between hours-long takeout dinners, running lines, hanging out with her sisters, and long talks by the pool.

Bex didn't want to pretend anything anymore. She wanted to simply let her feelings about Sam be her feelings, even if they were destined to be *only* her feelings because Sam had moved on.

It was too late for her and Sam, but maybe it wasn't too late for Bex to be honest with herself *about* Sam. To put the right labels on her feelings, past and present.

Sam stood up and held out her hand. "Let's go before you hurt yourself with all of those thoughts you're thinking. I'm going to tell Niels he can send the photographer to take candids one of these times we're recording the podcast. We'll let the fans see us as we are, since that's what they never stopped giving us."

"I like that," Bex said. "As a fellow producer, I approve this plan."

She took Sam's hand.

Finally.

Not a Little Drama

"**H**uh." Vic collapsed into one of the vaguely mid-centuryish chairs in Bex's brand-new producer's office, a lifeless beige space on the fifth floor of Cineline's Inglewood building, where the podcast was recorded. "Your view is so main character."

There was no mistaking the sarcasm.

"I didn't know that the HVAC things were so big on that part of the SoFi Stadium." Frankie leaned against the plate-glass window, taking in the uninspiring panorama. "They're casting a shadow on the parking lot."

"There's, like, nothing else to cast a shadow out there." Vic tucked her feet beneath her and rested her head against the wall, exhausted by the rigors of being alive.

Bex narrowed her eyes at her youngest sister, who was home from UC–Davis for a long weekend and in full vacation mode, wearing flannel pajama pants, athletic slides with nonmatching socks, and something that was an unholy hybrid between a hoodie and a blanket. Her long, pin-straight blond hair was lifting with static.

Bex always felt a little off her game these days when she had both of her sisters together. Now that they were adults, Frankie's brown curls and turbo-speed fussing next to Vic's tall, gloriously plus-size, Viking-like power slouch acutely reminded Bex of her parents. Killingly. But they were their own independent people who didn't need Bex to remind them to fold their laundry or turn in their AP history assignments anymore.

She hadn't figured out what they needed her to do, exactly.

"Did you wear that on your flight?" she asked.

"Minus the sleep mask and neck pillow."

"It's an hour-long flight," Frankie said.

"Scientifically, that is the perfect length of time for a power nap." Vic yawned. "And I had to get to the airport at seven thirty in the morning, which interferes with my final REM cycle."

"I love you both so much," Bex said. "Why are you here?" This was a rhetorical question, since both of her sisters had a highly developed radar for potential turbulence in Bex's life. "I thought we were meeting up for dinner. I'm working." She gestured at the laptop set up in the middle of the otherwise empty desk.

She'd thought if she brought her work here, she might be able to concentrate on the episode she and Sam would be talking about in just an hour. Every time she'd tried to do her rewatch, she'd been interrupted. She was supposed to have given Amethyst her clips by last night at the absolute latest.

"There's drama," Frankie said. "Even better, there's drama surrounding you. The last drama we had was Vic's breakup that went viral."

"There's no drama," Bex argued.

But undeniably, yes, there was drama. Rather a lot of it. The uptick in photographers staking out Bex's driveway and following her when she did errands was evidence of that, though so far the mainstream media were only interested in the new proximity of Sam and Bex. They hadn't figured out how to cover references to fanfic and long-ago on-set politics. "Not like you mean," she corrected.

"But you're spending time with Sam," Vic said. "Nature is healing."

"She's my coworker." Bex was appalled at how uncertain her voice sounded. She was an actor, for fuck's sake.

"And yet I've seen a lot of this lately." Frankie mimed Bex bent over her phone, texting madly. It wasn't a flattering imitation.

Vic was interested enough to lift her head from the wall. "Is she doing it late at night?"

"Yes, and she's skipping her nighttime routine to do it."

"Oh, wow. Wow, wow, wow." Vic widened her eyes. "You love your routine. With the stretches and the gross tea and the skin steaming. This *is* drama."

"Go away." Bex folded her hands on the desk. "Both of you. Go shadow Frankie at work or something. Take selfies. Get one of those fifty-dollar shakes with a whole cake on top."

"I'm off today," Frankie said. "And we already have an agenda. Vic's going to read CravingCraven fic with me, and we're going to figure out together who the writer was."

Bex's stomach pinched painfully. Why *was* it that her sisters only spent time with her when it was inconvenient? They were like moths, attracted to her primarily at moments when her distracted frazzlement made her want to burn them to a crisp, but ignoring her when she wanted to share a quiet dinner or watch a movie together. In September, she'd asked Vic if she wanted her to come visit for parents' weekend, and Vic had texted back, **obviously not**. Yet here she was, with Frankie, at the office Bex had never been to before this morning.

"Everybody's talking about the reunion," Vic said. "It was annoying when the special got announced in *Variety* online and everyone wanted to pull me into a conversation about it. Like, yes, I understand you're angling for access, Morgan, you don't have to pretend to be my friend, I've clocked the *Craven's Daughter* pin on your backpack. But even I couldn't resist the steaming cup of tea you call a podcast. Luciana is my idol. She excavated six years of toxic secrets in a half-hour episode."

Toxic was a strong word. Bex would hate to think *Craven's Daughter* was *toxic*. That she'd brought her sisters somewhere *toxic* nearly every day.

"No one at work can talk about anything else," Frankie said. "Half the crew of *Timber Creek Farm* is convinced this is going to end with a cold read of the script for the long-lost series finale, and the other half believes you and Sam are going to figure out what really happened to Jen."

Vic nodded vigorously. "Frankie and I have decided Craving-Craven is the key. This Big Name Fan is in the cast or crew. Figure out who they are, then interrogate them."

"We can't *interrogate* anyone. We're TV detectives, remember?" Bex tried to infuse her question with enough weariness to disguise the mixture of alarm and excitement souring her stomach. It was one thing to embark on a personal journey, of sorts, with Sam Farmer—even to invite their fans along for the ride. But that wasn't quite what Vic was describing. "What makes you think you and Frankie can figure out who CravingCraven is, anyway?"

Vic cast her eyes at the ceiling. "We were children on that set, but we weren't senseless blobs. We were *there*."

"I wasn't even a child by the end," Frankie said. "I did my first internship on *Craven's Daughter*, in case you've forgotten."

"How could I?" Bex asked. "You pretended not to know me for six weeks."

"Also," Vic continued without missing a beat, "we weren't distracted like you, and everyone was very indulgent with us or, even better, had no idea how to talk to children, and so they told us things they shouldn't have. I bet we know more than you and Sam put together about what was going on at Stage 46."

While Bex was suppressing the urge to defend herself against the accusation that she'd been distracted, Frankie jumped in. "Like where Dylan used to hide his vodka so he could drink between takes."

"Who's Dylan?" Bex asked.

"He was Jerry the gaffer's best boy until he got caught and had to leave," Frankie said. "They replaced him with Danisha."

"I liked Danisha." Vic smiled at the ceiling. "She had

encyclopedic knowledge of nineties grunge bands. She gave me a vintage Siouxsie and the Banshees poster to celebrate my first period. But she had to leave because she got into film school, and then it was that scary guy with the neck tattoo."

"Brian. He got the neck tattoo after his girlfriend filed the restraining order. It was a tattoo of her as Poison Ivy."

"Jesus." Bex blew out a breath. "Maybe I wasn't a fit parent."

"What?" Frankie laughed. "No. You were way stricter than I remember Mom and Dad being."

"There's this fic we're particularly interested in," Vic said, redirecting the conversation once again. She retrieved her phone from a giant kangaroo pocket in her blanket hoodie. "Let me pull it up, and we can discuss."

"Is it the one you sent me the quote from?" Frankie asked. "Because I have thoughts. I think—"

She was cut short by a gentle knock on the door frame. Bex turned to see Sam standing in the carpeted hallway, wearing what looked like a neon-yellow flight suit belted with a rhinestone belt bag. The suit's zippered cuffs at the ankle, wrist, and collar were a silky pink. "I'm interrupting," she said.

Bex read the hesitation in Sam's expression. She hadn't been expecting to find a full house of Simon women in the podcast office. Though Sam had remained close with Frankie and Vic, the four of them had not spent time together since *Craven's Daughter* wrapped.

Because, Bex acknowledged to herself, even though Bex and Sam had never been *together*, they'd definitely broken up.

"Come on in. It's your office, too."

Sam strode in. Vic jumped up and wrapped her arms around her.

"Hey!" Sam hugged Vic hard. "How'd your O-Chem test go?"

"Fucking nailed it."

"Not surprised." Sam sank down into one of the chairs, but she didn't lean back like she normally would have. She crossed her legs, her foot flipping one of her pink heels. The last time Bex had seen Sam this nervous, Bex had fucked it up and then didn't talk to her for half a decade.

Vic sat back down, and the four of them went quiet. Four women who were never quiet.

"This is awkward," Frankie said.

"I should've given you a heads up I was coming," Sam told Bex.

"You did not interrupt, and no heads up was needed." Bex opened up her voice to project the full-throated authority necessary to calm everyone down. "My sisters were just about to tell me about one of CravingCraven's fics that got their attention. You should join us."

"You're wearing a suit." Sam's attention was now completely on Bex. Her posture had relaxed. "Like a congresswoman."

Bex looked down at her brown pinstripe suit, the silk neckbow of her blouse tumbling over the top button of the blazer. "Our podcast guest today."

Sam held up her arms to show off her outrageous couture, which covered her from neck to ankle. "We had the same idea."

"What idea?" Vic asked. "Isn't your podcast guest Bradley Wilhite? Wait, I thought he was in Maine shooting a movie where he actually had to kill a bear and eat its liver."

"And jump out of a plane without a parachute," Frankie added. "But I guess thirty million is enough money for him to risk his pretty face."

"Disgusting," Vic said. "He's a hundred years old. Did you see he was dating Kara Montague? She's really nice, which I know, because she's my age! We've hung out! The last time we did, we went to an arcade and split In-N-Out. It wasn't that long ago."

"He's never dated anyone older than your age," Frankie said. "Your age is the top end of who he dates."

"He's not filming," Bex said. "He's back in town and scheduled to be on our podcast this afternoon to talk about 'You're a Mean One, Mr. Finch.'"

"I get it." Frankie nodded. "That's why you're both wearing the don't-grope-me armor."

"It's Bradley Wilhite's personal obligation as a very basic human-shaped multi-celled organism not to grope anyone." Vic pulled a pack of gum out of her sweatshirt blanket pocket. "If he's tempted by the appearance of Bex's shoulder in one of her ancient dance tops, that's entirely on him."

Frankie held her hand out for a piece of gum. "You're right. That is absolutely correct."

"Wait," Vic said, dropping gum into Frankie's palm. "Wasn't the *Craven* episode he guest-starred in the same one where you two touched pinkies?"

"Yep," Sam said. "The fans pick the episodes, and pinky touching is what they want." She pointed at Bex. "You haven't selected your clips. As your co-producer, I'm obligated to tell you that your tardiness disappoints me."

"Shut up a sec." Vic had one palm up, her phone in front of her face, and she was scrolling rapidly. "Sorry, Sam, I love you, but there's something in this one CravingCraven story. It's the AU where Henri and Cora are recast as pilots on a bomber in World War II."

Bex had looked at a few of the alternative universe stories, in which fans had imagined versions of Henri and Cora as captains on a spaceship, vampires living through historic eras, as Elizabeth Bennet and Fitzwilliam Darcy, and so much more. What every alternative universe story had in common was that Henri and Cora were in love.

Sam was already extracting her own phone from a zippered pocket on her thigh. "You should give it a read. No interrupted kisses in this one." She winked, startling Bex.

It was a Henri wink. Sam hadn't Henri-winked at Bex for years.

Hmm. Bex crossed her arms and lifted her chin at Sam to admonish her for taking liberties.

Sam smiled. She didn't seem nervous anymore.

"Check out the description of the German soldier they run across in the swamp when their plane is downed," Vic said. Frankie stood next to her, reading over her shoulder.

Sam tapped and swiped at her own phone, then stood to join Bex on her side of the desk, pulling up another chair and holding the phone so they could both read. Sam's arm against hers was warm. Bex leaned closer to see Sam's phone and read where Sam indicated. She scrolled through the detailed description of the character who AU Henri and Cora were observing from behind a bush. The German soldier hunched in a shelter made of tree branches that looked "more beautiful than it should for something hastily made." He had blond, thinning hair that was "strangely darkened" along the hairline.

"Well, that must be Josh," Bex said. "What with the awesome shelter, like it's an homage to his being a set designer, and how his self-tanner was always sort of bleeding into his hair. Which I don't think was natural blond."

"It wasn't," Vic said. "But keep reading, where Cora and Henri have captured him and managed to get him to an Allied encampment. The French soldier who interrogates him, the one with the beard?"

Bex read for a few paragraphs. Then the hair on the back of her neck stood up. "Oh my God, that's Carl. Camera One."

"The commandant fucking hates this guy," Frankie said. "The interrogation is some serious overkill. Which is surprising, because Carl is so easygoing."

"The nurse character must be Jen," Sam said. "She mentions headaches and health problems, and she has Jen's fair hair and green eyes." Sam clicked through to the story's last page, then set her phone down on the desk. "Okay, so, I didn't major in English, but if I had to guess, I'd say the author is suggesting there might be some issue between these three. The characters who are inserts for Jen, Carl, and Josh all despise each other, and they seem to have a dark past that pre-dates the war."

"Like when the Josh one says to the Carl one, 'I know what you did in the back alleys of the city, you conniving sewer rat'?" Frankie asked.

"And there's the fact that the Josh one calls the Jen one a 'fucking narc,'" Vic said.

Sam's eyes widened. "So Carl hated Josh?"

"It looks like it. And Josh hated the nurse, who is Jen?" Vic said.

Bex's head was spinning. This writer, who was surmised to be a cast or crew member of *Craven's Daughter*, was apparently someone who knew that Carl, Josh, and Jen had some kind of problem with each other. Did the writer know this from having observed their behavior, or because they were privy to issues that had arisen in the past? Bex had been there, too, and *she* hadn't known there was anything going on between the three.

If it was even real. Where was the line between fact and fanfiction?

Sam put down her phone and leaned back, brushing her arm over Bex's. "I'm not sure everything is meant to be literal. But when Luciana said there was bad blood running between everyone Aaron put together for *Craven's Daughter*, she wasn't kidding. I observed some of it. The CravingCraven writer seems to have known even more than we do about these dynamics." Sam tapped her fingers against the desk. "You know what I'm thinking?"

"That I still don't have my clips picked out, and Bradley Wilhite will be here in an hour?" Bex reflexively checked that her jacket was buttoned.

"*I* know what you're thinking," Frankie said to Sam. "You want to talk to Carl."

"Yeah, I would really love to talk to Carl," Sam said. "Also, I have a good reason to talk to Carl today, because Carl was the one who made 'You're a Mean One, Mr. Finch' what it ended up being."

Carl Moreland was a veteran camera operator who'd been Camera One for *Craven's Daughter,* a multicamera show. He'd had the most experience and the best artistic sense of the camera crew, not to mention a slow and steady temperament that made it possible for him to survive on a serial that replaced its director of photography five times in six seasons.

"Carl is the one who caught our pinkies touching on camera and fucking *zoomed in,*" Sam continued. "If anybody should be recapping what he was thinking when 'Mr. Finch' was made, it's Carl. Bradley Wilhite's guest spot on that episode lasted all of three minutes."

Bex was struggling to hold on to the different threads of conversation. "Look, I know we agreed to ask these kinds of questions so we could get some closure, but say we do talk to Carl about the dynamics we're reading into this fan story. He's smart. He misses nothing. He didn't miss that our pinkies were touching in a scene where both of our characters were crouched in a dark alley with bad-guy flashlight beams darting around. He will for sure know what we're driving at. And let's not forget, CravingCraven is a third party who is implicating Carl in a very complex history between complex people. He might have feelings about that, or have things he doesn't want discussed, or be angry, or—"

"—know the identity of the writer?" Sam said. "We can't ask Jen, and I wouldn't choose to talk to Josh Miller even if he was handing me an Oscar, but I like Carl, and Carl probably *would* know who would know all of this so well they could write about it. He might even be able to tell us if there are more clues we're missing."

"Clues," Bex said.

"To Jen's murder," Vic said. "Of course the fic has more clues. It also has a pretty interesting posting timeline."

"I noticed that," Sam said. "Whoever wrote those stories

was there from the beginning and posted for years. Luciana's right—they must be someone we know. And they know things no one else knew. Not the cops in Chicago, not the network, not us."

"Luciana said Aaron hired all the main players," Frankie said. "You know who keeps their enemies close? Guilty people, that's who."

"Oh my God," Bex said. "Are we making a *suspect list*?"

"You did play a detective on TV," Frankie said. "And you like to make lists. Cora Banks would already be busy with that chalkboard she brought into the office and wrote on with colored chalk."

"Cora Banks is not real," Bex said stiffly.

Though she did have her notebook in her purse, and it *did* sound like a good idea to get it out and start writing some things down.

"*This* is real, though." Sam tapped on her phone. "Craving-Craven is a real person who was among us. Who Aaron probably hired. Who knew everyone's secrets."

"Put CravingCraven on the suspect list," Vic said. "Aaron and CravingCraven. That's two. Also, Bette Holloway."

"The *writer*?" Bex cleared her throat after squeaking. "Why?"

"Because, first of all, she's a writer, so she could be Craving-Craven pretty easily. Second, she was Aaron's stepdaughter until her mom divorced him, which means she knew Aaron's secrets, she hated him, and her entire job put her in charge of deciding where everyone was and when. For example, Bette was the person whose scripts would decide how many exterior shots every season needed to be shot in Chicago, if any."

"Bette was cagey after the accident, too," Sam said. "Josh made heartless jokes, but that wasn't out of character."

"Put Josh on the list," Vic said. "He's basically the worst. Not as bad as Aaron, but sort of spidery creepy."

"Here's what I'm thinking." Sam crossed her arms. "We don't talk to Bradley. We don't interview him for the podcast."

Bex goggled. "He's the highest-paid actor in Hollywood.

You don't not talk to Bradley Wilhite. At least when you're under contract."

"I made us producers!" Sam countered. "You said this podcast was ours, and I'm supposed to tell you when you shouldn't have any fucks."

"I did, but the network will have no problem firing a couple of newly minted podcast producers who snub Bradley Wilhite. He's good friends with Niels. They go out on their yachts together."

"Like, side by side?" Vic mused. "Like riding horses?"

Sam blew out a breath. "Sure," she said to Bex, ignoring Vic's interjection. "But we don't have to talk to him in the sense of *talking* to him. He likes to talk to and about himself most of all. Amethyst can give him a prompt, let him yammer, and we'll record banter later about his performance that she can edit together with his self-congratulatory vomit. In the meantime, we invite Carl and talk to him about the episode."

That was a good idea. Still, Bex shook her head, reflexively feeling like it was her role to slow this train down. "Even if we could do that, we have no way of getting Carl here this afternoon while we have scheduled time in the studio, and we can't push the podcast back. The sponsorship agreements mean it has to be edited tonight and go up tomorrow."

"Carl's retired, so he can probably make your schedule," Frankie said. "He runs a seniors Dungeons and Dragons game at the community center in Hyde Park. He's basically always there. That's two miles away. Hire him a car. He likes that kind of thing."

"We don't know that—"

"Just hang on." Frankie was already texting.

"How do you know so much about what Carl's up to?" Sam asked.

Vic groaned in exasperation. "We told you! We were there! We know everything. We know every*one*. If you're doing this *Harriet the Spy* stuff, you're doing it with us. You'd be actually hopeless without our help."

Bex was opening her mouth to refuse when she remembered what Frankie had said on the set a few weeks ago. *Include us.*

Her sisters were adults. Their experiences with *Craven's Daughter* were just as valid as her own. And they'd lost Jen, too.

Frankie lifted her head and announced, "Carl said to send the car." She tapped her phone for another minute. "Amethyst is fine with the change in plans. She knows a PA for that talk show that films in Stage 16 who's Bradley's goddaughter. She's going to come down to the recording studio to make sure it goes smoothly." Frankie put her phone in her pocket. "And that's why there's no Hollywood without production assistants. We do all the real work while a bunch of people who don't know what they're talking about yell at us about how it's impossible."

Ouch. "I concede defeat." Bex gave Sam a look that she hoped was world-weary and not too desperate. "I guess we're sending a car to Hyde Park."

"Looks like it." Then Sam smiled down at her in a way that meant Bex had to take a centering breath, closing her eyes, which only made her more aware of Sam sitting right next to her, smelling amazing, and didn't help her figure out if any of this was a good idea.

"I'll help you pick your clips," Sam said. "If we hurry, we can get that done, then head up to the lobby to catch Carl up while Bradley's busy with Amethyst and the goddaughter." Bex opened her eyes to find Sam's blue eyes on her. "This is the part where you go from white-knuckled resolve to devil-may-care excitement."

"You mean this is the part where Cora Banks—"

"No." Sam stood up. "I mean you. You're way braver than Cora, and at least a thousand times bossier when you're not freaking out about stuff no one else cares about. Plus"—Sam touched Bex's neck-bow—"you can't waste this suit. It's painfully hot."

Bex wanted to get in a quip in response, even knowing Sam hadn't meant it and her comment was part of her habitual flirty patter, but before she could stop smiling and say something good, she caught a glimpse of Frankie and Vic in her periphery. "For heaven's sake," she said. "Get a bag of popcorn already."

Frankie plucked an invisible piece of popcorn from an imaginary bucket and put it in her mouth.

"This right here is why I booked a flight," Vic said with a grin. "It's my every dream coming true."

Bex didn't want to give her sisters any more satisfaction, but Sam should know it was okay to be here, to be hanging out with all of them together again. She reached out to find Sam's hand in the space between them, hidden from Frankie and Vic's view. When she found it, she touched her pinkie to Sam's.

Sam's hand moved toward Bex's touch. When she wrapped her pinkie around Bex's, *that* was the moment when Bex went from white-knuckled resolve to devil-may-care excitement.

It felt good.

Carpe DM

Carl Moreland leaned back in his chair, long fingers rubbing the silver beard that glowed against his dark brown skin, holding the tablet Sam had given him and chuckling.

Bex and Sam watched him read in the quiet recording studio. Presumably, the mics were live, but they'd only been picking up Carl's chuckles for some time.

He put down the tablet and his reading glasses, then crossed his arms over his CARPE DM T-shirt. "This is some good shit."

"One hundred percent agree," Sam said. "But do you get anything from it?"

"I'm not a psychic." He shook his head as though the whole situation left him bemused. "I know what you mean, though. The interrogator is me, and the downed German is Josh Miller. That nurse is Jen Arnot, and the two Allied soldiers are you two. That's clear as a bell."

"You didn't write it?" Bex asked. "Frankie was telling me about your Dungeons and Dragons group at the community center, and it sounds like you do a lot of storytelling."

Carl nodded. "True. And, truth be told, I've written quite a few homebrews for the fifth edition of D and D. That is"—he said this to the microphone—"I've put up on the Internet a developed D and D campaign of my own design for other players to use. I like writing, telling stories. I've even made a little documentary about my group that got screened over at the film festival in Venice Beach. But I haven't tried my hand at fanfiction. Quite a few of the folks I play with write it, so I've read enough to know that this is good. And I've certainly read enough to agree that whoever wrote it worked on Stage 46."

"Can you tell us what makes you say that?" Sam asked. "I'd love to hear your perspective."

After the hired car dropped Carl off at the studio building, they'd started out the session by filling him in on what they were up to and where they'd gotten so far. Bex had hesitated at first to take the plunge, worried that doing so would make Carl more reluctant to share, but Sam pointed out that they were both actors, so their entire job was reading people. They might as well tell everyone they talked to everything they were thinking, because it meant then they could listen not only to what they said in return but also to what they *didn't* say.

Plus, she and Sam had a whole audience of fans to follow up and do their thing after the episode dropped.

Carl shook his head. "I had forty-five years behind the camera, and I've worked with every kind of Hollywood—difficult, easy, didn't matter. I know my craft. You understand? I've seen dozens of different kinds of inventions and technology come through, and I mastered them all, because what matters at the end of the day is how well I can capture a director's vision or, lacking that, create a vision he thinks he had. I can get something in a fraction of the takes most other people need. I'm *on*. But some motherfuckers are dry rot on a project. Josh Miller has pretty sets, that's a fact. But good light and angles can salvage a mediocre set, so I'd rather mess with that than watch a self-aggrandizing piece of work like him ruin every good thing everybody else is trying to do, swerving out of his lane every chance he gets." Carl shook his head again. "Fool."

Bex was astonished. She'd known Carl a long time and never heard him say anything half so negative about another crew member. But then, she'd only known him on the set of *Craven's Daughter*, where they were subject to a studio hierarchy that kept them from saying everything they might have wanted to say.

"Okay. Message received," Sam said. "But was that it? The way Josh undermined the work on set was your whole problem with him? Because this fic makes it sound like there was something personal, maybe that went back a ways." Sam slid the tablet closer to herself. "Especially this part. 'I know what you did in the back alleys of the city, you conniving sewer rat.'"

Carl rocked in the ergonomic chair, thinking. "*Hmm*. I think that must not be entirely directed at me. That's the *Charles Salt* business."

Cold goosebumps lifted up along Bex's neck. "The *Charles Salt* business."

"That's right. I'm not unfair, so I will say the *Charles Salt* sets were some of the most beautiful I've shot. Looked good in every light, designed with impeccable flow, and they could be cleverly reset in a short amount of time. They inspired the cast, I know. They captured the grit of a demonic city so perfectly, you'd swear it was a place you'd driven through in your nightmares. And I love that kind of shit, besides. Science fiction fantasy is where it's at. So, credit where credit's due. Josh did the work."

"It was one of several projects Aaron and Josh worked on together before *Craven's Daughter*," Bex said to remind their audience.

"And Jen," Sam added. "Jen did the FX makeup for *Charles Salt*."

"Correct. I was one of three camera operators. I'd never worked with Aaron, Josh, or Jen before, and at first I was happy. But my respect for Josh Miller fell into the basement on a week-long shoot for a complex fight scene on an alley set that went way, way over budget."

"Tell us about it," Sam said. "What were the problems?"

"Every kind of problem. Fire escape pulled off when it was

supposed to support the weight of the actor, the continuity people kept catching the wrong paint and breakaway glass colors on
the set as it was repaired and reset between takes. Actors were
complaining the space was more narrow than the day before,
saying that was why they were missing their choreography. We
were all frustrated. I was doing my best to catch whatever I could
in the hope that editing could salvage it without wasting more
time. Jen Arnot was spitting mad."

"Why was Jen mad?"

"You seen *Charles Salt*?"

"Yes. Who hasn't?"

"So you know that was Jen at the top of her game. Unbelievable effects work. The horns and prosthetics, fangs and scales, all
that, looked *alive*. Cast spent hours in her chair. Those prosthetics took longer than a usual spackle and dusting to go through
makeup."

Sam crossed her legs, making the zippers on her jumpsuit jingle. "I remember reading that the lead who was half demon had to
spend four hours every day getting his makeup done."

"I'm sure. So they'd put in all this time in the chair, and then
there's these problems and delays, and the fight scene choreography isn't working, which means people getting hurt. They had
prosthetics for their fingers and claws that kept getting ripped or
mangled as they're doing take after take after take. Under the hot
lights, they're sweating, Jen's glue's not holding, she's having to
redo work she came in at three in the morning for. The worse it
gets, the more cavalier Aaron is about the budget. The complaints
about the set? The fact that Jen's having to remake expensive prosthetics? He doesn't seem to care."

"I can see why that would piss Jen off, but sometimes shoots
just don't come together."

"Yes. You're right. This is a complex business. But that extra
time Jen's spending on set means she sees some shit. And Jen, you

know, she's a talker. Not a reticent woman. She'll call the plays as they happen and postgame it with anyone who's nearby to listen."

Bex smiled, remembering Jen's fearless extroversion. Jen liked to say she had to be extroverted to survive as a woman in FX for fifteen years. "That's true," Bex said. "No secrets with Jen Arnot, but no lies detected."

Carl laughed. "I like that. So she's talking to everybody, including Josh. She's asking him why his sets are causing so many problems. No one loved that she was badgering him, considering he was Aaron's friend from way back, and they'd done everything together. Film school. First wives, first divorces, second wives, all that old boys' business. So you don't give Josh any more flack than you'd give Aaron, you know? Jen seemed like she was stirring up drama during one of the tensest weeks of the show, and no one liked it. *I* didn't like it. Sometimes it's best just to keep your mouth shut and your opinions to yourself."

"What did she see, Carl?" There was a thread of impatience beneath Sam's question.

"I don't know."

"*What?*" Bex involuntarily shouted. "What do you mean you don't know?"

Carl raised his eyebrows at Bex. "I mean I don't know. Toward the end of the week, the shoot is moved back two hours. Everyone's standing around. Jen's crew's doing makeup, but no Jen. Then we hear Josh and Aaron outside the set, screaming at each other. That went on awhile. Aaron comes in, red as a beet, accepts the first take the actors pop off, throws his script in the middle of the set, and leaves. We're standing around, and then those network folks come in. The ones who wear the sad, cheap suits. They give us a schedule to talk to them. Take us to a conference room one at a time, ask a bunch of questions about the shoot. Who got hurt, what happened, all that. Then we're back at it, no Aaron, no Josh, all through the next episode. Wasn't until years later that I heard a rumor that Jen reported Josh for sabotage on his own sets, causing a lot of those accidents on purpose."

"What would be the motive for sabotaging your own work?" Sam's cheeks had gone pink.

Carl shook his head. "Can't say for sure. Some like to see the world burn, and some like to play like they're gods, determining the outcome of it all in order to feel more power than they've earned. If I was guessing, Josh is some combination of the two, with a dash of desire to frame others for mischief."

Bex thought of the sugar glass that had cut her knee. *If it was sugar glass,* Luciana had said.

Could that have been sabotage, too? If it had been, it was possible Josh was trying to hurt her—or, taking Carl's point, to simply hurt *someone* on the set of *Craven's Daughter* in order to start something or to feel in control.

It was also possible that someone who knew about what happened on *Charles Salt* had set it up so it would *look* like Josh was trying to cause an accident because they were angry with him. Or seeking revenge.

"Was the rumor that Jen reported Josh something you can confirm?" she asked.

"I can't," Carl admitted. "The only thing I can say from my own observation is that from then on, there was real poison between Aaron and Josh, and it must've had something to do with that shoot and all of Jen's talking and questions. But if you ask me . . ." Carl trailed off, steepling his fingers beneath his bearded chin. His eyes had gone far away.

Bex waited several beats before she broke. "*I'm* asking you. Oh my God, Carl!"

He laughed. "Sorry. I'm saying if you ask me, Josh had a problem with Aaron, maybe from before *Charles Salt*, and we were all just walking into the middle of what Jen saw first. Maybe Josh was trying to make Aaron look bad. Could be he wanted something he wasn't getting. Could be there was romantic history nobody was talking about. What the hell do I care what these puffed-up white dudes get up to, so long as I get my money? But there's something ugly between them, and then they all show up on *Craven's Daughter*. Pretty fucking interesting. Interesting enough to write a story about, that's for sure." He tapped the tablet with the fanfic.

"But *you* didn't." Sam's voice was flat and distant, the way she sounded when she was thinking hard. "So who did? Who else knew enough about Josh and his sabotage, and whatever personal problems there were between Aaron and Josh, and Aaron and Jen, and Jen and Josh, to put it in a fictional story about two characters on a new show? Because whoever did might know more than they've said about what happened to Jen in Chicago."

Carl rubbed his beard. "Bette could probably tell you some things. She was young when *Charles Salt* was going on, but I remember her being around, and she doesn't miss much. Chaz, too. She always knows how everyone's connected. Who someone's roommate's boyfriend's dad was, how he got so-and-so pregnant and she had the baby in Rio. I don't know those stories."

"Chaz Morgenstern is the actor who played Rose on *Craven's Daughter*, the world-weary office receptionist who came with the agency when Cora inherited it," Bex filled in automatically. "She's eighty years old now and has been a working actor for an extravagantly long time, and it seems like everyone she's ever been connected to is in the business." Carl was right that Chaz would be a good person to talk to.

And Bex was thinking like Cora Banks would. Like a detective. She glanced at Sam, who'd steepled her fingers beneath her chin in a very Henri Shannon manner.

"You know something, though," Sam said to Carl with suspicion.

He chuckled. "Maybe I do. I was thinking how, with my homebrews, I put stuff in there that's interesting to me, and a lot of the time I couldn't even tell you why. But when I've got people in the room with me playing that story—acting it out, rolling the dice, making their characters come alive—I'm always surprised what they do with what I gave them."

Bex was thinking about the fans, and what Carl had just said, and fanfiction, but there was something stuck in her thoughts she couldn't tease out. "They don't add to your D and D story if they don't like it," she said, paraphrasing Carl's point. "If they're not having fun."

Sam was looking right back at Bex, her eyes bright with interest. "No, they wouldn't. When something is good, and feels good, it's inspiring, right? It feels more immersive for you than for other people who like it less. When you love something, the inside jokes come easy, and you feel like you can predict what everyone would say or how they would act, and it feeds the love, because imagining those things deepens your relationship."

"Yes!" Bex shouted. "If you imagine what your favorite character would say in your made-up scenario, it's like it happened."

"And what if you started writing those scenarios down?" Sam asked. "Then they *did* happen."

"You can fix things. Like our fans."

Sam pulled the mic closer to her face. "Exactly. And it's not just about seeing two characters kiss, it's about seeing yourself there, *your* identity, *your* love, as important. Writing fanfiction feels good, feels important, because it *is* important."

"Let Grandpa add a word," Carl interrupted. "What if you were knee-deep in something bad, or something you cared about, and needed it to have a different ending?"

Well. That was a thought. "Luciana told us that *Craven's Daughter* was an experienced team," Bex said. "These were people who either owed Aaron something or needed the chance he might be able to deliver on, or—"

"Knew he was good for a good paycheck," Carl said. "I've never owed that man anything."

"Right," she said. "But it makes sense that CravingCraven

would be someone connected to Aaron who wanted to process what had happened when it fell apart between Aaron and Josh."

"And Jen," Sam added.

"Yeah, but a lot of CravingCraven's fiction is about Henri and Cora and resolving their romance, so it wasn't Aaron writing the fic." Bex put her hand over her throat. "Aaron couldn't even pretend to care about the romance."

"Who else was on *Charles Salt*?" Sam asked Carl.

"Could be that there were other people who overlapped, but I can't recall anyone but myself, Aaron, Josh, and Jen."

Bex felt her throat go hot under her hand. "Do you think it was *Jen*?" She bent down and grabbed her bag and yanked her notebook out of it, paging until she got to her list of CravingCraven's fics. She ran her finger down the list until the last one. "There aren't any more CravingCraven stories after she died."

"Jesus," Sam whispered. "But is there a way to know for sure if Jen was CravingCraven? Maybe the writer lost heart after there was a death on our set."

"Wait, back up." Bex waved a hand in the air. "Before we forward theories for our audience that could break the Internet, we're crossing Josh off the list because . . . ?"

"Because fanfiction isn't about yourself," Carl said with finality. "Not really. Jen might have been working something out on the page, but if she was your Big Name Fan, like Luciana said—"

"You listened to the podcast with Luciana?"

"Yeah, of course. Gotta keep up with you kids. If Jen was your Big Name Fan, it's because Jen was doing it for all of them." Carl gestured around the studio. "For the other fans. For everyone making a place for themselves in the world of *Craven's Daughter*, like Samantha said. Josh Miller hasn't ever done anything that wasn't exclusively about Josh Miller. He didn't even design *for* the movie or *for* the show. He did it to get noticed. Or to be important. Win awards. That's why he didn't have a problem breaking his toys when someone wasn't giving him the power and control." Carl paused. "Just a theory. *I* don't know what motivates that man."

Bex heard a muffled thumping and turned around. Amethyst was knocking on the glass of her booth. She held up her tablet, then pointed to indicate the tablets on the table in front of them. Bex looked down at the message on her screen.

Talk about the pinkies.

"Right," she said.

Sam's smile creased the bridge of her nose. "Carl."

"Yes, ma'am."

"Tell us about that pinkie shot."

Carl laughed. "Roll the clip, ladies." While Amethyst bustled around in the booth, he framed out a scene with his hands in the space in front of the projection screen. "What we have here is a pivotal moment in episode thirty, 'You're a Mean One, Mr. Finch,' guest-starring Bradley Wilhite. Our intrepid private investigator, Cora Banks, has set a trap, using herself as bait, hoping to lure out a serial killer who's been murdering tax accountants during the Christmas season. The episode alludes quite heavily to Charles Dickens's *A Christmas Carol* and was written by Bette Holloway. Sam Farmer has caught wind of Cora's scheme and has walked into the middle of the trap in an effort to save Cora from herself. We're in a dark alley, and following the sounds of rattling chains is gunfire, over and over, but always from a different direction, as if there is a ghost. *Ooooooooh.*" Carl wiggled his fingers and laughed.

Sam and Bex laughed, too, as the audio from the clip filled Bex's earphones and the video started to play.

Bex watched herself crouch in the dark alley, Cora's hair blowing into the hood of her coat, which was navy with pink polka dots. A joke had been made earlier in the episode about the coat being the only dark clothing she had to wear while she was hiding as bait. Bex remembered pretending the stiff breeze from the studio lot was cold, whipping down a Chicago alley in December, instead of a warm Santa Ana wind whirling over fake snow.

Chains rattle, and Cora looks up at a fire escape just as a bullet comes from her right. She squeaks in fear. "I said I'd meet you here," Cora calls out, trying to sound brave. "No fair with the gun stuff."

The chain rattles again, this time from the dark shadows at the end of the alley, and Cora jumps, then crouches lower. "You told me you were coming alone, mister," she whispers.

Another gunshot rings out, this time from above, scattering the gravel at Cora's feet. She creeps to lean against the brick wall of the alley, shivering, and then a long, dark shadow fills the space she has just vacated.

"Okay," Cora says in a fierce whisper. "Stop being so freaking scary! Just come out already!"

"Cora!" Henri appears in the space where the shadow was. She drops to a crouch with her gun out, covering Cora.

"What are you doing here?" Cora asks angrily. "I'm trying to set a trap!"

The chains rattle. They sound like they're coming from behind the dumpster now. Henri swivels and points the gun at it. "Stay behind me!"

Cora immediately wiggles out from behind Henri, standing and putting her hands on her hips. "No! You're not supposed to be here! This is my secret trap! Literally a secret! As in, I didn't tell anyone but the bad guy. Are you the bad guy, Henri?"

Henri looks behind her at Cora, relaxing her stance and standing up warily, holstering her gun.

"No! I'm not the bad guy, Cora! You left your secret plan emails with the bad guy up on your computer."

"Oh." Cora furrows her brow. "Then why are you here?"

Henri's jaw firms. "Because you were emailing the bad guy and telling him to meet you in a dark alley in the middle of the city."

Another shot rings out in the alley, chipping the brick a little too close to where Cora is standing. Henri pulls Cora back down and against the building. "We are leaving this literal death trap right this minute." Henri unholsters the gun, holding it in one hand while pressing Cora against the alley wall with the other.

"But I haven't caught him yet," Cora whispers furiously. "It should be easy. He's obviously a bad shot."

A bullet slams into a brick right next to Cora's ear.

"Or we could leave right this minute." Cora grabs Henri's elbow, and Henri tightens her grip on her gun, backing them out of the alley while scanning the darkness. Suddenly there are chains rattling from every direction, too many to be from one person, and gunfire starts raining into the alley.

"Go!" Henri shouts, pulling Cora toward the weak streetlight and into safety. There is eerie laughter between gunshots. Henri manages to get them behind a pile of boxes at the mouth of the alley before gunfire pounds into the place where they were just standing.

Cora and Henri are breathing hard. Cora squeezes her eyes shut. "I'm so stupid."

When Henri looks over at Cora, her normally taciturn face softens. "No."

"I am."

"That's impossible," Henri whispers. "You're a teacher."

Cora laughs on a sigh, and both Henri and Cora realize the alley has gone quiet.

"What's happening? How did that happen?" Cora whispers.

"I don't—" Henri begins, and then there is the sound of chains again in the distance, and another eerie laugh. Cora shivers and for the first time looks afraid.

Bex held her breath. The camera found Cora and Henri's hands. *There it was.* Framed beautifully, for just a moment, was Henri's pinkie bumping Cora's, once. Twice. Then Cora sliding hers around Henri's, just as the camera panned back up to catch the look in both of their eyes.

Glad. Soft. Private.

The clip stopped. The sound clicked off in Bex's headphones.

There were tears in her eyes. She brushed them away, not looking at Carl or Sam.

The day they'd filmed "Mr. Finch," it was incredibly hot on the studio lot. Aaron had been in a crabby mood all week and had called her a "hack" the day before, blowing a hole through her confidence that the strong wind in her ears seemed to amplify. Vic was being bullied at school. When Bex had tried to wake her up that morning, she'd refused to come out from under the covers, then said some of the meanest things she'd ever said to Bex in her life, then burst into tears. Bex felt like a failure. She was late for makeup. The regular costumer had left the show, and the new one wouldn't stop talking about Bex's measurements, enraging her. The effects team had come up with a way to simulate gunshots in the alley that required Bex to remain poised and good-natured while small explosions were detonated next to her head over and over and over again.

And that day was the anniversary of her parents' death.

Sam knew. She was the only one who did. Which meant *Bex* was the only person in the world who knew that when Henri's pinkie touched Cora's, it wasn't Henri's pinkie. It was Sam's.

It was Sam, trying to make Bex feel just a teeny-tiny bit better on a horrific day by touching her finger to Bex's, a touch that they both assumed the camera wouldn't see. But Carl had seen, so everyone had. Watching the episode later with her sisters, Bex had felt her heart break apart and come back together in a way it had never done before, and so she'd known—she had—that she wasn't just coming to the edge of a cliff when it came to Sam. She'd already fallen.

"How did you even see that?" Sam asked Carl.

He looked at both of them, smiling. "You're kidding, right? Didn't need to see that when all I had to do was watch what was happening right in front of us."

Sam went uncharacteristically quiet and still.

"You saw what we were feeling for each other," Bex said, right into the microphone. To Carl. To the world.

She wasn't ready, and she didn't have a plan, but this time, she couldn't let that keep her from speaking the plain truth out loud. Failing to do that had hurt her and everyone she loved. "You saw, and so did our fans."

"And Jen."

It was Sam who said this. She looked uncharacteristically flustered by Bex's public confession. Bex couldn't raise just one eyebrow, but she could fluster Sam Farmer. That was satisfying.

"If we're right," Sam said slowly, "and Jen was our Big Name Fan, then that means a dear friend of ours has new things to say to us we've never heard before." Sam put her hand to her sternum, making her zippers jingle. "I wouldn't have thought doing this podcast, listening to the fans, would give me something like that. I'm so grateful."

Her cheeks were the same rosy color as the silky collar of her jumpsuit, and her blue-as-the-sky eyes were right on Bex. She looked like she meant it. Like she truly was grateful—to Jen, but mostly to Bex, for finally admitting out loud what they'd been told they never could.

"May her memory be a blessing," Carl said.

Then Bex, Sam, and Carl sat in silence together, because they'd just recorded a podcast that would hit number one again, and probably destroy the Internet, and possibly get Sam and Bex into trouble with the network if anyone high up at Cineline even bothered to listen to it.

And because Bex, for her part, was starting to feel like what she wanted to do next was turn to a fresh page in her notebook and make a list.

They had a mystery to solve.

A Real Detective

"**T**alk to me about this." Bex swiped open an attachment from her publicist and slid her phone over the pink travertine of the dining room table, which was littered with takeout boxes. They'd ordered in dinner from Vic's favorite taqueria, the traditional meal Bex and her sisters shared at least once whenever Vic came home from school.

Frankie glanced down at the screen, licking Tajín from her fingertips. "That's me and Vic."

Vic grabbed the phone and started swiping. "Oh, Franks. I told you that jacket was hot. Look at this one." She turned it toward Frankie, who leaned forward.

"Nice. You've got that whole cool-girl stride going on. The hair. The sunnies."

"Thank you very much. I wish they'd got one after I took off my sweater, though. Miu Miu sent me the top I was wearing underneath, and I could've made such a moment for them."

"Good lord!" Bex reached over and grabbed her phone from Frankie. "Obviously I meant to talk to me about why the paps were following you two around at all. What's going on?"

Frankie raised her eyebrows. "You're serious."

"I'm always serious about this kind of thing."

"Probably my secret baby," Vic said, reaching for the pineapple spears. "I'll never reveal the father."

Bex looked up at the rough pine beams that spanned the dining room ceiling, counting them and the skylights studded in between. It was an exercise she'd done many times around this table so she wouldn't lose her patience with her sisters and dishonor their parents' memories.

"It's your fault," Frankie said. "Yours and Sam's. Every time they see us, they think they'll see you, or Sam, or—the real money shot—you and Sam in the crosshairs of a long lens, too close to each other to be doing anything but—"

"All right," Bex interrupted, the back of her neck white-hot. "That's enough."

"You asked," Vic said. "And you don't have to apologize, by the way. This is the best school break I've ever had. I'm crushing intensely on my lab partner's roommate, Siobhan. Now she won't be able to check her engagement on socials without seeing my face. By the time I get back, she'll be yearning for me, and I can make my move."

Bex picked up her fork and pointed it at her sisters, neither of whom had bothered walking to the kitchen to get their own fork. Frankie had dripped chamoy on her shirt. Bex wanted to say something keen enough to arrest their attention but not sharp enough to sting.

She had no idea what that might be.

The second episode of the rewatch podcast had unleashed a maelstrom of the kind of attention Bex had spent most of her career avoiding. She'd always been given the impression by her agent and manager that she was *supposed* to avoid this kind of attention—the kind that was breathless to speculate more on her personal life than her current project—so it was strange to witness not only their rapture but also their eagerness to find a way to claim credit for the boost to Bex's popularity. There were texts in all caps with dancing emojis. A suggestion to lean in.

Lean into what, Bex wasn't sure. Maybe she had a guess. There was one paparazzi picture that her publicist had sent her accompanied by a long string of exclamation points. It had been taken with a long lens, probably from across the visitor's lot at Cineline, as Bex and Sam exited a coffee shop near the side entrance to the building. A bee had flown toward them from the planters by the door, and Bex had moved close to shoo it firmly away from Sam, who had an anaphylactic bee allergy that Bex took seriously. But Sam hadn't seen the bee or known why Bex was suddenly right next to her, and she'd caught Bex's wrist for a moment. The result was a picture of their faces very close together, with Sam smiling, a little bemused, and Bex's lips parted, her eyes wide, looking thoroughly disarmed.

She had the picture saved on her camera roll. Several times, she'd nearly deleted it. Her feelings about Sam toggled between elation, nostalgia, anxiety, and guilt.

"I had an idea," Frankie said. "For your investigation."

"*Our* investigation," Vic corrected. Bex shoved her plate away from herself and crossed her arms. "I'm not done talking about you two baiting the paps for clicks on your own social media."

Frankie nodded. "I can see that. But also, I was talking to Georgie Hayworth today. I happened to be running a light battery over to the shop, and she was smoking outside the Stage 20 lot."

Vic laughed. "Waiting for you, you mean."

"Well, yeah. I called her. But she did say she'd stop by *sometime* between one and three, so it is true that I ran into her unexpectedly. Semi-unexpectedly."

Bex tried to shift gears in her brain and found they kept slipping. Georgie Hayworth was the former Chicago police investigator who'd done consulting for *Craven's Daughter*. She'd advised Bette on scripts and occasionally gave Bex and Sam notes on scenes. Sometimes Bex and Georgie would talk about the best places to get good petite clothes off the rack, bonding over the challenges of life at sixty inches and below. "I thought Georgie wasn't in town anymore," Bex said. "Didn't she move to Chicago to be close to her grandkids?"

"She still consults and takes meetings here a few times a year. She told me to tell you hello and that the Rosleigh Boutique on Melrose is doing genius work with pants alterations."

Bex made a mental note, then shook her head to clear it. "But what—"

"I wanted to see if she still had any connections in Chicago that would give her access to the investigation the police did when Jen died," Frankie said. "If there are files to be gotten, how would somebody do that, or could she get them and look them over? That would be simpler and quicker. Georgie knows the ins and outs of Chicago investigation *and* our cast and crew and everything else." Frankie unwrapped a tamarind lollipop. "She said she'd see what she could do and let me know. Oh, and Amethyst's going to check if Georgie has an opening in her schedule to be on the podcast."

"Cool," Vic said. "That will give everything a real valid sort of feel."

"Hang on." Bex got up from the table, walked to the entryway by the garage, and retrieved the notebook and pen from her purse before sitting back down across from her sisters. "Back up." She needed a list. Probably some Post-Its. Maybe a cup of the tea her massage therapist sold her that was supposed to have adaptogens in it that kept a person from tackling their sisters in frustration.

"Georgie listened to the podcast and thinks she might be able to help," Frankie said. "She agrees there's something there. That's all you really need to put in your book."

Bex underlined *Call Georgie* and *Tell Sam*, feeling more settled and satisfied with her pen in her hand. It *was* nice to have both of her sisters home, sharing a meal, contributing to this project. She'd been unfair to think they only sought her out for drama. They'd been trying to tell her that their feelings about *Craven's Daughter* went as deep as hers did, and Bex was starting to see that this project, this podcast, had the potential to do more than help the fans.

Vic interrupted Bex's thoughts. "Franks, do you want to go

swimming with me at this guy's place in West Hollywood? I tore one of my contact lenses and can't drive."

With the abrupt change of subject, Bex closed her notebook.

After Frankie agreed to Vic's plan and her sisters left, Bex cleared away the mess from the table and wiped it down, thinking about how Jen's death had been like a stone in a still pond, rippling out from her family and friends and her work at *Craven's Daughter* to affect a much larger circle of people.

When Bex had driven two kids across the country to Los Angeles with a bank account budgeted so strictly it squeaked, her heart had felt like a bloody tornado, churning with grief, fear, resentment, love, and anger. She had been forced to grow up overnight and skip the parts where she was allowed to make a mistake. Her sisters mocked her lists and rituals, but those were the things that had given them a perfect Los Angeles night on a freeway headed to somebody's pool in West Hollywood, and every single dream in their healthy bodies.

It was one reason why Bex was so resistant to the very idea that something other than an accident might have taken Jen's life. She hadn't been able to feel it back then, but she could certainly feel it now—her fury that Jen was someone's daughter who had been made to feel safe in the creative world of moviemaking, and that safety had been a lie.

Returning to the table, Bex opened her notebook to one of the items on her list, pulled up the contacts on her phone, and tapped one to call.

"Hello? Is that you, Bexley?" It had been several months since she'd spoken to Jen's mother, Toni. Her voice was so much like Jen's, it choked Bex up a little. There was TV going in the background, like always, but Toni was already turning it down.

"It is! Hi, Toni."

Bex had first gotten to know Jen's parents when they visited the set, vacationing in L.A. to see their daughter. They were from Ohio, like her. She and Toni had bonded over shared knowledge of buckeyes, the OSU-Michigan rivalry, and the cream puffs at Schmidt's Sausage Haus in German Village.

"What a nice surprise! How are the girls? You know, we finally got a chance to get into the show Frankie works on, and every time they do one of those sunset scenes in the gazebo, I get excited because Frankie told me she assists with lighting those sunsets. I'll never get over it."

Bex let herself drop into an easygoing chat with Toni for a few minutes, catching her up on how Frankie felt about her job (mixed, with a lot of complaints that Bex couldn't figure out if she was supposed to help with or just listen to) and how Vic was doing at college (hard to tell, because Vic was circumspect about it, which made Bex worry, given that Vic was circumspect about nothing). It was so much like talking to Jen in her makeup chair, it made Bex's heart ache, and she knew she had to get to the point.

"I have to say, Toni, I'm calling for a reason. It's about Jen. I should've called sooner, and I'm sorry."

Toni made a sound that could've been agreement or a sad catch in her throat. "I got Sam's email about talking about Jen on the podcast. I think it's good."

"Have you listened?" Bex traced patterns on the tabletop, her stomach jumping.

"Oh, you know, I haven't listened to any podcast yet. I do listen to audiobooks in the truck when I'm running errands. I probably should give them a try."

"I'm glad I called, then. Are you in a place you can hear about Jen? Maybe even some tough stuff about how she died?"

"Bexley, the one subject I never mind talking about is Jen. Even how she passed. And of course it's the thing people mostly avoid talking to me about, so you go ahead."

It took some time to tell her everything. Bex was surprised by that. She hadn't appreciated how much had happened, and how quickly. With the murmur of Toni's TV in the background, looking out through her sliding doors at the recessed lights illuminating the ripples over the surface of her pool, she told Toni about fan-fiction and Luciana's having noticed that CravingCraven must have been someone on the cast or crew of *Craven's Daughter*. She walked her through the discoveries they'd made just by dipping into CravingCraven's stories, their conversation with Carl, and the theory that Jen was the most likely person to *be* CravingCraven. Finally, with her heart in her throat, Bex confessed to Toni what she and Sam had decided.

They wanted to know more. They wanted to help their fans figure out the truth.

"But if this upsets you—if you or your family don't want us to—you only have to tell me," Bex said. "I promise, I can put this horse back in the barn."

Toni started chuckling. "Now I'm especially glad you called, and I'm going to figure out this podcast business and tune in, because I can answer at least one of your questions. All those stories you're talking about? Those must be Jen's. I know that much."

They had been right. God. She couldn't wait to tell Sam.

"I bet the expression on your face is precious," Toni said. "And all this is because of Luciana de León! I used to watch her on that soap opera about the ex-convicts who lived together in Manhattan. Bonkers plot, but so compelling. When was that? Long time ago. Jen had just gone to L.A."

"Toni, if—"

"Don't worry, honey. Stop second-guessing. I'm tougher than you think. You know, I've had a lot of people contact me over the years, especially right after she died, who wanted to look into her death. Private investigators offering their services, that sort of thing. And it's not like I didn't want more answers myself, but all of those inquiries felt . . . invasive, I guess. If I could handpick who I'd want to have going over that time in Jen's life, it would be you and Sam. You loved her. I think you should find your answers. Jen would like that. She would like all of this. Especially, I think, she would want the world knowing she wrote all those stories. She loved to write. The good thing about *Craven's Daughter* for Jen was that with less FX work, she had more time to be creative in that way."

Bex made a reminder in her notebook to consider whether Jen's stories might have been nothing more than a creative outlet for a woman with more time on her hands, versus something to decipher about her death.

"You know what I always thought?" Toni asked, musing. "I thought Jen was trying to make things right in those stories. Anything that frustrated her, she'd write about it to get her feelings out. And it's true she had trouble with Aaron and Josh, but she'd had trouble with those two for years. It always seemed like the kind of thing that happens when creative people with control issues try to collaborate." Toni laughed. "Between you and me, Jen had weathered her fair share of professional and personal conflicts. She was a big person, a scary-smart person, but she wasn't easy."

On the other hand, maybe there *was* something in Jen's stories connected to her death. "Were there conflicts you knew about from that time that worried you?"

"Nothing that stands out above anything else, but for a person who liked to be in the middle of things, Jen was private. I learned to take it easy with questions and let her tell me what she needed to in her own time. She mostly talked about where she'd like to see the show go, her frustration with the network. When I asked her how she was coping, since I knew her health at that time could only take so much, that's when she told me about getting back into fanfiction. It was on the advice of her therapist to try writing again."

Bex hadn't known Jen was in therapy. They'd been friends, but she realized that Toni was right—Jen had rarely spoken deeply about herself. "She'd written fanfiction before?"

"Oh, yes. She begged for her own computer so that she could write and post on all those sites. I think if she hadn't been such a strong visual artist and had that internship in a special effects shop, she might have been a writer from the start. But she hadn't put that dream down. She always said life was long, and maybe I'd see her name higher up in the credits on a movie someday."

Oh, that was heartbreaking. Bex was glad to be a safe person who Toni could unburden herself to. They talked for a while longer, ending the conversation with Toni promising to listen to the podcast and share any of her thoughts along the way. Bex hadn't been able to come right out and ask her if she thought Jen had been murdered, but she took the fact that Toni hadn't protested their asking any and all questions about Jen's death as tacit acknowledgment that Toni considered it a possibility.

Or wanted it ruled out.

She went out to her chair by the pool with her notebook. It was her current favorite, tidy and leather-bound with a slim gold pen that was as much a worry object as a tool. There was already a smoother spot on the front where she'd repetitively rubbed her thumb.

Bex pulled her knees up and wrote down and bulleted her current thoughts as they came together.

Luciana and Carl were right that Jen hadn't simply been extroverted, as Bex had thought of her back then. She was *involved*. She asked disarming questions in the makeup chair and then talked about the answers for days. She would passionately argue with a crew member, then bring their favorite food in for their birthday.

Bex could admit that Jen had been easy to love but exhausting to be around. Even Toni hadn't been afraid to say that Jen was a complex personality. Combined with her moods, her enmeshment with those around her had taken her out of the category of invisible crew and given her status on a par with the people who had permission to behave as they wished—the executive producers, directors, designers. Jen had liked to say she'd spent most of her career swimming upstream to compete in the male-dominated special effects field, and "look where it got her." Suffering from a chronic migraine condition, unable to do the work she'd trained to do, she'd pivoted to doing makeup on a crime show and writing hundreds of pages of stories about the people she spent her days talking to.

Bex's pen paused. She had heard Aaron Gorman say more than once that if it weren't for Jen's talent, he wouldn't have worked with "someone like her"—someone difficult, he meant. Which was ironic, considering how difficult Aaron himself could be, not to mention Josh. But Jen was also someone Aaron felt had stolen attention that he deserved. She'd won her Oscar for her work on Aaron's movie, *Bloodright*, when he got nothing. He'd fought with Jen bitterly on *Charles Salt* while its dynamics fell apart. She had likely reported one of his closest collaborators.

Bex couldn't be sure where any of these thoughts led—not yet. But she did know that Aaron didn't shy away from conflict, and she'd never detected that he had what she would consider a moral center. It was important to note—which she did in her notebook with a star and a bullet—that to save his career with *Craven's Daughter*, Aaron had brought on two of the people he had been known to fight with the most: Jen and Josh. Many would think twice about creating such a pressure cooker, to borrow Sam's term. But Aaron wasn't the first person in Hollywood to build a pressure cooker in the hope he'd get a diamond out of it.

And he had, in the form of a shelf full of Emmys and Golden Globes for what was, in its heyday, the most-watched show in America.

Bex gazed at her sleek, black-tiled pool, its lights just starting to glow as the evening got dark. She never forgot she was an Ohio girl when she looked at the endless angles of her stone and timber and glass house tucked up in the Hollywood Hills. Never looked at her accounts without being aware of their promise she could breathe. Never looked at the framed pilot script of *Craven's Daughter* that hung in her bedroom and failed to appreciate that however hard it had been to get here and however much she'd endured, she was lucky.

It was the kind of luck she'd trade in a heartbeat for the chance to see her parents again, or to give them the opportunity to watch their little girls grow up, but it was luck just the same.

Luck and gratitude and money were the kinds of things that bred silence.

Jen had kept secrets. No one on the show had guessed she was writing fanfiction, at least as far as Bex knew. To Bex, that suggested there had been things Jen needed to talk about, but she'd only been able to talk about them in code. Maybe things she was afraid of.

Maybe things that could kill her.

"Hey."

Bex jumped, then yelped, dropping her pen as Sam appeared on the low-lit path along the back of the house. She grasped for it and fell halfway out of the chaise to keep it from rolling into the jacuzzi. "Where did you come from? Do I not have the security system on?"

Sam walked over and offered her hand so Bex could grab onto it to swing her legs around and sit up properly. "Sorry. Yeah, you do, but I disarmed it. I tried to call you to see if I could come over. When you didn't pick up, I texted Frankie. She said to stop by because you weren't doing anything."

Sam sat next to her on the edge of the chaise, stretching out her impossibly long California-girl legs and leaning back on her arms. Her running shorts, faded tee, and ball cap were proof that Sam "wasn't doing anything" either. They shared a preference for quiet nights in. "You have your notebook out." Sam tapped the leather cover.

"I've been trying to organize my thoughts." Bex put the notebook down, too conscious that Sam was looking at her. "I called Toni."

"She texted me a little while ago. That's why I thought to come over. It sounds like it went well. And Jen! Confirmed secret identity as CravingCraven."

Bex rubbed her chest. "I keep thinking about her writing all of those stories to feel better."

"Yeah. I think her fic gave a lot of other fans permission to feel better, too."

"It seems so unlikely that Jen was hurt deliberately. Not because she or her life were perfect, but because if someone hurt her, it was probably someone we knew. Or know. Maybe someone powerful who's gotten away with it for a long time. That's tough for me to take in. I think I've been putting a little bit of a glow on all my memories. I mean, can I agree that the set was dysfunctional, even toxic, maybe at times abusive? I guess so, to varying degrees, depending on who was involved. But a murderer?" She shook her head. "I don't know. I'm having a tough time seeing beyond what the police saw, at least so far. But I'm also realizing that back then I was seeing what I wanted to see."

Sam turned and settled into the back of the chaise, inviting Bex to face her at the foot. The light was purple, coming mostly from discreet fixtures inset in the landscaping. "When I think about you back then, Bex, what I mostly remember is how much you gave and everyone else took." Sam had removed her hat. Her eyes were sapphire in this light. "You were perfect on that set. The most experienced folks on the crew shook their heads in wonder at you. Aaron never said so. The network never did. The crew only told you by making everything as easy as they could for you, which is their way. I *tried* to tell you, but you didn't let me."

"I didn't let you tell me a lot of things."

Sam's eyebrows shot up. "No. But that's what I'm trying to say. Instead of getting the celebration and support you deserved, you were asked for more. Because you were so great. The network, and everyone else, exploited your talent. Your famous professionalism. Aaron exploited everyone on that set in the name of saving his own career. The network exploited our chemistry. And then I—"

Sam looked up at the clouded-over October sky and sighed.

It was all the warning Bex needed to know that Sam was about to take their conversation into uncharted territory.

"Bex, I was so tired of spending what we had on set in the name of Henri and Cora's chemistry. I wanted to have it for myself. I wanted *you* to have it. I wanted there to be an *us*. And imagining that, imagining how amazing we would have been together, meant I rushed our timing and then jumped ship when it didn't work."

"No." Bex leaned forward. "That isn't fair."

"It is. We haven't avoided this conversation. I didn't let us have it. I confessed my feelings to you and wanted you to return them, right then, on my schedule, because I was afraid you didn't feel the same way I did. When you tried to tell me you weren't ready, I received it as a rejection and ran." Sam huffed out a self-deprecating laugh. "I know you've been thinking this whole time that the reason we haven't really talked the last five years is because you rejected me, and I didn't bother to correct you, because I've been hurt." Sam twirled her ball cap on her fingertips, looking out over the pool. "I know you think I stayed as long as I could stand it so you and Vic and Frankie would get the benefits of syndication, but that was only part of it, a small part. I stayed because I never enjoyed myself more than when I was with you."

Oh, Sam.

Even a few weeks ago, when she met Sam at Stage 46, Bex didn't think she would have known what to do with this confession, but here, now, she felt completely connected to this moment—to the space between twilight and dark, to her breath, to Sam's ankle almost touching her shin, to what Sam was saying and how she was saying it. It gave Bex the courage to say what she should have told Sam long ago.

"I did feel the same way," she said. "But I knew you weren't happy after Jen died. I was afraid you were going to leave the show at any moment. I didn't know what I would do next. Where I would have to go. You asked to give me something I'd been told I couldn't even talk about, something I'd told myself I couldn't have if I wanted to keep the career and the stability I *needed*. You offered me your heart, but you did it at a moment when I believed all my options to survive were narrowing. It's true that if you'd asked again the next day, I probably would have cleared out a shelf in my closet for your baseball caps, but Sam, that was a *hard time*. For you, for me, for my sisters. Maybe we should give ourselves some grace."

Sam was looking at the pool deck, her eyes hidden. "Bex, I have to be clear with you. I have to tell you that all I want now, when it comes to you and me, is to be the kind of friend who helps you to get what *you* want. Whatever that is."

Bex took a deep breath. It was the same boundary Sam had given her before, at the studio, but it hurt a little more this time. She'd started to hope.

She wondered with a drop in her stomach if she told Sam about *Venice Memorial*, whether Sam would help her get that. It felt like she wouldn't, or wouldn't want to, but Bex wasn't sure why. Frankie had said she thought Bex was making a mistake. Combined with her uncertainty about Sam's support, Bex knew she had to be missing something when it came to her career plan.

She hated it when she was missing something. It meant she was going to have to start thinking harder about what she wanted.

Abruptly, Sam sat up with a sharp inhale. She reached over and touched Bex's notebook. "Tell me what you wrote down on your list, detective."

Completely unbidden, Bex felt tears welling up at the unexpected arrival of Henri Shannon calling her *detective*. The past and the present, reality and fiction, were all jumbled together. Bex touched her mother's earring to ground herself. "I was mostly trying to get things straight because my nepo baby sisters contacted Georgie Hayworth."

"No shit?" Sam slid her hat back onto her head. "I suppose we should probably get a real detective on this. Good idea, actually."

"She's going to try. She's in town taking meetings." Bex picked up her notebook. "If there is anything she can help with, I was actually thinking that maybe—"

"—she should be on the podcast?" Sam scooted closer, visibly excited. "Yes. Guess who I called."

"I couldn't. I don't have any foresight left. I'm purely hindsight and trying to hang on to what's going on in the here and now."

"Bette."

"Whoa."

"And she picked up! She sounded almost pleased to hear from me."

"I can't imagine how you would be able to tell." Bette Holloway was legendarily inscrutable.

"We had a chat. She's been listening to the podcast."

Bex flopped dramatically against the back of the chaise. "This is a *lot* to take in."

"But there's more. She's willing to come on as a guest. I'm thinking we have her and Georgie both, see what we can shake out."

"At the same time? You understand that Bette's currently on our suspect list."

Sam snatched Bex's notebook off the table and flipped through the pages, laughing as Bex reached for it. She held it away, though she didn't actually land on a page and read it until Bex gave her a nod. "Like, it actually says 'Suspect List,' and there is the name Bette Holloway. You are a delight, Bexley Simon." Sam handed Bex's notebook back to her and stood up. "You know, Bette had a lot of reasons with a lot of zeroes on checks to make sure everything about her stepdad's show went perfectly, which is the kind of thought that makes me read Jen's fanfic very carefully. I'm wondering if she knew something. But Georgie's a cop, so I figure if things go south in the Inglewood studio basement, she'll protect you."

"Who's going to protect *you*?"

Sam held out her hands. When Bex took them, Sam hauled

her to her feet, and Bex had to concentrate on not tipping forward and ending up with her entire body plastered against Sam's.

That was what had happened in the episode they would be recapping on the next podcast.

"Don't worry about me. Worry more about what you're going to say about the clip." Sam wiggled her eyebrows.

Right at that moment on her pretty patio, the night jasmine starting to release the day's warmth and its fragrance, Bex did not want to take Sam's bait or back down. If Sam could be friends and flirt with her at the same time, that meant Bex could be friends and flirt back even harder. "You mean 'You Must Remember This'? The only episode that may have had an earlier draft, according to on-set rumor, with a scripted kiss between Cora and Henri? The one where we had to do so, so, *so* many takes—"

"—but then they used the first one, because that was the only take where the gun going off and *interrupting us* was a surprise."

"Indeed. I am more than ready to talk about that episode, Sam. I have questions." Bex twirled a strand of hair around her finger, watching Sam for a reaction. "Many of which, serendipitously, are for Bette, including if she did, at any point, in any draft, script that kiss. But other questions are for you. I seem to remember that you started *waiting* for that gunshot. Like if you didn't keep your whole brain on it, then something else was going to happen in that closet. I am ready to find out what that something was."

Bex could not raise just one eyebrow, no matter how she tried, so she smiled at Sam instead, giving it plenty of coy dimple. Then Samantha Ellen Farmer actually looked down at the ground and *scuffed her feet* and *shoved her hands into her pockets*.

Bex had ruffled her. She smacked the notebook against her thigh and grinned.

That was one thing, then, she could say she wanted. To ruffle Sam as much as possible.

In the (Iconic) Closet

Bex dug around in her purse as she slow-walked down the wide hallway that serviced Stage 46. "Did you eat my snack bar? I know I had a granola-cashew-date thing in here."

"I can't have . . . oats," Frankie panted. She was behind Bex, attempting to push a huge cart with a balky wheel over a seam in the floor. The cart held a tarp-draped, bungeed-down, rectangular object. Amethyst had deputized Frankie away from *Timber Creek Farm* to help her today, which suited Frankie because it meant she could monitor the podcast recording. Neither of them would reveal what was on the cart. "Would you stop fiddling with your purse and *help* me?"

Bex turned around, exasperated. "You said you didn't want my help."

"I changed my mind after it became clear that wheels are only a useful invention when they work." Frankie shoved at the cart with her full body weight. It rolled a foot, then stopped. "Vic took your snack bar. I told her to replace it, and she picked up some Keto coconut oil and monk-fruit bars, but I think she ate them."

"God damn it." Bex clenched her back teeth against the tone in Frankie's voice, which threatened an argument about something Bex couldn't quite put her finger on or resolve. She applied herself to one of the back corners of the cart as Frankie moved to the other side. They shoved in unison. The cart began to roll, slow but steady.

"I have intel about the case," Frankie said. "I know someone who knows someone who was peripherally involved with *Charles Salt*."

"Who?"

Frankie stopped pushing and leaned against the cart, her expression annoyed. "First of all, 'Thank you, Frankie. I appreciate your going above and beyond, asking around your network for information about Jen while Sam and I walk in circles mistaking our butts and elbows.'"

"Wow."

Frankie pointed at her. "Also, it might have been a good idea to give Vic a high five for her help sometime around when she was moping about having to go back to school. She's been texting me every fifteen seconds that she's not sending me funny videos. She misses us. She misses *you*."

"I took her to the spa for the wrap with the hot oil, and we had lunch after at the vegan hot dog place that only she likes." Bex had congratulated herself for making time to treat Vic to an outing doing things Vic loved. Or maybe things she used to love. It was true that she had been a little lackluster at lunch and had complained about having to go back to Davis so soon, but if Bex worried about everything her sisters complained about, worrying would be the only thing she ever did.

Frankie sighed and tapped the side of the tarp in a transparent attempt to regulate her emotions. The object made a big, hollow sound that gave Bex a clue to the contents of the cart, confirming her existing suspicions. "But to get to my *point*," Frankie said, "and you might want to include this in your notebook, my source was old friends with Marilee Plungkhen. They went to high school together."

"Oh! Marilee had a big part on *Charles Salt*, right?"

"Yes, and what this source told me went down during a promo taping on the show's set."

"Who's your source again?"

"Look, I can't. They're a PA, too, and we can't pass along secrets and betray where they came from. Intel from each other is a currency. It's how we survive in an industry where there's not enough jobs and no one gets paid enough to cover rent and groceries."

"That's fair. I understand favors as a currency and will ask no further questions about that. For my notebook, Marilee was doing a promo taping on set. On Josh's set." Bex was starting to feel lightheaded. She didn't know if it was due to hunger, the exertion of pushing the cumbersome cart, or foreboding about the revelation Frankie was about to deliver.

"Yeah, so, Josh was skulking around when they were shooting, and Marilee had gotten friendly with one of the crew. Sounds like *friendly* friendly. But she had history with Josh."

"Josh Miller dated *Marilee Plungkhen?*"

"Josh can pull. Don't ask me why. Heterosexuality is a curse. But I guess they'd kept it pretty quiet. Anyway, there was a break in the filming, and the source found themself witnessing a screaming fight between Josh and Marilee, instigated by Josh, which was obvious because Marilee was trying to get away. Josh grabbed Marilee's upper arm, and my source was about to step in when Marilee escaped."

The hallway had opened up, the cart picking up a bit of speed. Bex could see light spilling out of Stage 46. Sam stood just outside the door with Amethyst, who waved at Bex when she spotted her and then disappeared onto the stage.

"Later on, the crew member who was flirting with Marilee tells my source that Marilee told *him* she sometimes wondered if Josh was sabotaging her on set. 'Trying to get me killed,' Marilee said. She told this crew member that if Josh hadn't been so close to

Aaron, and she could be sure it wouldn't get her into a mess with the network, she would've gotten a restraining order on Josh."

Bex's knees felt weak. "You're kidding."

"I'm dead serious. After my source heard the podcast, they called a couple people who were there to double-check the details, and everyone they talked to remembers it the same."

Bex was going to need to make a *lot* of notes in her notebook. A relationship between Josh and Marilee that went sour on the set of *Charles Salt* was an important avenue to look into—especially when it came with evidence of Josh engaging in abusive behavior and an accusation from a completely new source that Josh was a saboteur.

"Thank you," she said. "Sincerely. It sounds like you spent some capital to get this information."

Frankie looked at Bex, and for a moment Bex thought she'd get one of Frankie's grins in response, but her sister blew out a breath instead. "You're welcome. I did it for Jen."

Okay.

The cart was moving fast now. It thumped over a seam in the linoleum with a loud bang. Frankie and Bex pushed it up from the wide load-in hallway into the open space of Stage 46. Amethyst had already miked Bette, Georgie, and Sam, who were gathered around a table in a dark corner of the *Craven's Daughter* set.

"Delivery!" Frankie stopped the cart. She unhooked one bungee cord and ripped off the tarp with a dramatic flourish. "You guys ordered an iconic closet?"

"Wow," Sam said. "There it is."

Frankie started unstrapping the set piece. While Bex got herself miked and greeted their guests, Amethyst helped Frankie move it off the cart and into the middle of the Craven Investigations office, which had been denuded of its desk and props to make room.

"Remember, it's not anchored," Frankie said. "You can look,

but don't touch. We'll take some pictures after you record to share on the website."

"That's no fun," Sam said.

"Isn't that why I'm here? Because of how much audiences love the look-but-don't-touch thing?" Bette Holloway took a long pull from a matte black vaping pen. It matched her black button-up shirt, which she wore tucked into battered black jeans that Bex knew for a fact cost seven hundred dollars, because Frankie had a similar pair, and Bex had goggled at the price tag.

"We've been recording since the closet came in," Amethyst reminded them. "Get lively."

Amethyst led them through introductions. Bette had gone on from *Craven's Daughter* to a stellar career writing for mainly dark and gritty limited series that earned her enough Emmys and Golden Globes that her trophy shelf must be groaning.

"But *Craven's Daughter* was your first show," Bex said. "Did you have any idea that it would hit like it did? I know it was Aaron Gorman's concept, and that he wrote the pilot, but did you see his vision for it, or did you take it someplace different?"

Bette crossed her legs, reaching up to twist her dark hair into an elastic that had been on her wrist. She let out a big sigh that was loud in Bex's headphones. "I don't mind saying now that I hated my stepdad."

"Aaron," Sam clarified.

"Yeah. It would've been fine if he was a dick in his own life, but Aaron's a micromanager. So he marries my mom, who has a sixteen-year-old daughter, and decides he can play daddy. But I didn't need a daddy. I was the kind of sixteen, like, stick a fork in me, I was done."

Bex believed that Bette Holloway had probably emerged from the womb fully formed, with a tiny nose ring and a grudge against the pain of existence. "How did you end up writing for his show, then?" she asked.

"Probably the same way I became a detective in Chicago

despite being female, Filipina, and four-foot-eleven," Georgie interjected. "White-hot spite."

Bette looked over at Georgie, laughing, which was remarkable, because Bex was certain she had never before seen Bette laugh. Or smile? "There is nothing like hate-winning," Bette said. "I send a gallery of Getty photos of myself accepting awards to my ninth-grade English teacher every year. Not because she's proud of me. Because she gave me a D on our creative writing unit."

"You fought with Aaron during the run of the show," Sam said.

"Every fucking day," Bette agreed. "Because if I hadn't, *Craven's Daughter* would've been canceled before the end of the first season. Aaron didn't watch TV. He claimed it interfered with his creativity, but I don't know if you've realized that *Craven's Daughter* wasn't the first murder-mystery-of-the-week show in the history of American television, won't be the last, and Aaron could've been a legend if he actually loved what he was doing."

Sam was playing with the knot in her wide silk men's tie, loosening it so it looked even more artlessly cool with the tissue-thin T-shirt she'd paired it with. "Do *you* love it?" she asked.

"It might be the only thing I love," Bette said. "I'm not kidding."

"I believe you," Bex said. "If you were fighting with Aaron to make television you could love, what was your vision for *Craven's Daughter*?"

Bette leaned back and twirled her vape pen through her fingers. "I wanted to write a show about getting what you want. Or not. We know Cora's dad, Joe Craven, was a PI. We know he wasn't much else. Not a father, not a partner, not a friend. He hardly went home. He died in his office. Did he love it? Was his dogged obsession the same as love? Was giving everything up except for tracking down bad guys what he *wanted*? Cora is set up as the perfect kindergarten teacher. Is that what she wanted to do with her life? Then why did she abandon that job when she didn't have to? What about Henri? Went too hard at the FBI, was let go—or so she says when Cora hires her. Did she want to investigate, or did she just want to eat, or did she meet Cora and that was it, Henri wanted *her*? I think all that tension is why the show resonated with so many people."

There was something Bex didn't like about this pat speech, and not just because those questions had never been answered in the series. Bette was the writer Aaron had tapped to work with exclusively on *Craven*, and even though Sam was right that they'd frequently disagreed, when it came to discussing the show's vision, Bette had always deferred to Aaron. Why talk now?

"But," Sam said after a beat of silence, "no one has ever admitted, and I certainly have never heard *you* admit, that the show was about Henri wanting Cora. The audience never got any confirmation or closure on the issue."

Now Bette smiled at Sam. It made it seem as though she was a friend, here to hang out or do them a favor based on their personal connection, but Bex's relationship to Bette had never been personal. For years, Bette had written the scripts that told Bex what to do. Then Bex did it. "If it didn't come from me and Aaron, it must have come from the two of you," Bette said. "Which means there are a few options. One, I wrote it as a romance that never got consummated because, Sam, *you* heartlessly bailed before the series finale. Two, all that heavy breathing and inadvertent touching and lingering eye contact was something the two of you were doing because you were bored and fucking with us. Or, three—and keep in mind how very young and naive you were and how little you knew *how* to fuck with anyone—you were actually falling in love. Right in front of America."

Georgie coughed. Bex gripped the wooden arms of the director's chair. She didn't have a single word inside of her head. Not one. A blank cue card, then another. Nothing.

Anger had a way of doing that. Sam had pointed out that the network had exploited their chemistry, and Bex was starting to understand that *being* exploited had made it difficult for her to understand her own feelings. But what Bette had just said so flippantly removed any accountability from Aaron, from the network, *and* from Bette—making it Sam's fault for leaving, or the result of Bex and Sam's game, or because Bex and Sam weren't talented—that Bex was having a difficult time lining up all of her shouty, livid thoughts.

"Did you write the script?" Sam asked. Bex's focus came back with the harsh tone of Sam's voice. "For the series finale. Did you write the script for the series finale?"

Bette pulled the elastic out of her hair, and it snapped back on her wrist. "I did."

"What happened in it? Answer your own question. By leaving, did I deny our fans the catharsis of Henri and Cora's happily ever after?"

"The script doesn't belong to me," Bette said. "It belongs to the network. I can't say."

Now she had two hectic pink spots, high up on her cheeks. Bex wondered if that was because Sam was challenging her ego or getting too close to whatever secrets she kept. Or could it be that she needed to be more in control of this situation? Was she here because she was trying to shift a narrative that would eventually call her out?

"Come on, Bette," Georgie interjected. "There's more than one way to answer a question. Tell us what you *can* say."

"I'm sorry, I didn't know that I was a part of Bex and Sam's dinner theater murder mystery."

"I didn't know if you were either." Sam's tone was breezy, making it impossible to tell if this was edgy banter or accusation. Sam was a talented actress.

So was Bex. She *had* been young and naive when she started out playing Cora Banks, but she wasn't anymore, and Bette didn't write this podcast. She wasn't even a producer. *Bex* was. This was their podcast, hers and Sam's, and Bette's comments cheapened what they were trying to do, then and now. If Bette's scripts for

Cora and Henri had taken advantage of what she believed were Bex and Sam's very real feelings for each other, who was the hack?

Bex narrowed her eyes at Bette. She looked away, reaching for her vape pen.

"Maybe I could offer up some thoughts." Georgie leaned over and took a file off a table stocked with water bottles, then adjusted her deep burgundy skirt suit and slid on a pair of funky readers in a black-and-white pattern that matched her silver-shot gray hair. "Bette, you did let me go as a script consultant after the fourth season, but I want to tell you it never bothered me, because it was clear you'd listened to the heart of what I shared with you about investigative work. I don't get fussed about how close TV is to the real thing. I know how the sausage is made. No one wants to actually watch that. You wrote efficient mysteries solved by watchable investigation every week. Bravo. But Sam and Bex invited me here today for a different reason." Georgie tapped her folder. "Jen Arnot."

Bex sat up straighter. "Did you find something?"

"Real quick, we should catch up our listeners first," Sam said. "After last week's bombshell that Jen Arnot, who passed away on location after an accident, is CravingCraven, *Craven's Daughter*'s Big Name Fan in the world of fanfiction, we've had hundreds, maybe thousands of you digging into everything you could find about the show, the crew, incidents on set, Jen's career, and her alleged issues with both Josh Miller, our set designer, and Aaron Gorman. More than a few of you felt dissatisfied with how Jen's death was handled, and, after checking in with Jen's family, we gave Georgie the go-ahead to take a look at the original scene and accident report and give us her opinion. Obviously this isn't an open case anymore, and it wouldn't be Georgie's case even if it were, because she's no longer in law enforcement. But we respect her insight as a former investigator."

Bex's phone call with Toni Arnot had given her a very heavy sense of responsibility. She'd been having anxiety dreams, the kind where everyone was yelling at her. Right now, her agency and manager were thrilled with the spicy public attention on Bex for the return of her chemistry with Sam and the audacity of their decision to play detective with the fans, but Jen was *real*. Her family was real.

Bex's career supported a lot of people. She couldn't afford to move very far past spicy. Definitely not right into slander. Frankie's report of her intel had done little to relax her. Bette was pissing her off. The file on Georgie's lap was making her genuinely scared.

To center herself, Bex looked at Sam, whose voluminous wide-legged trousers and stacked patent red heels swished and shone as she crossed her legs. Her careless posture reminded Bex of how she had always played Henri as a woman with tremendous quiet power that she wielded only when she had to.

She'd modeled Henri's character on her dynamic with Bex, but not the way anyone watching *Craven's Daughter* might have guessed.

It had happened right away, at their chemistry read. Sam walked in, and Bex was already curious to meet her because Sam Farmer had appeared on the covers of a lot of magazines in not a lot of clothes, but the interviews she'd given in those magazines made Bex laugh.

She wasn't sure she could explain the low-down tug between them to anyone. How it was that Bex felt her posture perfect itself and a power she hadn't let out in forever size Sam up. How Sam waited for Bex to offer her hand to shake. How it was exciting but loose.

They sat on wooden stools across from each other. She relaxed, and then Sam did, too.

She smiled, and Sam looked down and smiled.

When they tried out Cora and Henri for the first time, Bex watched Sam make the choice to *switch*, taking up Bex's role in the power play that was already building between the two of them. It had been like sticking a metal rod into a white-hot arc of electricity.

Even now, thinking of it, Bex wanted to kiss Sam.

She let herself imagine in high definition if she would let Sam put her hands in her hair, or if Bex would hold her face, or if her kiss would be frantic or soft or very, very bossy. If Sam would make a noise. If she would flush under the sun-made gold of her skin.

Sam caught her eye, and Bex didn't stop to think about it— she just let what she'd kept tied up unfurl in the space between them.

Sam looked away, surprised, but her hands curled into fists. Her throat flushed pink. She'd caught what Bex sent in her direction.

Oops.

"First, I want to say that the balcony in Chicago doesn't meet modern codes for the height of its railing or how it's supported," Georgie said. "I think that's important, and so did the investigators. It's noted on the accident report."

"What?" Sam sounded deliciously distracted.

Feeling bad she'd let her brain off its leash, Bex took a deep breath to bring her surroundings and what she was supposed to be doing back into focus. Versus experimenting with how outrageous she was willing to get in mixed company to capture Sam Farmer's full attention.

"Open-air balconies are dangerous," Georgie said. "Even more so if they're unstable with poor railings and without a nighttime light source, which was also true for this location. The report's narrative is a reasonable interpretation of the available facts. It suggests that Jen was left behind at the apartment after she fell asleep, having complained of a migraine and taken medication that had been observed to alter her coordination. She woke up and walked onto a poorly lit balcony with a short railing, and then she either tripped and fell or sat on the railing and lost her balance."

"*But*," Bette said. "There's got to be a *but*. Why else bring Ms. Sherlock Holmes onto the show?"

Georgie took her readers off. "Bette, just like you, I don't do anything I don't want to. I'm seventy-two years old, retired, still have my health, my teeth, good hair, and a nice rack. Go ahead and question your own motives for talking to Sam and Bex today, but kindly leave off mine." Georgie put her readers back on. "As I was saying."

Sam burst into laughter.

"I apologize," Bette said to Georgie.

Georgie smiled. "Apology accepted. I would have no problems with this report except for a few things that stand out to me. I want to make it clear to any of my former colleagues who are listening that all of us know fresh eyes see new evidence, so no offense to the officers who closed this original investigation."

"We understand," Bex said. "But what did you see?"

"The inventory of Jen's effects doesn't include any medications. Not even a cough drop. Because of the circumstances, a toxicology report including alcohol was done, and there was nothing found in her system. Now if she was taking something like Maxalt for migraine—which, again, there's no evidence in her effects that she did—it's short-acting, and it would've taken a special tox panel to find it if there was anything still in her system to find. That wasn't done, as far as I can tell. Also, she's a little taller than me. Five two. I mentioned the railing was short, but it's still about as high as a kitchen countertop. I'd have trouble, even after a bad trip and fall, making it over that, and the railing wasn't broken, so she didn't come through it. We know that because photographs were taken. The balcony is small enough that a trip-and-fall would have had to begin in the interior room, but nothing there was disturbed. She might have hopped up to sit on the railing in the dark, all by herself after just waking up. That can't be ruled out, except—"

"The idea of doing that makes my stomach flip right over," Bex said. "I've done a few of my own stunts, and I still wouldn't sit on an old, dirty balcony railing over a pitch-black alley. Jen was a cautious person."

"Except with her mouth," Bette said. "She wasn't cautious with that."

"For heaven's sake, Bette," Bex said, because there wasn't any reason not to, and Toni Arnot was the only audience member she could clearly imagine. "Ease up."

"Look, the fact of the matter is, we didn't like each other." Bette crossed her arms. "We hardly crossed paths. There's almost no reason for writers to talk to makeup. It would dishonor her for me to act like we were friends."

"Then keep your mouth shut. It's like I used to tell my sisters when I served them food. Say you like it or say nothing. I don't need to hear every opinion that flits across your brain pan." Bex turned her attention to Georgie while Bette took a long drag off her vape pen. "Please continue. I feel like you've already presented enough to demonstrate it's worth another look at what happened."

Georgie closed her folder. "That's all of what I noticed from the scene and from the material evidence. The rest was reading the interviews with people who had been on location during the filming and who had last seen Jen. They went the way I would've expected them to, given the conclusions. The cast left together first. The apartment was packed up, and the crew left. Then your showrunner, cinematographer, film editor, and production designer all left together after finishing up a meeting. Everyone was interviewed. The interviews confirmed Jen had a bad migraine and didn't leave with the cast, crew, or director's group. This seems to indicate she was there alone."

"There were a lot of people in the building that day," Sam said. "It would be easy for someone to be missed."

"This seems to be a conclusion of elimination, not one of evidence," Georgie said. "That's not necessarily suspicious, though you're right, Sam, there were a lot of people in that building, and Jen's estimated time of passing means the majority left not even an hour before she died. I would say what I feel is professionally unsettled."

"It's worth talking about, you mean," Bex said. "Looking at it again."

"As long as her family continues to support it, yes. I'm in agreement with you."

"Thank you, Georgie."

"You're welcome."

Bex rose, studying the three-sided closet sitting in the middle of the set. The back wall was the inside of the closet's closed door. For the scene they were recapping, Bex and Sam had been filmed cowering behind it. "I think we're going to have to watch this clip. This is still technically a rewatch podcast, and no doubt our listeners are curious to hear what our thoughts are on all the heavy breathing, inadvertent touching, and lingering eye contact we got up to in there." She did not manage, or even try, to keep the bitterness out of her voice when she quoted Bette's dismissive words. "Sam, are you ready to look-but-don't-touch with me?"

"Pretty sure I left a scrap of my soul in this closet in season four." Sam got up, rubbing her hands together. "I was kind of hoping I'd get my chance to reclaim it."

Bex stepped into the box and held her hand out. Sam took it, and Bex pulled her in.

"You're not supposed to get in the closet," Amethyst said. "Frankie made that clear."

Bex looked up at Sam, her warm, ambery perfume heating the breath of air between them. "Frankie never listened to *me*," Bex said. "Play the clip. We'll give our impressions by method podcasting from this box."

Sam twirled her finger in the air. Amethyst huffed a sigh, but she played the clip, filling the projection screen with a shadowy close-up that Bex had seen in countless Internet memes in the years since.

"Don't make a sound," Henri says against Cora's cheek. Cora grips the front of Henri's coat, her eyes wide and terrified.

"We can't—" Cora is hardly whispering, mouthing the words as someone outside the closet is upending the office, pulling out drawers and knocking things over.

Henri shakes her head, then puts her finger against Cora's lips. Cora closes her eyes.

Henri stares down at her intensely, her brow furrowed as she removes her finger. Cora opens her eyes. They gaze at each other for a long moment, chaos outside the closet, hushed quiet in the small space they occupy. Henri bends down, her mouth hovering near Cora's long enough that Cora's fingers unfurl from Henri's coat and slide down. Henri moves closer—but then she turns her head ever so slightly, just as Cora closes her eyes again.

"Breathe," Henri says against the corner of Cora's mouth. Cora opens her eyes, furrows her brow.

"Henri?" Cora pulls herself closer to Henri by her coat just as a bullet breaks apart the wood of the closet door right above their heads.

When Amethyst stopped the clip, Bex released the two fistfuls of Sam's T-shirt she found herself holding. Her palms were damp. Sam's hands had found Bex's waist, resting on bare skin because Bex had worn another old dance rehearsal top that she'd cropped with scissors years ago. Had Sam pressed her fingers into Bex's sides like that back then? Bex remembered take after take of Sam's breath against her skin, how it sensitized *everything* in a way that made each reshoot of the scene more shaky, chaotic, and beyond her usual control than the last. She was at work. She was working.

She was a pro, in character, her character hiding in a closet with a crush on her colleague. Cora's boundaries were hashed, and so Bex's had been impossible to locate, just like they were now, with Sam's soft hair brushing against her collarbone.

Breathe. The fans had put it on T-shirts. They'd illustrated Henri and Cora, their faces so close, Cora's eyes huge. The closet door. Henri in her coat, Cora's hands at her lapel.

Breathe.

She wanted to kiss Sam. Right now, she wanted to.

And she fucking absolutely had wanted to back then.

"I changed my mind," Bette called out.

Moving as one, Sam and Bex turned toward her. She was crouched in the chair in a way that made her look like a bird of prey who had them in her sights. "I want to give you both the script for the final episode." Bette collapsed back from her crouch, letting out a harsh sigh. She looked somewhere into the dark of Stage 46. "Come what may."

Bex dropped her hands to her sides. Her palms hurt. Everything hurt. "You weren't fair to us, Bette."

She looked back to Sam, aware in some part of herself that they were still in the iconic closet, still miked, still at work. "None of them were fair to us," she said. "The network wasn't fair to us *or* to the fans. Aaron. Bette. They pushed us and pushed us until you were past your breaking point, and you know what? That's *confusing.*"

Sam shook her head. "We didn't know how to end this show. No one did."

"We knew," Bex said. "The fans knew. But that wasn't good enough." She stepped out of the closet and pulled off her mic and earphones.

"Send us the script by courier," she told Bette.

And then Bex walked off the set, starting to have a pretty good idea of what she wanted.

Fix-It Fic

"**A**nd here we've got the punch." Chaz Morgenstern put her arm around Sam. One of her six-inch-long gold tassel earrings caught against the collar of her linen tunic. "Be careful, though. It's easy to be deceived by all the fruit and fizz. You keep ladling yourself one more glass, you'll find out why they call it *punch*."

Laughing at her own joke, the elderly woman stepped away from Sam so she could put her other arm around Bex. "It's so nice to get together again. And to think I was dreading the reunion." She wrinkled her nose. "Just a *titch*. I thought the latest episode of your podcast was sure to cast a pall over everything, but it just goes to show how publicity is a fortune-teller's game." Chaz spoke as though everything she said was a scandalous secret, but that was nothing new. "So many of your listeners are tickled at how the two of you are blending a detective show rewatch with true crime. Others are delighted with the audacity of rebelling against the network. And everyone is dizzy from holding their breath." Chaz squeezed them both, her rings and smile flashing. "Waiting for that kiss they never got."

Bex smiled back, a little overwarm from Chaz's firm grip and the familiar strain of racing to keep up with her. Just thirty minutes into this party that Chaz was throwing to get the cast and crew together in advance of the reunion—now three weeks away—Bex was already exhausted. The moment she'd passed through the familiar double doors of Chaz's modest Eichler home in Thousand Oaks, she'd been stopped by former cast, guest stars, crew, and producers of *Craven's Daughter*, all of whom wanted to hug her, ask her about the podcast, and offer up their own theories. About *everything*.

Bex and Sam's willingness to entertain the subject of their feelings on the rewatch podcast had unhitched the entirety of the former cast and crew of *Craven's Daughter* from any semblance of decorum. Bex had never been winked at this much in her life. The innuendo was flying at her so fast, she kept catching herself with her hands at her earlobes, and then she'd have to take a few square breaths to remind herself that she was not naked, no one could read her mind, and the secrets of the most vulnerable, hidden chambers of her heart remained locked up tight.

"What I can tell you," Sam said, "is that Bex and I have been on a journey." She was a vision tonight in a floral silk romper. Tiny sunbeams filtered through the leaves of a huge lemon tree and broke up the colors in her hair like a prism.

"Ha! Have you two only just noticed?" Chaz ladled herself a glass of punch and toasted them. "Here I go, making my rounds. Please ensure you give these people a good reason for leaving the house on a Sunday afternoon to hang out with an old lady."

Then she was gone, and Bex could exhale. "Everyone in Hollywood is here." There were at least a few hundred people crammed into Chaz's open living area and backyard.

"*Hmm.*" When Sam stepped closer, the little hairs on that side of Bex's body stood at attention.

Bex took a long drink of her punch to quell the heat spreading over the sensitive skin of her chest. "Did you see Aaron?" She had nearly jumped out of her Fendi sneakers when she spotted him leaning against the cedar fence, glowering over a plate full of appetizers. She didn't think he'd seen her, and she'd been ducking him, resentful that no one had warned her.

"I did. And Bette, actually, at the same time. She didn't look like she hated him. They were both talking to Luciana, making some kind of unholy power trinity." Sam had put two fingers at Bex's elbow, steering her body slightly away. Bex knew that anyone who looked in their direction would see old friends, chatting as they surveyed the party together. She reassured herself they could *not* see the way that having Sam's fingertips wrapped around her elbow made her skin tingle.

Sam did read Bex's mind—not about her tingles, but about her unwillingness to deal with Aaron right at this moment. She steered them both to a shaded spot under an old arbor covered in camellia, which shielded them from the view of the other party-goers. But just as Bex was breathing a sigh of relief, she heard a man's voice, close by.

"It's fucking outrageous. Six kinds of slander. I'm looking forward to fucking owning them."

She knew that voice. It was Josh Miller. He couldn't see them, and they couldn't see him, but he couldn't be more than three feet away.

"Jesus, Josh. It's a party. Get a drink."

Bex only knew one woman with such a distinct South Bronx accent. Kim Ryerson, *Craven's Daughter*'s prop master. Bex looked at Sam to see if she had recognized Kim's voice. Sam nodded and put her finger to her lips. Confirmation they were officially eavesdropping.

"What have you heard from the network?" Josh asked.

"The network? Why would the network talk to *me* about a podcast for a show that wrapped years ago? Take a breath, buddy."

"I know for goddamned sure there hasn't been a single release given to my team or that's passed across my desk," Josh didn't seem even to be listening to Kim.

"A release for what? *Craven's Daughter* belongs to Cineline, and so does the podcast. Slander's only slander if it's not true. Can't say that I've heard anything, so far, that fits in that category. You don't have to like it, but what are you going to do when Cineline's attorneys pull out your incident reports from *Charles Salt*?"

"They're slandering Aaron, too. They can't say shit that damages the reputation of a project they've been a part of. And Carl needs to stay in his own fucking lane."

Kim laughed. "'Damages the reputation' meaning all the extra publicity? Listeners and viewers? Streaming numbers? Be quiet and be happy collecting the extra residuals. Unless you didn't negotiate residuals, and all this is sour grapes."

"Fuck you," Josh snarled.

"I mean, fuck you, too, Josh. My best guess is that the guys upstairs barely know what's going on. The only thing they're keeping an eye on are the fat checks the advertisers are writing and the numbers leading up to the reunion special in a few weeks. Which is to say, you're not *special*. Unless you're afraid they'll true-crime you into the number-one suspect spot."

"If someone did kill Jen Arnot, the only thing special about them was that they were first in line."

Jesus. Bex looked at Sam with wide eyes.

"All right," Kim said. "Good catching up. Here's to not talking again for another five years."

They heard her walking away, her voice as she hailed someone followed by fading laughter. After a long moment, Josh mumbled a curse and stalked off.

Sam low-whistled. "He's activated."

"Like he's straddling a nuke. But I haven't been around him in a while, so maybe he's only a few ticks over baseline. Still, it makes me anxious. It feels like a lot of responsibility to do things right, or we could get ourselves into heaps of trouble."

"Heaps?" Sam crossed her arms and smiled the worst, killingest smile at Bex. The light through the camellia made her skin look smooth and soft and perfect. It was hard sometimes—a lot of the time—to believe that Sam was a creature of this world. "Are we the Hardy Boys now?"

"You have to be nice to me," Bex said. "I ran out of my leave-in conditioner, and I can feel my curls leaving orbit. I'm going to have to avoid the entire Internet for days once the paps down the street put up their pictures."

Sam's grip on Bex's elbow tightened again, then fell away. "Come with me."

Bex followed Sam to a garden path along the side of the yard concealed by bougainvillea, then through a door into Chaz's garage, which wasn't really a garage. It had been converted into an apartment where Chaz often allowed friends in need to stay. Tonight, the caterers were using the ground floor to stage the appetizers and drinks, and purple-jumpsuit-clad staff bustled in and out of the room, exchanging empty trays for full. It was a job Frankie had done, as had most of the actors Bex knew.

Sam yanked two stools away from the wall. Bex sat next her as Sam pulled her phone from her sparkly clutch. "I couldn't sleep last night, so I read more of Jen's fic." Sam swiped the screen of her phone. "She has a series of, like, episode-related, head-canon, fix-it fic."

"Translate." Bex took the phone Sam handed her.

"Meaning, these are Henri and Cora stories that are either episodes told from their point of view, or they reveal what happens before, after, or in between episodes according to what fans generally believe to be true from their analysis of the show. They're stories that fix what fans feel isn't right. Take a look."

Sam dragged her stool close enough that her thigh pressed against Bex's bare knee. The floral romper Sam wore had cuffed shorts, the cuffs held in place with thin leather straps. It buttoned up the front, but Sam had left it unbuttoned to her sternum, with layers of gold chains draped against her skin. She smelled like a forbidden forest glade.

Bex had to twist a lock of hair around her finger pretty hard to pull her attention to the block of text Sam had highlighted pink.

I didn't know what it was about her. I collapsed into my grandpa's ratty recliner. I should've turned the light on. I should've grabbed the TV remote, but instead, I was sitting in the dark thinking about her.

Cora.

Every single relationship I had ever had was a disaster, and they had been with men and women who knew the score. Knew what I was like. Knew I couldn't be available in the traditional sense and was, let's face it, fucked up. When those trysts ended, no harm, no foul. But something like that wasn't possible with Cora, and worse, so so so much worse, I wouldn't WANT something like that with Cora.

Which was the problem, wasn't it?

For the first time, I wanted. For the first time, I could see the point. When Cora had asked me at the diner if I ever thought about "living the dream, the whole package, someone to love, a house, a dog, Saturdays planting flowers and Sundays reading books," the no was on the tip of my tongue. A reflex.

Which meant I couldn't answer her at all. Because I had never said "yes, I have thought about all of those things, but only with you" or anything like it, and that was the only thing I could say that was true, and the one thing I never could.

Cora deserved more than someone who would promise it all and then break every one of those promises.

It was clear now, after everything that had happened, and especially NOT happened, that what was being written was not a love story. The gods were making very sure of that.

Bex's eyes were burning when she finished. "But this is so sad. Poor Henri!"

Sam laughed. "Yes. Sure. But do you remember what episode Cora asked Henri those questions at the diner?"

One of the show's recurring bits was that Cora and Henri had a deal that if they couldn't agree on something, which happened not infrequently, one of them would say, "This is a conversation for the diner," and their argument would move to a grotty restaurant across the street from the agency where everyone had known Joe Craven and would give Cora and Henri folksy insight or insider information to help them solve their problem.

These diner conversations would often fade to black on a *moment* between Henri and Cora. The episode Sam was referring to had come late in the fourth season. It featured a quadruple murder that had somewhat jumped the shark and involved the guest appearance of Brother Mine, a boy band out of London that was everywhere at the time. The episode had been scored with the band's top love songs, and Henri and Cora interviewed multiple witnesses who talked a lot about romance and love. It all came to a head in that diner conversation in an angsty exchange that fans had analyzed at length, in part because of a pull-away shot where Henri's foot was visible sliding alongside Cora's under the table at the moment when Henri should have been answering Cora's question.

"It was 'Girl, I'll Never Say Goodbye-Bye-Bye,'" Bex said. "The buzz around that one was bananas."

"It was the episode that convinced fans and the media that the show *was* a love story. That Cora and Henri getting together was imminent. We met with execs and Aaron and Bette multiple times in that period."

"I remember."

"Jen wasn't, as far as I know, privy to any of those conversations, and we weren't supposed to talk about the direction of the show with any of the crew. Or, by that time, even speculate. Yet she writes here, infusing that scene with romance, that it's *not* a love story. That the *gods*"—Sam tapped the screen—"were making very sure of that."

"Well." Bex handed Sam back the phone. "I wouldn't be surprised if Jen knew more than she was strictly supposed to."

"I wouldn't either. But it would mean that Jen was talking to people who were in the know, and that they were talking to her." Sam's pale eyebrows drew down, her expressive mouth pursed in thought. "Fics she posted earlier, like the World War II one, have a lot of clues that the feuding was still active between her and Josh and Aaron. Last night, I realized that all of the fics posted from about the middle of season four on, ending with this one, don't have any of that stuff. They're almost entirely fix-it fics. The characters are limited to the original characters on the show, and there's little, if any, behind-the-scenes stuff. They're romances."

"You're thinking something healed between Jen, Aaron, and Josh?"

"Maybe, or maybe it had started exhausting her instead of helping her to write about it." Sam's palm lay on her chest, gold glistening and catching the garage light beneath her fingertips. She'd worn her hair loose, spreading over her shoulders. No stylist ever made Sam look this beautiful. Only Sam could.

"But what about how the end of this fic says the show is *not* written as a love story? Was Jen talking to Bette? Did she have inside knowledge about the ultimate direction of the show, and so focused on fix-its? But why, then, would Bette insist on our podcast that she hardly knew or talked to Jen? Why would she have said that she wrote the show as a romance but *you* messed it up by leaving?"

Bex could feel that she'd leaned in, pressing more of her thigh against Sam's to help anchor her so she wouldn't drift away, overwhelmed by the intimacy of this moment. It was so like what they used to share when they would have long, winding conversations or talk offsides about work.

Sam had said she *used to* have feelings for Bex. She'd never said anything about having feelings now except that she did not want to risk it. Bex needed to keep hold of that, because remembering all of this, examining it, meant the past and the right now were very much mixed together for her.

"We've already figured out that Jen was crafty in her fanfic," Sam said. "I think the only way for us to really understand if someone on set was involved in her death is for us to know the status of her relationships with people who had power."

Bex thought of the bulleted list she'd made in her notebook by the pool. Jen had acted like one of the people at the top who didn't need permission, even though, as a makeup artist, she shouldn't have had that much power and authority.

Aaron was a man who'd hoarded power around himself. Bex had a strong personality, but she'd found it hard to flex her muscles in that environment, even as a lead. If Sam was right, knowing more about Jen's relationships might help explain how she'd claimed some of Aaron's power for herself.

"It's a good thing we're here, then," Bex said. "What no one will tell us, Chaz will know, or at least will have heard more gossip about it than we have."

"And Aaron and Bette looking so cozy is worth poking at. Especially after what she said about him on the podcast. I imagine there are a lot more feelings swimming around this party like Josh's. Angry. Litigious."

"But Kim said it's only slander if it isn't true. I haven't had so much as an email from Cineline, so I have to assume she's right about that. True-crime podcasts speculate on whatever knowledge is at hand all the time, even if that means they're speculating about some real, non-incarcerated person being a suspect."

"You listen to a lot of true-crime podcasts?"

"You've driven in L.A. traffic. I can't be on my phone the entire time."

Sam smiled. "So do you think we should use this party to find out where Jen stood with the big players? Based on Josh's reaction, it could get dicey."

"Yeah, but when are we going to have all these people in the same place again? Not until the tenth anniversary, I'll bet. We have to strike while the iron's hot."

"Divide and conquer," Sam said decisively. "We should send Luciana in. She's offered herself up to the cause, and she has her own buffer of power."

Thrilled with the idea, Bex tapped Sam's knee without intending to do any such thing. "Do we trust her, Agent Shannon?"

Something dark passed over Sam's face. Not bad. Intrigued. Bex had to remind herself again that no one could read her thoughts or see inside her secret heart.

Even if Sam had always seemed to be able to do both.

"Um, hi."

Bex looked up to see a young woman whose deep brown skin came alive against the bright purple jumpsuit the caterers wore. She didn't look as nervous as her greeting had sounded. Her posture was open and relaxed.

"Hey." Bex offered her a polite smile. "Should we move on? Sorry we commandeered this corner."

The woman shook her head, and then Sam's face lit up. "Wait, I know you!" she said. "You played the fan in the boy band episode, right? The little girl who snuck into the hotel where Brother Mine was staying to get an autograph, then broke the case because you'd seen the killer. Wasn't that your first speaking role?"

When the woman grinned, Bex saw the resemblance that Sam had already picked up on. "Yes! I'm Dajahne Hammon. And, incidentally, that was also my last speaking part. But no worries, it was the gig that got me really interested in writing. I actually got my MFA in screenwriting from UCLA last year and just won a screenwriting contest. But that's not why I came over. Unless one of you is interested in producing a tender sci-fi about sisters who reunite after a war in the XE-62 galaxy."

"I mean, maybe," Sam said. "Give me your card and I'll pass it around, but first tell me why you came over."

Dajahne reached into her pocket and handed Sam a card. "Because, I'm sorry, I was eavesdropping"—she glanced at Bex, who ignored this reminder that she was constitutionally incapable of whispering, or even speaking at a volume below what could be heard from the mezzanine—"and I'd already been nerving myself up to talk to you if I had a chance. I've been listening to your podcast."

"I'm getting that a lot lately," Sam said.

"I'll bet. I wanted to tell you the reason I got interested in writing was because of Bette. She was great, actually. She let me see every draft of the script of that episode and explained how she decided what revisions to make."

Bex nodded to encourage Dajahne to get to her point. "Okay."

"Yeah, so, I wish I could say a kiss had been edited out or something, but that's not it. You know who was always with Bette when I was hanging out with her during that whole shoot? Jen Arnot. They were close. Close enough that Bette gave Jen plenty of access to her laptop, and I learned a lot from *Jen* about how to write a good story."

Bex's brain temporarily went to static, then zapped back online. "You're saying Jen, the makeup artist, was writing with Bette? And they were friends?"

"Yes. I wouldn't say friends, maybe more like collaborators. Especially looking at it in retrospect, when I've done my share of writing with other people, that was the dynamic. And that means, you know, you two are on the right track to talk to Bette again, because my jaw was on the floor when your latest episode dropped. I don't think I entirely realized until your podcast that Jen didn't have *any* writing credits. I went back and checked to make sure. I was going to make a comment on the forum or link you to my TikTok, but I haven't had time, and I thought I'd maybe get a chance to see you here. Chaz always puts me on her list for the caterer to hire since I went back to school at UCLA. She was super-nice to me on the set."

"Look," Sam said to Dajahne, after giving Bex a wide-eyed, wordless *Oh my God*. "Bex and I were friends with Jen. We both knew her family, and we have never heard this."

"You wouldn't, though, right? The two of you were, like, up front." She made a gesture with both hands, cupping a space in front of her. "In the lights. There was a whole backstage world you weren't part of. That was what convinced me I didn't want to be an actor. All the action was behind the scenes."

Frankie often said the same thing. "We are the wrong people to be investigating this mystery, aren't we?" Bex asked.

"You did play detectives on TV." Dajahne smiled. "And like I wouldn't take medical advice from Meredith Grey? Absolutely, I would."

"Thanks," Sam said. "I'm going to give your card to my agent to give you a call and talk. I hope everything works out for you. And we can call you if we have questions?"

"You better. You're in my network now. Anyone I talk to is going to hear about my close, personal connection with Bexley Simon and Sam Farmer."

"Give me your phone." Bex held out her palm, and Dajahne pulled a phone out of her pocket, unlocked it, and handed it over, taking it back only after Bex texted herself with it. "We owe you one."

Dajahne grabbed a tray she had put down nearby before she'd talked to them. "I'd be careful with Bette," she said. "I liked her, and she did me a big favor with her mentorship, but the podcast reminded me that there was something scary about her."

They watched Dajahne pass out of the garage, her full tray of champagne glasses held aloft. When Sam stood up, her expression told Bex they were about to go swimming in the deep end. It was a very Sam response to what Dajahne had told them. Sam wanted to know more, and she wanted to know it immediately.

Good. So did Bex.

"I'm assuming Frankie's here somewhere, networking?" Sam asked.

"Vic is, too, actually. She got ahead in her classes to fly home yesterday because she wanted to see everybody and 'gather evidence.' I'm seriously starting to worry about what her GPA's going to look like at the end of the term." Bex slid carefully off the tall stool while holding on to the hem of the short, off-the-shoulder T-shirt dress she wore because she hated cocktail wear and knew that if her platform sneakers were tall, sparkly, and exclusive enough, she could get away with cotton jersey everywhere else.

"How do we do this?" Sam asked as they paused by the garage door. "Do you have a plan?" She sounded unbothered, almost a little *too* unbothered.

Bex wondered if there was more on her mind than getting to the bottom of the show's dynamics. "Let's put Vic on Bette," she said. "Vic's disarming and immune to the ironic distance of a millennial goth. And, fuck it, I'm going to talk to Aaron. I'll see if I can figure out how much of all this he knew about. I'm going to tell him Bette's sending me the script in case he didn't hear the podcast."

There was obvious approval in Sam's smile. "Good luck with that. Frankie should be the one to talk to Chaz. I'll tell her not to stop until she's sure she's dredged up every last iota of gossip about Jen's personal life and her relationships with the rest of the crew."

"Yeah. Good. Frankie could squeeze blood from a stone. I want you to see if you can get Luciana and Josh in the same conversation. If the rumors about that series finale are right, we'll need both of them. Especially Luciana's star power."

Sam held the door open with her hip for Bex to slide through. "Why?"

"Because of the reunion. Honestly, Sam, who wants to watch an hour of all of us sitting on the set talking about things everybody already knows when they could properly say goodbye to Cora and Henri once and for all? I think we should ditch that plan and film Bette's episode instead. It's the finale!"

Then, without breaking eye contact, Bex moved through the doorway, making sure she was closer than she needed to be to Sam's body when she passed beneath her outstretched arm and the warm cotton jersey of her dress made contact with Sam's cool floral silk in a way that could have been an accident but definitely was not.

"Tell you what, Bexley Simon." Sam laughed. "You are full of surprises."

Maybe Sam *was* surprised. The last time Sam really knew her, Bex didn't do anything off-script. Sam was welcome to get to know what Bex was like when she improvised.

And, of course, the first rule of improvisation was to always say yes.

Kicking the Hornet's Nest

"I turned it down, of course. When that new woman executive from Cineline called, what's her name—Margaret? Marta? Trying to tell me how exciting it would be to sit on a stage with a bunch of people I bought a place in the Bahamas to get away from." Aaron Gorman shoved his hands in the pockets of his cargo shorts. "Couldn't have paid me enough to get involved."

Bex tried to think if she'd ever beheld Aaron out of cargo shorts and an oversized, unbuttoned polo shirt washed free of any color or shape. Had he worn a tux at the award shows? His flip-flops looked ancient enough that Bex wondered if she had seen this exact pair before. His auburn curls were thinner and grayer, the creases in his freckled skin deeper, but his appearance was otherwise unchanged. Even Aaron's mannerisms were the same— quick looks to the right and left as he spoke, fiddling with the scratched and worn Rolex watch on his wrist, pulling at his bottom lip. So much so that Bex had to sternly remind herself that he had no authority over her. Not anymore.

"You turned down the reunion show, but you came to Chaz's party?" Bex glanced over at Sam and Luciana. They were both dealing with Josh, who was talking too close, gesturing angrily. Bex would be concerned, but that was Josh. She had more feelings about the way Luciana had snaked her arm around Sam's waist.

"I was in town." Aaron shrugged. "Chaz doesn't skimp on the champagne."

"Don't miss us a bit, huh?" Bex had to wonder why Aaron *was* in town. Could the podcast have rattled him? Did he have ducks he needed to get in a row?

"Do I miss herding cats under the thumb of asshats like Niels Shaughnessy when I can collect a producer's coin on a white sand beach?" Aaron's eyes flicked toward the studio head where he stood laughing with Aaron's ex-wife. "Fuck, no."

"Must be nice to catch up with Bette." Bex took a sip of champagne. "Have you been listening to the podcast? Chaz thinks that's why so many people showed up today for her get-together."

"Not really my medium. I'm sure fans will latch on to anything new, though."

"So I guess you didn't hear that we're going to film the finale." Bex hadn't heard this either. She had only said it once, aloud to Sam, but she had done so at ordinary Bexley Simon volume in the vicinity of a garage full of emerging actors, so she didn't doubt the world would know soon enough.

"Yeah, I heard," Aaron predictably said. "Wondered how you got that by Shaughnessy."

"Why would Niels object? Because of the direction Bette's script takes?"

Aaron sighed. "I know you think we're the bad guys, but the business is a lot more complicated than that." He pushed his fists into the bottom of his pockets and rocked back on his heels. "*Craven* was a vehicle for thirty million eyeballs to get their fill of their favorite stars as a corpse, with enough procedural to entice the men to watch. In other words, money. So my idle curiosity about Shaughnessy greenlighting the finale is directly related to my knowing *Shaughnessy*, not anything Bette might or might not have written. I know what Shaughnessy cares about. Breakfast cereal. SUVs. Branded credit cards. Prescription drugs. It's about what keeps enough people in the seats to watch the *real* show, commercials." Aaron took a hand out of his pocket and pulled on his lower lip, right on schedule. "I'm surprised you haven't figured it out yet. I guess you're still on your TV-sweetheart-to-movie-star pony ride. Someday soon when your agent can't get you cast as anything better than the next young thing's mom, maybe you'll see my point."

It was exactly the sort of cynical speech Aaron used to make when he wanted to cut her down to size. Bex was pleased to discover it made her feel nothing stronger than mild boredom. "Maybe what I see is that the world is a lot bigger than your point," she said. "The world is actually pretty interested at the moment in finding out if a crusty old institution like Cineline will right one of its wrongs for everyone to see. That's what the papers will write about—*Craven's Daughter* getting the queer romance ending it always should have had but the studio execs were too cowardly to deliver. No one cares whether the *men* tune in. But it could be you've been out of the game and in the sun too long, with a few too many whiskey sodas under your belt to understand how things work now."

Aaron scoffed, but his eyes darted to the side, and his neck went red. "Maybe I did see the way the wind was blowing, and that's why I got out. Didn't want to end up canceled, did I?"

Bex felt her body slow down, just as it did when she got surprised in a live performance when someone flubbed a line or a prop broke. On the surface, Aaron's comment sounded like a standard Boomer-esque complaint about the world leaving him behind, but her actor's senses told her there was more to it. "I don't know why you'd worry about that. No one we've talked to about you on the podcast suggested it was a possibility."

"You mean Carl or Luce? Bette?"

"You *have* been listening."

"I know people who do, and they keep bothering me with their worries about it. But why should I care? I've done and seen it all in the business. Fucked up and printed money, both. I've always been damn good at what I do. Let anyone say what they want."

"Including that there was serious trouble between you and a woman who died on location for your show?"

Aaron recrossed his arms. Bex couldn't get over the fact that he still hadn't walked away. Something about this interested him. Or worried him. Again, it could be just his ego keeping him in the conversation, but even someone stroking Aaron's ego could never hold his attention for this long. Bex had finished a whole glass of champagne.

Had she ever given enough thought to why *Aaron* left *Craven's Daughter*? When Sam decided not to come back, her decision necessarily affected the legendary chemistry between Cora and Henri, but actors, even leads, left network serials all the time. If Aaron really had believed the show's success didn't depend on Cora and Henri, why hadn't he recast Sam's part?

Why had a director who could've dragged his career out another fifteen years retired to the Bahamas instead? Did Aaron need to know what she knew? Was that why he was "in town"—to make sure some five-year-old cover-up stayed covered?

"On-set deaths are rare," Bex said, watching closely for a reaction.

Aaron's expression didn't move from its usual crumpled, grumpy collection of frown lines. "Here we go."

"I'm serious." Bex matched his frown. "Jen died. Even before that, though, how many of those incident reports did we all have to sign during the run of *Craven's Daughter*?"

Aaron winced. Whenever there was an on-set accident or injury, every cast or crew member who was even peripherally involved had to sign off on an incident report for the studio's official record. Incident reports meant potential lawsuits or fines, so every one was a ding on the showrunner's reputation with the network. "A few," he admitted.

Bex had been involved in or witnessed more than "a few"

herself. The glass that cut her knee was one. A partial stair set that wasn't anchored had skidded away from the brick wall when she was being lit for a different episode, and she turned her ankle. There had been a water scene they shot in a pool on the lot—in it, Cora fell into the Chicago River—and when Bex wrapped her arm around a false piling, it broke, sending her backward with a splash. She'd had to be evaluated for a concussion. There was also the incident with the broken prop bed, which was going to come up again in the next podcast, since the episode was one of the fan favorites.

"You don't remember a number?" she pressed.

He sighed. "Eight."

Bex had only been following a hunch, but eight incident reports and an on-set death in six seasons was a seriously bad safety record. Borderline negligent. The network heads must have been more than worried about a lawsuit after Jen died.

"That's eight more incidents than I've ever had to sign off on any other set," she said. "And even if you're not listening to the episodes, I bet someone's told you that Carl Moreland came on the podcast to reveal that *Charles Salt* had its own thick folder of reports, at least one of which was bad enough to bring the network lawyers down on your head after Josh and Jen had a blowout argument. Your production was temporarily *shut down*."

Aaron looked at her with a kind of animalistic malice that Bex could admit raised her hackles in an icy trail down her neck. She'd never gotten more than a resigned reaction out of Aaron about anything, and even when he barked and shouted on the set, it was easy to shrug off. This was different. Personal.

"A shutdown bleeds money," she pushed. "You felt the pressure of that. If a TV show is a commercial for the commercials, then that incident on *Charles Salt* was you, personally, costing the network money. I have a source—"

"A source." Aaron rolled his eyes so hard his neck bent back, and he looked at the sky. His sigh was a gust. Bex could feel it stir the curls on her head.

"Yes. A source. One who made it clear Josh had a problem keeping his feelings in check when it came to Marilee Plungkhen. Jen wouldn't have liked that, same as she didn't like you bad-mouthing her over the Oscar she won for *Bloodright* just because you didn't get one for directing."

"Jesus Christ, Bex. You know you just played a detective on television, right?"

"And yet I'm standing here coming up with such good questions to ask you." Bex cocked her hip and raised her eyebrows.

"Best of luck with that." Aaron gave her a brisk wave and turned to leave. "Like I said, I walked far, far away from this shit for a reason."

Watching him saunter into the crowd of partygoers, Bex let out a jittery sigh. She'd known Aaron wasn't going to be warm and forthcoming. She hadn't known how far she'd take it until she hit his limit.

This was what it felt like to do exactly what she wanted, apparently. She hoped her heart would recover.

"Hey, gorgeous." Vic appeared at her side. Her cheekbones were bright red, and she'd pulled her long hair into a scrunchie bun perched precariously on top of her head. Her cocktail party attire was a pair of red sequined overalls she'd found at an estate sale years ago, which she'd paired inexplicably with a swimsuit. "Bette's cracked. I love her."

"That tells me nothing. Negative nothing."

"She's one hundred percent capable of killing someone. That's number one. Also, she absolutely figured out instantly that you had sicced me on her. I just rolled with that. Then we talked about organic chemistry. Her partner's a doctor—"

"Bette has a partner?"

"—and she used to make them O-Chem flashcards. She's thinking about a cat, so I told her about Hannah Hearts Rescue and what they really care about on their draconian adoption application. Then I asked her if she had a vendetta against Jen and killed her over Jen's wanting writing credits on the show, because we'd just heard from an inside source that Jen secretly wrote the scripts for the seasons when Bette was winning solo Emmys. Then, swear to God, her eyes turned red like a demon's, but she told me to fuck off, and here I am. It was a ride. Like, a whole story. Very Tolstoy."

"Oh my God."

"I'm only home for a couple days. I had to be efficient. Also, Sam and Luciana are in the back bedroom—"

"*What?*"

"—with Chaz and Frankie, and I'm supposed to come get you." Vic put her hand over her mouth. "Did you think Sam and Luciana were *making love* in the back bedroom?"

Bex's entire physiology caught on fire. "Jesus! No! Victoria Clara Cunningham Simon, just . . . shut up, okay? Shut up. Gah." *Making love.* Why was Vic like this? It was not Bex's fault. Vic had always been like this. Although Bex had failed at parenting the Vic-ness out of her.

"Hmm." Vic looped her arm through Bex's, but Bex's stomach sank as she caught a fleeting moment of hurt flicker over Vic's face. "You can see how I'm so good at investigation. I know how to get information out of people. You have just told me so much."

"Can you elaborate about what exactly Bette said?" They started toward the house.

"What I just told you. She freaked out when I suggested Jen had been collaborating with her on scripts, and she's angry or petrified about something. Whether it's something she knows, or something she did, or she's afraid of it coming out about Jen, I don't know. She flounced." They pushed into the crowded kitchen. "Frankie's got a hot tip off Chaz, though. She wouldn't say what it is until I brought you."

They walked down the birch-paneled hallway to Chaz's guest room, where their hostess had posted another young hopeful in a purple jumpsuit to take bags and personal items to store and watch over. The young man nodded at them. "They're waiting for you inside," he said.

"So much drama," Vic whispered. "I'm living for it."

Sam and Luciana sat on low built-in benches by the windows with their heads together, talking, and Chaz and Frankie had moved a row of purses out of the way to sit on the end of the bed.

"Hey." Frankie stood, smoothing down her black linen strapless sundress. It had been their mother's and was the only dress she owned. "So get this—and not even Luciana knew it, so it's big. I made Chaz come in here after she told me so she can make sure I have the details right."

"What is it?"

"Aaron Gorman and Marilee Plungkhen were seeing each other," Frankie said. "Like, when Josh was screaming at Marilee that day my source told me about, she was already with Aaron. And Aaron was still with Bette's mom."

"Illicit affairs," Vic said. "Clandestine adulterous chicanery. Love it."

"Also, Jen and Marilee were really close, and Jen told Marilee she should leave Josh, although Chaz doesn't think Jen meant for her to head in Aaron's direction. And all of that happened around the time everything was going wrong on the *Charles Salt* set, when Jen reported Josh, but also, because of some part of Aaron's contract, Aaron had to pay a fine, and his management dropped him." Frankie took a breath and looked at Chaz. "That's the scoop, right?"

It was a pretty big scoop, in Bex's opinion. It sounded like the relationships between Josh, Jen, and Aaron had given both men reasons to be angry with each other *and* with Jen. Her response to Josh's choices had caused both Josh and Aaron to pay professional penalties.

Angry enough to hurt Jen? Bex couldn't be sure.

"Wait." Sam smacked the lavender carpet with the flat of her palm. "Chaz, did you know this when you came onto *Craven's Daughter?*"

"Ooh." Vic dropped to the floor and folded effortlessly into Lotus pose. "Chaz is a suspect."

"Wouldn't that be exciting? No, Jen started confiding in me around the end of season four. I had to confess to her that I'd had some touch-up work done during the hiatus, and there were a couple of incisions that weren't healing properly that she would have to work around. It was a great deal for me to reveal. I'm over that kind of thing now, but then I was still trying to book in the middle-age range. Jen was exceedingly lovely about it, and the longer sessions in her chair and the secret between us meant we started talking. She missed her mother back in the Midwest and didn't like to worry her with the dramas inevitable to working in Hollywood. I was someone who felt maternal but could take the ugly side of things."

Bex sank to the floor next to Vic, trying to integrate this new information with what she'd learned. "Aaron couldn't get out of Hollywood fast enough after *Craven* ended, and he was rattled by my talking about Josh's involvement with Marilee and the aftermath. More to the point, he's *here.* If he really doesn't care anymore like he claims, then why let me talk about this stuff? Why react to it? I implied these soured relationships and Jen's report had something to do with her dying, and he made a less-than-graceful exit from the conversation."

"About halfway through the last season," Sam said, "my manager let me know I was having a meeting with Aaron and Niels." She sat on the bench with her arms crossed, her long legs stretched out in front of her. She'd kicked off her shoes, and her feet were bare. Casual, cool, California Sam. But the razor-sharp edge to her tone had the attention of everyone in the room. "No word what it was going to be about. No one else invited. Just me, Aaron, and the head of the network. Niels sat there stone-faced while

Aaron told me if I didn't stop talking about Jen's passing, he would ensure I was written off the show."

Bex felt sick. She hadn't known this. To her, it had been a comfort that Sam was willing to talk about Jen's accident. To find out that Sam had been threatened, and to remember that Bex had never checked in with her after she *did* stop talking about the accident, even when she grew increasingly distant, made Bex feel horrible.

She hadn't been a very good friend when Sam needed one.

Vic stuck her finger in the air. "Bette hated it when I told her it was getting around that she wrote with Jen. *Hated* it, hated it. But she didn't deny it. Would that secret have as much poison in it as this cursed and unholy triangle between Jen, Aaron, and Josh?"

"Speaking of Josh"—Luciana leaned back on her arms, her diamonds catching in the light and scattering little rainbows over the room—"I don't know that he isn't going to kill someone by the end of this party. He's unhinged."

"I walked past him, and my eyes about crossed," Vic said. "He smells like he's been drinking all that spray tan." She made her eyes cross. "Fake coconut and narcissism."

Sam barked out a surprised laugh. "Vicious. But true."

"Is he working?" Bex asked. "Before the reunion, I hadn't heard his name in a while."

Frankie shook her head. "No current projects. Nothing in the can."

"That's what he was raging to Sam and me about for one thousand years," Luciana said. "No one has any vision anymore, no one dedicates themselves to their craft, no one has any resilience, no one knows the difference between AI and art. He's been spending most of his time trying to trademark elements of his old sets so he can go after productions that have anything that, at a squint, looks like something he's done."

"Did you mention Jen or Aaron?" Bex asked.

Sam tossed her hair. "Didn't have to. Josh has been listening to the podcast. He said the word *slander* so many times, I was worried he was going to break one of his front teeth. I'm certain we'll have a cease-and-desist letter from his lawyer by morning. However, what makes him the angriest, it seems, is that he and Jen were 'good.'" Sam made air quotes and imitated Josh's nerved-up baritone. "Jen was just trying to protect Marilee, which he can understand if someone was 'looking on the outside,' and he 'fucking loved Marilee,' so he can't have any issue with Jen for that. Jen's report about sabotage was a lie, he says, and he had the receipts to prove it, but it's water under the bridge. He won't speak ill of the dead. They were tight in the end. He was 'broken' when she died. And so on."

Frankie made a noise in her throat that drew Bex's attention back to her. She was standing with her feet set wide apart and the scowl line between her eyebrows sunk deep.

"What is it?" Bex asked.

"It's nothing."

"It doesn't look like nothing." She scanned the faces in the room. "This is a safe space. I'd like to hear what you want to say."

"I don't know if you guys will even get it. You're old Hollywood." Frankie swept her arm over Sam, Luciana, Chaz, and Bex.

"Hey!" Sam said, as Luciana made a *hmph* noise and Bex suppressed her response because she'd just promised to be safe.

Chaz only smiled and nodded, which meant Frankie focused on her when she spoke again.

"Well, it's true. And it applies here. Because, like"—Frankie ran her hands through her curls—"you're talking about very scary events that took place, first of all, *at this party*. I know there's a culture that creatives are expected to clash, and that sets are stressful, and powerful people are 'difficult' or 'passionate' and so we excuse, on set, what is actually abusive behavior. In actual fact. And not enough people have woken up to the fact that this is not acceptable."

Now even Luciana looked chagrined.

"In the last hour," Frankie went on, "almost all of us have been yelled at or menaced in some way by powerful people. At a *party*. Because a culture like Hollywood has a way of spilling over into private life. The history of this place is actually infested with stories of intimate partner violence and murder, domestic control issues, financial abuse. The Me Too movement brings in a generational trauma. Decades of this stuff, all coming back to the dynamics on set, where some people have the power to treat others however they want, and everybody else has to keep their fucking mouths shut. I don't know how anybody stands it long enough to make a career. I'm one shitty incident away from quitting my job the next time some super-important person is unable to regulate their emotions like an adult."

Frankie grabbed a vanity stool in the corner and sank down onto it, looking blotchy and defeated. "*Craven's Daughter* was a textbook example of what I'm talking about, so we have to take the ongoing abusive behaviors of everyone we've talked to seriously. We *have* to. They want to yell and threaten and cut down and shoot demon eyes at others? Okay. Then let their actions talk for them, but don't count them out from having engaged in criminal behavior just because this stuff is supposedly normal."

God. Frankie was right.

She usually was, when she went off like this. Frankie could be counted on to see injustice clearly and speak up about it. Usually with zero diplomacy, but Bex had learned from helping her grow up that diplomacy wasn't nearly as important as telling the truth.

"Hey, Franks?" Vic said from the floor. "I'm sorry. I'll dial way back on my relishment of the drama."

Frankie nudged Vic's knee with her foot. "It's okay. I know you're just excited to be included." Vic sniffed and nodded. Frankie looked around the room in admonishment.

Bex wasn't sure what alarm currently going off inside her she should respond to. There were multiple. How she should be thinking about Hollywood or her career. How she'd just been treated by Aaron, or how her baby sister had been treated by Bette. How unhappy Frankie had seemed lately, and did it have to do with her work? Was Vic sad? Should Bex have a family meeting, even though her sisters hated them? Why did she keep noticing how beautiful Sam was? Where was her *notebook*?

"Thank you, honey," Chaz said. "What you're reminding us of is important. I hope looking into the past teaches us something about moving forward."

Frankie nodded. "Yeah. Okay. I'm good."

Sam adjusted her posture in a way that changed the feeling in the room, acknowledging that they'd all heard Frankie and were doubly interested in getting back to business. "I want to share what I keep thinking about, which is how I was so close to Jen, or so I thought—and Chaz, it sounds like you were, too. It turns out Bette was. Even Josh claims they were 'good.' Who *wasn't* Jen's bestie? But after she died, no one wanted to say her name. She didn't get so much as an episode dedication in the credits. What was that about?"

Bex fiddled with the glittery shoelaces of her sneakers. "Maybe the problem was Jen. Not in a victim-blaming way, but she *was* a lot. Maybe she was someone who, when she was around, turned up the temperature of other people's issues as they tried to project them on her. Not really what I want her family to come away with."

"No." Vic was picking at the carpet. "I get why you'd say that, but me and Frankie basically lived in makeup. Bex, your call was so early, and half the time the show was shooting we didn't have school. We sat under the counters, or we'd be curled up in the hallway outside the door. You'd be running your lines and want us not to bother you. Jen was . . ." She looked helplessly at her sister. "I can't think of the word."

"Like the key light turned all the way up," Frankie said.

"That," Vic agreed, nodding vigorously. "That's why we hung around her. If she was a focal point of people's problems, it's because everybody liked telling her their problems, and *Craven* had a lot of problems. It wasn't because Jen was a problem."

Bex felt her body relax against the wall at how good that was to hear.

"Such a lovely way to put it, Victoria. For what it's worth, I agree with your assessment." Chaz rose slowly to her feet. "My darlings, I have a soiree to host, so I will leave you to it. Bex and Sam, you are not permitted to do an Irish goodbye at my party. Once you're finished here, make an entrance and mingle. I have a reputation." She swanned out of the room.

"Frankie, hand me my bag, please," Bex said. Frankie found the battered shoulder bag in the sea of leather goods and tossed it to her. Bex fished around inside it until she located her notebook. It was getting full. She flipped through to a blank page, then turned her pen to open. Everyone sat quietly while she jotted down some quick notes.

When she looked at everything that had come out since Sam joined her on Stage 46 less than a month ago, her head spun.

Luciana stretched and stood up, too. "This finale. If it happens—and I plan on going out there and massaging Niels until he thinks it's his brilliant idea to shoot the finale three weeks from now instead of the boring talking-heads reunion interview we were going to do—then I'm in. You do know I was meant to be cast in it? That part of the rumor is true. My agent had told me, speculating that I would play an evil twin of myself or something. In any event, an homage to how the series got its start. If Bette doesn't send it over promptly after her tête-à-tête with Victoria, then leave it to me to get my hands on it." She leaned over and kissed Sam on the cheek, making Bex's heart pinch for a moment. "Let's lunch soon." Her gaze found Frankie. "I appreciate the call-in. If you decide to quit your job, consider giving me a ring."

Frankie nodded.

"I'll go with you, Luciana." Vic stood and adjusted her outfit. "You can get the photographers to catch you whispering in my ear while I make wide eyes. It's good for my love life to have myself documented enigmatically. Come on, Frankie."

The trio left, and Bex lay back on the soft carpet to stare at the beam in the ceiling. Sam moved off the bench and lay down next to her.

"So," Bex said. "This is all under control."

"Like a tornado," Sam agreed. "Hurricane." She turned onto her side, propped on her elbow. "How are you doing with that?"

Bex didn't want to talk about it anymore. Her brain was playing a loop of Aaron's mannerisms and bluster transposed over Bette's bitterness about recording the podcast, memories of Jen, Josh spitting mad. What Frankie had said. She needed a break from kicking this particular hornet's nest.

She put her arm over her head to gaze at Sam, letting her thoughts drift as she scanned from the mole on her jaw to the spot where she hadn't quite managed to get the cowlick at her hairline to behave. It occurred to Bex there was something their estrangement had kept her from saying that she could tell Sam now. "You've come to every one of my shows in New York. It meant so much to me."

She didn't think Sam had any way to know, but news of celebrities attending Broadway shows tended to make its way to the cast and crew via the ushers, most of them aspiring Broadway actors. The first time it happened, Bex had been glad she hadn't found out Sam was in attendance until afterward—but the anxious flutter that Sam might be out there in the audience had accompanied every performance that followed.

Sam closed her eyes for a moment, her cheekbones flushed pink beneath the smattering of peachy freckles she'd collected skateboarding with her brothers. "I have."

"I'm glad. It made me nervous, but frankly that's good for me."

Sam looked down at the carpet. "I have a confession. I was excited to learn that after *Craven's Daughter* you were taking a principal role on Broadway."

"Oh, yeah? The last five years in movies and on Broadway have been a literal best-of-times worst-of-times, but it's been good for my career."

"Sure, but I wasn't excited because of your career. I mean that I was excited, selfishly. Here's the thing. When they told me who my costar would be, I wasn't surprised, because the chemistry read we did together was killer. I didn't know a ton about you—"

"What was there to know? I had no credits."

"—but I'd seen you on the cover of *American Theater*. The group shot of Broadway up-and-comers."

Bex smiled, remembering. "That was a best-of-times best-of-times."

"You were lying across the laps of two other actors wearing an unlaced corset under a blazer and almost nothing else, and you had your Tony sticking up between your spread thighs."

Bex's heart kicked up a very fast rhythm in response to the way Sam was looking at her. "It wasn't my Tony," she said. "It was a plastic Tony."

Sam shook her head. "*So* not my point. I'd already seen that picture and been killed by you, specifically. By the time we had the chemistry read, I knew you'd won your Tony and had two pilots under your belt, so I found a recording of the show that got you the award. I was on a run, listening to the whole album. You didn't have a solo until—"

"The sixth number."

"Yeah. I actually stopped in my tracks. I didn't know anyone could sound that way, and I would never have guessed it, meeting you and reading with you. I mean, you're loud, Bex. You were good in the scenes we did together and right for the part. But when you sing, it turns the world in a different direction. It's like this superpower you carry around with you that, once someone has seen it, they can never stop looking at you like you're a miracle." Sam reached out and pulled a curl. "And your hair. There was no hope for me. Worse when it turned out you were a good person."

"I'm sorry," Bex whispered. She didn't think her chest could get any tighter without something breaking.

"Don't be. Nothing felt better than being in love with Bexley Simon. It was like having the best, most delicious secret ever."

"I had the same secret about you," Bex said. "I kept it so well it was nearly hidden from myself." She kept her tone as light as Sam's, like friends talking about their old crush and feelings in the past, but all of the new feelings were making themselves known to Bex, too—painfully, fantastically—spilling over everything inside her with crushing, pining, spikes of jealousy, horniness, flashes of hope, romantic daydreams.

"Tell you what, Bex—" Sam started to say, smiling a little to acknowledge the deliberate echo of Henri Shannon.

But then she stopped herself.

There was a time when Sam had stopped herself from saying something to Bex a lot. She would make a joke or change the subject or shake her head and walk away. Bex remembered feeling relief when that would happen—the relief of getting a little bit more time to grind her way to the part of her life where she could live for her own dreams again. She had always thought that once Sam told her what she wanted—once Sam asked Bex what *she* wanted—that she would be ready. But she hadn't been.

She'd learned the hard way that "ready" wasn't a feeling. People felt love or felt afraid or felt wild ambition, but there wasn't a way to feel ready for what life offered in its own time, any more than there was a way to turn the clock back and live the life she'd had to leave behind.

There was only this. The right-now.

"I'll tell *you* what," Bex said. "This time, I'm not going anywhere. We have plenty of chances to figure everything out."

It was only part of the truth. Bex would race through all of the conversations and discussions that needed to happen and rush to the ending if it meant that, right now, this minute, she could put her arms around Sam Farmer and kiss her. She wanted to let Sam feel everything she'd kept muffled and suppressed for years, and everything since they reunited that was crystalline, hot, and loud.

She would cut in line if she could. She would skip this part.

But Sam had said that what she wanted was to be Bex's friend. Only that. Bex had to honor it, even if she fervently hoped the day would come when Sam told her something different.

"I'm all in on figuring everything out," Sam said. "Including what you want. I know you've been making a lot of hard choices lately."

Bex heard the shift in Sam's tone that meant there was something she wasn't telling her. "You do? Hard choices like what?"

Sam wiped her hand over her mouth. "Like what we talked about when the studio set up that campy meeting for us on the old set—though I'm glad they did now—and you had to think about the fans and approaching me again. I imagine all of this has unearthed a lot of other feelings and choices. We talked about how I want to be there for you like I used to be when we talked through everything and tried to figure out what we wanted."

Bex narrowed her eyes. As a rule, Sam was not inarticulate. Not unless she was lying. Sam was a terrible liar. "I still feel like I'm missing something."

"You likely are." Sam sighed and looked at the opposite wall. "Some things are so easy about being with you again, and other things I'm struggling with."

"Okay." Bex felt that. "I can leave it there. But I'd like it if you could promise to talk to me about what you're struggling with sooner rather than later."

Nodding, Sam reached out and touched Bex's shoulder. With Sam's skin on hers, Bex knew with an unshakable certainty that there was something new here between them. Not just the discomfort of what to say and not to say or what to talk about, but something that injected Bex's brightest, sharpest, most hopeful hopes for what they could be together with a determination to make it happen.

"I'm going to change the subject now." Sam grinned. "What's our next episode?"

"'No Room at the Inn.' We're scheduled to do it with Kim Ryerson so she can talk about the famous prop hotel bed malfunction. Amethyst's begged us to give her at least twenty-four hours' warning if we're going to switch the guest again."

Sam stood and offered Bex a hand up. "Let's not switch the guest. Our prop master probably knows more about Josh Miller than anyone else. We'll carry on in our pursuit of truth."

The truth, Bex thought, *and* the end to this chapter in their lives that had never been finished.

She would do everything she could to make sure that this time it had a happy ending.

Vintage Hollywood Mythology

The audio crackled in Bex's earphones, but the picture on the podcast studio's wall-mounted screen was perfectly clear.

> Cora and Henri unlock a dingy, battered door facing a street lined with neon lights and occasional sirens. The numbers on the door hang askew. Henri has to shove the door open with her shoulder to unstick it, and what they find is a dark, oppressive motel room, very much past its prime and barely inhabitable. At the same time, they both notice the one very small bed, look at each other, and then look away, visibly uncomfortable.
>
> "And here I thought investigating in the field would be glamorous." Cora tentatively steps into the room, her festive holiday sweater, flared skirt, and heels in obvious contrast to the environment.
>
> "Maybe if you started charging people real money, it could be." Henri wrinkles her nose and shuts the door behind them. "You can take the bed, I'll . . ." Henri looks around rather desperately, then walks over to a door hanging off its hinges to reveal a tiny shower and a sad toilet and sink. There is no

sofa or bathtub to sleep in. She looks at the bed in panic. "I can take the floor."

"Don't be ridiculous." Cora bustles over to the bed and gingerly sits on the edge. "Plenty big for both of us." But she sounds uncertain.

Henri nods, pained, and shrugs out of her blazer, draping it over a rickety chair while Cora averts her eyes. Cora steps out of her heels and unpins her hair. Henri glances over at her just as the bright red curls tumble down her back.

"After you," Henri says, and Cora climbs on top of the covers. Henri eases down next to her. The bed is extremely small. Henri flips off the lamp, and the room goes dim except for the glow of neon lights coming through the threadbare curtains. They both stare at the ceiling above.

"What was the best Christmas present you ever got?" Cora asks in a low voice.

Henri smiles a little in the dark. "Badge," she says. "My dog. I'd asked for a dog for years, and then when I was twelve, she was waiting for me in a laundry basket under the tree with a bow around her neck."

Smiling, Cora turns her head to look at Henri. "Good dog?"

"She was the best." Henri's eyes move around Cora's face. "Loved everyone. Got me out of my shell. Helped me make new friends. She woke up excited and gave me a reason to look forward to something every day."

Cora swallows and turns her head back, unable to maintain eye contact. "Mine was a book. Frog and Toad. I was disappointed because I had wanted a pretend makeup set I saw at the toy store, but when my mom read it to me, I just . . ." Cora's eyes drift back to Henri. "I didn't know books could be like that. That book made me hungry for other books, and then made me want to be a teacher."

"Do you miss it?"

"There are things I miss about it. But lately I'm realizing that the rest of the world may need kindergarten teachers as much as kindergartners do."

Henri stares at her for a long moment. "Cora, I . . ."

Cora's gaze moves up. "Oh! What's this?" Her arm reaches over Henri's head to touch a coin-operated box. Henri props herself up to look and then rolls her eyes.

"It's a bed massager. You put a quarter in, and it shakes the bed."

Cora looks confused.

"For . . . relaxing." Henri winces.

"Do you have a quarter?" Cora's smile is guileless.

Henri raises her eyebrows, but she gamely fishes into one of her pockets and produces a quarter. Cora takes it and reaches up to drop it in the box. She pushes the button. At first, nothing happens. Then the bed starts to shake violently.

"Is it supposed to do that?" Cora yells over the jackhammer-like noise. "It's not very relaxing!"

One of Henri's hands is gripping the edge of the mattress. She turns to Cora. "I don't think so. It will probably stop."

There is a huge bang, and the bed collapses, breaking right down the middle. Cora screams, loud. Cora and Henri are trapped inside, face-to-face, Cora's leg over both of Henri's, their noses touching.

"Are you okay?" Henri tries to arch her back and

escape, but this just tangles them closer together. They're both breathing hard, looking wildly around until their eyes lock and they go still at the same time. Cora's body seems to soften, and her hand moves over Henri's arm. Henri brings her face a little closer while they gaze at each other.

Then the motel door slams open with a crash, Cora screams again, and a figure with a ski mask lurches in, coming for them both.

The audio clicked off in Bex's earphones. The screen on the wall went dark. Kim Ryerson had both hands over her face. She was shaking with silent laughter. Bex's own mouth had gone dry. She tried to center herself by looking at Frankie, who sat behind the glass of the recording studio's booth with Amethyst and Luciana, head bent over one of the instrument panels.

Bex really needed to get back to watching these fan-favorite scenes *before* she had to sit through them in a small room that had Sam in it. Especially if Sam was going to keep wearing such minuscule clothes.

"There you have it. The scene that launched a thousand memes." Kim tucked her glossy brown hair behind one ear. It immediately slid back to cover her face as she interlaced the fingers of both hands in the air in front of her, making the sleeves of her waterfall cardigan slip to her elbows. "We've got Henri and Cora smashed like a taco in a vibrating bed, which was not in the script, but a good example of what can happen when things do not go according to plan with the cameras rolling."

Sam's laugh sounded choppy. Bex wondered if she was remembering, like Bex, the parts of that moment that weren't visible to the cameras. Like how Bex had been able to feel Sam's heart pounding against her chest from the shock of the bed unexpectedly breaking around them. How, even as she'd anticipated hearing Aaron yell

"*Cut!*" at any moment, she had used her thigh to pull Sam's hips closer to hers, and Sam's eyes had gone dark.

How Bex had never, ever wanted Aaron to end the scene so the crew could rescue them, because until he did, they were suspended in a completely private, stolen moment in which anything could happen.

"What went wrong?" Sam asked Kim. "And I should say, just for clarification for any listeners who don't know the full story of that episode, what we just watched was the *only* take of the scene."

"It had to be, because the one and only bed was toast!" Kim stretched her hands above her head again, wiggling. "Okay, so, first, the bed wasn't a bed. Aaron insisted on a vibrating bed, and I thought I could find one because they were sort of a staple in comedy from Aaron's generation, right? But the studio didn't have one, and none of the places I sourced props from did either. Our team had to make it."

"I remember that," Sam said.

"I bet, because it was quite the job. What we made was a frame on wheels with a piece of light foam, and then it was dressed to look like a bed. We needed the vibrations to read for the camera, so we modified a pair of shocks, like what you use for a car, right? Pneumatic truck shocks, because those were bigger. We hooked them up to springs that spanned the frame, and there were motors moving the shocks. We went through a couple of prototypes, having to upgrade to bigger and bigger springs and shocks and motors as we tested it with our crew lying on it, but we finally got it just in time. It was remote-controlled."

"I remember you asked me what I weighed," Bex said. "This is never a good question when it comes to someone making your props or rigging up aerials for you to be strapped into and flung across the stage. I always give the person who asks a good twenty pounds over, just in case."

"Wise move," Kim agreed. She pushed her hair behind her ear again. "And to be clear, I had my whole crew, plus Tiny, the best boy, whose name was paradoxical, pile up on this bed with it running at full shake. I'm a safety-first kind of girl. It's part of my job. Everything checked out. We rolled it in, and I had both of you climb on before the first take."

"Worked perfectly," Bex said.

"Yep. And then it was rolled off set to get a few cameras rigged on it, a mic, and Josh's team had to dress it for the motel room, right? We set up for the take. I had the remote control. You did the first part of the scene, and then you were both on the bed. I had already asked Aaron if we could do one continuous take first, so we could see how the bed played for the camera with the script. What you see in the episode, from the moment Cora and Henri get onto the bed, is that."

"If you look close, watching in sixteen-nine aspect," Sam said, "you can just see the very edge of a boom mic in the upper right-hand corner, because for a take like that, to check everything, we might not be as strict about setting up."

"Right!" Kim nodded. "So we roll, everything begins, you guys are fantastic as usual, I turn on the bed on my cue, and"— she clapped her hands together—"blammo! I turn off the motors and start to run onto the set, as do several other folks, but Aaron holds his hand up, making everyone stop. He keeps rolling. Magic happens. Good actors. Clever director. Bad prop. Magic."

"Amazing camera work, too," Bex said. "I think Carl was the one who had a clear shot through the gap in the folded-up mattress."

"Hang on." Sam leaned over to reach into a big pink tote. She pulled out a script and put it on the table. "I brought the script with me for this episode." She flipped it open to a page she'd dog-eared. "I wanted to point out that there's a whole page of dialogue that's missing because of the broken bed. What was supposed to happen was that Henri asks Cora, while the bed vibrates, for her opinion on a gift Henri's purchased for someone she's seeing."

Luciana's voice came over the recording studio's sound system.

"What?! I demand a full explanation. This is Luciana de León. I am in the booth and on the scene, reporting directly to fans, who will be as shocked as I am right this minute."

Sam laughed. "I thought you read CravingCraven fanfic, Luce."

"I do!"

"Well, the script isn't even what's interesting here. What's interesting, once again, is the fic—namely, one of the in-episode AU, alternative-ending stories is titled 'Henri Rides Off into the Neon Sunset.' In that story, the bed doesn't break, Henri tells Cora she's met the love of her life, Cora doesn't let Henri see her cry but dies inside and then decides all she wants is for Henri to be happy, so she encourages her to follow her happiness, telling her nothing is more important than the love of her life. Then the bed stops vibrating, and there's a lot of angsty internal monologue on Henri's part. The bad guy comes in, and Henri fights him off, putting all of her broken heart into it because she's not really in love with this other person, she just thinks she can't have Cora. Then, after it's over, Henri walks away. Cora lets herself cry. There's a big ten-year AU interlude involving Henri's brokenhearted stint as a bounty hunter with a gray moral center and Cora's failed marriage, and then a rescue-style meet-cute that ends in rated-M-for-mature reunion activities on the top floor of the Chrysler Building."

"*Oh*," Luciana breathed in a dramatic whisper.

Bex couldn't speak, momentarily stuck on the way Sam had just looked at her across the table when she shared how the fanfic ended. Bex was going to have to steel her spine and find out once and for all if Sam had a girlfriend. Also maybe double-check how firm Sam was feeling about the we're-just-friends thing.

But this was not the time. Bex sternly swept those thoughts away to focus on what Sam had brought to the table. "You're suggesting that Jen Arnot knew what was in the original script?" she asked. "Or at least that Jen knew Henri was going to tell Cora about someone she was dating, not all the other stuff with the bounty hunting and failed marriage."

"Yes." Sam folded her elbows on the table, leaning toward Bex. "But also I wonder if it indicates there was another direction for the show in the minds of Aaron or Bette or other powers that be, and the bed broke it."

"Is this the part where I get to have a dramatic reveal?" Kim asked. "Because I have one."

"This is everything," Luciana said. "I could die of it."

"Hold up." Amethyst came out of the booth wearing an expression of stern resolve and holding wireless sets like what they had used on Stage 46 for the podcast episode with the closet. "Kim gave me advance warning. You've got to wear these, or the sound will be garbage."

She miked them up. Frankie and Luciana had spilled out of the booth along with her, and everyone milled around, chattering excitedly, while Bex tried to act normal. She avoided looking directly at Sam, who'd worn her hair down after braiding it up wet, so it made ribbons of wavy texture across her bare shoulders and slid over her biceps when she moved. Her sleeveless minidress was covered all over in embroidered butterfly patches, making her look as though she'd lain down in a field and been covered by a blanket of butterflies, and when she moved, they might all startle and fly away.

Too much to handle while Bex was also preparing herself for her reaction to Kim's surprise. She didn't know what Kim planned to reveal, but she knew the decisions she and Sam made to do this podcast and find the truth had cracked something open, and the crack would keep widening, bringing in more and more people, more and more truth, until it swallowed up every lie they'd been made to live with.

It was a breathless feeling.

"I had something brought over to the loading dock of this building from studio storage," Kim said with obvious satisfaction.

"Shall we go downstairs and take a look?" She opened the door of the podcast studio to lead them out. Luciana and Frankie tagged along, though Amethyst had not given either woman a headset.

Amethyst had asked them to keep their mics live so she had enough to work with in post-production. Bex and Sam kept up a stream of chatter with Kim as they took the elevator down, eliciting behind-the-scenes insights into some of *Craven's Daughter*'s more notorious props. Then they walked through a garage-like door in the basement that led to the loading dock, its own doors open to the light and a hot, asphalt-smelling breeze from the parking lot. Bex spotted the bed sitting on a big cart—still broken, but without any covers on it. Just a mangled sandwich of wood and foam and black mechanical parts.

"Here she is!" Kim said. "I want our listeners to know that I took a whole bunch of pictures that will be up on the *Craven's Daughter: Cold Case* website, along with the usual video clips."

"How'd you get this here?" Bex asked. "We're recording in Inglewood," she remembered to tell their audience. "Did you steal it from storage at Cineline Studios?"

"Nothing like that," Kim said. "This is completely aboveboard. I filled out the paperwork and everything."

Bex and Sam walked to the bed and looked it over. "To be honest," Bex said, "I have no idea what I'm seeing. It could be modern art, or it could be what happens when I try to put together Ikea by myself."

Kim laughed. "Here's the frame, made like any bed frame, specced to support five hundred pounds. Here"—she stepped up onto the cart and placed her hands on a large black metal cylinder with springs hanging off it—"are the parts that make it vibrate. This is where my big reveal is." Kim stepped over part of the frame and crouched down to where the bed was broken. "Sam and Bex, could you lift the foam off it? Just wiggle it out."

Bex stepped next to Sam, and they grabbed on to the foam,

yanking it out of the V-shape the broken frame made. Kim indicated they could put the foam on the ground.

"Now look. What do you see?" Kim pointed at the break.

Bex inspected it for a moment. "To be honest, not much? Broken wood. It looks like each side of the bed is a separate piece, folded up."

"Exactly." Kim grabbed on to the bottom of each side and flapped the frame like wings. "Two bed halves."

"But there *weren't* two halves put together," Sam said, crouching down next to Kim and touching the frame. "This looks like it was one big square with the slats, and a couple of supports running opposite the slats."

"Right. And look here, where it's broken."

Bex watched Sam run her fingers over it. "It's clean. Like, there *is* splintered wood, but the crack looks like it was *made*."

"Exactly." Kim stood up and brushed off her clothes. "If a bed breaks, especially the way I had the vibrating mechanism hooked up, I would expect that one of the wheeled legs would come unattached, making a wide, sagging break, or crushed edges of slats in whatever area took the most force. More of a controlled collapsing. This is folded in half. It *snapped*. We see that in the episode. And it snapped because it had help. All along the middle, where you noticed the clean break and the splinters, is a cut made with a tool, extending halfway through the wood of the frame."

"What!" Bex barked. She crouched down. "No."

"I reported it. There was an investigation done, and my crew was questioned. I admit that it would be difficult to be truly injured from how it was tampered with, but anything that *is* tampered with, even if it's to mess up a shot, is a big deal."

"What was the outcome of the investigation?" Sam asked.

"I got a special safety official added to my crew by the network who watched everything we did and documented our props and builds. But you know who I think should have been watched?"

"Oh, God," Bex said, remembering Kim arguing with Josh at the party.

"Well, he *thinks* he's God," Kim said. "But he's only a set designer. Remember I said that the bed left my purview to be miked, lit, and dressed? I just want to say for our listeners, that's not even how things are supposed to work. A prop is whatever's in the script that's used as part of the scene. This bed is a prop. I'm supposed to handle everything about it, I'm the prop *master*. Set design is only supposed to be involved with dressing, which is aspects of the set that aren't used as props. The moldy old shower in the motel room that nobody uses or goes inside—that's set design. But Josh had worked it out with Aaron before I was hired that I had to let him approve and dress all my props. He took this bed to his workroom to dress it."

Sam's liquid-silver gladiator boots made her even taller than usual, so her frown was more than a little intimidating. "Hey, so you don't have to talk about this," she told Kim. "I don't want you to have to deal with any aftermath."

"Thanks, but it's fine. I made my thoughts known at the time, and the report is technically public record. I'm allowed to talk about my theory, which is that Josh tampered with the bed to mess up the shoot, probably because he was fighting with Aaron. When I ran this theory by Josh, he told me to go ahead and say it if I wanted to, that I was wrong then and I'm wrong now. But the joke's on him, because all's well that ends well. In this case, his sabotage ended in a ratings-busting episode."

"An episode that might have turned the arc of the show in a direction different from what Aaron and Bette were planning," Sam pointed out.

Bex had too many things to think about at once. She remembered when she read the original script years ago, her stomach had felt sick and hollow when she got to the scene with the vibrating bed. It was almost cruel how it had made her character into a joke, a woman so naive that she misunderstood and ruined a moment that should have been a turning point in Cora and Henri's relationship.

But they hadn't filmed it like that, because the bed was sabotaged by Josh or someone with access to Josh's workshop. And because Carl had captured part of what was happening *in* the bed, and what he'd captured made good television, Aaron hadn't asked them to come back another time after the bed had been fixed to shoot it again. He'd rolled with it.

"Either Bette or Aaron was trying to break up Cora and Henri," Bex guessed, thinking aloud. "But because Aaron didn't stop filming and didn't have us reshoot, he must have changed his mind. Or overruled her. One would presume."

"And maybe Jen was the only one who could have documented, for the fans, how it might have gone instead," Sam pointed out. "Since Cora and Henri's relationship wasn't something we were allowed to discuss in interviews."

"But what would be Josh's motive to do something like that?" Bex twisted her earring. "I know he has a reputation as being difficult to work with, and we've had other guests who've had theories about Josh and on-set drama, but it *is* true his primary reputation is for perfection and exemplary design. I honestly can't think of a single reason he would want to hurt us or mess up Aaron's shoot."

"Yet," Sam said tightly. "We can't think of a reason *yet*."

"Well, you're the detectives," Kim said. "I've told you everything I know."

Bex was listening to Kim and Sam talk some more about how props become unwitting actors and writers for a story, especially in the case of the bed, when she noted two people approaching from the sunbaked parking lot.

One of them wore a suit. No tie.

Before she could voice a warning, Niels Shaughnessy and Josh Miller were standing by the cart with the broken bed, Niels was making a "come on" motion with his hand that Amethyst correctly interpreted as "mike me up," and then both Niels and Josh had on headsets while Sam narrated the unfolding event—rather calmly and sardonically, Bex thought—and Kim's mouth hung open.

Network men were so *incredibly* theatrical.

"Thanks for the intro, Sam," Niels said. "I see we've got the infamous bed out from its snug rack in Studio City."

"Yes." Kim looked like she was going to say more, but Niels broke in again.

"Fantastic. As the fans say, 'iconic.' Cineline has a way with iconic, right? And what a story! Intrigue. Mystery. All of it magically leading to one of the highest-rated episodes in the show's history. What synergy."

"I guess?" Bex finally found her voice. "Or it must be, if our fearless leader is here, hiking up the ratings of this episode."

Niels chuckled beatifically. "I'm coming along for the ride, that's all. The rewatch, the behind-the-scenes speculation and rumors and campfire stories. It's vintage Hollywood mythology stuff, right?"

Oh, Bex thought. *Son of a bitch.*

Sam raised an eyebrow and gave Bex an imperceptible nod that meant she understood what Bex was thinking: Niels was here to paint this episode-in-progress—and, by extension, their entire podcast—with the brush of "Hollywood mythology." He was deliberately blurring the line between entertainment and reality, reducing Bex and Sam to the role of hosts whose efforts to uncover the truth of what had happened to Jen fell into the same category as reality TV. He wouldn't say none of it was true, but he would certainly remind listeners that their truth was being produced, maybe even scripted.

The fire of Bex's rage started to build at the base of her spine, hot in her belly. But what could they do? He was Niels Shaughnessy. He could pull the plug on the podcast with a snap of his fingers. He could sue Bette for breathing a word of the existence of the final episode with a single call to Cineline's in-house legal department, and Bex and Sam and the rest of the cast and crew certainly couldn't film that episode or release it without his blessing.

She was enraged with him, but equally enraged that she'd put herself in a position to work with him again, that she hadn't been able to see anything clearly years ago, and that so much about what had happened then, when she was working so hard and doing her best, should be coming to bear in this moment. Bex supposed she should try to be thankful for that—not just for the chance to make it right but for the clarity that would prevent her from making a huge mistake and working in proximity to this man ever again.

She couldn't. And she wouldn't. *Venice Memorial* was off the table.

But right this minute, she and Sam were stuck, the exact same kind of stuck they'd always been in, and they'd been fooling themselves to think they could avoid ending up here.

Sam put her hands on her hips, directing the power of her celebrity and her height and her glorious look-at-me fashion to force Niels and Josh's attention back to her. "*Mythology* is such an interesting word to use," she said. "It's not as though Cineline has ever pulled this bed out of storage and put it on the studio tour."

"Maybe we should," Niels said. "Fans would get a kick out of that. We could put up a display with the original script"—he swept his hand over an imaginary wall, and Bex hated the way he moved, the way he acted as though everything here belonged to him—"and, if we had permission from Jen's family, as they've been so gracious about supporting this project, we could put up pages from her fan story, too. A whole display about how some of our favorite moments in television get made. What a delightful idea."

Bex was a little surprised by her sudden physical revulsion for Niels. But *was* it sudden? Or was she in fact letting herself feel something that had built up over months and years, her body haunted by the things she'd been put through when this man sat at the top of the hierarchy, calling the shots?

And why was he even *here?* Did he have a live feed out of the recording booth? Or were there people talking to Niels behind the scenes who were steps ahead of Bex and Sam and what they'd been discovering?

No. Kim had said there was paperwork. She'd requested the bed be removed from storage and transferred to Inglewood. That request would have been flagged, would have traveled up the chain of command as something Niels might want to know. And here he was—with Josh, even. These two men had piled into a car together. They'd had to endure each other's company and make small talk on the way from Studio City, and that meant that what Sam and Bex were doing genuinely bothered them.

Good.

"You know, Niels," Sam said, "since we have you here, I'd love to know what *you* thought about where Cora and Henri would end up. Did you see a happy ending to the implied romantic arc, or were you more interested in keeping fans guessing forever?"

"Those are decisions for the creative team. I'm just the pencil pusher upstairs trying to make sure we keep our bottom line in the black."

Just the pencil pusher upstairs. Bex's hands curled into fists.

"So it was up to Aaron," Sam pressed.

Niels's laugh made Bex taste bile in her throat. "It's more complicated than that, but in a general sense," he said noncommittally. "You know what you should do is have Aaron Gorman come on as a guest. I bet he'd be willing to talk to you girls and share some of the stories about how he comes up with all of this." Niels gestured toward the broken frame of the bed. "Vibrating beds that break at just the right moment. Hilarious, honestly."

Bex wrapped a strand of hair around her finger and tugged hard enough that she let out a little huff. Sam glanced at her, and

Bex read her expression as easily as though Sam had spoken her feelings aloud.

Fuck this. We don't have to do this.

Her own chest was tight with the same feelings she'd had after she'd walked off the photo shoot and refused Niels.

This was what that refusal was about. Because she'd been here, exactly here, sitting in Niels Shaughnessy's office next to Sam, across from Aaron, across from men in suits whose names she didn't know and no one bothered to introduce her to. She and Sam had pleaded their case for Henri and Cora and the fans to this same unyielding wall of bland hierarchy. They had *tried*. She honestly couldn't remember how many times they'd tried, how many meetings like that there had been. She had thought those meetings had left her resigned because she had so often felt she hadn't said enough or been as fiery and proactive as Sam, but no. Those meetings had left her angry. Hurt. Disgusted. But she'd been stuck in survival mode, afraid of losing the show that was her job and her home, her security and the place where she saw her best friend—her *Sam*—and so Bex hadn't given herself permission to feel that anger, hurt, and disgust.

She had to feel it now.

"Kim," Josh said with laughter in his voice, "I loved this bed so much." He came to the cart and put his hands on it, the sun slashing across his five-hundred-dollar sunglasses. "*Craven's Daughter* was such a pinnacle of craftsmanship, you know? We had to really toe that line between gritty procedural and the camp of detective tropes, and make it feel big enough, grand enough to hold the celebrity of our weekly guest stars. I love that kind of challenge, and I miss collaborating with you and your team. I remember Aaron telling me, 'We've got to do a motel room with a vibrating bed.' I was like, 'Aaron, man, you know those don't exist anymore. No one's gonna know what it is.' But he insisted, and he was right. Putting Bexley and Samantha in the vibrating bed together made the joke fresh."

With that, Bex's control snapped. How dare he? How dare he wink to the queer chemistry that she and Sam had made and fought for while everyone else sneered or rolled their eyes or protected the soda companies or were so wrapped up in their own galactic-sized egos that they didn't care about anything but old grudges and constant credit?

Bex had had enough.

"You miss collaborating with Kim?" she asked.

Josh rubbed his mouth. "Yeah, and that's high praise. I've had prop masters tossed from other projects. I have a rep in this industry for being obsessed with getting the art right. I insist on perfect colors, perfect faux finishes, exact replicas of shots on location. I care about how the camera reads my work. Bad props look like toys, but Kim's props are good."

Kim stared at the bed, her face drained of color. Luciana was engaged in hushed but heated debate with Amethyst.

"And Aaron? Sounds like a lot of synergy between the two of you?"

Now Sam had noticed Bex was up to something with her questions, and she raised an eyebrow.

"Aaron's a legend."

"So I'm guessing that you and Aaron already signed on to be part of taping the long-lost series finale, then?" Bex allowed sly excitement to edge into her voice, enough to suggest she was in on what Niels was trying to do, and she found the vagaries of this radio-drama reality show podcast delightful.

Josh scowled at her. Several loaded seconds went by without a response.

"*I* have." Luciana strode over to the cart, her silky white joggers hugging her curves. She held a small mic to her mouth that she must have wrested from Amethyst. "Luciana again. I can't resist. I was going to make my announcement on *Late Night,* but this is more fun. More clues for the audience! And, God, I think this finale will be something no one has ever done in the history of television. Pick right up where you left off in front of a live studio audience of fans who've been on the journey with you from the beginning, and give them what they yearned for every minute of those hundred-plus episodes. Ultimate catharsis."

Luciana now faced Niels, having edged slightly into his personal space. His expression was several creases past irritated. She lowered her voice and adopted a confessional tone. "*Craven's Daughter*, you know, has been my favorite show for years. So for me—a guest star, a fan, reader of the fanfic and greedy for every new minute of Henri and Cora—a decision like this from the network is emotional. Affirming. Validating. *Political.*" Luciana's smile was feline. "Niels, you're a *genius.*"

As head of the studio, nothing could stop Niels from burying this podcast episode in a vault beneath the Cineline building. *Technically*, nothing could. But Luciana's insertion of herself into the recording was more than a delightful bit of theater. It was a threat. Luciana wanted Niels to know that if he threw away this episode—if he turned his back on the series finale being filmed—she would leverage her own power and the power of the *Craven's Daughter* fandom against him.

Niels laughed. It wasn't a friendly sound. "Doing my part."

When he looked at Josh, it wasn't a friendly look. It was a look that said, *You were supposed to bring the weapons.*

Josh wiped his forehead with the back of his hand. "Haven't had a chance to catch up with Aaron, but if he's down, I guess I am, too."

"Not a hamburger's worth of beef between the two of you," Sam said cheerfully. "Like always."

"Vintage Hollywood mythology," Luciana breathed. "So much of it starts just like this." Then she switched off her mic, dropped it on the ground, and pointed at Bex and Sam. *Call me,* she mouthed.

Kim unhooked her own mic, glowering at Josh. "This bed is

fucking cursed." She wove between Amethyst, Bex, and Sam and disappeared into the building.

Niels grimaced and switched off his mic. "I'll have some suggested edits for this podcast episode."

Bex looked at Sam and saw her own thought reflected back in Sam's eyes.

Not if we edit it first.

Two Birds with One Stone

As soon as Bex had walked out of the sightline of the loading dock and no one who had been gathered around the bed could see her, she started to run.

There was a raggedy, weed-clogged sidewalk along the side of the building, and she flew down it, glad she'd worn her expensive running shoes for the podcast today, glad she'd kept up with dance, glad she could still empty her mind like this, the same way she liked to do before a big number in front of a full house.

She wouldn't take the part on *Venice Memorial* even if that man got on his knees and begged. Her face went hot thinking about Frankie telling her she was making a "colossal mistake." She had. It had been wrong of her to take direction from Niels, agreeing to manipulate Sam into doing the reunion special and the podcast *for the fans* without copping to her real reason. Of *course* Frankie was right.

Bex's heart broke with the recognition that she'd believed steady work on another television series that she wasn't even excited about would be a chance for her to find joy in her personal life again—the same joy she remembered feeling on *Craven's Daughter*, through good times and bad. She had utterly missed what the joy on *Craven's Daughter* had been about. The joy was about *Sam*.

Sam, Sam, Sam. Her heart had tried to tell her what it wanted, but Bex hadn't listened.

The running and self-recrimination and how her entire body and emotions were going off like a torch were why Bex didn't hear anyone yelling at her, and probably why she screamed in surprised frustration when arms came around her middle, holding her in place.

"Bex, Jesus." Sam's arms. Sam was panting in Bex's ear. "You are so fast, it's uncanny."

Bex pulled away. Sam was fanning her face in her offensively microscopic fairy dress and shiny, laced-up heels, and Bex's brain took up all of the angry chemicals that had been racing around her body since Amethyst retrieved their mics and Niels and Josh walked away. Her throat had gone fire-hot. She heard herself yelling before she even knew what she was saying.

"What was that? What *was* that!" She stomped her feet and looked up at the hazy blue of the cloudless sky. "Why can he *do* that? Walk into our thing, our time, our story, and do that? Why does he get to say it's pretend, it always was, that it's not real, that we're not real, like he's some kind of Orson Welles and we're doing *War of the Worlds*, not talking about our own actual experiences? He's calling our audience fools. He's speaking for Jen, who's—"

Bex pressed the heels of her palms against her eyes, staving off the burn of tears. She didn't want to cry. She was too angry.

"—who's *dead!* She's *gone*, and we're trying to tell a story about her that's important, but he only had to walk across the parking lot and call it 'vintage Hollywood mythology,' and it's fake. It's nothing." Bex stamped her foot. "You know, Sam, I never forgot about the meetings we took with Niels and Aaron, but I did forget what it feels like when you're giving everything you've got to tell a story, a human story, and *one man* can come in and make it so it wasn't real. It wasn't anything. It was stupid. A stupid, shameful, embarrassing *girl* thing."

Bex knew the tears had come, but she didn't bother to swipe

them away. This anger was rising up from so many different directions, she was certain if she stopped crying about one loss, she'd start crying and yelling about another.

"It was real for me," Sam said.

"I know that! It was real for me, too! That's what I'm saying! That's why I'm angry!"

Sam ran her hands through her hair, then dropped them to her sides, her brows furrowed.

Bex closed her eyes. "You're not the problem. It's me that's the problem. Do you know—do you know?!—that I was actually considering, not even considering, *hoping*, that I would work for that man again? On a new show." Bex pressed the backs of her hands against her flaming cheeks. "I thought because I was so happy on *Craven's Daughter*, with my family, in general, that I could be happy like that again. Can you believe that? How did I not know that what made me happy was you? How did I not understand that when Frankie and Vic grew up, my relationship to them would change? Tell me exactly how dense, how *ludicrous*, I can be, and I will add a superlative to that amount."

Sam bit her lip, looking to the side. It wasn't the response Bex had expected. It was Sam holding back, and it sent sweat-prickles of fear down Bex's spine.

"Sam?"

"You weren't wrong at Chaz's, when we were talking and you noticed I wasn't telling you everything. I let you think it was because I wasn't sure about getting close to you again, that I was being careful of my feelings. I am very much kicking myself for that." Sam huffed out a laugh. "Like I have ever been careful with you, Bexley, oh my God."

"What is it?" Bex wanted her ordinary breath back, not this running, angry, keyed-up wheezing. "Tell me right now."

"Frankie told me about *Venice Memorial*," Sam said. "She was hopeful that if you brought it up while we were working together again, I could remind you of the reasons why it wouldn't be good for you. I should have never agreed. Part of it was my inability to tell your sisters no, which is on me, because you're right, they aren't girls anymore, and if they want to be treated as adults, they can't go behind your back. But the other part is that, yes, my experiences on *Craven's Daughter* and with Niels weren't the same as yours. I saw more because I *could* see more. And the other part is that—" Sam put her fist to her mouth, her collarbones and neck bright red, her famous composure nowhere to be found.

"What is the other part?" Bex couldn't figure out if she was hot or cold. Her voice croaked out of her throat in a way that would have genuinely alarmed her if she cared about anything but what Sam was about to say. "What is the thing that made it okay for you to tell me that you only wanted to be my friend and who was here to help me figure out what I wanted, and flirt with me and have *moments* with me even though you said you weren't ready for moments, the kind of moments that have made me so hopeful I am drawing hearts around your name in my head? *What?*"

"That!" Sam barked. "I'm sorry, I don't mean to yell, but it's *that*, it's that I never stopped wanting a chance with you, Bex, I just didn't. I never stopped wanting the whole fucking world for you. And I'm biased about what the world *should* be for you, I admit that. I admit I don't think what you deserve most of all is a role where you wear scrubs and a lanyard and rush around having dramatic romantic subplots with men whose hair looks like it's made of plastic. But also I can understand that my bias is patronizing. I don't want to be in charge of you, Bex. I want to love you. And, God help me, I agreed to every fucking thing to have a chance at it, including the reunion and the podcast, even knowing why you were asking me, knowing I shouldn't, knowing why Frankie wanted me to." Sam had her hand on her heart, pressing. "Frankie loves you. Don't be mad at her."

Bex felt hectic, boneless, hot. Was she happy? Should she be? She wanted to explain everything, to Sam, to herself, but she wasn't sure what to say first, and one of Sam's hands was still pressed against her chest like she was holding her heart in, her eyes searching Bex's face.

But then she turned away.

Bex realized it was because Frankie was jogging down the sidewalk, pale, her eyes red. *God damn it.*

"Where are you going?" Frankie demanded.

"Nowhere," Bex said. "I'm not going anywhere. I was upset."

"Don't *do* that."

"What?"

Frankie stopped four feet away. "I'm not a kid. You don't have to do that thing where you smooth everything out and smile and ask if I want to go home or get something from the vending machine or get a book from your bag."

Bex's heart skipped at the accusation in Frankie's tone. "That's not what I was doing."

"I could hear you yelling. I haven't heard you yell in years."

"I yell. You know I yell."

"Not like that."

"Like what? Like my sister went behind my back and discussed my career decisions with someone else after I had already told her what I wanted to do?"

"You don't *know* what you want to do! You don't know so much, you can't even tell if anyone else is doing what *they* want to do!"

"What the fuck does *that* mean?"

Sam winced.

"Can't you just be my sister?" Frankie asked, moving closer. "Can't you stop trying to be Mom, finally, and look around and notice that I don't need you to worry about my non-dairy needs but it would be really fucking nice to talk to *my sister* about my actual *life*? I'd like that, Bexley, for *once*!" Her nostrils flared. She opened her fists, shook her hands, and dropped them to her sides.

Bex knew from experience that Frankie wasn't done, so she didn't venture to speak.

"I'm the age you were when Mom and Dad died," Frankie said, a little quieter. "I hate doing laundry. I can't stand that I have to feed myself three times a day, day in and day out, like, the fucking tedium of being an adult is unreal. Dishes. Getting out of bed every morning. Going to a job and doing what they say, and everyone tells you you're so lucky to have it when it's vile. For the first time in my life, I can imagine in granular detail what you had to do for me and Vic. And every single time you're smoothing over some mistake I made or some trouble Vic got herself into, or you cancel something for yourself to do something we're capable of doing on our own, I want to scream. I don't want your sacrifice anymore. I don't want you to fix anything for me, nothing, *nothing*."

"I don't want to fix anything either," Bex said, trying not to yell. "I didn't want to fix anything *then*. You told me about that picture of me with my Tony award getting pizza, and I had to look it up. I hadn't ever fucking seen that picture! In that picture, I was drunk. I had to be carried into the pizza place by my elbows because my feet were bleeding from wearing stupid shoes and drinking too much champagne at the after-party. That night, I made out with at least two of the people in that photo, and possibly I went home with both of them. I was so fucking high. I was so fucking happy. My brand-new theater agent had told me I would be Broadway's new princess, like Bernadette Peters. I was already in rehearsals for my next show. It was the adaptation of *Pride and Prejudice*. I got Lydia, the part with the biggest, raunchiest number, and it was more money than I thought I deserved until that night. That night, I deserved it all. And goddamnit, Frankie, I had to leave *Pride and Prejudice* because my *parents died*, and my sisters needed me. I watched that show win a gazillion Tonys and sell out again and again. I watched the original cast album hit the chart for weeks. I watched it go to London. It opened the night I made a list of lawyers in case I had to fight Dad's alcoholic sister for custody after her threats at the funeral.

I had actually *just* screamed at you because you wouldn't let Vic sleep in your bed again."

"Bex." Frankie's tear-soaked voice didn't soften Bex's heart at all. It was about time Frankie heard this. She *wasn't* Frankie's mom. No one would ever be but Theresa Simon. But she was Frankie's big sister, and Frankie was right, it was time for Bex to act like one.

"No. Let me get to *my* point. It wasn't a sacrifice. That's my point. You know why? Because Mom and Dad were dead. For them *not* to be dead was all I wanted. For *me*, I wanted that, and especially for you and Vic. I was twenty-four years old, so, yeah, I didn't want to get up early every day and make meals and take kids to school and deal with Mom and Dad's estate and bury Vic's fucking hamster while she cried that everything she loved died. But I did want a family, Franklynn. When it was just me and Mom, my secret wish for Christmas and my birthday every year was for a family. I wanted the drama and praise and for Mom to drive a minivan. Mom meeting and falling in love with Dad was my wish come true. And then you. And Vic. I remember the first time I told someone, 'I have two sisters.' I felt so good. 'I have two sisters. I have two sisters and a mom and dad. Our house is the big one near the park in Clintonville. Me and my sisters are named after neighborhoods in Columbus, yeah, my mom and dad are funny like that.' I was never, ever going to give it up. Can't you see that? Broadway, or *I have two sisters*? It wasn't a sacrifice. It wasn't even a choice."

Bex pressed her palms to her eyes, drained in some ways, even as she still wanted to stomp her feet and scream.

"I just want you to be happy." Frankie choked out another sob. "I just want you to ask what would make me and Vic happy instead of thinking you know."

"Then leave my own happiness to me, and I'll leave you and Vic's happiness to you and Vic, but could all of us just fucking meet in the middle and talk about it?"

Frankie pushed both hands through her soft curls. Nodded. "I love you."

Bex glanced at Sam, who had one arm wrapped around herself and her phone in her hand. She looked wrecked. Bex felt sorry for all of them. What a long goddamned day. If Vic needed some kind of catharsis, she would have to have it while Bex was horizontal on her bed.

"If I could make a suggestion," Sam said. "We go to our office upstairs and regroup. I just got an interesting text."

"From who?" Bex asked.

"Bette. Apparently, a courier will be here pretty soon with the series finale script. Don't call her, she'll call us. She used a lot of periods in this text. The vibe is spiky."

"But we'll get to read the final script, so it's difficult to care." Bex squared her shoulders. "Okay. I am ready to regroup." She put her arm out to her sister, giving her a quick side hug. "And I love you, too, you absolute monster."

They made their way back into the building on wobbly, coltish legs, at least in Bex's case. They got to the cart with the bed, and Frankie pushed it into the bay, wheeled it to a corner, and pulled a tarp down over it. On the elevator up, they were quiet.

By the time Bex had finished freshening up in the restroom, hoping she could cold-water splash the day away, and they'd had coffees delivered, it was time to meet the courier and sign for the sealed envelope.

She opened it in the elevator. The cover page was pink, with lots of huge red font warning the reader that the script was the property of Cineline and this copy was only for authorized persons.

She slid it back into the envelope.

In the office, Sam was on a phone call at the desk. Frankie sat on the loveseat in the corner with a pile of vending-machine snacks. Bex dropped onto the cushion next to her.

Frankie tapped the envelope on Bex's lap. "I desperately want to yoink this and run away to read it."

"Try me. I had to sign for this script. It's in my official custody." Bex's phone buzzed. She pulled it out of her back pocket. It was Vic.

> something's happening
>
> i can feel it
>
> u were recording today & now there is a crackling energy in my blood
>
> tell me or i will skip class & put a plane ticket on your card

Bex held her phone out to Frankie. "Debrief your sister." She tucked the envelope under her arm and crossed to sit on top of the desk next to Sam, who was just hanging up her call.

"How bad is the bad news?" she asked, reading Sam's expression.

Sam's smile was rueful. "Niels and Josh signed appearance contracts for the podcast. As producers, we could edit them out, but my intuition is to continue being as transparent as possible. I don't want to hide the fact they came on."

Bex looked at Frankie. "You know Amethyst best. Do you think she can handle the editing in a way that will pass muster with Niels but also make it clear to our fans that he and Josh are assholes?"

"Not like that will be hard." Frankie's thumbs hammered the phone screen, texting Vic. "Amethyst's good. She'll edit it fast, and she'll make sure it's just as barely compliant as it can be while also making a statement Niels can't understand and won't censor."

"But the fans will get it?"

"The fans always get it."

Sam plucked the envelope from under Bex's arm and turned it upside down so the script fell into her hand. She read the cover page. "You know, Bex, this is the first thing today that's really pissing me off. I didn't love Shaughnessy showing up with

Josh, but I knew there would be consequences for shaking the branches so hard at Jen's party. But *this*." Sam dropped the script on the desk and stared down at it. "I hate that this has existed for five years and no one showed it to me."

Bex patted the spot beside her on the desk. "Read it with me now."

Sam sat, and Bex had a sudden sense memory of their table reads, both of them laughing over their overacting, joking with the guest star, and trying to guess who the killer was. They'd often end up sharing a script just like this, thigh to thigh and shoulder to shoulder, one of them holding it and the other turning the pages.

Bex knew they should talk more about how they felt, and soon, but she wasn't ready yet. She wanted to let the dust settle on everything they'd confessed in the parking lot. She'd told Sam she wasn't going anywhere.

Now she had faith Sam wasn't, either.

Bex licked her finger, just like Cora Banks would have, and turned the cover sheet of the script so they were looking at the first page.

The establishing exposition before the title sequence introduced Luciana's character as the episode's villain. It established a mystery as to whether this character was the same person Luciana had played in the serial's first episode after the pilot—alive, even though she'd *seemed* to die in that episode—or if she was that character's twin-slash-doppelganger, bent on revenge.

"Classic," Sam said. "Love an old-school trope."

"Hmm." Bex turned another page. "I'm more curious about how this will explain the way Henri and Cora left each other in the last episode."

"You mean if Cora is going to accept Henri's letter of resignation at face value or see through it and realize that Henri's series-long secret is that she was kicked out of the FBI because she took the fall for her former partner, who was a mom and had to feed her family, and this secret has finally come to a head because her former partner grew a conscience and confessed to the FBI?"

"Got to love a six-season series conflict that could've been a conversation." Bex turned another page. "Okay, this is bizarre. Are you caught up to me?"

"Yeah." Sam adjusted her hold on the script and flipped to the next page. "Yikes."

Bex read the scene, then recoiled. "God, double yikes." She looked at Sam. "Do I need a snack and a glass of water, or does this suck as bad as I think it does?"

Sam turned another page and scanned over it. "This sucks *worse* than I think you think it does. What is this dialogue? I feel like I'm back in my freshman-year screenwriting class."

They started the next scene together, one set in a warehouse with Luciana's original character, who in fact had *not* been murdered in the first season, and then they both reared back at the same time.

Bex flipped the cover back over the script and dropped it on the desk. "It doesn't even matter if Cora and Henri get their happy ending if this trash fire is the beginning and middle that leads up to it. Is this a draft? Is this *it*? Surely Bette sent over the wrong envelope."

Sam leaned over Bex's lap and flipped to the last page. "It's signed off."

"By who? I know three people in craft services on my last movie who could write a better script than this."

"I guess that's why Bette never let anyone read it." Sam's brow furrowed. "But she had no way of knowing it wasn't going to be read. Possibly ridiculed."

"Definitely ridiculed. Sam, we can't film this."

"Jen was dead," Frankie said, putting her phone down. "We know Jen had been writing with Bette. And Bette hasn't had solo writing credits since, only collabs and writing rooms. Maybe Vic wasn't off base when she tried to shake a murder confession out of

Bette by telling her we knew Jen was writing her scripts. We really could be looking at a Cyrano de Bergerac–type situation where Jen was secretly ghostwriting the whole show for Bette."

"But why?" Bex was shocked, and she'd been in Hollywood a long time. "There isn't a writer in this town who doesn't collaborate. It would have been a standard move for Bette to open up the writing room."

Sam tapped her chin. "Because of Aaron, maybe. Because he didn't do that, which meant she couldn't. He gave her a chance. He didn't have a lot of choices, he was pulling favors, but this was a favor *Bette* had managed to pull. And, remember, Aaron had been cheating on Bette's mom on the set of *Charles Salt*. That was pretty fresh. Bette had a lot of leverage just then, but she was young. She's got pride."

"How would she have known Jen?" Bex pulled up her legs. "Jen was older and didn't have any writing credits that Bette would have known about."

The room went quiet for a beat. Then Frankie sat up straight. "The same way *I* knew Jen. Remember, Carl said—Bette was there when Aaron was directing *Charles Salt*, like Vic and I were for *Craven's Daughter*. Jen was the key light. She would've been nice to Bette and taken her under her wing. If Bette hung around Jen, she could have found out Jen was a writer. Maybe that's when something started, like Jen mentoring Bette."

Bex looked around for her purse. She needed something to eat. And her notebook. "I have so many more questions. Why did Bette send this over? Is it because she doesn't think she can cover it up anymore? Or because she thinks we have no discernment and can't tell it's horrible? And what the fuck is up with Josh? What was that with the bed? Halfway sawing through the supports of a weight-bearing prop in the hope it will create an on-set disaster is *outrageous*. I want to believe Kim is paranoid, but Josh supposedly did the same thing on *Charles Salt*, though he still denies it."

"I guess if Josh was pissed that Aaron stole his girlfriend,"

Frankie mused, "I can sort of see revenue sabotage on *Charles Salt* as a motive, since it makes Aaron look bad. But I've just been hashing this out on WhatsApp with Vic, and we can't recall anything like that on *Craven*."

"Jen's the common denominator," Sam mused. "She connects Josh, Aaron, and now Bette. Other than that, I've got nothing."

"So what's next?" Bex asked. "I want closure for our fans. Especially now. Josh, Aaron, and Bette are all horrible in their own way, but almost everyone in this town is horrible. The only reason we're even worried someone had something to do with Jen's death is because the studio did such a crap job of explaining what happened. We knew Jen, and it never made sense."

"And Georgie said there were no meds in her system, plus she was too short to fall over the balcony railing easily." Sam scrubbed her hand through her hair. "Go on."

"I was just going to say I agree that Jen's connected to this mess, but that doesn't mean there was a murder."

"But this is a lot of secrets," Sam said. "Aaron post-divorce, on his last chance. Josh dealing with fallout from a potentially career-ending incident that shut down production and got him in deep water with the network. Three-way affair. Plagiarism. People in L.A. have killed for less."

"So, again, what now?" Bex asked.

"Now," Sam said, jumping off the desk and putting her hands on her hips, "we kill two birds with one stone. Niels just came on our podcast and tried to suggest what we're doing is a crass commercial stunt. But his claim dissolves if we find out what happened to Jen. The other bird is to stop thinking we're *only* TV detectives."

"What's the stone?" Bex asked.

"Chicago," Sam said. "Shouldn't this podcast record on location?"

The Makeup Artist's Secret

"**C**an you believe this? I can't believe it."

Cicely Greene had been interjecting this every so often as Amethyst set up her apartment for the podcast. Cicely sat on a loveseat with a tartan throw. The beads decorating her goddess twists matched her orange cat-eye glasses. She snuggled more deeply into the throw and stage-whispered, "I just can't believe it."

When Bex had first tried to call Cicely after learning that the apartment with the balcony had been sold by the studio and was occupied, she was so difficult to get hold of that Bex had resigned herself to knocking on her door once they got to town. But then Cicely called back and launched directly into a monologue about how she and her partner had "already done" plenty of interviews and photo shoots related to *Craven's Daughter*, they weren't interested, everything they'd ever said could be found online, lose my number, et cetera.

Bex had to wait for a small pause to blurt, "I'm Bexley Simon," then hang on through several more seconds before Cicely paused her diatribe, which sounded entirely justified. Then Cicely was hard to talk to over her extreme excitement.

Bex and Sam had taken a private flight to Chicago courtesy of a producer friend of Sam's. They had wanted to avoid the inevitable disruption and the possibility of photos leaked to the media by fellow travelers. Public interest in the pair of them had only gotten more intense since the last episode with Niels, Josh, and Kim dropped.

"Can *you* believe it?" Cicely asked her wife, Eleanor, who sat beside her on the sofa, buttoned into a navy-blue suit and flats. Eleanor had come home early from work so she could be here for the recording of the podcast.

"I cannot," Eleanor said solemnly. "I'm operating on the assumption it's a dream."

Amethyst was talking to Johnny Kerr, who would be their guest this week. Her edit of the podcast episode they'd done with Kim was perhaps the most subtly brilliant example of audio manipulation Bex had ever witnessed. Niels's office had approved her first cut. No requested changes. Bex suspected Niels might have reviewed a transcript without actually giving it a listen. *Everything* that had happened in the parking lot was captured, played through without cutaways or commentary. Nothing had been added to explain it. The only introduction Niels and Josh received were the impromptu remarks Sam made as they approached.

But Amethyst had left in things that she normally would have edited out. Things like the quick, involuntary inhale Bex had made when she spotted the two men—still there in the recording. Or the way Sam's voice sharpened with suspicion, and the heavy sound of Niels's breathing. When he first spoke about "Hollywood mythology," there was a long, awkward pause, and the wind caused something to rub over one of the mics, a loud and irritating sound that made it obvious how Luciana pitched her voice at a purr to smooth over the tension.

Listening to the recording, Bex couldn't *not* notice that the meeting had been contrived by Niels and Josh. It sounded artificial. Stilted. Plenty of fans heard it, too—enough to create a loud hum of anticipation and Internet sleuthing. Bex couldn't look at a computer, phone, TV, or stone tablet without running into a lot of words about, well, *kissing.*

She had started to dream about kissing. She kept having to

nerve herself up to make eye contact with Sam when they were alone, lest she pull Sam down to her mouth by her nape and make her. She had no idea if Sam had noticed. Bex didn't know how to navigate a situation where both of them had talked so much about their past-tense feelings and alluded to their present-tense ones, and a lot of time was spent in close proximity, which had made thoughts about kissing unsettlingly vivid.

Definitely, there was a conversation they should be having and were not.

"I'm just about done here," Amethyst said. "Let's get you two miked, and we'll do the balcony with Johnny."

Johnny Kerr was a Chicago-based actor who had played the recurring comedic character of the building's mysterious super, Mike, on *Craven's Daughter*. Cora and Henri were forever trying to find Mike, but they only ever managed to track him down in a nook by the ancient boiler in the bowels of the building. Bex and Sam used to film all their scenes with Johnny for the whole season on the same day when they came to Chicago for the location shoot.

"Gotcha," Bex said. Sam ambled over to stand next to her in the dining room. They had both been avoiding the balcony. Bex did not want to *do* the balcony. At all.

"Nothing looks the same." Sam looped her arm through Bex's, and that helped. "I don't think I ever realized what a pretty apartment this was. Eleanor says the coved plaster and the woodwork are all original."

"Whenever we were here, it was covered in equipment, everyone's stations, and there was never any furniture except folding chairs. It was work."

Amethyst stood in front of Bex, frowning as she tried to get the microphone to attach properly to Bex's jean jacket, which Bex wouldn't take off because November in Chicago was a completely different situation, weather-wise, from November in Los Angeles. Even Sam wore a sweater. Cropped, because Sam, but still.

"Yeah, but *Chicago* wasn't work," Sam said. "The filming hours were short. We could play in the city. It's nice to be back here. I didn't expect that."

Bex lifted her chin—Amethyst had given up on her jacket and was trying to pin the microphone to the ruched neckline of Bex's top—just in time to catch Sam looking at her.

"Remember when we went to that escape room?" Sam asked. "It was so dark in there, and we couldn't figure out the very first puzzle, but even though they'd said we could call on the phone from the room and ask for a hint, you refused, and we ended up sitting on the floor in the entryway of the haunted mansion for an hour while you complained about your feet hurting from walking around all morning."

"I remember how we had to tell the kid who'd check in over the sound system that we were okay. That we *wanted* to spend fifty bucks per person to sit on the floor."

"Still one of the best dates I've ever had."

Bex messed up and accidentally met Sam's eyes. They were a deep blue in the clear light of the apartment, and so, disarmed by Sam's incomparable eyes for a split second, she imagined what it would be like if this were *their* pretty apartment. If she woke up to the sun filtered through the beveled glass doors of the bedroom with her leg wrapped around both of Sam's, Sam's hand tangled in her curls, knowing Sam was hers.

Mine, mine, mine, her heart sang. Bex swallowed.

"For me," she said, "it was when we took that long walk by the lake after going to the last hour Shedd's was open, and we got back so late to the hotel that there wasn't any food, and you made me nachos with food from the vending machines, the minibar, and the hot plate part of the coffeemaker."

"The nachos were after my miniature grilled cheese sandwiches made from bagel chips failed."

"Best food ever." Bex found she couldn't say it and look right at Sam. Chicago had always been just a little dangerous for them, unsettling their routines and opening up space for feelings they hadn't acknowledged to each other.

Like the feelings Bex was having now.

The worst trip to Chicago, the best time they ever had here, was the last. It was the night they'd gone to Zanies to see one of Sam's oldest friends do a stand-up set. They'd been given seats in a small roped-off section near the stage. No one had come up to talk to them or taken pictures, enabling Bex's fantasy that she and Sam were just like everyone else in the audience. She'd ordered fries and a cocktail, then another, laughing and laughing at the outrageously confessional set, and after the show she and Sam had taken Sam's friend, Coco, out to a dark pub for drinks, where Coco and Sam competed to see who could make Bex laugh harder at their stories about growing up in Oakland. With Sam's arm around Bex's shoulders to keep her from falling out of their tiny booth, Bex crushed against her side, hot and damp, raucous and leaning in to half-shout into Sam's ear and smell her perfume while she felt the press of Sam's body against hers.

They left the bar holding hands, Bex swallowing over the raw feeling in her throat, too happy to think seriously about whether she'd injured herself, and she didn't know what would happen next, but she *hoped*. Chicago was enchanted. She could let something happen in Chicago.

What did happen was they saw flashing lights, a knot of men shouting their names, and they pulled apart.

In the morning, Bex woke up to the news about Jen.

"Johnny?" Amethyst asked. "Are you ready?" He'd wandered over to sit between Cicely and Eleanor, his arms spread across the back of the sofa as he chatted with them both. At Amethyst's prompting, he leapt to his feet.

"All yours," he said.

"We're recording?" Bex asked. Amethyst gave her a thumbs up.

"Welcome back to the fifth and next-to-last episode of *Craven's Daughter: Cold Case*," Bex said, pitching her voice at a warm purr. "It's a special one today, because we're in Chicago. That was Sam's idea, so blame her if it goes awry, but with just two weeks left before the big *Craven's Daughter* reunion to get all of our questions answered, we decided to take this week's podcast directly to the source. We have an amazing guest to introduce—fans might guess who it is. And, to be honest, I was so worried about seeing the balcony again, but I'm looking out at it, and it's not so bad. The owners of the apartment, who are lovely, have all their plants and little lights they've strung up. It's okay. I'm okay."

Sam stood behind Bex, just to her side, with one arm braced in the opening that led to the balcony. "Did they tell you they've got the lights and plants out there on the balcony because they can't use it? There's a contractor coming in next week to tear it off and put up a new one. Georgie was right. Our listeners will remember that Georgie was the retired Chicago detective who had a second career as a Hollywood script advisor. Georgie came on the podcast and told us what she thought of the report that was filed on Jen's death. She said the railing wasn't up to code. She also said she thought the railing was a little too high for a tripping accident, even if Jen did have meds in her system, and I have to say, looking at it, I hadn't remembered it was quite *this* small and rickety. I'm thinking about how dark it would have been on this balcony without the lights for filming."

"After last week, I don't mind saying, it's been hard not to feel like we've taken this too far." Bex offered Sam and Johnny a shaky smile. "But I know Jen's family doesn't want her to be forgotten. Jen's mom welcomed our decision to look into this. She said she thought Jen would love it."

"I wouldn't be here if not for that," Sam agreed.

"So let's keep going. Make this ours. Let's make this time our fans' time. Isn't that the whole point?" Bex had wanted to say that or something like it—to remind the fans that she and Sam were on their side, and this podcast was not scripted or fake, as Niels had implied.

"Yeah, Bex, it is. You know what I can't believe, though? I can't believe Johnny Kerr is still around."

Johnny laughed. "Chicago can't quit me." He dropped into one of the chairs that Eleanor had placed near the balcony, and Bex and Sam followed suit.

"He just got a spot with the Groundlings," Sam told their listeners. "At sixty! He's in rehearsals for a Chicago Shakespeare Theater production of *The Tempest*, so we're lucky to nab him."

Johnny had been bald for decades, which showed off an angular bone structure the camera and theater lights loved, but today he wore a long, gray, wavy hair system, installed for his part in *The Tempest*. It set off his dark eyes and pale brown skin.

"I always feel lucky to see Johnny," Bex said. "He's an extraordinarily talented actor who Sam and I have learned a great deal from."

"Do go on." Johnny laughed.

"It's true." Sam leaned back in the overstuffed armchair she'd dropped into. "I learned Henri's South Side accent from Johnny. Everyone should be glad Mike the Super was in the pilot, or there would have been way too much evidence of what a Northern California girl thinks someone from Chicago sounds like."

"I'm a lot more interested in what the two of you have going on," Johnny said. "I've been listening to this podcast." He rubbed his hands together. "Of course, I knew Jen. We got on well."

"You both would go down the street during breaks in filming and carry out granitas from that Italian place." Bex had forgotten that until this moment. She was surprised at how this apartment had stirred so many strong memories for her, and how many of those memories were good. Really good.

"Yes! Oh, Jen was fun." Johnny stopped, and Bex realized his eyes had gotten shiny and he was looking out at the balcony. "Tough how she had to give up parts of what she loved so much the last several years of her career. But the silver lining is that she finally found time to devote to her writing."

"Her fanfic?" Sam's surprise was clear in the tone of her voice.

Now Johnny's smile was sly. "That, she did for fun. What no one knows, and I don't mind sharing out, is that a few weeks before Jen passed, she had a spec script optioned by UBC that was going into pilot development."

Bex sat up straight so fast, her little microphone tumbled off her neckline, and she had to hold it up. "What?"

Johnny crossed his legs and resettled the pleat in his trousers. "I think *I* only knew because I was the priest for this particular project of Jen's."

"The priest?" Bex asked.

He scrubbed his hand over his stubble, contemplative. "Sometimes when you're making a big change in your life, you find yourself confiding in someone who doesn't have a single horse in the race. Your priest. Like how you might talk to a coworker about being afraid your man's stepping out, or to your hairstylist about going back to school."

"That sounds like what Jen was to me," Sam said. "She was a good sounding board."

"Coulda been a therapist, I told her, but she said she had too many opinions for that. But with her script, I think she was keeping it under wraps with all of you in L.A. because it was with UBC, and she had her contract with Cineline, who's the competition. She didn't want anyone upset with her."

And she didn't want to mess up whatever writing relationship she had with Bette, Bex thought. "Do you know anything about the script? Genre? How far it went in development?"

"I don't. Not a bit. I imagine UBC has still got the option, but it would be with Jen's estate." Johnny folded his hands on his lap and looked from her to Sam. "Which just makes everything more of a damn shame. People should see their dreams live themselves out."

This new information was starting to feel heavy in Bex's heart.

"And you two talked about all of this on the last location shoot, is that right?"

Johnny folded his hands in his lap, solemn now. "We did. But if you remember, the weather was bad. Rain and storms, which riled up her migraines and pain in her arms and hands. She had her station set up with her ergonomic chair and footrest, and that special light she liked to use for headaches. I think a few crystals, too. She was throwing everything at it."

"I remember." Bex did.

"So I hung out in her corner between takes on the shooting days. She was having a hard time. Not just the migraines."

"Why else?" Sam asked.

"Well, my friend, because of you." His eyes were kind when he told Sam this. "She could tell you weren't happy, and you'd talked to her about leaving the show. She knew the sixth season would likely be the last, but she felt like you could decide to take off at any time."

"And that's my fault," Bex said. Sam shook her head, wiping away a tear. "No, it's okay. I don't mind saying. Sam and I were closer than close, as the whole world guessed. I willfully ignored, at the time, that there was an entirely very *extra* layer of are-they-or-aren't-they on top of the show's will-they-or-won't-they, because I just wanted to spend my time with her. It made it difficult for Sam. That week in Chicago, we were reaching a breaking point."

"Aaron isn't known for his sweet nothings, but the vibes, as they say, were pretty dark," Johnny said. "Tense. We finally wrapped, and the circus was packing in. This is the night Jen had her accident."

Bex stood and took a step closer to the balcony, letting her eyes roam over the pretty potted plants, the white fairy lights wound around the railing.

"Yeah," Johnny was saying behind her. "The cast took off quick, including you girls. Jen and I talked while the crew struck the set and packed up. Aaron was in a meeting with cinematography and the new editor and Josh. The muscle came in and loaded the equipment down the stairs and into a truck, and the crew left. I remember they asked us to go with them to this corner somewhere along East Fullerton, where a woman had a tamale stand. Jen and I were still deep in the life talk, having a good time, so we turned them down. Don't know what the boss men were talking about, because that door with the fancy glass was closed, but they finished up, and Aaron left with the cinematography and editing folks. Josh got out his camera and was taking pictures."

"He took a lot of pictures when we were on location," Sam said. "He never stopped fussing with the exterior stage set back in L.A."

Bex walked over to a small table she'd put her bag under. Johnny's recollection of who was left behind in the apartment, Bex was sure, was different from what was in the police report. She pulled out her notebook and flipped through it. "Johnny, remember when we had Georgie on the podcast?"

"I do."

Bex found the copy of the police report Georgie had talked about on the show. "She looked at the original investigation into Jen's passing. Their report says that Josh left with Aaron."

"No one ever reached out to me." Johnny sounded uncertain. "I did call Cineline to offer any assistance. I told them Jen ended up getting a terrible migraine and said she was going to lay down for a minute. I heard the podcast, but I couldn't say if she took any medication or not. She had a fold-out camping cot and her migraine light."

"You told Cineline?"

"That's right."

"But not the cops."

"Cops never contacted me. I did call them, too. I talked to someone at the station. When I did, I explained I was part of the cast and a friend of Jen's. They asked me if I could confirm she wasn't feeling well, and I did. I'd gone from the building to a meeting, so

I gave them the name of the person I met with to confirm my alibi. Not sure if that ever happened."

Bex looked at the part of the report where Georgie had a note about who left at what time. "Oh fuck."

"What is it?" Sam held her hand out, and Bex passed her the pages.

"The report says when the *cast* left and lists cast members, but it doesn't give each cast member an individual time. I don't know if the detectives who handled this investigation ever got Johnny's message, because they clearly didn't know Johnny was one of the last people to see Jen living."

"I think we have the same problem here." Sam tapped her finger on a line in the report. "This puts the people who were meeting with Aaron as all leaving at the same time."

"But aren't there individual interviews with those four?"

"Yes," Sam said. She flipped and read further. "Josh does, in fact, say in his interview that he left with Aaron's meeting group. He *doesn't* say he stayed behind and took pictures. Or that he knew Jen and you were there. When did you leave?" Sam asked Johnny.

"Not long after Aaron, since Jen wasn't feeling well. I offered to drive her back to her hotel, but she needed to pack up her station, and she thought she'd lay down for a few minutes, have some coffee, then pack. She didn't want me to stay and help."

"She wouldn't," Sam said. "Jen was meticulous about her things."

"So I left. I waved at Josh, and he nodded at me. I texted Jen about an hour later to make sure she didn't need anything, and I didn't hear back, so I thought she must have fallen asleep."

Sam was still flipping through. "None of this is in the report Georgie talked about on the podcast." She put it on her lap and looked from Bex to Johnny. "What you're telling us is that Josh Miller was the last person to see Jen alive."

"If you believe me," Johnny said. "Though he could've left

soon after me, not knowing Jen was resting in the other room, and not have seen her."

Amethyst stepped forward. "Let's pause here. I want to get in the clip and any comments you have about it. We can see where this conversation goes from there."

At first, Bex didn't understand what Amethyst meant. She felt electrified, her skin buzzing and tingling. They were getting close. The only thing she wanted to do was get closer, not play a fucking *clip*.

Jen was alone in the apartment after everyone left. That was how every account Bex had ever heard of her death began. *Jen was alone in the apartment. It was a terrible accident.*

But she hadn't been alone. Josh was there—Josh, who didn't get along with Jen, because he'd threatened Jen's friend Marilee, and he'd been sabotaging actors on the set of *Charles Salt* until Jen found out and turned him in. Josh, who'd made the vibrating bed into a trap and caught Bex and Sam inside it.

If Jen hadn't been alone in the apartment—if Josh was there with her—the implications would upend everything the police had reported as fact about Jen's supposedly accidental death.

"Breathe," Sam said, her voice close to Bex's ear.

When Bex turned and looked up, her hand resting on Sam's fuzzy sweater over her bicep, she found enough steadiness in Sam's blue eyes to give her the composure she needed.

Amethyst had set up the clip so it played for Sam, Bex, and Johnny on Cicely and Eleanor's television. It was the balcony scene at the end of the last episode of the fifth season. Bex watched herself and Sam—Henri and Cora—on the balcony that was less than ten feet away from where she stood now. Johnny, as Mike, was in the frame but standing in the apartment. Cora wore a huge T-shirt and a pair of sweatpants she'd found in the agency's closet, because in the episode she'd chased a suspect over catwalks in an abandoned factory, ruining her clothes. She had cuts on her forehead from the chase, and her hair was huge, curls going every direction, with a haze of frizz.

Bex knew exactly why the fans had voted for this episode.

"Thanks, you two." Mike rubs a hand over his face. "Thank you."

"Thank us by having the talk you need to have with your daughter," Cora says. "You both survived. You owe each other that much."

Mike nods and smiles, then turns away and disappears into the apartment. Cora watches him leave.

"How are you feeling now?" Henri asks, leaning against the railing. The wind is whipping Cora's hair around, and Henri's hair is loose around her shoulders, down from its customary ponytail.

"Better." Cora smiles at Henri and holds up a paper cup. "Thanks for the coffee."

Henri turns away to look out over the street. "You really scared me today. I've been a part of bomb defusals that were less tense than watching you climb fifty-year-old factory ladders in heels."

Cora smiles. "Compared to the Halloween party in a kindergarten classroom once the candy's been passed out, that was downright relaxing."

Henri doesn't laugh. "Don't do that."

"What?"

"Minimize what you did with a joke. Not just the danger, either. You were smart. You made a lot of intuitive, split-second decisions that seasoned agents in the field couldn't make. I know I give you a hard time, but I hope you know how much I admire you. Every day, for a lot of different reasons."

Henri steps closer, right into Cora's space, and meets her eyes. Her voice drops to a near whisper.

"I'm doing this job to learn to be half the detective you are, but I don't think I've done a good job of letting you know that I'm also here because you're the best . . . friend I've ever had."

"God, Henri." Cora blinks and looks away for a moment. She swipes away a tear with a little laugh. "You have to warn me before you get sentimental like that. Sentimentality is my kryptonite. You know that."

"I do. I used to think how sensitive you are would make you bad at this job. But you've shown me that investigative skills are learned. What you have is innate and a gift." Henri smiles and tucks a big curl behind Cora's ear. "However, if you're never in mortal danger again, that would be too soon."

Cora looks into Henri's eyes, but she doesn't laugh. "I never mean to get into trouble. You might be surprised to know that I've actually always been extremely good. But there's more to life than following the rules." Cora reaches up and quickly, tentatively, touches the lapel of Henri's jacket, and before Cora can drop her hand, Henri catches it.

Cora steps closer. Henri dips her head down. They look into each other's eyes, nose to nose, for a long time. And then Henri suddenly moves her cheek against Cora's, and Cora's lashes flutter down.

The camera moves to Henri's face. Her eyes are wide open as she gathers Cora into a hug. Slowly, the camera starts to pull back in a single, continuous shot, revealing Cora and Henri's arms wrapped around each other. It slides away over the balcony railing so the viewer can see Cora's and Henri's legs intertwined, and then farther still, back and back, until only their silhouettes remain.

The camera had been attached to a remote-controlled drone, something that had never been done before on *Craven's Daughter*. The scene faded to black when Cora and Henri were nothing but an indistinct shape against the brick side of the building, leaving the question of what happened next to hang in the air until the series resumed.

The season six opener hadn't answered that question. It started up weeks later, in the middle of a new case, leaving audiences wondering if they'd ever get an answer or a happy ending.

The apartment's television screen went dark. Bex looked at the balcony shining in the sun, so different from in the clip.

"The last line was meant to be delivered as wit," Sam said. "A little funny. I think the script has Cora tip her coffee to Henri, and they both lean against the railing and look out at the city." Sam was gazing at the balcony, too. "This was another one of those first takes that somehow got into the episode."

"And tell me," Johnny said, "how much of it was craft?"

"I think I'm doing a very good job of giving tired and injured," Bex said. "I can really feel Cora's bone-deep exhaustion." The back of her neck had gotten warm. "But possibly there is one of those organic, emotional intersections of the actors' feelings with the script that is motoring the power of that moment."

"Organic, huh?" Sam smiled. "That's one way to put it." She stood up and then held her hand out. "Come on. Let's go take a look around on the balcony."

Bex let Sam lead her the few steps outside. "Well," she said. "I can't believe I'm saying this, but it's nice out here."

Sam drew her to the railing. "It is. What is this?" Sam rubbed a soft leaf in one of the planters, turning and directing her question to Eleanor and Cicely. "Mint?"

"Lemon balm!" Eleanor called out.

"Lemon balm, say our lovely hosts. It smells amazing."

"Jen would have been into this," Johnny said. He'd joined

them. "Very dramatic, but with a redemption arc that brings in sunshine and flowers and old friends."

Bex let out a surprised laugh. "I think you may be right. You know what?" She put her hand on the railing. "I'm glad we came. I'm glad you're here with me, Sam. I'm glad we're out here and have reframed this difficult memory. Now, when I think about Jen, I'll think about her writing, and having a good priest, and also I'll think about lemon balm." Bex squeezed the railing.

Then screamed, just a little.

"Oh my god!" She must have squeezed too hard, because a piece of the railing had come away. "I'm so sorry! I broke it!"

Sam knelt down, and Bex backed up, then squealed again because the railing had come apart from top to bottom, where it met the deck of the balcony. "I *really* broke it."

Johnny had joined Sam to look. Sam pulled gently on the part that had come loose, then asked Johnny, "Do you see that?"

"I do. Might I ask our hosts to retrieve these plant baskets hanging from the railing?"

Eleanor rushed out and took the plants, so that the part of the railing Bex had wiggled free was bare. Then Bex saw it, too. "This whole part is a different shade from the rest of the wrought iron."

When Sam and Johnny moved the section of railing back and forth, a perfect rectangular piece pulled out. It was the full height of the railing and about two feet wide. Sam held it up and waved it around. "That's because it's not wrought iron." She tapped it against the deck. "It's plastic. Or resin, something sturdy. It's a patch."

"That's the part they fixed," Cicely said from the living room. She was frowning, but she looked confused, not angry. "You didn't break it. It's been like that."

"It's where she went through," Eleanor clarified. "Where they had to patch the railing up afterward."

"But that can't be," Bex said. "Georgie read in the police report that Jen stumbled and fell *over* the railing, not through it. Georgie made a point that this bothered her because Jen was relatively short, but she *must* have gone over it somehow, because the cops looked for a broken spot in the railing, both up here and on the street. Even loose bolts. You said they fixed it? Like, who?"

Cicely was still frowning. "I guess we don't know. When we bought the apartment from Cineline, we weren't told anything about the particulars of the accident, and as fans, we didn't want to know. We wanted to keep our memories to just thinking about Henri and Cora. But after a couple of years we noticed the patch because it weathered and faded. We assumed it was to fix where the railing broke in the accident, so we covered it with plants because it made us feel bad. It's part of why we're replacing the whole thing. Other than the fact it's dangerous."

Sam held the section of railing, running her fingers over the curlicues of the faux wrought iron. "I don't know that there's a super or landlord in the whole city of Chicago who would patch a railing with anything more elaborate than a piece of plywood and a hundred zip ties. This is perfect. If it hadn't faded, you would never know it wasn't part of the original hundred-year-old railing."

Every cell in Bex's body had gone numb. "Josh was the last one here."

"I've cut the mics," Amethyst said. "I already have it recorded that the police report is wrong according to Johnny's recollection of events. That's enough to pass on to the authorities from my end. Whatever else you guys decide to report, I'm leaving it off the official record."

"He said he wanted things to be perfect," Sam said. "Perfect replicas. On the last podcast, remember?"

Bex did remember.

She had only wanted to remember the sunshine and the lemon balm.

Brave Like Carrots

The lobby of United Broadcast Corporation West was a mid-century homage to the golden age of television, including several displays of original costumes and props from the studio's most beloved shows.

"Is that Daisie Shine?" Sam kept her voice low in the hushed lobby, but she took Bex's wrist and pulled her across the empty space to the huge glass case. Illuminated inside it was a four-foot-tall, orange-feathered puppet, the star of UBC's longest-running show for children, about an owl who couldn't stay awake at night and had to adapt to daytime living. "She was my favorite. I had Daisie Shine sheets, a Daisie Shine toy, the Owl House with the clock in it, and her best friend, Mouse Trax. He was remote-controlled and made little squeaks."

"I liked Carrots," Bex said, referring to the bold singing bunny who had an unlikely on-again, off-again situationship with Robert the Fox. Hyperaware of the press of Sam's fingers against her wrist, she took a deep breath and sang,

> What I know is how the fields call my name,
> how no flower looks the same,
> and every brook bubbles best when it rains!
> Everything that's beautiful is what makes me brave.
> Come with me, come with me, come with me!

She ended the song with Carrots's signature nose wiggle.

Sam had turned toward Bex during her performance, and now she stroked her thumb over Bex's wrist and said, "Marry me."

Bex's heart turned into a thousand butterflies, but she staved off the resulting blush with pure willpower. "This is sudden." She almost managed to disguise the tremble in her voice with bravado, but Sam kept sliding that thumb back and forth over where she must have felt what she was doing to Bex's pulse.

"I told you how weak your singing makes me." Sam's hair slid from behind her ear as she leaned closer, her smile beguiling. "Remember when I had that holiday housewarming party when I bought my house, and you sang 'Send in the Clowns' with that three-hundred-year-old composer—"

"Stephen *Sondheim*. My God, Sam, show some respect."

"—at the piano, and I cried so hard that I had to be brought back around by Emma Stone's special recipe for a lemon martini? And then I was tipsy because gin dissolves my boundaries, and I spent half an hour describing a dream I had about the first out queer president to Ewan McGregor?"

"I think a lot of people remember." It took everything Bex had not to yield to the pressure at her wrist and step closer, close enough so the only thing she could see was Sam Farmer smiling at her, talking about how great she was.

"That's what your singing does to me, Bex. Nothing bad, but also nothing reasonable."

"You're saying it makes you lose your cool." Bex tried to raise one eyebrow. Failed. She didn't know when her hand had drifted up, but her fingers were suddenly close to touching Sam's bare collarbone. She made herself curl them into a loose fist, which she rested against Sam's shoulder in a way that was definitely normal.

"I'm only cool around you when I'm flirting or trying not to," Sam said. "Every other way around you is very unprocessed."

Bex's fingers had abandoned their fist in favor of smoothing over three inches of Sam's bare shoulder. *All* of Sam's shoulder was bare. She'd worn a nothing scrap of black patent leather that was ostensibly a strapless top, with high-waisted blue-and-white houndstooth trousers. Her shoulder was polished and smooth and incredibly soft.

"I never found it difficult before you to ask a woman out *or* flirt with her," Sam said. "That's always been easy, the easiest thing. But nothing I've ever done with you has been easy, Bexley."

"Sam." Bex couldn't hear over the banging of her heart.

Amethyst had carefully edited the last episode. Not wanting to interfere with any official investigation into Jen's death, she'd kept the focus on the revelations about Jen's writing career, leaving out the information about who had remained in the apartment and who left at what time on the night of Jen's death, as well as Sam's commentary about the railing.

With Georgie's help, Sam, Bex, and Johnny had been connected with someone at the Chicago Police Department and spoken with her about what they'd discovered, but the detective had been cautious and could only promise she would pull the original report and take a look at it.

Cicely and Eleanor had agreed to hold off on their balcony renovation for the time being.

However, what *had* been revealed in the episode was enough to lift public interest in Sam and Bex and *Craven's Daughter* to what might be described as a fever pitch. Bex had been unable to sleep and was texting Sam at every conceivable pretext. Chicago had busted everything open, and Bex couldn't stop remembering parts of their friendship, small moments, and crying, or laughing, or sometimes letting herself think what would have happened if, in that moment on the balcony at the end of season five, Bex had threaded her fingers through Sam's beautiful hair and kissed her.

Bex had not been as brave as Carrots. Or even as brave as she thought of herself.

Enough.

"Are you seeing anybody?" she blurted. The question came

out exasperated—Bex *was* exasperated, with herself, for torturing herself for such an extended period of time—and it also came out much too loud, loud enough that the young person at the reception desk who'd given them name tags and called upstairs to announce their arrival looked up with wide eyes.

Sam's exhale whistled out of her. "Bexley."

"Just—yes or no," she said in the quietest voice she could manage. "I need to know. If you have someone."

"No." Sam shook her head, the skin over her sternum blooming with pink blotches. "I'm not seeing anyone. I don't have anyone. I hope that was obvious."

"I'm not either," Bex said. Maybe unnecessarily, but she said it anyway, and she was glad, because it earned her one of Sam's slow smiles—its own kind of torture.

"Good," Sam said.

"Good," Bex repeated.

They were smiling at each other like fools when someone called their names.

"Sam! Bex!" Saanvi Kaur made her way across the terrazzo floors of the lobby, her arms open wide. Saanvi had enjoyed a meteoric rise to the C-Suite at UBC and had a stellar reputation for a studio exec. "Do you embrace?" Her Oxbridge accent clipped her speech, but her smile and eyes were warm. "You must." She hugged them both, then turned around to the person at the reception desk. "They don't have teas. Or a drink. Maddy, did you offer them drinks? They are standing here in the middle of the lobby like they were left behind by their tour guide."

"She offered us drinks," Sam said. "And snacks. And use of the sofa in your outer office. We were taking in the displays."

"I'm glad." Saanvi nodded at Maddy, who looked grateful to be off the hook and went back to her computer. "Let's go to my office. Do you like white wine? I just opened a chardonnay."

They followed Saanvi through a series of interconnected and beautifully decorated lobbies until they arrived at her open door.

Her office was a study in the heyday of California modern, with glass and wood finishes setting off an abundance of natural light. She led them to a circular sofa upholstered in creamy leather and poured them wine in glasses so delicate Bex hoped the rim of hers wouldn't break off in her mouth.

"So." Saanvi leaned back with her glass. "I have been gobbling up your podcast the absolute second it drops. It's either the most smashing dramatic performance I've ever witnessed or the two of you are on one hell of a ride."

"The latter," Bex said. "So much the latter."

Saanvi laughed. "I miss my scandal era. The last twenty years have been so dull. My daughter is expecting my first grandchild, and I worry I won't have enough juicy things to tell them on my knee. How can I help you with this delectable mess?"

After going to the police, Bex and Sam had spoken with Toni, Jen's mom. As the executor of Jen's estate, she'd received a series of payments related to Jen's work for UBC, but she hadn't understood that they were for something different from the residuals, account settlements, and small-potatoes employment insurance payments that had come through from a variety of studios Jen had done work for over the years.

With Toni's blessing, Bex and Sam had decided to talk to Saanvi and confirm any details they could get about Jen's script with UBC. What they'd found out in Chicago certainly put Josh in a suspicious position in Jen's death, but they simply didn't know enough to sort out the dynamics between Jen and Josh, Aaron, and Bette in a way that would point to a clear motive for murder for any of the three.

"We wanted to learn more about what Jen had in development with UBC," Bex said. "I believe her estate sent through paperwork?"

"Yes." Saanvi waved her hand. "Everything is proper. I am very sorry for your loss. At the time of the accident, I was still at UBC East in New York. When things like this happen, it's a chance for all of us to review our safety protocols."

"Thank you. I really appreciate you saying that." Sam let out a long breath and leaned forward. "A lot of things came up when we were recording the last episode of the podcast that didn't make it into the recording, but they mean that we want to be as careful as possible going forward."

Saanvi inclined her head to indicate her understanding.

"First, we'd like to check our facts and officially confirm with UBC that Jen did write a pilot that was picked up for development. And second—this is really sensitive, but we wondered if you knew or had records to indicate whether Jen had any other writing credits. Or had mentioned writing anything she didn't get credit for."

"You mean, was she carrying Bette Holloway and secretly writing *Craven's Daughter*?"

Bex coughed over a swallow of wine. "Um. Yes. That."

Saanvi set her empty glass carefully on the table in front of her. "You have to understand that if we think we can make money, we'll buy scripts and treatments from almost anyone. I just bought something written by a nineteen-year-old who went to Burning Man with one of my assistants that is the most ridiculous flaming poo bag I have ever paid six figures for, but my assistant is right that it will likely dominate for enough time on the streamers that I get my investment back twentyfold, at least. But Jen's script was special in a way you rarely see." She sat back and crossed her legs, thinking for a moment before she continued. "At first, she claimed she'd honed her craft writing fanfiction. I wasn't convinced. There was a way her script had of finding the one moment in all of the action that made something particularly romantic. I knew that Jen worked on *Craven*. I've been around a long time. Sometimes job titles don't fully describe what a person is really doing in their role." She raised an eyebrow. "So I asked her point blank."

"And she told you she was writing for the show," Bex said.

"She told me, and she confirmed when I asked directly that Aaron knew of this arrangement."

Bex blinked, momentarily speechless. Aaron *knew* Bette wasn't writing *Craven's Daughter*?

"Whoa." Sam's eyebrows met her hairline. "Nepotism is a hell of a drug."

Saanvi laughed and draped her arm along the back of the sofa. "People use the tools they have to solve the problem of their hurt. It may not seem so, but Aaron had a lot of grief around blowing up his marriage to Bette's mother. He loved her, and he loves Bette. A better man would have gone to therapy. Aaron pulled strings, called in favors, and kept secrets. I'm not excusing it. It's simply all he's bothered to learn how to do. According to Jen, Aaron asked her to help Bette. Jen had given Aaron treatments and scripts to look at more than once. He knew she was talented. Who knows? Maybe that's why he brought her onto *Craven* even though Josh was there and there was bad blood between them."

"This is a mess," Bex said. "Shakespearean-level messy. End of Act Two, ghosts everywhere, father-daughter-showdown messy."

"Like a performance of *Lear* where it rains on the stage," Sam said, but she sounded distracted.

"What is it?" Bex asked.

Sam took a sip of wine. "*Craven's Daughter* was doing what Aaron needed it to do. It was a hit. It was winning awards. Aaron had a clear path to leaving a legacy, and he was giving his stepdaughter a chance at a big career in Hollywood. He wouldn't want any of that to be disrupted by a revelation that would ruin Bette's career and compromise his unblemished record with *Craven's Daughter*. That means he has motive, and it means he set Bette up to have motive. Aaron was there in Chicago. Whatever happened to Jen that night, he or Bette could have been responsible. At the very least, they contributed to the network's minimizing Jen's death, which benefited them both because it kept the wheels of the show running on the tracks through one more season."

"That's chilling," Bex said. "But I can't disagree with the reasoning."

"Johnny said Josh would have been the last person to see Jen alive, as far as he could know. Josh hadn't stopped his sabotage, if sabotage is what his messing with the balcony railing was. We know he's abusive. Aaron's focus on Bette's career made it vital for Jen's ghostwriting to be a secret."

Bex picked up the thread of Sam's thought. "Did Josh know? Was Aaron after Josh? Was Josh blackmailing Aaron? Did Jen get caught in the middle? Or was Josh jealous of the opportunity Aaron was giving Jen? We know that Josh hated Jen. We know she stalled his career with her reports and order of protection. But—"

"I'm trying to figure out how it's simple," Sam interrupted. "Josh evidently did replace part of the railing, but Jen could have still gone through it without his interference. In other words, it *could* be that Jen was alone when she fell, and it just so happens that Josh fixed something that he broke at a different time, in the course of getting materials for our set."

Saanvi held both her hands up, smiling. "You're having a conversation that I am delighted to be privy to, but it's one my lawyer would kick you right out of my office for. I should probably ask if there is anything else I can help you with."

"I don't know." Bex regretted the wine, which had soured her stomach. "I think we need to talk to Georgie's contact with the police again and let them know the general shape of this. At least that Jen was writing for Bette without credit, and Aaron knew."

Saanvi rose to her feet. "Use my office as long as you wish." Before she left, she squeezed them both on the shoulders. "It's nice to remember there are really good people in this town. I'd love to get dinner with the two of you once everything is settled down."

With that, she left. The door snicked closed behind her.

"I hate this." Bex plucked at her waistband. In deference to meeting a network executive, she'd worn real pants, what she mentally called *hard pants*, and it was a decision she regretted. "I hate that I was living a green-screen version of my life on that set, and now I'm looking at the final cut, and there are monsters and dragons and evil forests everywhere that were real to everyone else but me."

Sam let go of the pose she'd been sitting in for the meeting to starfish herself on the low sofa, her hair staticky against the leather. "*I hate that I was running around asking everyone what the hell was going on, and those assholes told me less than they told your kid sisters.*"

"I should've seen more. I talked to Jen almost every day. I thought of her as a close friend, but I didn't know she was a writer at all? That she'd shown treatments and scripts to someone like Aaron? That this was her dream? What kind of friend was I?"

"She *was* your friend. She was my friend, too. If Jen didn't want us, or her mom, to know about that part of her life, I'm inclined to think the reason has something to do with agreements she was making with people who had huge stakes in her discretion." Sam turned her body toward Bex. On this sofa, in this light, in her outfit, she looked like a *Vogue* cover. "Before you launch yourself into an anxious spiral about everything you failed to see, Bexley, remember that you didn't call the shots on that set. We wanted to make it right, and they told us to stay in our lane. What we did was the best we could do at the time."

"That is probably a healthy perspective." Bex took a breath in through her nose and pressed her index fingers to the corners of her eyes, then shook it out all over, like she was getting ready to go onstage. "You know what I want?"

"I don't. At all. Please tell me so I can make it happen."

That made her smile. "I want to talk to Aaron. I'd rather not talk to Niels if we can avoid it, but I want us to sit down with Aaron Gorman and see if we can't get him to level with us, once and for all."

"What about Josh?" When Sam stood up, her pants sluiced down her legs in a way that was a little hypnotizing.

"I think we have to leave Josh to whatever Georgie's detective friend decides to look into, unless something changes." Bex stood and straightened herself to her full five-feet-plus-four-to-six-inches-of-hair, and then, without letting herself think about it, she put her arm around Sam's waist. Sam laid her hand over Bex's where it curled around the soft wool of her waistband and held it in place.

Easy.

As they left the office, Sam's gaze scanned the whole room one last time. "I think I could really get into an office like this."

"I don't doubt it." Bex waved at Maddy, the receptionist, on their way across the lobby. "You've always had very strong executive energy."

"Black and oily?" Sam laughed.

"No, gold and tentacle-y, reaching out, gathering in." Bex made a beckoning motion with her free arm. "Inviting."

"I will put octopi on my stationery."

"Don't think small," Bex said, as firm as she ever got. "Put a thirty-foot-tall golden octopus on the front of your building right beneath your name."

Sam smiled, not at Bex, but at the world.

Bex liked that.

Literary Analysis

Vic sat shoeless in one of the poolside chaises, her bare legs crossed and disappearing beneath the hem of an oversized Irish fisherman's sweater. She read aloud from the screen of her phone.

"You're nothing! Nothing! Less than nothing. You weren't here when the old man needed to be propped up after a bender and had to take another case to pay the bills. You weren't here when he had his first heart attack."

Jared brought his fists down on the desk, the brass lamp crashing over the edge, making Cora jump. If she had thought that tracking down this man, her half brother, was a good idea before, she'd like to have a word with past Cora. Unlike her, Jared looked like their father, the pale hair brushed back over his head, the broad shoulders, too much color in his face, but she wondered if her dad had a temper like this.

Her mom could have never survived a temper like this. She'd barely survived Cora's stepdad.

"I wasn't around." Cora tried to keep her voice firm but deescalating. Like the time Aiden Kowalski had climbed to the top of the swings with a nap blanket tied around his shoulders like a cape the day he wore his Superman T-shirt. "I didn't even know there was someone to be around for. You had to deal with a lot."

"You don't know the half of it." Jared wiped his mouth with the back of his hand and started pacing back and forth. "You don't know about his funks when he couldn't solve a case. You don't know about the money trouble. Who rescued him from the bill collectors? Wasn't you. You especially don't know about what he was like when he decided he'd lost the love of his life and his little girl. And what he was like, Cora? Stupid. He was stupid. Because your mom wasn't worth giving up on the relationships that were actually in his life. The people"—with this, Jared pounded on his chest with a fist, making Cora wince—"who were always sticking around for him."

"Jared."

"No. You ruined him. You and your stuck-up fucking mom. We might've been able to do something, we were supposed to do something. That sign"—Jared pointed at the glass in the door painted with CRAVEN INVESTIGATIONS—"was supposed to say AND SON. And Son! That's what. And then you're back here, 'cause he gave it to YOU. You find me. What? You wanted a pretty reunion? Fuck you. Suck on an exhaust pipe."

Jared kicked over the metal chair in front of the desk, sending it toward Cora's legs, then slammed open the door and started out. But before he left, he doubled back, looked at the glass in the door, and smashed his fist through it. Cora squeezed her eyes shut, her hand gripped around the phone in her pocket where she had pre-dialed 911. On her brother.

She hadn't expected a reunion, but she'd expected to share something with him. Given their history.

She didn't let herself cry.

She picked up the chair and the lamp.

She got a broom, and a mop and bucket, and cleaned up the glass, and the blood. She taped a piece of cardboard over the hole. And then, for a long time, she sat behind her dad's desk—so long, actually, it got dark.

She was so lost in her thoughts, and in her stupid, stupid grief, she didn't hear when Henri came in.

"Cora?"

Henri was in her extremely cool jeans, her tough girl jeans, and a leather jacket. A tough girl leather jacket. Cora would never be a tough girl. She'd thought she was tough, taking on Craven Investigations, but she wasn't nearly as tough as she believed. It was hard to do something better with her dad's crummy business. Jared was impossible. All she had run into since she started was secrets and lies.

"I really was too unsophisticated to take this on, wasn't I?" Cora still didn't let herself cry, but she wanted to.

Henri sat down in the metal chair. "Only someone who really cared would have taken this on. I haven't ever cared as much about anything as you do about making this work and helping people who need you. Don't tear yourself down for what makes you the very best person I know."

Cora hardly ever got so many sentences in a row out of Henri Shannon.

And Henri never lied. Cora knew she had secrets, but she didn't lie.

"Besides, kindergarten teachers are a lot tougher than I thought." Henri stood up. "You wanna go downstairs and take a ride on my motorcycle?"

Cora started to laugh and say no, but then what? She would get her purple backpack out of the closet, walk to the El station, and go home and microwave a pot pie and feed the hamster?

She was tough. She could be tough.

"Yes, I do," Cora said, and loved that Henri looked surprised. Loved it even more when she blushed. She especially loved sitting on the back of Henri's bike, her arms wrapped around Henri's middle, watching the streets whip by in a blur.

She promised herself, right then, she wouldn't get cynical. And she would make all of this her own.

Vic lowered her phone to her lap. Frankie sat beside her, ramrod straight and vibrating with energy in her head-to-toe black with black boots. She was sipping a vegan date shake from the shake shack where she liked to stop on her way home from work. Snack wrappers, papers, cell phones, and a tangle of charging cables littered the small table between her and Vic.

This was how Bex and Sam had found them after receiving an urgent summons by text. Bex had been staring at a display of dragon fruit at Erewhon and thinking—like she had for the past couple of days since their meeting with Saanvi—about Sam. But Frankie's message had alarmed her, so she'd hastily put back the three things she'd managed to gather into her grocery basket between daydreaming, and by the time she was parked at home, she could see Sam wearing her favorite green ball cap and walking along the trail behind Bex's backyard that she always took from her house ten minutes away.

Or, at least, she used to. And now she was again.

And here Sam was, sitting on one of the pool chaises, watching Bex pace around while Vic read Jen's story, which was not an emergency after all, but which Bex was trying very hard to attend to, except it was difficult, because Sam was watching her.

She had been right to avoid feeling like this. Women in their thirties shouldn't have to deal with this feeling. The songs she'd been singing in the shower lately were completely embarrassing.

"Can you even get your head around this fic?" Vic asked. "It's all here. Everything. I can't believe it's been online where anyone could find it—that Jen was, in fact, the fandom's Big Name Fan, so *thousands* of people were reading this—but no one but us insiders could have known what they were looking at, and even *we* didn't know until we started digging around, discovering where all the bodies are buried. Knowledge is power, right?"

"The best, most killing part is the title," Frankie said. "It's called, 'I Can See Now Why You Didn't Consider Yourself Father Material.' Like—" Frankie made an exploding bomb with her hands with the accompanying sound effect.

"Cora's first line. From the pilot." Sam said this from behind sunglasses, hiding her expression. She patted the spot by her hip. "Bexley, sit. The pacing is driving me up the wall. It's so fast and darting. Like one of those scary chihuahuas guarding a front porch."

"In a minute." Bex pointed at her sister. "Vic."

"What?"

"I don't get it. I don't get what you and Frankie are talking about. I think you're trying to say there is some symbolism here? About fathers, maybe? But the motorcycle ride at the end throws me off."

Vic sighed. "It's shocking to me sometimes that you're in the arts. I just came off a week of back-to-back-to-back labs, which were mostly math and a lot of revolting growth on agar, and when Frankie made me read this, my heart literally beat out of my chest with all of the repressed feelings Jen got in here. I went straight to the airport and bought a ticket."

"Business-class ticket," Bex said. "Did your urgency require more leg room and meal service, or . . . ?"

Vic stuck out her tongue.

"You guys can break this down for me and Bex without being mean," Sam said. "This story is different from Jen's other ones. Very—"

"*Real*," Vic interrupted. "*So* real. *So* emotional. She wasn't wrapping things up in layers here. This is raw. That's what I see. Raw and bald." Vic wiggled her hands in front of her. "This fic is working shit out. It's giving me self-care, I really feel that."

"If you don't mind, could you walk me through it like you are the English teacher you clearly think I didn't have?" Bex reached out a hand to Frankie. "And give me some of your date shake. You always get the large and then leave half of it melting in the cup on the counter like you can't learn."

"Fine." Vic sighed again in melodramatic exasperation. "The brother, Jared, is Josh. The way he looks, and how he talks, and his relationship to the office, which is the same as the office on the show. He acts like it belongs to him. He should have inherited it."

"Josh doesn't act like other designers," Frankie broke in. "He was always there on *Craven*'s set. Fussing with it, barging in on other people's jobs, constantly talking to Aaron like he was some kind of co-director. Like he owned the place." She handed Bex the date shake.

"Right." Vic held up her phone. "And this Jared, in the story, has the same kind of ownership and *thought* he was close to Joe Craven, his father, who's supposed to be his business partner, but that didn't work out. They weren't as close as Jared believed they were. And here in the story, he's breaking his father's office, but it's someone who looks just like Josh breaking his own set! And then we have Cora cleaning it up. Which is why I'm pretty sure Cora is an author insert."

"Jen, she means," Frankie said. "This time, in this story, Cora is *Jen*, not you. This scene describes Josh losing his shit at *Jen* over her getting stuff he doesn't think she deserves. Not the makeup job, probably. The writing job."

Sam slid her sunglasses into her hair. "So we're thinking the Joe Craven in this story has got to be Aaron."

"'I can see now why you didn't consider yourself father material,'" Vic said, quoting the line from the pilot. "It's giving disappointment, anger, retrospection. Remember, *Aaron* wrote that line. The pilot was his, and he'd disappointed a lot of people, professionally and personally."

"Bette and her mom," Frankie said. "Aaron failed as a father to Bette. He let her down, even though Bette said he made a big deal about wanting to do a good job. Like Vic said, it was Aaron who wrote the pilot. He's haunted by not turning out to be father material. He's calling himself out. He's projecting. He gave the show to Bette to write, gave her *Craven's Daughter*"—Frankie emphasized the show's title—"just like Joe gave Craven Investigations to Cora to make up for what he did to Cora and her mom."

"But Josh didn't want Aaron to share," Vic said, "same as Jared didn't want Joe to share. Josh took this out on everyone—remember the sugar glass? But mostly he took it out on Jen. Jared in the story takes it out on Cora, who is Jen. And Jared and Cora are half brother and sister to represent that Aaron cheated on Bette's mom with Josh's girlfriend."

"This is getting very Greek," Sam said.

"*Charles Salt.*" Bex took a long drink of the date shake. "Their argument on that set nearly shut the show down. Josh's career didn't recover until Aaron hired him for *Craven's Daughter*, so it makes sense that Josh would have hoped *Craven's Daughter* would be a successful fail-up."

"But Jen was hopeful, too," Vic said, bouncing a little. "Like, it's not Cora's fault that right when she managed to track down her dad, it was to find out he was dead, but he'd left her the agency. She didn't want the agency. She wanted a dad. Instead, she's got this new work to do, and she never expected it, but it's exciting. She likes the work. She's good at it."

"Jen had always been an FX artist who aspired to big things," Sam said. "Aaron gave her this job in makeup, yeah, but he also up and handed her his show to write. It must've been scary but amazing. But terrible."

"I wish Jen hadn't gone along with it," Bex said. "Writing for no credit and no pay! It's the worst."

Frankie shook her head. "Let's not. Jen was a grown-ass woman making her own decisions. In this story, she gets on the motorcycle. There are rewards no one can take from her, and she can go somewhere else and get what she wants and needs. That's what she did in the end. She engineered her own escape, in the sense that Jen was pursuing her interest in writing and pivoting to a new career."

"I think it's Josh who's more interesting here," Vic said. "Josh wanted to be Aaron's right-hand man. He wanted acknowledgment for his hard work, and to finally get the rewards he was owed for his loyalty. Instead, Jen got those things for herself, which he could not accept."

"The part I hate," Sam said contemplatively, "is the violence. If we really are tossing ourselves down this rabbit hole headfirst and reading this story as having a one-to-one relationship with reality."

"Yes. I think we have to pay close attention to this violence," Frankie said. "He shouts and storms around and destroys the office. We see him breaking the glass. Yelling. Calling Cora names and scaring her. And the story starts in the middle of this abuse. It's implied there was more of it the reader didn't see. Blood. Cora has to clean up with a mop and a broom, and she sits in the dark feeling traumatized for a long time. She doesn't tell Henri what happened. There is no one she can tell. She can only go after what *she* wants."

"If Josh anticipated that good things would come to him from working with Aaron again," Sam said, "then he would have a lot of complex feelings about what Jen was getting."

"Passed over for writing credits?" Bex asked. "Exploited by Aaron and Bette?"

"Sure, but ghostwriting for Bette also put Jen in a special relationship with Aaron. It put her on the inside, sharing a secret with them, helping Bette, who was important to Aaron. Josh perceived Jen as someone who had betrayed him. He wouldn't have thought Jen deserved all that access."

"Maybe," Bex said, unconvinced.

"Well, another angle to consider," Sam said after a moment, "is that there's a common thread to all of the stories about Josh. He was quick to work with Aaron again. He respects him. As soon as he was threatened, he went straight to Niels, and as long as Niels was right there, he was on his best behavior, even complimenting Kim Ryerson, who Bex and I had witnessed him yelling at during Chaz's party. Luciana has a lot of power in this town, and I'd like to think I wield a decent amount myself, but Josh had no problem dressing the two of us down together."

"Women, you mean," Frankie said. "His worst behavior is toward women. Marilee Plungkhen, Jen, Kim, and any incidental woman who gets in his way. But he's deferential to men." Frankie scrubbed her hand through her messy curls. "Like, it's so boring and ordinary, you know? Misogyny, I mean. It's the lowest and easiest path to take in a patriarchal society other than racism. Couldn't he be an *interesting* literary character?"

Bex started trying to formulate a response, then realized she'd run out of steam. She sat down next to Sam, put her hand on Sam's lap palm up, and Sam, thank God, took her hand between both of hers. Bex ignored the way her sisters stared. "It's interesting to think about the story as expressing some of these emotional dynamics between Josh, Aaron, and Jen," she said slowly. "But I'm not sure how seriously to take it. Everybody's seen Josh yell, but I never saw him break anything."

"He put real glass in a breakaway window knowing we were going to be crawling around on the ground," Sam said.

"And he sabotaged the bed." Bex thought about that. "We could've been hurt."

"I don't even like to think about Josh replacing part of the balcony railing." Vic wound a scrunchie she'd had on her wrist around her fingers. "Because what am I supposed to imagine, that he pushed Jen through it, or something like that, then covered it up? He was very hard to deal with, but he once helped me with a diorama I had to make for school. I got an A-plus."

"I have a theory about Josh," Frankie said. "Not so much a theory, actually, because I already acted on it, but you can't be mad, because I haven't had a chance to tell any of you yet."

"What?" Vic turned to her. "You didn't even tell me. Why? I paid for Internet service on the flight so we could message. Where are my messages?"

"I had to check some things. Then I called this emergency meeting." Frankie took a deep breath. "You know how Bex had nepotized me into a six-week internship on the *Craven's Daughter* set when I was taking that class on lighting design at college?"

"Nepotized," Vic said. "That is so good. Like getting deputized, except it's unearned privileges."

Frankie rubbed her palms over her thighs. One of her knees was bouncing in a way that reminded Bex of what she'd been like during the internship—how focused and driven.

"I remember I thought it was strange that Josh had changed the railing," Frankie said. "Before, the railing was just straight-up-and-down bars. Like a painted wooden handrail all around, and the other part was black spindles. But he'd replaced it with this much fancier railing. A lot of what Josh did was hard to understand, but this was above and beyond. I asked a couple people about it who didn't know what I meant. For Vic and me, the set was like our house. We *knew* it. I hated Josh changing that railing out." Frankie hitched in a breath. "I don't know why I hated it, but I did. Then you told me about the cutaway piece of railing that was patched in Chicago, and how it was plastic. The thing is, the wrought-iron-looking railing on set is made from a plastic resin. I checked the episodes in season six to make sure I remembered right. I compared them to the pictures you took in Chicago. It looked like the same railing to me. So this morning, I went back to Stage 46."

Bex's vision grayed at the edges. What Frankie was about to say felt palpably dangerous, ringing through her body like a phone call Bex wasn't sure she wanted to pick up.

"That was reckless," Vic said.

"I didn't go alone. I took Juan Ramon with me." Juan was a senior stage manager for Cineline. He was responsible for the larger challenges and maintenance tasks associated with having multiple sets on the same facility at any given time. "The balcony set is on a cart. It's been pushed in the corner because the stage hasn't been dressed for the reunion yet. Right away, we could see that the railing matches the railing in season six, but not the railing in season five. Juan stepped onto the balcony and took a lot of pictures and looked close at every part of the railing. It actually took some time, but he found it."

"What?" Sam croaked out the question.

"A piece that was patched in. The same size and shape as the one that was missing and replaced with the fake on the balcony in Chicago. But this piece, on Stage 46, is wrought iron. *Real* wrought iron." Frankie was rubbing her thumb over and over her wrist. Bex's heart broke for her, for the little girl who loved the excitement of making TV, and the one who loved Jen, and the one who had only gotten to enjoy a little bit of charmed life between tragedies.

"Good goddamn," Sam said. "You're saying Josh took evidence

from what happened in Chicago and—and built it into the set? Why would he do that?"

"There's no reason to assume it was evidence," Bex said. "We have to stick to what we know. All we know is there was a piece cut from the Chicago railing, and it was patched with a cast-resin patch that not even the police noticed was there until years later, when it had faded from the sun. Josh is the only logical person who had the skills and access to do that. We know he redid the replica balcony's railing after that trip to Chicago. But now we *also* know he took the railing piece he cut from the balcony in Chicago to L.A., made a new railing for the set to match Chicago's, and inserted the wrought-iron piece. Josh was a perfectionist. Wanting an accurate, authentic railing *is* his style. So say he took it, cast it, and patched it so he wouldn't get called out for destroying property. Then he used it to make the set in L.A. It could be that he just liked having that real bit of wrought-iron balcony there as an homage or as proof of his skills. I'm describing vandalism, at most."

"I don't think so," Frankie interrupted. "Like, for real, I don't know, but I don't think so."

"Because the other possibility is that he was hiding evidence of a crime or an accident he witnessed," Sam said. "He pushed, or Jen fell accidentally through the railing, and he covered it up. Maybe he covered it up because he was the only one there and didn't want the heat."

"Or maybe he covered up Aaron's crime." Bex squeezed Sam's hand as the possibility came to life in her mind. "A crime Aaron committed for his own reasons, or committed for Bette because Jen was going to come forward. If he covered up something, then Aaron owes him."

Frankie shook her head like she didn't want to think about it. "Juan took pictures and roped off the balcony and locked the whole stage down. Probably he has to talk to studio lawyers? Execs? I told him that you guys had been talking to someone at Chicago PD, but he didn't say very much after we found the patch."

"That means we don't have a lot of time if we're going to figure out some of the truth for ourselves." Sam stood up. "I'm sure there's a hundred different reasons that explain what you and Juan found, but most of them aren't pretty. And, look, we all know firsthand what the studio did when they were faced with what happened to Jen. They covered their asses, first and foremost. Nobody's priority was to get to the bottom of anything or to maintain transparency or, you know, ensure the police's investigation covered all the bases so that people could be safe on that soundstage. Honestly, it may already be too late. There could be a truck headed to an incinerator right now with a Niels Shaughnessy bobblehead on the antenna."

"What do you want to do?" Bex asked.

"Aaron's in town. You said you wanted to talk to him. He's not returning our calls, but he always stays at Chateau Marmont like he's a docent of old Hollywood. I'll drive."

Bex stood up, too, but before she could follow Sam, she went to Frankie and hugged her. Then Vic hugged both of them, and Sam wrapped her arms around them all.

Josh had underestimated Jen, and everyone had underestimated Bex and Sam.

But just like the old *Craven's Daughter* set, nothing ever really died or was thrown away in this town.

All the stories were right here, waiting for their light.

She Kissed How She Listened

"**I** suppose you want a drink." Aaron scowled at Bex and Sam where they sat on the hard, low sofa in his suite at the Chateau Marmont. He'd finally called after Sam texted they were in his hotel's Mission-style lobby, and a fan was filming them with his phone who said he'd seen Aaron in the restaurant earlier, and so was narrating his video with rhapsodic speculation about the series finale.

Aaron's call consisted of him barking his room number and hanging up.

"I'll have a Coke," Bex said. "With some ice."

"With some ice," Aaron muttered, tonging ice rather aggressively into a glass. "Sam?"

"I'll have one of those Perriers on the bar. You can just hand it to me before you combust from hospitality."

Aaron huffed and grabbed the green bottle, shoved the beverages at them, and collapsed on the matching sofa across from them. He pulled his phone out of one of the pockets of his cargo shorts and tapped at it. "Out with it. I have an appointment for an IV vitamin drip in an hour."

Bex decided to be the one to dive in. "Has Bette talked to you about what Vic discussed with her at Chaz's party?"

Aaron kept poking at his phone and didn't answer. Bex lifted her glass to her mouth, aware of the soft sound of bubbles popping in her drink as Sam shifted in search of a comfortable position on the sturdy sofa. The suite was spacious, appointed with seating clusters that gave its occupants a clear vantage of the gorgeous grounds through charming mullioned windows. The French doors were open, and enough of a breeze came through to ruffle Sam's hair.

Bex heard a gentle beep from behind the closed door of one of the adjacent bedrooms. Aaron looked up from his phone as the door opened.

Bette stood on the other side of it.

"I have talked to him about it, yes, Bex." Bette slid a laptop computer into a sleek crossbody bag. She sat down next to Aaron and held out an orange bottle to him. "You didn't take your blood pressure medication again." She rattled the bottle and looked from Bex to Sam. "It's the silent killer. But, to be clear, *I'm* not the silent killer."

Aaron grabbed the bottle from Bette. He fished his meds out of the bottle, washing them down with a juice that had been on the coffee table. "Looks like she can answer your questions." He finished off the juice and leaned back.

Bex considered Aaron and Bette. They were easy with each other. Bette had watched Aaron carefully as he took his medication, and the exasperation and worry in her voice when she told him he'd forgotten was real. Bex thought about what Sam had said about how they'd behaved at the party—not like estranged family members but like father and daughter.

"We've heard from more than one credible person that Jen was, at a minimum, your co-writer and likely a lead writer on much of *Craven's Daughter*," Bex said. "In fact, from what we're being told, it was an arrangement *you* made, Aaron. Want to tell us about that?"

"You know what? Fine. Fine." He spun his battered Rolex in a circle around his wrist. "*Charles Salt* was a blue-ribbon shitshow," he said. "People were hurt. Jen was right to make the report she did. Marilee"—Aaron pulled his big hand over his gray and ginger curls, and Bette's jaw clenched—"Marilee is a good person who got stuck in the middle of a bad relationship with Josh and my knack for self-sabotage, and she was still bringing her best to every day of that shoot. Jen and Marilee were close. You know what Jen was like."

Aaron looked from one to the other of them, his face ruddy against his pale and wiry eyebrows. Bex couldn't speak to his early career, but by the time this man became Bex and Sam's showrunner, he had not been brilliant, nor had he been easy to deal with. He was inconsistent, paranoid, small-minded, and difficult. But there were times, now and then, when the work would break through to him, and Bex would catch a glimpse of what he must have been like once. What he could have been like.

She saw that Aaron now.

"Josh lost his goddamn mind when he found out about me and Marilee, and nearly lost his career. That was fair. I lost my family having that affair with Marilee, and that was fair, too. Jen was there for Marilee, even when people who didn't know the whole story openly froze her out for being a snitch and hard to work with. Which she wasn't. She was just the only professional on a set that had become a free-for-all."

Bex was sure her face had traveled through at least twelve different expressions of shock. Sam had frozen in the act of twisting off the cap of her mineral water.

"Jesus, Aaron, you're a lot more forthcoming than you were at the party," Bex said.

"At the party, I didn't know that your unfiltered six-foot-tall Visigoth of a sister was going to drag out the entrails of a gentleman's agreement in a public setting that could ruin my daughter's career."

Bette barked out a laugh. She folded her legs beneath her on the sofa. One of her hands was in a tight fist. "We fought a lot, in the end," she said. "Jen and I. For a long time, I think I let my mind slip over the fact that she was writing most of those episodes because the experience was so collaborative." She shook her head. "Jen was giving me so much of what I had always wanted, but no one had taken me seriously. As I learned more, I did write more. I think as I got better, and more of the show lived in my head, I got closer to Dad in the aftermath of what happened. My self-esteem was improving so much, I lost the plot."

Dad. Bex had been right to think that Bette and Aaron were closer than it had seemed five years ago. Against her will, Bex felt a pang of sympathy for Bette, who had been younger than Vic was now when the man who loved her mom and had tried to be her father imploded their family. How much might Bette have needlessly blamed herself for what happened between her mother and Aaron? And had Aaron, desperate to make amends, tried to do it by giving her a dream she wasn't ready for?

Jen would have known it wasn't entirely Aaron's guilt that had given Bette the opportunity. She would have known it was mostly for Bette. And Jen wouldn't have let a young woman fail.

"I started thinking of Jen as interfering, not teaching or collaborating," Bette said. "And because her arrangement with Aaron didn't include writing credits, I felt confident in my right to be an asshole. She was patient about that. She probably expected it. Sometimes I would think about why she *wasn't* getting credits, if not on *Craven's Daughter,* on another show or a movie. I told myself it was because she wasn't good enough. So many mental gymnastics on my part, just to function."

"It was my fault," Aaron said. "I put them in that position, and once it was going, I never stepped in. I didn't listen to anything Bette was trying to tell me and what Jen was telling me straight. It's why I couldn't listen to you, Sam, about that business with the direction of the show and what the fans wanted. Jen and Bette were already fighting about it. I couldn't care. I was working not to hear the consequences of a very personal circus I had created. And I was dealing with Josh. Again."

Sam firmed her mouth at Aaron. "You threatened to fire us if we said anything about Cora and Henri in the same breath as the word *romance*. Maybe I could be convinced you didn't personally care very much, but *someone* must have felt pretty fucking determined about keeping a queer relationship off any Cineline channel. Who was it?"

Aaron looked at Sam steadily for what seemed like an eon before he finally shrugged one shoulder. "It was still my show. God knows romance had never been the kind of story I told. The execs had their Big Data that told them not to mess with whatever formula was working to get the ratings we were getting every week."

"Simple as that." Sam's voice was hard.

"I guess not so simple for an idealistic 'artiste' like you, but for someone who has to go to quarterly stockholder meetings, yeah. As simple as two plus two."

"Our fans don't agree with that equation."

"No one but you folks in front of the camera think about the fans. Those guys upstairs are thinking about the *other* twenty-five million viewers who are sitting in their recliners in Harvey, Indiana, to watch a celebrity get murdered so they can decompress from putting computer chips in Honda Civics all day. The ones who watch a commercial for laundry detergent and remember to make a grocery list."

"What about the queer kid in Indiana, Aaron? Who's thinking about them?"

Aaron shook his head. "You know the answer to that already. And television never promised to save the world."

"Oh, for fuck's sake." Bette's frown made her look more like herself. "Television promises to save the world *all the time*." She turned to Sam. "We couldn't make the show without Jen. That's the ugly truth. The sixth season scripts—the ones she hadn't already helped me write before she died—were a series of cheap stunts and stale cliches that only your and Bexley's acting rescued from inconsequence. You read the series finale. Jen must have told me a dozen times that shoving Henri and Cora in a closet but never letting them kiss was a mean trick with an expiration date. That finale is the curdled milk I asked for and deserved." She cast a jaded look at Aaron. "Data's not everything."

"Well," Aaron said, his expression sour. "I guess I'm just an old man, then, with limited uses of my own."

"Now you're getting it. Besides, you love sitting on your lanai and bossing me over FaceTime. *Dad* suits you just fine."

Aaron rubbed his hands over his knees. A shadow fell over his expression. "Well. If I'm being honest—and it's likely about time I am, at least now and then—it wasn't just the guys upstairs." He grimaced at Sam. "It was like what Luce said on your podcast. It was one particular guy upstairs. Jeff Gantry."

Sam leaned forward, her eyes lasering on Aaron. "Your brother-in-law, who Luciana said gave you the chance to do another show with Cineline."

"That's right. He was going to be the only one who gave me the kind of budget I knew how to work with, and you heard the story from Luce about how I called in every other favor I had—all true, and also the same thing everybody does in this town. But it had to be a hit, and it had to pay the debts I'd racked up to people like Bette's mom and Jen and Josh, and if I wanted Jeff to stay on board, it couldn't be a show that swung for the fences. It had to be a show that stayed at the top of the ratings and didn't make waves."

"Because my uncle Jeff is a fucking bigot," Bette said.

Aaron bobbed his head. "Something like that."

Bex put her Coke down. She crossed her legs, leaned back, and draped her arm over her eyes. She needed a minute.

This man, to put Band-Aids on the bullet holes he'd caused in his *own* life, had cashed checks with credit he drew from other people's lives. Bex's life. Sam's life. The lives of their fans, who *did* count.

And Jen's life. Especially Jen's.

So many people had been recruited to repair and polish Aaron Gorman's career. And it worked. It fucking worked. He'd had his third big TV hit, the biggest, one of the highest-rated and most beloved shows of all time, which trained his daughter in her field, employed everyone he'd hurt and owed something to, papered over and ignored harms, and threw away real people's professional accomplishments, credits, and—and *loves*, all so that Aaron could have an estate in the Bahamas, accolades, and a stream of invitations to guest-lecture at film schools.

She sat up. Her anger was a hot coal in her throat. Never a good sign.

"You know what?" Bex pointed at Aaron. "I have always been someone who knew what I wanted. From the time I was small."

"Okay." His sarcasm was impossible to ignore.

Bex lifted her chin and gave him a *look*. It was the same look she'd used to force her sisters to put down their bullshit and straighten themselves out.

It worked on Aaron. He twisted his Rolex and waited for her to speak.

"Until the sixth grade," she said crisply, "I was the only child of a single mom, a mom who'd gone to fucking Julliard on a piano fellowship, but instead of traveling around the world from concert hall to concert hall, she lived in an apartment over a garage in the Bexley neighborhood of Columbus, Ohio, so she could teach piano lessons to wealthy people's kids. I saw her dither and almost cry over whether she could afford to throw a box of Cinnamon Toast Crunch in our cart at Kroger, and what *I* wanted was for her to be able to do whatever the fuck *she* wanted. I saw her sacrifice and her talent, I took note of the way she never complained about anything, and what I wished for most of all was for someone with power and money to fall in love with her and let her set the world on fire and make me siblings."

Bex made herself take a deep breath. Sam had put her arm across the back of the sofa behind her.

"Which, okay," she said. "I was eleven. I'd been raised in a patriarchal society, I realize I could have wanted more, but it happened. She met someone who adored her, this enormously tall Viking of a man who was the kindest person I've ever met, and she was free to do her thing. She got a spot in the Columbus Symphony Orchestra, she recorded, and in our first big house in the Franklinton neighborhood, I got a sister who I adored. In our even bigger house with real turrets in Victorian Village, I got another sister, who made our family complete. That meant I was free to make another wish. I'd been lucky, so I wanted something even bigger."

She let herself fall back against the sofa. Sam's arm came across her shoulders, which was what she'd hoped would happen.

"Broadway. That was my dream. When the American Conservatory in Chicago accepted me, I could go because of my dad. And when I finished and wanted to live in New York and audition for Broadway, my dad double-parked a van in Washington Heights and walked every box of my worldly goods up four flights of stairs to my shitty railroad flat that was pretty good for New York. He told me to break a leg and gave me a 'break in case of emergency' debit card. I *wanted* it, so I drove my neighbors crazy practicing and showed up early to every audition. I wore out my dance shoes at a crappy dance studio right by the George Washington Bridge. I took so many acting classes, probably too many, and I did it. I got it. *If you can make it there, you can make it anywhere*, that's what they say, and I was on top of the world until I wasn't, because I got one of those eleven-p.m.-on-a-weeknight phone calls from Ohio."

She could hear her voice start to get shaky, but Bex didn't care.

"And *then*, Aaron, *then* all I wanted was for my sisters to not lose anything else. I wanted them safe. I wanted them to feel like they still were part of a family. So I moved here to the only two-bedroom apartment I could afford, very, *very* far south of the studios, and I had enough money from insurance and what there was in the estate to feed us in that apartment for two years."

Sam squeezed her shoulder.

"I signed my contract with Cineline with six weeks to spare. That was nothing but luck. I got lucky. So the next thing I wanted was for *Craven's Daughter* to give my family enough uninterrupted paychecks that, just like their mom, my sisters could do whatever their hearts desired. Every time I was in front of your cameras, Aaron, that's what I was thinking about. The *only* time I didn't think about that was when I was with Sam. But you know the fuck of it? I didn't think to want the love of my life! And that's not okay."

"I don't see what any of that has to do with me," Aaron said. "You got your paychecks. I wasn't telling you what to think or do when you weren't on my set."

"But I was always on your set! And when I wasn't there, I was getting ready to be there, or giving interviews about the show, or getting recognized and talking to fans about being Cora. For six years, I was Cora. The character you invented. And *you* were the one who decided that Cora's feelings for Henri, and Henri's feelings for Cora, were only good enough to zoom in on, not good enough to grow. You made me the human embodiment of unfulfilled romantic and sexual tension. That was my job, Aaron—to depict yearning, to want, but to never, ever let my character get what she wanted, because if I did, *Jeff Gantry* might be uncomfortable. Never mind that queer fans were *erased*."

Bex took a breath. Discovered she was still mad.

"Fuck that," she said, decisively. "Fuck putting the bar on the floor. Fuck straight, cis, white men like you giving crumbs to queer and marginalized creators and fans so they can have more for themselves." Bex was pointing at Aaron again. Her hand was shaking. She let it fall to her lap. "I made mistakes. I own them. But *your* decisions ruined any trust *I* had in how I felt about Sam, and ever since, I haven't known what I wanted. Can you believe that? Me! Bexley Simon, who has a voice that can break your heart even if you're sitting in the worst seat at the back of the Gershwin Theater, hasn't known what she wanted for five years. That's real. It's real that if you create a homophobic work environment, you hurt people. Imagine that."

Bex perfected her posture. She could hear her speech ringing in the corners of the room, the way it did when she hit just the right notes, so she waited for Aaron to meet her eyes. If she needed to say this, he was damn sure going to hear it.

"*Craven's Daughter* took something important away from me. I want it back, because I just found out the real reason that light went out in *me* is because *you* cheated on your wife, had a dry spell in your career, and were beholden to your homophobic brother-in-law. So now, Aaron Gorman, you are beholden to *me*. You're beholden to those fans you hurt."

Bex put her hands down onto her knees. Her voice was very loud in ordinary exchanges, and so her angry speech—which she could admit had gotten away from her in the depth and breadth of its autobiographical elements—had been much louder than an ordinary exchange.

The silence after, by comparison, was churchlike.

Bette cleared her throat and opened her messenger bag. "I can't pretend to have the ability to answer to"—Bette looked from Bex to Sam, whose expression was unreadable—"a lot of that. However, Dad and I have been working on something that might help." She pulled a stack of paper out of the bag and handed it to Sam, perhaps guessing that Bex needed to maintain her position and posture until she got a hold of herself.

Sam took the papers from Bette. "It's a script."

"For the series finale. To film the series finale instead of a reunion. As the reunion."

Bex had more or less given up on this plan after reading the script Bette had couriered over. They only had ten days left to pull it off.

Bette looked at Aaron. He managed another one-shouldered shrug. "If you end up doing this thing, I'd rather it not be crap." Aaron shifted on the sofa, and Bex realized that he was uncomfortable. As in, emotionally.

She couldn't not stare. It was like seeing a white tiger in the wild.

"Why did—" Bex started.

"Not because of anything to do with the two of you, in the event you start to believe you can hassle me or anyone else and get what you want," Aaron said. "Despite my anchor to the reality of corporate Hollywood, I do, on occasion, care about the art." He wiggled his fingers in a mocking gesture, as if saying such a thing threatened his masculinity. "I can appreciate that the series has some loops to close. I talked to Niels. The network's given it a green light. Your people will hear from their people, blah blah blah." He gave a wave of his hand.

The room went quiet again.

"You're not going to get any thanks from me," Sam said. "If that's what you're sitting there waiting for."

"I wouldn't dare imagine I could get anything from you at all, Samantha Farmer." Aaron's voice had gone petulant, so Bex supposed the magnanimous weather of his soul had blown over. It never lasted long. "By the way, I'll be directing."

Definitely blown over.

"Thanks for the Coke." Bex stood up.

Sam stood, too. "Don't bother yourselves, we'll make our own way out." She tucked the script under her arm.

Bex picked up her bag, feeling how this visit had shifted the scales in the direction of justice. They had specifics and confirmation where before they'd had questions. She'd finally spoken up for herself. They'd eliminated Aaron as a suspect.

But they couldn't bring Jen back or give her a chance to live her own big dream. It was hard not to feel as though the moment the lights went out on Stage 46, so many beautiful things and hard things and sad things had gone dark and crumbled into dust, and only the ghosts were left.

She followed Sam to the door. The moment Sam opened it, Aaron called them back.

"Fuck. Wait."

"What?" Bex turned around to see Aaron looking at Bette, who gave him a tight-lipped nod.

"Look. I had decided this was none of my business, and Bette disagreed, but now that I think about it, she's probably right. What do I know? Seems like everything I decided to do my way had a way of making shit worse." He sighed heavily. "It's about Josh. I wanted to leave him out of it, but maybe it's time I stopped making excuses." Aaron looked down at his hands, flipping his phone over and over between his palms. "This isn't easy to say, so I'd rather you forget I even said it, but despite what anyone may think, I loved Kathy. Bette's mother. Still do, though I fucked it up. Marilee was . . ." Aaron sighed again. "She was Jen's very good friend, even before she started dating Josh. Which is why, when Josh started up with his bullshit—"

"Abuse," Bette interrupted. "Please, call it what it is. Controlling. Gaslighting. Isolating. Then throwing things and punching walls, which led to cornering, screaming, grabbing, shoving. Assault."

"Yeah." Aaron sounded defeated. "Marilee had been talking to Jen about it, and Jen was Jen. She made a big fucking deal out of things, usually things nobody wanted her to. She was talking about restraining orders, removing Josh, calling cops onto the set, the whole nine yards."

"It sounds like she was making the right amount of deal about it," Sam said, her voice hard. "It sounds like she was doing the minimum amount of deal to avoid the pain, trauma, and even death of someone she cared about."

"I think when you know a person like I know Josh—"

"You minimize," Bette interrupted again. She looked at Bex

and Sam. "We've talked about this in family therapy. We've read books and articles. He's supposed to be learning." Bette turned back to Aaron. "You rationalize, you justify, you invent reasons, you project feelings and background information on a person who is doing what they are doing for no reason except they *want* to. Because they have learned that abuse is a way to get what they *want.* Those rages had a goal for him, and it was to control her, just like every other dirtbag who abuses people. He's not complicated or misunderstood. He's someone who is focused only on his own comfort and getting every possible thing he can for himself through any means possible without anyone holding him accountable. There is no fucking *reason* a person abuses another person."

"Yeah. I get it." Aaron nodded, his face sad. "So Josh didn't like it. He—he started sabotaging shoots. At first to make Jen look bad."

"How would Josh's sabotage make Jen look bad?" Sam asked.

"Because after the shoot in the alley that Carl talked about on your podcast, anything that went wrong Jen would make a big stink over, act out. It made her seem unreliable, especially because at that time she was starting to get sick and missing a lot of work. But what Josh was doing backfired on him. It cost too much money, so the network had to get involved. That was when Jen made her report. Josh got kicked off the set, and his designs were left to his studio to build and execute, because no network is going to care how good a series looks if they're losing money."

"But he didn't stop," Bette said.

"No. Being Josh, he didn't. And I didn't stop him, either. I think Jen underreported how much he had turned his bullshit on her, because for Marilee it had let up some, though Jen wouldn't stop coming to me still worried about Marilee, with these statistics about how dangerous it is when abusive relationships end. To get her to calm down, I said I'd help out with Marilee. Give her someone to talk to—a man, I guess—and give her some advice, make sure security was tight, all that. And I didn't understand . . ." He darted a glance at Bette.

"Wrong."

Another sigh. "I was ignorant and self-serving, and I didn't think about how what I did might confuse Marilee, who was vulnerable. I just went with it because it felt like it was happening so fast—"

"Nothing was 'just happening.' You didn't cheat on Mother by accident. Your life takes place at the same speed as everyone else's. This is not what our therapist has been helping you with."

"Accountability." Aaron tossed his head. "Here it is. My accountability. Take it or leave it."

"What?" Sam barked.

Bex's hands had gone numb, and she felt like she was floating slightly out of her body. "You're saying Josh was threatening Jen? And then you and Marilee? And then you had Jen and Josh on your *show*?"

"After he got Jen to drop the restraining order she'd been awarded against Josh," Bette said, her face tight. "So he could have his last, big hit with *Craven's Daughter*."

"Just like Luciana said." Sam's voice was dark with anger. "You only cared about who was good."

"Creatives work well under pressure," Aaron said mournfully.

"Oh my God!" Bex screeched. "I had my sisters with me on that set! My tiny baby sisters!"

"Did you not think to tell the Chicago police that they should look into the fact that Josh had this history?" Sam asked. "That Jen had been awarded protection from him?"

"By then, it had been years and years." Aaron rubbed his face. "I'm learning, all right? I'm trying!"

"Why are we supposed to fucking care that you're *trying*?" Sam yelled. Everyone was yelling except Bette, who looked like she was imploding.

"Listen!" Bex dropped her bag on the ground and put her

hands on her hips in a way she hadn't since Vic was in high school. "Why did we even have to come here, Aaron? Why were you ignoring our calls? You're *not* trying! You're certainly listening to our podcast, so you know what Luciana said, what Carl noticed, what Georgie reported, and Kim Ryerson! You have the history with this to put together what the Chicago police, right now, are looking at. *Who* they're looking at. If there is even a chance Jen passed away because of something other than a terrible accident, why wouldn't you want that brought to light?"

He shook his head. "You still don't get it. It's not about me or anything I can do, and it's not about you and anything you think you can do. If the network doesn't want anyone to know something, they won't. Even if someone says it right out loud."

Bette was the most animated that Bex had ever seen her, rocketing up from the sofa to put her hands on her hips. "How many times do I have to explain—"

Sam's reaction was just as fast and twice as furious. "I swear, if one more person tries to tell me—"

"Stop!" Bex demanded. "Stop, stop, stop!"

It worked. No one could harness the power to shut up a room faster than Bexley Simon.

She closed her eyes and gathered herself for what felt like the tenth time in this stupid suite alone. "Here's what's going to happen now," she said, putting steel behind every word. "We're going to walk out that door, and we're going to tell the Chicago police what you've told us about Josh. Sam and I have already told them some things you don't know about that mean our next phone call is likely to get their attention. We're going to tell them that Jen— who was last seen alive by Josh, by the way—was strong-armed into dropping what sounds like a very reasonable restraining order against him. And that Josh was already known to retaliate by sabotaging his sets, and there is a big chunk of the actual crime scene balcony railing missing in Chicago that somehow ended up being incorporated into the Cineline balcony."

"What the fuck?" Aaron's eyes widened in alarm.

"That's right. What the fuck is right. So what I need to know is where your chips are going to fall when things start happening. You tried to silence Sam and me before. I need to know you won't do that again. I need to know that, if necessary, the two of you will sit with both of us in front of a press corps and tell them the truth, because that's the only thing that's going to prevent horrible things like this from happening to good people in this stupid town again."

Bex was crying. Yes. She was crying because Jen had died, and she *should not have.*

"I'm there," Bette said. She sucked in a shaky breath. "In fact, I'm in 'discussions'"—she used air quotes—"with my people about restoring writing credits to Jen. Getting her name on awards. I can't and won't promise how this will happen, and it will likely be in such a way that I don't take as much heat as I deserve, but I won't stop until it's done."

"Fine," Aaron said. "Go save the world. God help you." He waved his hand at them.

But Bex noticed that his eyes were shiny.

Sam was not crying. She looked very cool, actually, as though she'd never shouted at Aaron or felt anything more than mild disappointment in a man in her life.

"If we don't like this script, you *will* rewrite it." Sam said this to Bette.

Then to Aaron she said, "You can be trusted to run with a bonkers premise, but I'm not trusting you to get the feelings in there. Bex is right. You suck at feelings. After everything you've made our fans put up with over the years, they deserve the kind of ending Jen would have given them, so this"—she brandished the script at them—"had better be the best thing either one of you has written in all your lives."

She leaned down to pick Bex's bag up off the floor, and when she straightened, she looped it over her own shoulder and nodded at Bex as if to say, *I'm with you.*

Bex left. She stomped her way through Chateau Marmont, angry that it was this fucking hard for a woman's voice to be heard.

When they were in Sam's car, buckled in, they both sat in the silence for some time, letting the fire of that encounter burn away from their bodies. Bex felt limp. Spacey. Just at the moment she started to notice how long it had been, and that her heart rate was normal, Sam looked over at her.

"You know that day I came into your dressing room right before we filmed what would end up being the last scene of the show?"

"Yeah?" Her heart started up again.

Sam twisted around in the driver's seat until she was fully facing Bex. "Here's my truth now. I'm falling in love with you all over again."

She seemed relaxed. Sam wasn't the type to ruminate or worry. She acted. *I'm falling in love with you all over again*, she said, as though there wasn't anything to worry about, and then she sat ready to listen to Bex the way she always did, her blue eyes steady and a smile ready, offering Bex permission to say anything, be anything, try anything.

She was so irresistibly, delightfully Sam.

Before Bex could think or make a list or come up with a reason not to, she unbuckled her seat belt and slid across the passenger seat until she could breathe in the sugar and musk of Sam's perfume. She didn't look away when Sam's perfect eyebrows rose in surprise, or when her freckles faded with her blush, or when both of them sighed when Bex put her hand against Sam's jaw.

"Thank you for telling me," she said. Bex rubbed her thumb over Sam's cheek. It made every bone in her body go hot at once, softening her all over in a silky awareness, turned on, heart thudding, fearless.

Sam reached up and gripped the lapel of Bex's jacket, pulling her even closer. "You're welcome."

"I want you," Bex said. "I'm falling in love with you again, too."

That was the first time she kissed Sam Farmer. Just once, closing her eyes, glad to feel Sam's mouth against hers. Just that—the soft press of Sam's mouth and the way she gasped and then kissed Bex back—and Bex had never felt so wanted in her entire life. Sam let go of her jacket and put her arm around Bex and did what Bex had imagined her doing so many times. She put her hands through her hair and kissed her while smiling, which gave Bex the opening to pull Sam's lower lip into her mouth when she didn't quite expect it.

Sam kissed like she listened, and Bex told her everything. How hot Sam was, how good, how important, how much and how long she'd been wanted. Bex told her, too, about everything she'd imagined or fantasized about by kissing Sam deeper, and scraping her teeth against Sam's neck in a way she'd thought about so many times that she was surprised when it felt so singular and new and gorgeous.

There were so many things they'd been waiting to tell each other.

Bex slid into Sam's lap, wrapped her arms around her, kissed her soft and deep and told her more.

Sam was such a good listener.

Reunion

"You've got Craven Investigations, deposit required." Chaz took a long drag off her prop cigarette and stubbed it out in a grubby coffee cup.

"Cut." Aaron sat on his stool gazing down at his handheld camera monitor. "Got it, Chaz. Let's set up for the office pan."

An alarm beeped, and crew came onto the office set, arranging lights and moving walls, taking pictures, peering at light meters, and wrapping and relaying cords.

"Is it strange? Haunted?" Sam recrossed her legs in her canvas set chair. Wardrobe had put her in dark trousers, loafers, a white shirt, and a blazer, and makeup had done her hair in a low pony-tail with a strip of gauze pinned around the hairline to lay down flyaways before she went on camera. The scar from the cut Henri sustained in the second episode had been applied to her forehead, along with a lot of makeup designed to be no-makeup, including just a few individually applied eyelashes.

Bex wanted to kiss her again.

"No and yes." She shifted in her own chair, wincing. The costumer who'd fit her in this green A-line skirt and frilly blouse had made a lot of *hmm* noises and done a great deal of yanking.

"What's strange," Bex said, "is Aaron behaving like a real director. I think it's freaking people out. A PA was in Luciana's light, and he politely asked him to move and then thanked him when he did. It made me drop my line in shock."

"You should've yelled at him years ago," Sam said. "Make sure you give him some kind of treat at the end of the day so he associates his good behavior with a positive reward."

Bex laughed. "I think his treat is working with his daughter like that." She indicated where Bette was sitting on a stool next to Aaron, a script binder open, talking to him and Aaron's cinematographer.

"Yeah. That never happened before. One thing's the same, though." Sam wrinkled her nose as a shout came from somewhere off set. Bex couldn't hear words, but she recognized the voice.

"Josh." She tried to nod in a knowing way, but every muscle in her neck had frozen. Her eyes darted over to a tall, broad-shouldered PA who'd unobtrusively made her way closer to the source of the shouting. Her name was Judy Lawson, and she was a detective from the Los Angeles Police Department working in cooperation with Chicago.

Undercover. On a detective show.

Bex hadn't been able to sleep last night, anticipating today, so she'd pulled up CravingCraven's fanfic on her phone. Frankie and Vic had been analyzing and talking about the fic all along, and Sam had made herself familiar with the entire body of work, but Bex herself had never read back through the stories after finding out Jen wrote them.

This time, what she noticed was the love.

The first time she sat down in Jen's chair to have her makeup done for the pilot, Jen had pulled Bex's hair away from her face with an elastic and then crouched down in front of her and put her cool, light fingers on both of Bex's cheeks, turning her face to the side, then back, tilting her chin up, studying her from every angle. *Don't you just adore how different people's faces are?* Jen had asked, her green eyes wide. *The more I look at people's faces, the more I feel like I'm looking right into their souls.* She smiled. *I like the look of your soul, Bexley Simon. I think we'll be friends.*

Jen had offered friendship to so many people.

The stories she'd written about *Craven's Daughter* had shuffled and reshuffled the people she worked with every day into different roles, imagining the jokes they might tell and the arguments they might have, the speeches they'd give and the feelings they couldn't bring themselves to express. Bex believed the stories had been mostly for Jen, a way for her to journal and process what she was living through, but she'd shared them so generously, written so much and so well, that the world had identified her as *Craven's Daughter's* Big Name Fan—someone whose love for the series came across in her work in a way that made the world of the show more expansive for everyone.

It was the same thing Bex tried to do as an actor. Show her feelings, and do it big enough so other people could read them, feel them, and make things with them. Make *more*.

"All right, folks." Aaron clapped his hands and rose from his stool. "Rewrite on scene three. Affects Luciana, Marcus, Chaz, and background group one. Grab your new pages in ten from Sal. Everybody else, get out of here until three, because we're gonna get this office pan in and then do the reshoot. Memorize fast."

Another alarm sounded, and Bex and Sam got up. As they walked off Stage 46, Sam grabbed Bex's hand.

She'd never done that before. Not here.

"Are you going to the dressing room?" Bex swung their clasped hands between them as they moved into the hallway, relishing Sam's firm grip and the fact that people were looking, had *noticed*.

"No, we're going to our spot," Sam said. "Frankie and Vic are out there with what they're calling a 'picnic,' but I'm skeptical." She pushed through the door to the studio lot and held it open for Bex. Sam's costume shirt was so tight that it pulled out of the waistband of her trousers, and she had to let go of Bex's hand to tuck it back into place.

"Probably it's the kind of picnic that's a pile of stolen craft service food on a paper towel," Bex said. "But that sounds amazing. I'm so hungry. Do you think they got any of those mini-quiches with the shallots and bacon? I only put one on my plate when we got that break at ten, and when I went back for more, they were gone."

"Hard to say." They wound through the abandoned carnival equipment and past a row of gongs. "I've barely seen your sisters today."

"They've been squirrelly," Bex agreed. "I keep sensing they're up to something, but I haven't figured out what, and whenever I try to pin them down, they wriggle away."

Bex knew her small talk deserved the biggest cringe, but ever since the moment everything changed in the parking lot of Chateau Marmont, there had been an unsettled energy between her and Sam that felt like they were both waiting for the other to break. She was trying to be patient. They didn't know the ending yet, and probably what she was really feeling was yearning. Power. Anticipation. Horniness. Hope. Vulnerability.

Five years of it.

Eleven years of it.

"Is that you guys?"

Bex heard Vic's voice just before she and Sam emerged into the open area that the *See You Never* stoop set was parked in.

"Close your eyes! We're not ready."

"We are, too," Frankie said. "They don't have to close their eyes."

"That's probably good," Vic said agreeably. "If they close their eyes and Bex falls down and splits her costume in two, we're the ones who will end up getting yelled at." She was waving both arms when Bex finally saw her standing halfway up the steps of the fake brownstone. Bex's throat tightened as her eyes filled with sudden tears.

"Oh, no!" Vic said. "What's the matter?"

Bex shook her head. "Nothing. You just looked like Dad."

"Shit!" Vic bounded down the steps and wrapped Bex into a hug. "It's his birthday today. I mean, you know that. You texted us about it last night, with the picture, which I meant to say thank you for because I don't think I've seen it, but I was hard-flirting with Siobhan when the text came, and then I forgot."

"I miss him," Bex said to Vic's shoulder.

Then Sam was hugging her, too, and she could feel Frankie's wiry body behind her, which was nice until she stumbled a little and Frankie's knee caught the back of her thigh, making Bex yelp and wrench herself free of the hug.

"Sorry!" Frankie's voice had a suspiciously emotional rasp to it. "We made you a party. Come see. It's not completely put together because we planned it for later in the day, but this works." She got her bony fingers around Bex's elbow and pulled her toward the set, which Bex now saw had been decorated with white streamers. The landing outside the false door was covered with a white plastic tablecloth stolen from craft service, and there were a few trays piled with mini-quiches, a bag of chips, some grapes, and a two-foot-tall white cake covered in white and yellow roses.

The cake said, CONGRATULATIONS BEX & SAM!

Bex looked from Frankie to Vic, perplexed. "Congratulations on what?"

Frankie made an irritated face and pointed at Bex's hand, which had drifted back to gripping Sam's hand without her noticing. "For that. Long, long time coming on that, and we weren't positive it was ever going to happen."

"And, you know, *this*," Vic said, gesturing broadly toward the studio building. "The finale. The podcast. The fact that there's an undercover—"

"Shut up," Frankie hissed.

"No one can hear us." Vic crossed her arms. "We just wanted to, you know, acknowledge you. You always got us a cake if we, like, did something hard. So we thought—"

"Vic thought you should have a cake," Frankie said. "I said it had better be really fucking fancy, because if we were supposed to be buying you cake this whole time, we have a lot of cakes to make up for."

"It's a wedding cake." Sam said this in the way that Bex knew meant she was trying not to laugh. "With our given names on it." She put her hand over her mouth. "Was that— Did you have any concerns, there, when you ordered it from a bakery? The information might—"

"It's from Genevieve Roberts's bakery." Vic leaned down and swept her finger through one of the icing roses. "She gave me a deal on it, plus she's extremely very discreet."

"Lucinda Seymour Roberts's youngest, yes?" Bex asked. "The one who got her nose done over winter break in eighth grade. And dated the bass player who made headlines when he spit on the morning show host. Has had at least two reality shows. She's extremely very discreet?"

Vic shrugged. "It's just a cake. It was supposed to be for Megan Renna and Darby Hare's recommitment ceremony, but then DeuxMoi broke that Darby was seen at Frost making out with an unnamed model in the VIP section. But it's perfectly good. And also gluten-free. Megan doesn't do gluten. Or dairy. Or egg. Or sugar. And Darby can't have tree nuts." Vic bit her lip. "I do not know what this is made of, and Megan and Darby's names were scraped off, but isn't it pretty?"

"It's beautiful," Bex affirmed. "Somewhat bizarre, and there is no way our names iced on a wedding cake isn't already all over town, but thank you."

Vic seemed to smile and started grabbing drinks for everyone, but she was also slamming plastic cups down on the landing, and her cheeks were red in a way that made an alarm go off deep in Bex's chest. "Vic? What's—"

"I need to rant. Just a tiny rant." She pinched the bridge of her nose, then looked at Bex. "I'm sure you meant the cake is bizarre and not the fact that I wanted to make a party for you, but I'm sorry, it feels the same. I just—" She pinched the bridge of her nose again, screwed her eyes closed to keep herself from crying.

"Vic."

"No, gimme a minute." She flapped her hand at Bex. "I know you think I should be at school, or if I'm not at school it's because I'm having a crisis, but I'm not. I just *like* this. I like all of us being together and doing something together, and I like that there's a detective on the set because people finally care what happened to Jen. I like doing things with you guys that make me feel like part of a family." She looked at Sam, wrinkling her nose. "With you, too. Remember when I was in middle school and we all went to Cabo and practiced my school Spanish ordering street food and buying souvenirs? That was the best. The best weekend. The most fun. But this podcast and the investigation and hanging out, and seeing you and Bex talking to each other again, that's been pretty good, too."

Vic sat down on the step, pulling her scrunchie off her wrist to put up her hair, staring hard at Bex with big, watery eyes. "I don't want you to come to parents' weekend or invite me to dinner where you ask me a thousand questions to make sure I'm not secretly drowning in college. I just want to talk out by the pool again. I want to watch you and Frankie do your curly hair routines together while I narrate the parts of a movie you're missing when your head's upside down over the diffuser. I want takeout runs on the rare nights we're all in the same place at the same time." Her eyes had gone red. "I remember Mom and Dad, I *do*. But it's like an album of pictures in my head, or sometimes a feeling I try to play over and over again. But Bex, I use your co-wash on my hair at school because it smells like the people part of home, even though it makes my hair look like rotting seaweed."

"*Victoria*." Bex felt the layers of her makeup begin to soften and sift down her face with her tears, but she reached up and rubbed her face anyway, trying not to sob.

"I know we still see you," Vic said to Sam, "and you call me once a week like you must have it on a phone reminder, 'check in on Vic,' but that's not what I'm after, you know? I don't want to be left out. I don't want anyone to be left out. I'm the *baby*." Vic sniffed, her chin trembling, and turned to Bex. "I told you I didn't get into UCLA because I thought . . . I thought you wanted me to spread my wings." Vic choked. "But I did get in, and I wanted to go there and live at home."

Bex had known Frankie's problems with her were coming for them after months of their being tight with each other, but she hadn't known Vic wanted to live at home. No one had said. She hadn't guessed.

"I'm sorry." Bex sat down heavily on the step, ignoring the plastic crunch and wet seeping of a food container that had smashed under her butt and meant she'd ruined not just her makeup but also the costume she was sewn into.

And maybe her family. Maybe she had ruined that, too, because then she remembered saying the same thing to Frankie on the *Craven's Daughter* set weeks ago. *I'm sorry.*

She'd told them she was sorry so many times, as if she should be able to make up for what they'd lost. Instead of telling them something more like . . . *I know. I know how you feel. I feel that way, too. I miss Mom and Dad like a huge hole in the middle of my heart, and this is hard, this is so hard, sometimes I'm afraid. You are the best two things that ever happened to me, and I will not fucking lose you, too. I won't, I won't, I won't.*

Bex had kept that inside of herself like it was the seal on the bottle she was saving her family in. Like her actual feelings would break them apart, when those feelings were something the three of them shared.

"You're not the only one who needs a new plan," she said. "I've kept nagging you about if you're supposed to be at school because I feel like that's what I'm supposed to do, but actually I would like it better if you went to school here and moved back in. Maybe I'm not supposed to say that. I haven't known what to do with myself since you guys have been . . . not on your own, but grown up. I haven't known what I wanted. I hate that it's Jen's death that has made up for things we've been needing, but maybe that's just Jen, you know? She was always getting into everyone's business and trying to make everything go better, and maybe that's what this is. Jen getting into our business one last time."

Bex pushed the backs of her hands against her eyes as if she could save what was left of her makeup. They came away stamped with mascara and shadow. "Who was it who said you know you've made it when all you want is more of what you already have? I've made it. Or I've almost made it. What hurts so much is that I could have made it long before now." Bex put her hands on Vic's shoulders and then quickly kissed her forehead. "I'd like more of my family. It's great. Move in, or I'll visit you more often. Whatever you want. You're my baby sister."

Vic pressed her lips together and nodded once, sharp and fast. "Okay. I feel like my rant was successful. I knew you cared, I promise, but I can't deal with your *Party of Five* vibes. I like drama on the streets, but with my peeps, I need it easy."

Bex laughed. "I get that."

Sam was leaning against the handrail of the stoop, her jaw clenched. Bex's heart stuttered.

"This is probably not the time," Sam said, "but I haven't been able to figure out when to say this. I'm doing a movie on location in Iceland in two weeks. I haven't even gotten another minute alone with you, Bex, since we were in the car at Chateau Marmont—"

"What?" Vic wrinkled her nose. "*Eew.* But also, that's kind of perfect. If my sister's not involved, it's amazing, actually, but . . . *eew.*"

Bex ignored Vic. Her middle was achy and spinning around with . . . she didn't even know what. Something bad. "Iceland?"

"With Mackiovitz." Sam winced.

"No!" Bex felt an extremely unreasonable tantrum coming

on. "This is the worst! You'll be trapped in Iceland forever. Mackiovitz took half a year to shoot *Lavin* and made everyone on set learn French." Bex put her head on her knees. "You're going to meet someone fantastic on a glacier and spend the rest of your life eating skyr and lutefisk while collecting Oscars like they're arctic berries."

"That is such a surprising mash-up of two very different kinds of jealousy." Sam sat down next to Bex. "It's part of why I wasn't sure about this reunion, because it was cutting it so close to the movie, but I could never say no to you, and I was never going to. I don't know how we'll figure this out. I've felt so bad about everything between us for so long, and I haven't had very long to feel good, and I'm leaving. But couldn't we try?"

She leaned close and made Bex look her in the eyes, which were as pretty and blue as ever. The little green speck in her left eye was unfair. She was so *Sam*. Always Sam.

Bex couldn't look at her and not think, *There you are. Where have you been? Mine.* She let out the breath she'd been holding. Sam seemed to understand it as a good sign.

"I'm quitting my job," Frankie's voice broke in. They all looked at her in shock. "Since we're doing this." She picked up a plastic knife and sliced into the top tier of the cake, tumbling a fist-sized wedge onto a paper towel. "Anybody else want some?"

"What?" Bex reached behind her and yanked apart the stitches that were holding her into her skirt. It was either that or be eviscerated by the waistband.

"I haven't been happy being a PA for a long time. But it's been hard to talk about, because I know how impossible it is to get this job, and I only got it because I'm your sister. But I went to college and studied stagecraft and dramaturgy and set building and design, and I spend most of my time here waiting and then moving ten things around in three minutes, then getting yelled at. I was all over *Craven's Daughter* as a kid, in every part of the show, and I need something like that. I got an internship at the

Barrymore Theatre's design shop in New York. If I take it, I'll be gone for nearly six months. Then I'll come back and be unemployed, or maybe I'll be offered something there. I don't know. I don't know very much right now except that this feels right."

"I think you must have tried to talk to me about this all the time we almost fought, recently," Bex said. "Maybe you've tried to talk to me about this a lot of times."

Frankie shrugged. "I was mad at you, but there were layers. We have a whole thing going on at the house with our routines. I've been worried about you. It's gotten so I can judge how the day will go based on what you sing in the shower in the morning, and that can get real dark." Having already given cake to Vic and Sam, she cut a piece for Bex and held it out to her until she took it.

"I'm glad we fought. I hope you can be happy for me, because I'm excited. I feel like I haven't been excited about something in forever." Frankie forked into her cake and shoved a bite into her mouth. "Huh. This is delicious. I have no idea what it is, but I'm okay with that."

"That should be our new family motto," Vic said, shoving cake into her mouth. "We have no idea what this is, but we're okay with that."

Sam pulled on Bex's hair. "Yeah. Maybe our motto, too?"

Bex didn't want Sam to go to Iceland. She wanted all the time back she had ever wasted so she could spend it on this woman in a way that involved a lot of horizontal surfaces and pent-up creativity. Then she wanted more time just for talking. Another decade for kissing.

But Sam needed Bex to be okay. So for now, she could do that. She dropped her voice to the softest whisper she could manage. "If you're okay with it, I can *learn* to be okay with it." She pressed her knee against Sam's. "But, fair warning, I can be incredibly dirty on FaceTime, and I will not pull punches if Mackiovitz's shoot runs long."

Sam's blue eyes went darker, and her jaw clenched in a way that was very Henri-enduring-her-longing-for-Cora, which Bex enjoyed, so long as she maintained the upper hand.

A crashing cacophony made Bex clap both hands over her ears. They all looked up to see a PA scrambling to his feet, having just stumbled into the row of gongs stored near the carnival sets. He started jogging across the lot toward them. When he made it to the stairs, he ran both hands through his messy hair, his glasses slipping down his nose.

"Dudes. Aaron's pissed. No one could figure out where you went. I had to ask security to check the cameras." He noticed Bex. "Oh, fuck. Caro and Matt are going to be enraged. It will take an hour to put you back together." He blinked at Frankie, having just spotted her. "Hey, Frankie."

Then he blushed.

"Hey, Haris." Frankie leaned against the railing with an expression of indifference she must have learned from Sam.

Bex caught Vic's eyes. Vic sent Bex an *oooooooh* look. Later, when things settled down, they would have a good time *investigating* this Frankie-and-Haris situation.

Bex stood up, brushing crumbs off the skirt. "Is Aaron ready for our scene? He said three o'clock."

"No," Haris said. "But you should get back. Niels Shaughnessy came down and stopped the filming. He threw a fit and insisted somebody find you. What did you do?"

Bex had no idea.

She guessed Jen wasn't done meddling yet.

Pretty Speeches

"It's not going to work." Aaron crossed his arms and craned his head toward the door so pointedly, Bex worried he might fall out of his chair, given the extremity of his slouch.

"We believe it's the best chance we have," Detective Judy Lawson said. "It may be the only chance we have. Josh Miller's been clearing out his apartment. Based on interviews we've done with people in his circle, we think he's going to leave town as soon as tonight. If that happens, we can't do anything to stop him, and we don't know where he'd go."

"He's not gonna leave town. Who told you that?" Aaron's skepticism couldn't conceal his doubt.

"His girlfriend." Detective Lawson raised an eyebrow at Aaron as well as Sam could have.

Aaron looked away. Bex couldn't help it, she felt for him. He'd known Josh for a very long time. Talking to Aaron at Chateau Marmont, they'd seen evidence that he had cared a great deal about Jen. In fact, a lot of Aaron's problems seemed to stem from caring about people but also possessing way too much self-serving motivation and poor impulse control. It was a tricky moral center, to be sure, but he clearly wanted to do the right thing.

Bex couldn't say what Niels wanted. He was uncharacteristically quiet, sitting at the far end of the table without so much as a notepad or a cell phone, listening.

It turned out Niels's bluster was just for show. Detective Lawson was the one who had called them together due to a story that had hit the entertainment news. After Frankie and Juan Ramon found the piece of wrought-iron railing on the balcony set and Juan locked the set down, he'd turned over the railing to the police. Someone at the crime lab, or someone who knew a crime lab technician, must have leaked that a lab report was pending on a few specks of what might be blood.

The fast-spreading story apparently took away the leverage Los Angeles and Chicago might have had to question Josh, since he now knew they had the railing, with blood on it that the lab was testing. Lacking the leverage provided by the element of surprise, the police had nothing but unprovable theories. The rumor that Josh was about to leave town made it imperative to force a confession, if possible, today. They wanted to use the reunion taping to create pressure.

"It seems like a dirty trick." Aaron sighed, a sure sign of his imminent capitulation.

"Says the man who deliberately created similar pressures on set to get good results on his projects," Bex said primly.

"I understand, and I'm sure you understand, that we can't go forward with this without your cooperation," Detective Lawson said.

Niels finally spoke. "Cineline has agreed to cooperate."

The detective nodded. "What we have planned happens after the end of the final scene."

"On the balcony, you mean," Sam said. For the first time in all of this, she looked tired, which made Bex worry, because Sam never looked tired. And once Bex started worrying, she worried about everyone.

Vic, for example. How miserable she had been out there in the wilds of Northern California, away from home, thinking that Bex had essentially kicked her out in order to finally be free. Had they really resolved that? What could Bex say?

And New York liked to chew people up and spit them out. Bex knew folks associated with the scene shop at the Barrymore. Kari Leder, for example, carried a knife in her boot and had once screamed so loud at someone hanging a light on the catwalk, they dropped it, smashing one of the seats in the mezzanine. Would Frankie be working with Kari?

They would have to start looking for apartments. She could call in that favor with her broker. Frankie would have a bedbug-free unit in a building with a doorman that was on, not adjacent to, Forty-Eighth Street, so that she wouldn't have to ride the subway to work, or Bex would build it herself.

"Bex," Sam said. "Hello?"

"Yep." She shook her head. "I'm here. Sorry. My question is how. We're already right up against it with the network's insistence that we'll get the highest ratings if we simulcast the finale in four time zones and then play the final scene live. We're shooting and editing under pressure to make the nine o'clock broadcast slot on the East Coast, and now we're on a stop. Fine. Somehow, we'll make it happen. But you're saying you want us to film and broadcast our live final scene with a skeleton crew, go to black, and then immediately execute this plan to pressure a man to confess to a crime?"

"Yes," Detective Lawson said, unbothered. "We understand from the studio that a live broadcast captures the maximum attention of everyone on the set. We know it's likely Josh will be in the most revealing psychological head space if his attention is on that balcony set while he knows that evidence may have been discovered."

"Jesus," Sam breathed. "This is altogether colder than anything former federal agent Henri Shannon could come up with."

Bex found her eyes drawn to Niels at the end of the table. She had never been asked to do anything quite this unconventional in all her years in television. She didn't think it was her jadedness that had her wondering where the lawyers were, with their fat stacks of NDAs.

Sam was looking at Niels, too, and her eyes were pure fire. "I'm sitting here thinking, where are the suits? Where's the paperwork?" she asked.

"Also what I'm thinking!" Bex interjected.

"But the lawyers don't know, do they, Niels? They don't know whatever it is you found out soon after Jen died that meant we were all sent home and told not to say a word. Why there was no *Hollywood Reporter* article about Jen's option with UBC and if there would be posthumous development of her show. We didn't even run a black screen with a three-word *RIP Jen Arnot*. Instead, I was hauled into your inner sanctum three separate times—again, no lawyers—and told not to talk about Jen. And when I walked into your office after the last episode to tell you I wasn't going to stick around for season seven, you slid a termination agreement across your desk, already typed up, and handed me your Mont Blanc to sign it with. What did you know, Niels? Did someone call you up and tell you Josh was alone with Jen? Did you catch Josh hiding a blood-covered balcony railing on the set? Or was it even worse—were you on your hands and knees that night on the balcony, before anyone called the police, cleaning up a crime scene with Josh Miller?"

"That's enough," Niels said quietly.

Detective Lawson had risen to her feet during Sam's speech. Now she took a step toward her. "Ms. Farmer—"

Sam held up her finger at the detective, frankly looking more like a detective in her Henri Shannon costume than Lawson did. "I'm not fool enough to think I'll get an answer. When this is finally solved, I'll give the credit where it's due, which is going to be the Chicago PD, the LAPD, and probably the FBI."

"And us," Bex said, starting to feel her own power. "Our podcast. Our fans."

Aaron shook his head. "He's not going to tell you what you want to know," he said. "But I will."

"Aaron."

He pulled on his bottom lip in sullen defiance of the warning in Niels's voice. "You don't have a thing on me anymore, Shaughnessy, and I owe a lot of people something and don't have many ways to pay the debt." Aaron looked at Sam. "I called him up," he said. "Same morning Jen was found. Got him out of bed to take my call. I knew if people started talking, it was going to come out about UBC picking up her show for development, and there had to be more people than just me and Jen who knew she'd been writing with Bette. I didn't know what happened to Jen, but I wasn't going to let the aftermath fall on Bette and ruin her future. So I told Niels the whole thing."

"Goddamn," Sam said, softly.

"Thing is," Aaron said, "I knew how it would turn out. Niels would make it go away. In Hollywood, either everything's fine, or it's a fucking mess but you don't talk about it, so it's still fine. I'd been through it with *Charles Salt*. The price I paid is there was never going to be a season seven. Every conversation I had with Niels after that, he mentioned retirement. His favorite places to golf. How much he thought I'd enjoy learning to sail."

Bex narrowed her eyes at Niels. "So why did you green-light this reunion show and the podcast? Why dig up the bodies? Pardon the crass metaphor."

Aaron chuckled. "Wasn't up to him, was it? That's because of the merger. Cineline and Magnum Opus. It didn't get much press—Magnum Opus wasn't a big outfit, but they owned a ton of IP, and they were savvy. When they agreed to the buyout, they had their own list of Cineline's IP they wanted the right to revive at any time. That moved the *Craven's Daughter* IP out from under Niels."

"I don't get it," Bex said. "He's still the head of the studio."

"Yeah, but *this* decision isn't on his desk. It's that new IP department. It was up to that woman—Magda, Martine? Can't remember. She's who called me when they made their minds up to do the *Craven* reunion. Told me she was out of her mind with excitement. She's a huge, huge fan."

"Ha!" Bex pointed at Aaron. "Fans! How unimportant are they now, huh?"

Sam's disgust was focused on Niels. "You never thought that anyone would be interested in *Craven's Daughter*, did you? You never gave any credit to the fans who wanted to see a queer, right-out-loud, prime-time romance on a procedural. The tease kept the sponsorships and the conservative suits happy and people in the seats, right? Win-win-win. But you didn't get it. You never understood that the fans trusted *us*. You never got that the 'Hollywood mythology' you like to talk about is just talented people working together, so you never counted on a Carl. Or a Jen. Or me and Bex. You thought the data was the whole picture. But *people* are the picture, you asshat."

Detective Lawson snorted, and Aaron coughed to cover his laugh.

Bloodless beneath his tan, the studio executive stood up and buttoned his jacket.

"Before you go, Niels," Bex said, "I wanted to give you the courtesy. You'll be hearing from my agent tomorrow. I'm stepping back from *Venice Memorial*. Between us, I don't think television is the right medium for me at the moment. The vision's just not big enough, you know?" She smiled her most brilliant Broadway-baby smile at him.

"Break a leg, everyone."

With that, he departed, leaving nothing but the sandalwood ghost of his expensive cologne.

"Fix yourself up and be in places in twenty. We have one more scene to get in the can before we set up for live." Aaron pulled on his bottom lip. "This is it," he told the detective. "If it doesn't roust up whatever confession or reaction you're looking for, get out and never come back."

"Understood." Detective Lawson looked at each of them in turn. "Any questions?"

"No," Sam said. "Bex?"

"No." Bex's stomach felt like she'd swallowed a brick. "I just have to keep telling myself that Jen would have enjoyed this. Otherwise, I am a disaster."

The detective left. Aaron pointed at both of them as if doing that communicated the feelings in his heart before he also left. Bex looked at Sam. Her color was rosy, and her eyes sparkled like diamonds. Or lasers. "What do you really think Niels was trying to cover up?"

"We're never going to know, but I got my answer from the fact he was even down here with no lawyers, and he didn't say a word in his own defense. You watch, Bex. From here on out, it's going to be nothing but spin from the network."

"Ugh. I hate that." But it did make it easier for Bex to understand Frankie's decision to leave L.A. for New York. "I think I need to put a pin in it until we've managed to get through filming, or I'm going to flub my lines on live television."

"You would never." Sam rested her head against the back of her chair. "What I keep thinking about is when I met you on this set weeks ago, after not really talking to you more than a polite three minutes in years, and I already knew I was going to say yes because it meant I would get to spend time with you, but also I didn't know if that was going to be good for me. What has happened since has been the legal definition of a mixed bag." Eyes still closed, Sam propped her feet up on the desk. It was the pose Henri Shannon always adopted when she delivered her cynical rundown of Bex's progress with a case.

Tell you what, Cora. Tell you what.

"Would I have said yes then," Sam asked, "if I knew I would be setting a trap for an alleged criminal who I've known for fifteen years and who allegedly hurt one of my best friends?" Sam stroked her chin. "I can't answer that. What if I knew about the criminal trap, but I *also* knew you'd crawl into my lap in my car and kiss me like it was the only thing you've thought about your entire life? I mean, I would have said yes, but also I might have wondered why I had to pay such a price for kissing. Even kissing *you*, which, in my opinion, should have always been free."

"Wow."

"Hold that thought. What if I had been told that I would be skulking all over town asking wild questions and being provocative on a podcast and looking for clues in fanfiction? Well, then, I would have *so* fucking said yes, because that part has been a blast, even knowing what we were doing it for. So what I think is that I can barely think at this point." Sam dropped her feet off the desk, leaned close, brushed her finger under Bex's eye, and came away with a false eyelash that Bex had lost in her stoop-picnic weeping. "Make a wish."

Bex laughed. "I wish that all's well that ends well." She blew on Sam's finger, and the falsie fluttered.

"Me, too. And I wish you might be up for wasteful, semi-spontaneous forty-eight-hour trips to Iceland, and that you don't give yourself hives as Vic comes home and Frankie moves away, and that we won't wrap tonight and then let this get away from us, which, now that I think about it? I would have agreed to anything if it was with you, Bexley. All of it. Especially the part where your jumpsuit ripped."

This time, Bex didn't laugh at Sam's teasing. She leaned forward and kissed her instead, because she could. Because she'd held Sam's hand on set. Because she'd felt what her heart did when Sam said she was going to Iceland, and she'd been in this town long enough and lived through enough that she knew for sure when something was real.

This was real.

Including the way Sam messed up the rest of Bex's costume

that had to look perfect in twenty . . . now fifteen minutes by fisting the frilly little shirt and pulling Bex close, and before Bex could stand on her tiptoes for her second kiss with Sam Farmer, Sam had moved her mouth to Bex's throat, licking over a spot that made Bex make a noise that was *not* quiet, because Bex could never be quiet, which made Sam laugh against her neck and gave Bex goosebumps.

"You know what?" Bex smiled at how breathless she sounded. "I'm glad my plan didn't work and I haven't had a chance to make a new one. I filled up every page of my notebook, which is unprecedented. I can't actually imagine what happens next."

"Will that kill you?"

"Fair question." Bex thought about it. "Obviously not. However, so many things have happened in my life that I didn't imagine and didn't have a plan for, and I've survived one hundred percent of them. Believing that my odds will change just because I've gotten this far would be magical thinking."

"Bex." Sam raised her eyebrow. It looked so good when she did that.

"Maybe it will kill me. Yes."

Sam laughed. "If you don't get yourself together—"

"Gone!" Bex hustled out of the room.

She wasn't sure who would be more upset with her, the costumer or makeup, but Aaron—or, more likely, Haris—must have warned someone in advance, because they were ready for her and worked their usual miracles, only grumbling a little. It helped that at no point had anyone involved in the production of *Craven's Daughter* been able to enforce continuity over Bex's hair from shot to shot, so a good part of what they needed to do, they immediately gave up on. The fanfiction sites had entire categories for CORA HAIR LORE. She was just providing them with inspiration.

In the final version of the finale script, Luciana played the evil twin of her character from season one. Or, more accurately, the twin who had been smuggled by her father to Guatemala as an infant in a bitter custody battle with the mother, who was rich and raised the other daughter in the luxury of Chicago's Gold Coast—a backstory hinted at in the first season because Luciana's character was being hunted by an unknown enemy whom Henri and Cora were unable to defeat, solidifying their determination to never lose again. In *this* episode, Henri and Cora were able to solve that first murder by uncovering that the killer was the twin sister.

Bex had spent not a short while with the script getting it all straight, but as they got the episode in the can, she started to feel excited. Everything was clicking. Though he'd retired, Carl had been invited on set due to the popularity of his podcast appearance, and the crew was relishing his easy mentorship and taking his notes about the show's classic angles.

And the set looked good. Really good. Bex had only seen Josh in passing, but those glimpses had given her a stomachache. He was talented. He had a *gift*. It struck Bex as such a tragic waste.

Bex guessed that Josh had spent a lot of his life afraid, defensive, and then violent, in order to get the things he wanted. She didn't have sympathy for him, but she did feel in her bones what Vic had been saying on the stoop and Sam said in the conference room—that everything felt better together, in collaboration, building relationships, nurturing family where you found it. It was a miracle to Bex that where that was absent on *Craven's Daughter*, the fans had filled it in. Their investment in a love story had created community. It had created more stories and encouraged collaboration. She was determined to show the fans what their investment in important things led to.

It led to what they had always wanted.

Which was, at the moment, the pleasing vision of Luciana de León handcuffed to a chair in the Craven Investigations office, her glossy black hair falling in unkempt waves to her waist as she panted in a way that drew attention to her legendary cleavage framed by the open neckline of a leather suit scuffed and marked from the hand-to-hand battle that her stunt double had engaged in with Cora's stunt double in a scene shot earlier in the day on a houseboat.

Which was, additionally, the return of Henri Shannon, silent, staring, her jawline firmed and her feet propped up in her favorite thinking pose.

And which was Cora Banks, leaning against the desk near the brass lamp, copying one of Agent Shannon's poses, crossing her ankles and her arms.

"Action!" Aaron called, and the scene came alive.

"She was your *sister*," Cora said reproachfully.

Annamaria Pompellini snarled and spat on the floor. "Blood doesn't make a sister."

"No." Cora furrowed her brows. "You're right. It doesn't. But you didn't try to solve the problem in your family any other way than the way the problems had started in the first place. Violence. What are you left with now?"

Annamaria smiled, but tears spilled down her cheeks. "My honor."

At this, Henri got up from the creaky chair behind the desk. "Tell you what, Annamaria." She walked closer to the bound woman. "Tell you what. I know something about honor. In my case, I decided to preserve someone else's, someone I had loved and thought deserved it more than I did. But the best way I could've shown my love was to be honest. To face reality. More often than not, honor leaves you alone, which I've learned"—at this, Henri turned to Cora, and their gazes caught—"is not the point. Love is the point. I've learned a lot more in this life from a kindergarten teacher than I ever learned from *honor*."

Cora turned quickly from Henri and blinked away her tears before bringing her attention back to Annamaria. At that moment, Annamaria pulled her hand from behind her back, and the metal handcuffs clattered to the floor. She leapt up, reached down to retrieve a switchblade from a strap at her ankle, and flicked it open. Then she seized Cora, holding the switchblade at her throat. Henri immediately crouched into a fighter's stance.

"I don't need your pretty speeches." Annamaria pressed the knife into Cora's throat until a drop of fake blood ran down her neck. "I already have everything I need." She pulled the blade away slowly, replacing it with her finger, and smeared the blood slowly down Cora's skin. "Do you?"

Henri lunged, and Annamaria turned, knocked over her chair, and ran from the office. Henri jumped over both the desk and the chair in pursuit. Cora moved to follow, but the base of the lamp caught her skirt and ripped it right up the back.

"God *damn it*," Cora huffed. She pulled out her phone to call in Henri's backup.

It was the first and only time Cora Banks had ever sworn on an episode of *Craven's Daughter*. That little moment had been Bex's idea.

"We've got it." Aaron looked up from his monitor. "It's a wrap on that scene." He was making an expression that was something like a smile. Bex was afraid it would break his face. "Stay nearby while we set for live. I've sent this to editing."

They'd already filmed Henri chasing Annamaria into the hallway, where she was apprehended with the help of Chaz and a handful of beloved recurring secondary characters who'd spent the serial's run passive-aggressively complaining about having to share space in the same building with a detective agency.

Aaron visually surveyed the cast and crew. "I'm dedicating this episode to Jen Arnot." He waved away the beginnings of the applause. "Stop. Should've already happened. Be ready for our next fucking stunt, and until then, don't need me."

He stomped off the set. Amethyst immediately manifested in Bex's peripheral vision holding a clipboard stacked with headsets.

"What a marshmallow," Sam said. "I bet he gives the best hugs."

Bex laughed while Amethyst miked her for a different last

episode. They had decided to delay the conclusion to *Craven's Daughter: Cold Case* and record it on set in the intermission between filming the series finale and its national simulcast, which would end with the last-ever balcony scene, broadcast live.

They sat at a small table where Amethyst had set up a tablet cued to the episode they would be discussing. This podcast was scheduled to drop immediately after the conclusion of the broadcast. They had one last fan-voted clip to talk about, a moment from the final episode of the sixth season that had been made to stand in for an ending for five years.

Bex pressed her hand against her belly to make the nervous flutters stop while someone from the studio took pictures of them recording in their Henri and Cora costumes and makeup.

A few dozen people were gathered around, some leaning against the walls of Stage 46, others sitting on the floor in groups of two or three. Most were actors who'd finished their work and changed into their street clothes but didn't want to leave yet. Some were crew on break until they were called back to set up for the final scene. Bex recognized a few Cineline staffers. She waved at Dajahne, the background actor who'd helped her and Sam at Chaz's party, and then at a group of folks she'd met from Frankie's work on *Timber Creek Farm*.

"Ready?" Sam asked.

Bex nodded as she said, "No, not remotely."

Sam laughed and tapped the tablet to play. She pushed the volume up until the audio for the filmed clip playing on the tablet— just for them, this time—reverberated through the soundstage.

> "Sometimes I think about going back to teaching." Cora takes a long sip from her soda, watching Henri's reaction across their table at the diner.
>
> "Do you want to?" Henri's voice is short. There is a purpling bruise across her cheekbone, and her normally pristinely white button-up is rumpled and

torn. The waitress sets a burger down in front of Henri and shakes her head at Henri's appearance.

"When I think about it, that's what I ask myself. Do I want to?" Cora looks directly into Henri's eyes, her expression determined. "And the fact is . . ." Cora swallows. "I don't know."

Henri doesn't look away. "I have no doubt they still want you. That they would take you back in a heartbeat."

Cora smiles gently. "That's the thing." Her voice has dropped to a whisper. "I don't know that they would."

Henri looks down. "They would."

"I think there's only one way I would go back to teaching." Cora pulls herself up straighter.

"What's that?"

"If you decide to leave. If, after everything we've been through, you left." Tears suddenly spill from Cora's eyes, and her mouth trembles.

Henri squeezes her own eyes shut. She looks pained and almost angry. "Cora."

"No, listen to me. We've made something here, me and you. It's not what my father made, and in different ways, neither of us have known what we're doing, but it's a real thing, and it's helped people, and I don't want to lose . . ." Cora trails off. Henri isn't looking at her, but the camera catches the desperate uncertainty in her expression.

"What?" Henri returns her gaze to Cora, but now with her familiar and self-protective steely distance. "What don't you want to lose? The agency? Is that what you're talking about?"

"You." Cora stands up, throwing the napkin on her lap on the table. "You. All of it, but mostly you."

Cora leans down. She touches her fingertip to the scar on Henri's forehead, and Henri reaches up as if to grab her hand, but then Cora picks up her bag, puts money on the table, and leaves.

The episode fades to black on the ringing bell over the diner's door.

When the clip ended, someone on the set began to clap, and then all of them were clapping, the sound sweeping over the set. Bex waited for it to settle down. She knew what she wanted to say about this scene. It was what she'd always wanted to say but never thought she could. "Sam."

"Yeah."

"We filmed this minutes after you asked to talk to me in my dressing room, and then we didn't really talk to each other again about anything until we started doing this podcast."

"Yeah." The corner of Sam's mouth quirked up. "That's a fact."

"I want to discuss what you said to me in my dressing room that day."

Sam's eyes widened and got suspiciously bright, but she gave Bex a smile. Not a smile for their audience or for the cell-phone cameras pointed at them. A smile for Bex and only Bex. "Yeah. All right. Let's talk about it."

"You came in. I was already nervous. I'd been avoiding talking to you alone for weeks. I knew you wanted to say something to me."

"What did you think I wanted to say?"

"What I would've said if I hadn't been so afraid I had to keep everything going exactly like it was or the entire universe would fall from the sky like marbles rolling off a table."

Bex took a breath to help her talk. "You weren't in costume," she said. "Even though you should've been by then. You were wearing a yellow T-shirt with a smiley face on it and bike shorts, and you looked like my favorite Sam. The one who would stay too late at my house, both of us punch drunk and unable to laugh anymore because it hurt our ribs. I want you to know that I never wanted that Sam to go home, even though she was often the Sam who would stop laughing for a moment and look at me and say my name in a way that meant I felt like I had to change the subject. Or what? I didn't know. I just knew I had to keep you from saying whatever you were going to say after my name."

"Bex," Sam said, just as tenderly as she always had.

"Like that. And that's how you started in my dressing room. 'Bex.' And then you said, 'Please let me say it.' I started to cry, because what you were going to tell me was the thing I most wanted to hear, but the one thing I didn't think I could do anything about. I didn't stop you. I couldn't make words. You said, 'I want you. I want us. Please say we can have us.'" Bex felt a few tears. Her throat was tight, but it wasn't difficult to share this with their fans. Not anymore.

"And you said, 'I don't know if I can,'" Sam said, without a trace of the grief her face had fallen into that day. Between them, there was nothing left of the awful, screaming silence that had followed Bex's inability to tell Sam what she'd wanted to hear.

"I did," Bex said. "Because right then, all I could tell you was 'I want.' And then I couldn't find a way to finish the sentence. What did I want? I knew in my heart, but I couldn't work out in my head how to ask for what I didn't believe I could have. You said, 'Let me know when you figure out what you want.' And then you left and got into your costume, and I didn't see you again until we had to film the scene we just watched. Our fans, I think, voted for that scene because there isn't any way to watch it and not feel at least some of what we were feeling. As soon as we wrapped it, I looked for you."

"Tell them why." Sam understood, like Bex did, that this conversation wasn't really for the two of them. It was for the fans who'd never been given any of the answers they wanted.

"Because by then I *did* know. I was so terrified, every muscle in my body was shaking, but I was looking for you everywhere, and somehow I knew I had ruined everything. I never found you. You had gone directly to a meeting to negotiate your contract, which was already holding up everybody from knowing if they should start work on the next season, and you told them you were out. Effective immediately."

"You knew where to find me if you wanted to talk about it."

"I did. But I received your leaving the show as a statement in response to how I answered you."

Sam laughed. "Bexley Simon, there was not a single time in the last five years when, if you had shown up on my doorstep, I wouldn't have yanked you into my lair."

Bex felt the back of her neck go red-hot. "Meanwhile, no one showed up at my doorstep." She tried to raise one eyebrow. Failed.

"False. I was there all the time."

"Hanging out with my sisters."

"And mooning over you."

"Who says *mooning*? What even is that?" Bex couldn't stop smiling now. She'd finally said out loud what had happened, how it felt, what had gone wrong. Her heart hadn't exploded. She hadn't died. It was just her and Sam and the lightness of knowing it really wasn't too late.

"Tell the people," Sam said, leaning on the table and holding the mic to her mouth. "What has it been like this week to finally give them what they want?"

"Hmm. As of right now, which is just a short time before we go live with the final scene, we haven't given them *everything* they want."

"No. How are you feeling about that?"

"Well, as you know, it can go one of two ways. It's our choice, according to the script. Which, first of all, that's something I haven't been offered before as an actor. I like it. But also, we haven't talked about it. There's a very sweet final exchange, and then there's a spicier version that doesn't involve any lines."

"I was going to see how it went. I like the risk of a live camera on me while I consider my moves."

"Huh. So what I can tell the people right now, who are listening after the broadcast, is that whatever they saw is exactly what we wanted to happen in the moment."

"You can. You know what else I would like to tell the people?"

"What's that?"

"You folks are going to see a lot of news coming out of this last episode." Sam was speaking directly to the fans now. "There's a good chance that most of it will be focused on the studio. Cineline as a hero, Cineline as a victim. But, ultimately, everything we've been doing since we started this podcast is for Jen. She was our friend, and she was our Big Name Fan. That's a title you, the fans, bestowed on her. So I hope that if the show that airs tonight gives you any inspiration, ideas, or feelings at all, you'll consider writing a fanfiction and dedicating it to Jen Arnot, the original Big Name Fan of *Craven's Daughter*."

"She would like that so much," Bex said.

"Plus, how else is anyone going to know what happens after our last balcony scene?" Sam asked, raising an eyebrow. "There's so much prime-time network television still shies away from."

"That's perfect. I love it. I have something different that I'd like to tell everyone." Now Bex leaned forward on the table and stared into Sam's eyes.

"What is it?" Sam asked this with her trademark witty insouciance, but her eyes were bright and very focused.

"I finally know what I want. And maybe it will be hard, and maybe we'll have to figure a lot out, and maybe we still have so much to catch up on, but it's us. It's our ending, Sam Farmer. I want you and me."

Sam's smile was a brand-new one that Bex had never seen before.

She couldn't believe she'd waited so long for it.

Broadcast Live from Studio 46

"Shell casing for your thoughts." Henri held out the bit of smashed brass.

Cora settled her hands on the balcony railing and looked out over the dark street, the street light illuminating her face. "I will give you my thoughts without evidence of violence. How about that?"

"Better."

Cora grinned, throwing Henri a look that made her swallow in response. "I was thinking about how the world connected us to these two sisters. The first one, because she was betrayed by loving a man who had stolen her heart but who only wanted to end her life. After that case, I'm not afraid to tell you, I nearly packed up my cardigans and ran back to my classroom because I felt like such a failure. The second sister seemed like her motivation was hate. Revenge. Not revenge for her sister's life, but because of everything that unfolded since they were born and their parents' relationship fell apart. But I don't think it was hate. I think it was hope. I think she was hoping to come to the same place her sister had, to talk to the same people and get a different outcome. Somehow, in some way, to get her sister back."

Henri moved closer to Cora. "The way you got your father back?"

"No, because I never had him. I've been getting to know him

through finding out what it means to be Craven's daughter, and it's clear he wasn't father material. I don't think there's anything I could've done in this agency to make up for that. But I was thinking about it, and I realized that knowing what to do about love and hope and things you're afraid of sometimes doesn't get figured out for years. Sometimes you need a lot more experiences to help you find the right answers."

Henri edged even closer, until Cora had to tip her head back to keep from breaking eye contact. "I had a question the day we met," Henri said. "When I tapped on the glass in your office door."

"You were looking for a job."

"You thought so. The truth? I was looking for the bathroom. Your light was on. I could see through the window. You were just a shape." Henri outlined the shape of Cora's hair around her head, smiling a little. "But you said to come in, and you thought I was here for an interview. You talked so fast, I could hardly keep up. When you found out I'd been an FBI agent, you acted like it was a foregone conclusion I'd been sent here to work for you."

"*With* me," Cora said. "I hoped."

Bex let her eyes drift over Sam's face the way Cora had never before been permitted to. Cora had memorized Henri in glimpses, glances, waiting for moments to look when Henri wouldn't notice her looking. "What was your question?" she asked.

"You were so bossy. I wanted to know what it would be like"—Henri laid her hand on Cora's shoulder, gripping it in a way that wasn't quite professional—"to let someone like you be in charge of me."

Cora's laugh came out choked, and she coughed just a little before reaching for bravado. "It's been six years, Agent Shannon. I hope you have your answer."

Henri's smile was crooked, a little sheepish. "Just more questions." But her hand had drifted down to grip Cora's arm, and they were so close to each other, Henri was staring at her mouth. "Every day we're together, it seems like there's another mystery to solve. A dozen new questions to get the answers to. A hundred things to learn."

"I'm a good teacher," Cora whispered, and then let out a breathless sigh that was almost a moan, because Henri's fingers were in the hair at the nape of her neck, and Henri's wintergreen breath was on her cheek.

"The best," Henri said. "I was right about you. I was right all along."

"Maybe I'm the one who was right." Cora slid her arms up and around Henri's shoulders and wrapped one hand gently around her ponytail. "Tell you what, Agent Shannon. That's how it usually works."

"You've always been right, Cora."

Henri's kiss didn't start soft, or tentative. It was sure, and sexy, and made both of them inhale sharply before going in for another kiss.

And then another, this one while they smiled.

The camera pulled away, leaving them both in silhouette, kissing on the balcony, revealing the moon over the building and a glimpse through the door leading to the office of the glass window with CRAVEN INVESTIGATIONS painted on it in gold.

"Cut!" Aaron barked. The set exploded in applause as Bex and Sam stepped apart from each other, laughing. The crew were laughing and shouting, and someone screeched out that social media was already on fire.

"That should do it," Sam said.

"Oh, we did it." Bex felt her chest go tight with pride. They had given *Craven's Daughter* the happily ever after it always deserved, and now they had one more thing they were being asked to give. For Jen.

"Are you ready? Josh is in a chair next to Aaron's."

Sam looked over at Aaron, who inclined his head slightly. He had decided to keep Camera One rolling, its feed sent directly to his handheld monitor. It meant that only Aaron and Josh could see it as the crew started breaking down parts of the set, talking, joking, checking their phones, and other cast members congratulated each other with champagne provided by craft services. Aaron had framed the shot in close, as if it were the opening sequence to another episode. Another mystery.

Which it was, in a way.

Sam dropped to a crouch, slipping off her blazer, and Bex walked into the office to make a new entrance onto the balcony as her character. One last time, she became Cora, just as Sam became Henri.

"What is it?" Cora carried two coffees for her and Henri, a folder for a new case under her arm. "Did you drop a donut?"

Henri looked back. "Donuts are processed poison. No. Look at this."

Cora put the coffees and folders on the ancient table on the balcony and crouched down next to Sam. "What am I looking at?"

Henri slid her fingers through the design in the wrought iron, gripped, and gave it a wiggle. "That."

Cora put a finger on the railing, then dragged her finger down, tracing what Henri had revealed. "It didn't break like this. Someone's cut clean through it."

Henri wiggled more. A whole section of the railing lifted out.

"Careful." Cora reached for Henri's upper arm and walked them both back away from the exposed edge of the balcony. "If you fell, I would be so angry."

Henri gave her a wry grin. "Angry, huh?"

Cora sniffed. "Safety first." She touched the section of railing. "How long do you think it's been like this? Did someone break in? Is someone trying to hurt people in this office? We come out here all the time."

Henri shook her head, inspecting the section of railing. "I think it's been like this for a while. There's rust at the edges where it was cut. But it's obvious whoever did this didn't want anyone to notice that this piece had been removed." Henri looked closer, her brow furrowed. "Hmm."

"What?"

"Hold this, just a sec." Henri dashed into the office, then returned, and Cora put the railing down on the table when she saw what Henri held in her hand.

Henri opened the small plastic case and removed a dropper bottle and a swab. She carefully swabbed the railing and then dropped the reagent on the tip of the cotton. They both watched as the end of the swab turned bright pink. "Blood."

Cora looked at Henri with horror. "I don't want to point out unpleasantness, but we both know we've removed deceased fauna from this balcony more than once. It might not be—"

"Human?" Henri picked up the section of railing, got a hand on either side of it, and, in one motion, swung it in front of herself like a weapon, making Cora gasp.

"What the fuck!"

Where there had been chatter on the stage, it went quiet when the exclamation sliced through the scene, breaking Bex's connection to her character and stopping her and Sam in their tracks.

"What the *actual fuck*?" It was Josh.

Bex heard something crash, and then he was stomping across Stage 46. She couldn't believe he'd moved so fast. Anger contorted his face in a way that made him look horrifyingly not *Josh*, even though she'd seen him angry plenty of times.

He made it onto the balcony set and tore the railing away from Sam, but he'd grabbed it so hard, he stumbled back.

He was expecting it to be wrought iron. Heavy. But it wasn't. That section of real railing was in a lab somewhere, getting scrutinized for evidence. This railing was a plastic prop. When Josh realized, he hurled it over the balcony set so hard, Bex could hear it whizz through the air past her head. It smashed and clattered somewhere in a dark part of the soundstage. "You think you're so fucking clever!" he roared.

Josh looked out at the crew, frozen and silent. Because of the lights, Bex couldn't see where Detective Lawson was. She was supposed to be nearby, along with security guards who were really police. She'd promised not to let anyone get hurt. Bex's heart was racing in her chest.

Then she heard her sister's voice. "Bex!" Vic screamed. "Bexley!"

Her eyes burned. Vic sounded terrified. She hadn't been told about this new plan. Other than Niels and the police, only Bex and Sam and Aaron knew. Bex made a move to run past Josh, but he put his big body in front of the opening that led to the office set.

"You know nothing. You all"—Josh turned around, taking in everyone on the stage—"think you're so smart, but you don't know how conniving she was, how she was using you to get what she wanted."

"You mean Jen." Sam's voice was calm. Her hand clasped Bex's, and that was a relief. "Jen Arnot."

"The sainted." Josh pounded a fist against his chest. "She was always talk-talk-talking behind everyone's back, but everything she said was a lie. Writing for Bette. Covering for Aaron's days off the wagon. Learning everybody's secrets so she could play us off each other. First she sets me up on *Charles Salt*, gets me fired, and flushes twenty years of hard work down the shitter. I can't get a job painting backdrops for high school theater, and just when I think I've got a chance to put something back together again with Aaron, I turn around and find out he's hired her for *Craven's Daughter*. So yeah, I was fucking mad! You tell me what it means when all of a sudden she magically doesn't need a restraining order against me on *this* set. What does that tell you? That what she was protecting all along was *her* plans. *Her* career. Knock me off of my opportunities so she could get ahead. Everyone around her suffered something like that, all so she could get her big deal at UBC."

Sam had started to slowly move away from Josh. They'd been acting partners so many times, Bex was acutely aware of how Sam moved her body and how she expected Bex to move in response. Sam wanted to back out through the gap made in the railing. They could walk around the set into safety. Bex squeezed Sam's hand so she knew she understood.

"I don't think I get it." Sam's tone was crisply businesslike. "She was the makeup artist. You and Jen and Aaron had known each other forever. This was an experienced set."

"Jesus Christ. You've been pointing fingers on your Nancy Drew podcast for weeks. Then this stunt. You think I'm stupid? I know about the railing they sent to the lab. Did *you* know cops are allowed to lie to you? 'We have evidence,' they say. 'Someone saw you there. We know you were alone with her, we know she started fucking yelling some shit at you about the hole in the balcony.' Like I was trying to assassinate one of her precious cast with what she called 'my stunts,' when the cast was already gone, and I was just waiting for a quiet ten minutes to do my fucking job. Whatever bullshit the cops want to tell you, they can, just to get you to confess what they need to put you away. I'm not stupid. That"—Josh gestured at the hole in the railing—"was just what I cut out to make a mold so our set wouldn't look like trash. You know they were using camera drones for those shots in Chicago? They got angles that made it clear that our set was a weak dupe. Here I am, fucking holding the integrity of this show on my shoulders while she's three-quarters out the door, but you're accusing *me* of snapping and, what? Knocking Jen through the balcony like a croquet ball through a wicket with a piece of wrought iron?"

Bex felt her face contort at the violence of that minimizing, grotesque simile.

"Did you?" Her voice emerged from her raw throat even louder than usual. "Is that what you did?" She looked back at the gap. "Because she was my friend. I know her family. I talk to her mother. They have to live without her. You didn't like her, okay! Fine! But Jen had a right to her life. Her dreams. What the fuck did *you* think you had a right to, Josh?"

He scoffed. "Every step she took led her to this." Josh wrapped his hand around the railing beside the hole and shook it. "It was her fault, and she would've done the same to me. Left me bloody in the street."

Suddenly, there were police everywhere. Sam seized a moment when Josh surged forward to back through the gap in the railing with Bex. The last thing Bex saw before they were out of the light was Josh's gray face and the way he pushed his body against the officers in anger as they cuffed him.

Then Josh and the police looked far, far away, like they were on a stage, which they were. Lit up. On camera. It gave Bex the out-of-body sensation of unreality, but it was actually happening.

Vic and Frankie ran toward them. Bex wrapped her arms around her family, crushed between Sam and Vic and Frankie, and held on tight.

Then she felt a tap on her shoulder, and she turned around, the group hug breaking up. It was Haris, the PA who'd retrieved Bex and Sam from their picnic on the brownstone steps earlier.

"So, weird news. In the midst of a lot of weird news." He pushed his glasses up.

"What is it?" Frankie asked. "You look . . . weird."

He nodded. "Turns out someone, we don't know who yet, which is also weird, didn't cut the live feed."

"*What?*"

He looked away from Frankie and winced.

"But they cut to commercial, right? To the news? To anything else?" Frankie stepped forward when Haris didn't answer. "Right?" she whispered, so close to his face that someone looking from a distance might have thought they were kissing. Haris's hands were curled into fists at his sides.

Possibly Haris wouldn't mind if Frankie *was* kissing him.

"Also weird, it seems . . . not." Haris swallowed, stepped back, and steepled his fingers and tapped his chin with them. "There was possibly some confusion? Since you guys stayed in character, and the monitor for controlling the feed was in another room, and this is all kind of a—"

"Don't say weird," Frankie interrupted.

"—*unusual* project, and I guess the thing with the cops was sort of not communicated . . . widely enough."

"*But*," Frankie said. She took Haris's shoulders between both of her palms in a way that commanded his complete attention and flushed his neck. "You know something. You saw something, or someone told you, or you figured it out because you are dazzlingly sneaky—we both know it's the trait I admire most about you." Frankie dropped her voice in a low register that Bex had never heard before. "You give up your secret *right now*, Haris Ahmadi."

"Bette," he croaked. "Bette did it. But if you tell anyone I said so, she'll murder me."

Bex put her hands to her cheeks, looking from her sisters to Sam to Haris, thinking, *Bette.*

She'd wanted the world to know the truth. Finally.

"I'd never tell," Frankie said fiercely, letting go of Haris with a brisk brush of her palms down his upper arms and a small squeeze that, if Bex hadn't been watching closely, she wouldn't have seen. "Thank you."

Vic was already on her phone. "*Cowabunga*," she said. "This is so *much* Internet."

Sam put her hand low on Bex's back. When Bex turned to look at her, she said, "Let's leave before the lawyers get here."

Bex closed her eyes. "Yep. Frankie, could you . . . ?"

"Yes." Frankie's curly hair made a wild halo around her head. "I am going to get the car. Meet me by the emergency exit door that's broken." Frankie gave Haris a dark look. "Make sure nobody gets in their way." She jogged off.

When Haris hustled them away from Stage 46, still wearing

their costumes, Bex didn't turn to see what was happening behind her.

Everything she cared about was up ahead.

Frankie met them by the emergency exit door. They piled into the car. Everyone talked too fast, too much, as they worked through what had happened from each of their four perspectives, filling in the details that the others might have missed, sharing how it felt to finally be at the end of a story they'd lived in through the hardest, longest, worst-best years of their lives.

They agreed to turn off their phones.

They went to In-N-Out, and they toasted Jen with sodas.

Sam told them about where she would be filming in Iceland, and Frankie talked about a call she'd had with, yes, Kari Leder from the Barrymore, who Frankie seemed to have actually hit it off with—which made sense when Bex thought about it, because Frankie was exactly the type of person that people with knives in their boots liked.

They all talked about old times and new times.

They enjoyed *this* time. For the last time.

The Mystery of What Comes Next

"That can't be everything." Bex surveyed her foyer filled with the neatly stacked pale blue containers she'd bought to pack up Frankie's things for her move to New York.

Frankie had conceded—after more of a fight than Bex expected—to the apartment in a doorman building that the broker assured them was regularly treated for pests. It was a bit farther off Forty-Eighth than Bex would have liked, but it was an interesting walk or a one-stop ride on the subway to the Barrymore.

"It's everything." Frankie put her hands on her hips. "I'm very minimalist." She'd grown out her hair a little, and it coiled around her ears and neck. She wore the soft dark green sweater Bex had bought her for Christmas, but her jeans and boots were black, because this was Frankie.

"Minimalist?" Vic snorted. "There's ten times this much in your room. Plenty to loot for *my* room after you're gone."

"Don't you dare." Frankie stuck her hands in her back pockets. "I left behind everything I really care about."

Smiling, Bex willed away the tears that wanted to come because Frankie meant her stagecraft models and vintage movie poster collection and guitars, not Bex and Vic. Probably.

"For crying out loud." Frankie's expression was exasperated when she looked over at Bex blinking too fast, but she put her arms around her anyway. "You know I care the most about you and Vic, but I don't even leave until tomorrow. We're supposed to be having fun tonight."

"Yeah, there's only eight more days until UCLA starts," Vic said. "I'm staring down the barrel of Evolutionary Biology with a prof who people on TikTok call 'the Steel Wolf.' I want to hit this holiday thing before the A-listers show up at the club and ruin the mood." Vic had dressed the top half of her body for the party in a bedazzled pink tank that picked up the pink tips of her outsized false eyelashes, but her bottom half was still cozy in pajama pants and fuzzy slippers.

Bex would not be going to the "holiday thing." She had a date. It was on Zoom, and she would be providing her own food and drink and ambiance, but it was with Sam, so those kinds of details didn't matter.

"Come snuggle with me on the patio before you get ready," she said. "I'll turn on those lighted floating globes I got for the pool and bring out hot chocolate and blankets."

"It's sixty-five degrees," Vic complained. "I wore my Uggs today to try to get into the spirit, and my feet sweated so much, my toes pruned."

Bex sighed.

"But I will take a hot chocolate." Vic bumped her shoulder and followed her into the kitchen.

After some bickering, boiling over a pan of milk, and digging through three storage ottomans for the outdoor blankets, they were settled into the big wicker sectional, looking at the lights on the water, and burning their tongues. Shockingly, they were quiet for a long time.

It had been a hard day.

"Are you doing okay after Chicago?" Frankie didn't look at Bex when she asked this. Bex could tell that Frankie and Vic had been trying to give her a lot of space since she returned from her trip yesterday evening.

"Yes." Bex took a deep breath. "Based on the questions I

was asked and what the police were willing to tell me, it sounds like Jen's death happened how we've thought it did, and how the press has speculated. Josh was removing a section of the railing to cast it onsite so he could take it back to California and build a new railing for the balcony on set. Jen woke up from her nap, most likely thinking everyone had left. She probably hadn't taken any medication. Georgie was right about that. She saw the balcony with the hole in it, Josh messing with it, and had good reasons to assume sabotage. They got into an argument over that. Georgie's review of the old file, combined with the additional interviews that were done with Johnny Kerr and some other people, put Josh there. It sounds like where Jen was found in the alley was more consistent with her having fallen *through* that gap in the railing, not over it. We know from the press that there's DNA evidence. I assume it's the blood on the railing, but no one's confirmed that or told me if it's Josh's or Jen's."

"It's Jen's," Vic said. "I know it is. I know he hit her with it. Because who stands close enough to a big hole in the railing to just fall through it? You avoid it. And the cut-out piece of railing would have been so heavy. It would have been easy to *make* her get close to the edge with it. And everyone in America heard that gross thing he said about croquet." Vic sniffed and touched her fingers to the corners of her eyes to keep from ruining her eyelashes with tears. Frankie put an arm around her.

Just before the holidays, they'd all flown to Ohio to visit Toni Arnot. They'd laughed a lot and eaten too much, and Vic had signed them up for a behind-the-scenes gorilla encounter at the zoo that made Toni cry over how much Jen would have liked it.

It was a lovely visit. They hadn't talked about Josh at all.

"My statement to the police was mainly about everything I'd done to open up the case," Bex said. "Who I heard what from and when, and where I had everything documented—"

"Your notebook," Frankie said. "Now you'll never be without one. Your notebook habit has been vindicated."

"It has. There were a lot of questions. It took a long time, but I was glad to do it for Jen. I was sad thinking about what steps Josh could've taken to help himself a long time ago, and how many lives would have changed for the better if he had. On the plane back, I thought a lot about Sam. How she knew something was wrong and was suffering because no one would hear her."

"But what about you?" Frankie asked. "Sure, you're glad to help Jen. You've said so over and over. But what are you *feeling*? For *you*."

Bex picked at the fringe on her blanket. The question didn't surprise her. It would have, before, but she understood her sisters a little better now. "I don't know if there really were ghosts on the set," she said. "If there were, I think we sent them on their way. That makes me feel better. It's been hard pushing forward with so much weight dragging on me from what didn't get finished. I remember when we first moved here, I had really bad insomnia. That's why I started my night routine, by the way"—she aimed her most parental look at Frankie, then at Vic—"and I would lie in bed thinking about everything Mom and Dad were missing. It was impossible to accept that we'd *finished* being a family with Mom and Dad."

"What helped?" Vic sipped her hot chocolate. "Or maybe it's still like that."

Bex shook her head. "Sam. You two. Making new memories. Time? That I am myself all the way through and can't really imagine myself any other way? You can't sing in front of thousands of people and have a very big capacity for regret, I guess. Right now, I'm pretty interested in what's next, and that helps. Having interesting possibilities up ahead."

"Drama." Vic nodded. "Exactly. Confession—I can't wait to meet this Steel Wolf guy. I'm secretly hoping it's completely out of pocket. Like where TAs cry and an evil subplot is discovered."

"I don't know why you'd think we don't know that about you," Frankie told Vic. She stretched out and crossed her ankles, throwing off the blanket. "When you were a baby and got vaccine shots in your thigh, you wouldn't walk for a week. Mom had to keep you home from preschool. It was a whole thing, just because you couldn't get enough of the *event* of bursting into tears every time you tried to take a step."

"Now that you've gotten a taste of it"—Vic looked at Bex but reached around her and yanked Frankie's hair, which meant a slap fight started behind Bex's head—"do your interesting possibilities up ahead include more, you know, detective stuff?"

"What?" Bex reached behind her head and smacked both of Frankie and Vic's hands so they would stop. "That is not a thing."

"Completely a thing," Frankie said.

"It was barely a thing with this *Craven's Daughter* reunion special mess, which the press has not calmed down about. I can't imagine, what? Painting SIMON CELEBRITY INVESTIGATIONS on the side door with the glass in it?"

"*Hmm.*" Vic threw off her own blanket. "You came up with that name pretty damn quick."

"Go get ready." Bex sat up, holding her hands out for their mugs. "I hired a car for you, so don't use cabs or Uber or anything like that. Set up a tab, check your purses, keep your drinks in sight, watch for anyone vulnerable who needs help, and leave before the men come who are dating women younger than their own children."

"You're not my mom," Frankie said, with none of the heat she used to say it with.

"No, I'm not. Because if I were your mom and you didn't do what I wanted you to do, I would just fret and read a parenting book and maybe yell a little. But since I'm only your sister, I can threaten to throw away your Funko Pops or maybe scatter them in the driveway and drive back and forth over them until they are Flat-o Pops. Or put Nair in your shampoo. I have a lot of ideas that I haven't had a chance to deploy due to all of this pesky responsibility."

"Let's go finish getting ready before we find out too much more about what she's really like," Vic said. "Bex can keep up with us at the party by checking my socials."

Her sisters went inside, and Bex cleaned up. As soon as she saw the lights from the driver's car and yelled out her goodbye, her text came through.

Ready?

Bex tapped the thumbs up and raced into her bedroom, grabbing her tablet off a hall table and taking a quick look at herself in a mirror, then wishing she hadn't because she didn't have time to fix anything. As soon as she propped herself in bed and put in her ear buds, she made the call, biting her lip.

It was only three in the morning in Selfoss, Iceland, but Sam was already in a wig cap, her shoulders protected by a drape, and she had what Bex knew was a coffee with two espresso shots and lots of sugar. The shoot had been grueling.

"Hi." Bex drank her in, trying to pick up on every detail.

"Frankie called and told me she thought you looked sad when you got back from Chicago, but I thought that couldn't be, because you texted me that you were doing well." Sam raised one eyebrow.

Bex gave Sam a stern look back. She did not want to waste their precious time together on the same discussion she'd just had with her sisters. She had other plans that were one hundred percent related to the fact that she'd locked her bedroom door. "I told you everything I could about it. I can't imagine it was much different from your experience, even if you were allowed to appear by Zoom. You told me you were okay after. Should I doubt you?"

Bex did not try to raise an eyebrow at Sam. Recently, putting on makeup in the mirror while talking to a particularly shocking Vic, she had realized that her own personal version of Sam's eyebrow-raise expression involved the appearance of her left dimple and left dimple only. She had been practicing making that dimple sink on command.

She did it now, but Sam just laughed.

"Touché." Sam folded her arms on the table she was sitting at and gazed at Bex for one beat longer than would give Sam plausible deniability she was thinking about anything other than what kind of call this would be. Bex took advantage of Sam's self-conscious grin with a look she didn't have to practice in order to know it was very thirsty.

Sam had left before the worst of the aftermath died down. In fact, she'd left almost a week early because her director wanted her focused for filming. It had been so, so, so long since they'd seen each other. More than a *month.*

"Here's something."

"What? Give me something, Sam Farmer."

Sam smiled in the way that was very new between them and made Bex ache. "We wrap in Selfoss in three weeks. Then there's several weeks of studio and green-screen filming in L.A., but I'll be home. Around. Not here, freezing through my faux fur costume."

Bex's stomach flipped. Contrary to what their avid global fan-base seemed to believe, she and Sam had barely gotten started as . . . as Bex and Sam, whatever they ended up being to each other. When she'd told her sisters she was looking forward to what came next, she'd been talking mostly about Sam, who'd been stealing time away from grueling sixteen-hour days on location as much as she could to talk, joke, reminisce, analyze, and, yes, *flirt* with Bex. Lately, there had been a very intense undercurrent and some *extras* to the flirting that made Bex both inconveniently horny and a teeny-tiny bit nervous about seeing Sam again in person. In a good way. Mostly.

"God, that would be amazing, I—"

Bex stopped.

"What? Did our connection freeze? Can you hear me?"

"*Shh.* Yeah. I just remembered something." Disappointment swamped Bex's excitement.

"What?"

"I'm going to Kansas." She collapsed back on her pillows, defeated.

Sam's eyes were wide, and Bex could tell that she was trying to be cool but failing. "Why would you do that? When?"

"In three weeks. Shauna Kane called me before I went to Chicago."

Sam whistled. "Shauna Kane! That's . . . a really big deal. Like, an incredibly big deal. Had you been working on this without telling me?"

"No, nothing like that. I kind of forgot about it because of the Chicago thing, as far as telling you before this moment. A year ago, she wanted me for her Western. The one with queer cowgirls. I wanted to, but I was in New York, and she even tried to change around her shooting schedule, but it didn't work. Someone else was cast who backed out. She called me, and now I'm going to Kansas for location filming in three weeks when you'll be home but stuck in L.A."

Sam had her fingertips to her mouth, listening to Bex. "How long?"

"A month. Then L.A. The set build will be done then. Will you be in L.A. in three weeks and one month?"

"Maybe? They haven't settled on a location for *Theomina*. The dragon-riding movie. It was supposed to be L.A., but now they're talking about Vancouver for the tax break, and I guess there are 'good trees,' whatever that means."

Bex flopped her arm around her head dramatically, wondering why she hadn't become a financial advisor like her dad. Damn genetic talent. "I'll be here between Shauna's wrap and New York, but only for a month."

"One month." Sam firmed her jaw. "My people are going to

call these *Theomina* people, today, and tell them I'm allergic to Canada."

Bex would've laughed, but she couldn't because she'd melted in a hundred different places at Sam's determined expression, at the way she listened, and especially at the evidence she was as eager to see Bex as Bex was to see her.

It was scary. Sometimes she caught herself staring into the middle distance imagining what it would be like to see Sam again in person. To be able to touch her, and whatever would happen after that, and *everything*, everything. "Do you think we'll ever work together again?"

Of all the questions Bex had thought to ask Sam, she was surprised that was the one that escaped. They'd idly talked about working together after getting the same question many, many times in the interview frenzy that followed the series finale, but mainly in a way that seemed sentimental.

Somewhere far off in her notebook-carrying, list-making brain, she knew she'd asked it because of the conversation they were having. Iceland, L.A., Kansas, New York, Vancouver, Paris, Croatia, New Orleans, London. The *work*. Endless and hard and time-consuming in a way that explained the end of so many celebrity romances. When would they next be in the same place at the same time for long enough to really have each other?

Bex had wasted so many years already. Years she might have been with Sam.

"I mean, together, we're pretty overexposed at the moment." Sam smiled. "But I think I know what you're asking."

"Ohio's nice," Bex said. "You went to Yale Drama. How do you feel about directing high school students in what I'm sure would be a very fresh production of *Our Town*? I can give piano lessons. Voice. My mom's old students probably have kids of their own now. Instant network."

"Bex." Sam leaned in and put her head on her hand, looking her over through the screen.

She thought Sam might've meant to sound like she was teasing, except Bex heard the longing, and she heard Sam's understanding that Bex was pretty far gone. All in. Terrified, but for it. "Well, maybe not. Or, how about this? Vic suggested a detective agency."

"In Hollywood? Then we'd never get time off between the cold cases and the ongoing shenanigans." Sam cupped her hand behind her ear as though listening to a faraway voice. "But I do like the sound of Farmer Investigations."

"Sure you do. We'll have to keep it in mind for a retirement career. Simon and Farmer Investigations."

"You mean Farmer and Simon. Alphabetical, as is customary." Then there was a grin, and Bex put away the worries and the thousands of miles between them.

She listened to Sam, and Sam listened to her. They kept each other company the best way they could while the sun rose in Iceland, and Frankie and Vic danced in Los Angeles, and Jen's family spent another holiday season without her—but at least now they had a story to tell.

Bex liked to think it was a story Jen would have been proud to be a part of.

She had been bluffing, just a little, when she told her sisters she was looking forward to whatever the future would bring. But Bex had been bluffing, just a little, her whole life.

That was how she always made it through the mystery of what came next.

Acknowledgments

Every once in a while, there are characters who impatiently in their magical reception room and who don't hang around waiting for the author to open the door and call their names—they just kick the door down. Bex and Sam were these characters for us, and they were assisted in their escape by Annie's agent, Tara Gelsomino, who mused on socials about her desire for a reunion show romance. We owe a great deal to Tara, as well as to Ruthie's agent, Pamela Harty. They are tireless, inspiring, and collaborate with the Big Magic of our authors' imagination to get books like *Big Name Fan* in the hands of readers.

Our children, August and James, remain our closest conspirators in this life, and while Annie has saturated herself in fandoms and fanfiction for decades, it was our kids' dedication to fix-it fic, AUs, fandom dust-ups, unlikely ships, and the queerification of every corner of every fandom that provided light and humor to the process of writing this book. We love you. No superlative could capture you two adequately. Thank you for our house of laughter and nerdery.

Susan Rogers remains a rock for our family and shoulders the lion's share of support for our life as authors. She reads everything we write, she deep dives into publishing lore with us and learns the lingo, and she celebrates every milestone, even when we forget to. Our kids couldn't ask for a better auntie. Thank you for flying on planes to be at our signings and hand-selling our books. We love you immoderately.

Barbara and Barry Homrighaus have offered us unconditional and faithful support, listening to the trials of submission and deal-making and every one of our aspirations. Thank you for all of it. We're so glad you're copilots to our adventure.

Shannon Plackis was the rare editor who was also our number one target audience for this book. A veteran of fandoms and fanfiction, books, and queer community, she offered powerful support to this book, and her heartfelt insight meant that Kensington's mighty publishing team was activated to find it as many readers as possible. It's not surprising that the gifted Shannon found a fantastic new opportunity in publishing while the three of us were having fun editing Bex and Sam, and while changing editors *can* be an uneasy time, Alex Sunshine swept away any worries and took us on with grace, smarts, and powerful ideas. We couldn't have been better taken care of by Shannon and Alex as well as the entire Kensington team.

Finally, we couldn't have done this without the ongoing love from our queer community and found family, from author friends who get it, and from booksellers and librarians who broker in imagination, magic, and take care of you, readers—the reason why we're here at all. Thank you.

Don't miss the next book in
Annie Mare and Ruthie Knox's
TV Detective series.

Bex and Sam return to crack
another Hollywood case in . . .

Love a Comeback.

Back in the
Leather Corset Again

Crouching on a dirty soundstage, Sam Farmer tried to find the place inside herself where she had invited her character, Theomina, to live.

Small bits of grit bit into her naked kneecaps. When she adjusted her position, the boning of her leather corset caught painfully against her rib cage. Ignoring the discomfort, Sam listened for the voice of the dragon rider inside her.

Theomina had lost everything she loved. Her father. The witch who was the only mother she'd ever known. Her beloved dragon. She was tough, but she'd reached her limit. She was tired. Her heart *hurt*.

A tear raced down Sam's cheek as she stared up into the ice-blue eyes of her costar, Chad Bevington. His eyes were the only part of him she could see clearly, since his face was covered in the green fabric of his chroma key suit. The evenly spaced markers sewn into it would allow the CGI people to do their post-production digital magic and turn him into the soul-sucking beast that Theomina was fighting.

It wasn't hard for Sam to access the part of herself that believed Chad made a credible soul-sucking beast.

"Cut!"

Sam relaxed her body as much as she could in the dragon-riding leathers of her costume. She looked past the lights pointed at the studio stage. "Did we get it?"

"Your nose is running every time you cry." The assistant director sighed and looked at her clipboard. "Take five while we decide."

Goddamnit. Sam had wrapped this movie almost two months ago. She'd wrapped it so hard, thrilled beyond description to be finished in Vancouver and finally able to unpack her suitcases at home in the Hollywood Hills. But compositing issues with some of the green-screen shots meant she'd been called to a borrowed L.A. soundstage at StudioHonor for reshoots at 5:00 a.m. on the same day her former costar, recent sleuthing partner, and current long-distance girlfriend, Bex, was finally coming home.

"When I need to cry on camera, I like to remember when my dog died," Chad said, stretching his arms above his head. "Nice, clean tears." He winked at her.

Ugh. Sam didn't mind so much that Chad was vain and entitled. Vain entitlement came preinstalled in this town. What she did mind was his tendency to try to control everyone and everything that happened on set. This was a man who'd threatened to call his "legal team" so often that it became an inside joke among the cast and crew.

Sam, I'm afraid I'm going to have to grab you real quick to adjust your wig.

Really? Sam would raise her eyebrow at her snickering makeup assistant. *You can try, but you should know I'll be calling my legal team.*

Other than lightly mocking the man out of earshot, Sam had said nothing about Chad's behavior. Like the character she played, she was tough. She'd grown up with four older brothers and knew how to fight hard and dirty to maintain her ego under the attack of entitled boys.

Though Chad was not a boy. He'd begun his career as an icon of nineties cinema, and he remained as familiar to movie and TV audiences as popcorn.

Still. Not worth the energy.

After a long stretch of lights going on and off, crew yelling directions, and conversations between the director and his assistants, the main bank of lights went down. "Thank you, theydies and gentlefolk, that's a wrap!" the director yelled. "Get the fuck out of here and stay out of my face until I see you at the premiere."

Sam blew out a breath in relief.

"Except for you, my queen." The director turned to point at Sam. "I'll see *you* in a week."

Sam gave him the wide, affable smile that was her trademark, most recently reproduced on the plastic face of her Theomina action figure's prototype. "Looking forward to it."

She was not.

Making movies about magic was not a magical experience. Sam had adored *Theomina* when it was a postapocalyptic fantasy novel. She'd given copies to her nieces and nephews, and they'd been the first ones she called when she was offered the part in the film. *I'm going to play Theomina!* she'd told them over Zoom, and everyone had cheered.

Then she'd spent most of the shoot grateful beyond words that the novel's author had promised to only ever write *one* Theomina book. No more books meant no sequels. Sam would never have to play Theomina again.

Or so she'd believed.

The author's artistic convictions, it turned out, didn't stop her from licensing her IP to Howell Motion Pictures. Just yesterday afternoon, Sam received an excited phone call from her manager letting her know that blockbuster-maker Bradley Wilhite had attached himself to a *Theomina and the Dragon of Shadows* limited series in the role of Theomina's romantic interest.

The one and only novel characterized Theomina as ascetic,

with no other love than for her kingdom, and definitely not for a giant creep of a man who was more than twenty years older than her and didn't believe in intimacy coordinators. But Theomina and her fictional principles were no match for heteronormative Hollywood.

Bradley Wilhite wanted Sam to report to his ranch in Telluride in seven days for a chemistry read, and Sam was expected to pack lip balm, drink plenty of water, and smile.

The director gave her a wave on his way out. Soon, Sam was surrounded by costume assistants who unbuckled her from the leathers down to the singlet and bike shorts she wore underneath. Chad was still being freed from his suit when she booked it to a dressing room to remove her makeup and fake blood. She brushed the special effects dirt out of her hair and slammed on a pair of jeans, a T-shirt, and a ball cap. They were her comfy clothes, designed for utility and escaping the set quickly. In her bedroom at home, Sam had something a lot more special laid out for when she saw Bex later.

On the open-air top deck of the studio's parking garage, she unlocked her Audi and flung her hat onto the passenger seat. The first thing she did after a long, desperately needed exhale was dig her phone out of her bag, swipe past three million notifications, and tap the only name in her saved contacts that she'd marked with a star.

Bexley Simon.

"Hello?"

Sam winced. The familiar voice sounded distracted and like there were a lot of people around. "Bex?"

"Sam? Fuck! Hold on. *I've got it, for Christ's sake!*" Bex said this to someone else. *"It's a carry-on. I'll carry it!"*

Sam's girlfriend was a small woman, short, curvy, and deceptively adorable, with a face that could make a person fall in love or weep across an entire theater and into the cheap seats, but she was not quiet. A Broadway theater critic had once admiringly mused that, given the pair of lungs on Bex, her body couldn't possibly contain much else besides her artist's heart—and, what's more, she needed nothing else but that heart and those lungs to keep herself upright, dancing, and singing.

Sam put the phone on speaker and turned down the volume.

"Okay. My *god*. Sam? Are you still there?"

"I am."

Bex gusted a breath out into the phone. "Give me one second, I'm at the entrance of the VIP lounge." The background noise dropped away. The sound of Bex breathing into her phone became all-encompassing, then inaudible. "Now I can hear you. Can you hear me?"

Sam laughed. "I can hear you. You must be at the airport."

"Indeed."

"LAX, I hope?"

"I *should* be at LAX, but my flight out of JFK was diverted to Denver because apparently it's hard to fly through something called a derecho?"

"Sounds fake." Sam made her voice as loose as her hands, which she laid palms-up on her thighs to keep from squeezing the steering wheel in bloodless fists.

"Doesn't it? I just got off the plane, and I'm supposed to stay in this room they are calling a VIP lounge. At some point there will be a new crew, and I will get back on the plane." Sam heard a loud rustling that she recognized as the sound of Bex digging through her bag for whatever gross nutrition bar she currently believed would solve her problems. "I should've taken Frankie up on her offer to drive cross-country with her, but I feel like it's possible I'm not made for road trips."

"Absolutely you are not." Bex was a lot of things—a world-class singer, a joyful dancer, an actor with charisma for days—but a woman satisfied with any kind of passenger seat was not one of them.

Sam loved that about her.

It was a helpful reminder. She held onto it and made herself take a few beats to recenter. She'd been looking forward to Bex's return more than was altogether good for her. Possibly, a little bit, Sam had been clinging to a fantasy of what Bex's return would be like. Daydreaming about surprising Bex at the baggage carousel. Flipping through a mental carousel of potential outfits and imagining how Bex would react. Thinking up menus for a romantic evening meal they would share poolside, just the two of them.

None of that was going to happen. Even so, it was a perfect May afternoon in Los Angeles. Hot, but with a nice breeze. The sky was clear. She'd been released from the clutches of *Theomina*. Nothing was fucked here, as her brother Fergus liked to say. No one had abandoned her. Sam would see Bex soon, even if soon turned out not to be tonight.

Six months, though. It had been six whole, entire months since they'd been in the same room. Their work had pulled them apart, throwing their relationship into the kind of long-distance, not-quite-there-yet limbo that made Sam worry, lying awake in the middle of the night, that she'd left it too long and missed her one cosmic chance at love.

She and Bex had been together almost every day of the six years they spent costarring on *Craven's Daughter,* a TV procedural about a kindergarten teacher (Bex's character, Cora Banks) who takes over her dead father's detective agency and teams up with a disgraced former FBI agent (Sam's character, Henri Shannon) to solve one murder per week. They were fraught years for Sam, heady and frenetic, with an undercurrent of doomed pining for her fellow TV detective.

Then, after Sam confessed her feelings to Bex and Bex didn't instantly admit to feeling the same way, Sam had fled, quit the show, and spent half a decade accepting any role she was offered, so long as it enabled her to avoid her quiet house and her own company (Sam's condition) and moved her up another rung in the ladder of Hollywood celebrity (her management's stipulation).

The result was that Sam had reached a fuck-you level of stardom with the money to match. She was very rich and very, very famous, but without Bex she wasn't happy.

They'd figured it out. Their reunion six months ago had turned out to be the most delicious do-over Sam could have asked for, and in the here-and-now it wasn't her fault *or* Bex's that their schedules were packed. The commitments keeping them apart had been decided before they got together. And Sam was a patient person. Level-headed. Extremely chill. Everyone said so.

"You're doing the thing where you go silent," Bex said. "So I'm doing the thing where I panic."

"Right. Sorry." She wasn't brilliant over the phone. They'd suffered through a lot of calls at weird or inconvenient times over bad connections. They texted constantly at first, but small issues blew up too easily into big misunderstandings, and so they'd been relying heavily on voice memos for the past few months. Sam had started to feel like she was sending letters by carrier pigeon from the warfront to her fiancée back home.

"I am disappointed. I miss you." Sam delivered this line with, she thought, a degree of affability that convincingly hid her vulnerable yearning. "But we can't control the weather. When do you think you'll get in?"

"They seem pretty confident a fresh flight crew will be here in a couple of hours." Bex sounded as crushed as Sam felt. "And by then, the storm will be past. With the time difference, I could be in L.A. in time for a very late dinner at Tatsu Ramen."

"Perfect." Sam bit her lower lip. She could feel every place her stiff costume had dug into her ribs, leaving hurt places that would bloom into bruises tonight while she slept. Alone, most likely.

She rolled her eyes at herself. Give a girl a mom who wasn't cut out for parenthood and a dad with multiple marriages, and she'd be stuck with abandonment issues forever.

"This is what we're going to do." Bex's voice had gotten crisp, exactly like an older sister who'd had to raise her two younger sisters with literally nothing but pure faith and terrifying ambition. Which she was.

"Tell me."

"This plane is pulling away from the gate in one hundred and twenty minutes or less, or I am calling Kevin Costner, who happens to owe me a favor, and who I know is at his place in Denver right now, and he will fly me to L.A. private."

Sam smiled at this pronouncement. At its heart, Hollywood was a small town, which meant it did a brisk commerce in favors, boons, and handshake agreements. One of the things that made Bex so delightfully *Bex* was that she kept track of every single one in a secret notebook she kept in a zippered pocket of her bag. "Why not call him this instant?"

"I want to use my favor as judiciously as possible, due to a thing not worth going into with his management. But in ninety minutes or less, I want you to go over to my house. I know you wanted to pick me up from the airport, but I'm assigning you to another mission." Bex's voice had become formidable. "Turn on the pool lights. Make sure there is food, a lot of it. Nothing vegetarian. Frankie's taken me to every plant-based deli, cafe, and bar in Manhattan, and I am getting frail. Tonight, we're going to eat a devastating number of something extremely bad for us and listen to all of Vic's major and minor dramas, and then we will curl up together on the big pool chaise and talk or not talk until we fall asleep or a drone camera catches a picture of my thigh between your legs and my mouth welded to yours"—Bex paused to take a breath—"and the rest of us, you and me, will start early tomorrow."

Hearing Bex's description of their thighs intertwined had Sam actually blushing. She pulled at her lip, acknowledging a pang of misery that she and Bex couldn't be immediately alone. Fortunately, it was a small pang. Bex and her sisters, Frankie and

Vic, were a package deal. It didn't bother Sam, who'd grown up in a family where privacy was scarce and raucous conversation the norm. "That is a *plan*."

She tried out believing every word of it, just to see how it felt.

It felt wonderful. For three seconds.

Then the good feeling slipped away.

Sam's dad had been married seven times. The longest romantic relationship ever embarked upon by Caesar Polonius Farmer, Oakland periodontist, lasted thirty-six months, and it was on supplemental oxygen by the end. In defiance of these familial odds, Sam had always hoped to find her person—her *one* person—and pair-bond until death. This meant that while the press liked to paint a picture of her dating habits that featured a revolving door of women, the truth was considerably more . . . governess-like. Proper. "No contingencies?" she asked.

"No. This is the only plan. It is a good plan, and, what's more, it's the plan we deserve."

"It is a Bex plan."

"Yes. Which means it will happen, or something else equally remarkable will, and then I'll make a new plan. But get ready."

Sam could easily imagine Bex in plan-making mode, her cloud of unruly auburn curls bent over one of her notebooks as she made a list. It was a sight Sam looked forward to seeing again soon. "We're almost there," she said, mostly to herself.

"And once I'm back, we'll have six weeks," Bex said. "A week for every month we spent apart."

Except that I'm going to Telluride.

Sam pushed the thought and everything it represented down somewhere deep inside herself. At thirty-five, she was a couple of years younger than Bex. She didn't feel ancient yet, and her paychecks told her she was far from irrelevant, but in this industry everyone balanced on the knife's edge of celebrity. The bigger her team got in order to manage her prestige projects and growing stature, the more that team depended on Sam's work bringing in the kind of money and attention that fed the beast. Which was why she hadn't found a way to tell them that taking time away from her six weeks with Bex to schmooze with studio people and Bradley's team, talking at and around another Theomina project, was not something she wanted to do.

No one had asked if Sam wanted to. *Bradley* wanted her to.

Sam didn't doubt that after she showed up at his rustic abode there would be other things he wanted from her, one after the next, until her six weeks with Bex had broken up and disappeared like the surf when it hit the sand. But if she even attempted to refuse the meeting, her team would be thrown into a panic. There would be a leak expressing something along the lines of Sam's desire to leave show business. Bradley's people would either start planting shit pieces or assume she was playing hardball and offer more money, which she wouldn't be able to refuse once her people saw all the zeroes.

Sam had to go to Telluride. But she didn't have to think about it, much less mention it, until after she'd indulged in at least a few days' worth of quality time alone with the woman she loved.

"Sam?" Bex spoke her name with a hint of concern. "You're acting . . . I don't know. You're *acting*. What's up with you?"

Sam was staring through her car's windshield at the studio building, trying to figure out a way to convincingly answer this question, when the exit door opened and her costar, Chad Bevington, walked through it. He'd changed into plaid board shorts and a loose tank that showed off his waxed muscles. His luxurious blond hair system was styled in the same tousled waves he'd sported since he was twenty and could open any door in town.

A second man followed him out. The sunglasses and black fedora he wore combined with the man's slight, dancer-like stature to give Sam an instant sense-memory of the Juicy Couture perfume samples shoved inside the celebrity magazines she'd pored over as a preteen.

That was Sloan Lennox.

Sloan Lennox, walking out of the studio with Chad Bevington.

Sloan Lennox *talking* to Chad Bevington, with one of his habitual unfiltered Lucky Strike cigarettes pinched between his first finger and thumb (on a strictly no-smoking lot), gesturing to Chad with a trail of smoke fading in his wake.

"I'll be damned." Sam couldn't believe her eyes. Seeing the two of them together was like watching a long shot from the classic film *The Lights of Marfa*, which had made both of these men legendary.

Together, Chad and Sloan had anchored Hollywood's Ice Crew, a six-pack of gorgeous young celebrities who held court in the nineties from the Velvet Chair Lounge on Sunset Boulevard. Chad, Sloan, and a third leading man, Christian Stanstedt, became famous for their roles in various Tom Kessler productions opposite Ramona Watts, Macie Finn, and Juliette Draper.

But Chad and Sloan hadn't been photographed together for at least twenty years, and probably closer to thirty. Not since Juliette Draper drowned.

"You'll never guess what I'm looking at," Sam whispered. She didn't have to whisper—she was encased in an Audi Q8 with the air conditioning on full blast—but the gossip value of what she was staring at made whispering feel like the only appropriate response.

Or maybe it was Chad and Sloan's body language. There was something furtive in the way Sloan kept scanning the parked cars.

"What? What are you looking at?" Bex's impatience burned through the phone line.

"The Ice Crew, if you can believe it. Chad Bevington is in this very parking lot with Sloan Lennox. They're striding across the pavement like it's *Lights of Marfa* all over again. Sloan just flicked the butt of his cigarette at the pavement, skipping it like a goddamn stone on a pond."

"Oh my God!" Now Bex was whispering, too. "Send me a picture."

Chad and Sloan had stopped in the middle of the lot and were talking to each other. There was a lot of gesturing. Sam shot off a quick series of photos and sent them to Bex.

"Unreal!" Bex was still whispering, although her whisper was always more like a stage whisper. "Chad and Sloan *together*? They loathe each other! Their feud is legend! I was completely obsessed with the Ice Crew in high school. I watched *Karma Revisited* so many times I wore out the DVD, and my mom ended up buying it from Blockbuster. They were my moody teen ideal."

"I don't think they were teenagers when they did those movies. They're at least ten years older than us, and that's only if they're not lying about their ages, which Chad definitely is."

"But wasn't that part of the appeal? Depressive twenty-somethings wearing too much eyeliner, pretending to be my age. I went through a phase my sophomore year where I wore brocade vests with leotards exactly like Macie Finn. I *so* should've known I was queer. No one who was obsessed with Macie Finn turned out straight, that's for sure."

"I worked with Macie." Sam said this distractedly, absorbed with watching what was now a heated conversation. She took a few more pictures.

"Whaaat? How do I not know this?"

"They were a guest star on *Utopia*." Sam had started out in Hollywood in the ensemble cast of a hit sci-fi drama. She didn't miss the tight and shiny jumpsuits that costuming had made her wear for her role as a half-android, half-human starship captain, but it had been fun to work with a big ensemble cast and some truly remarkable guest stars.

Bex made a tiny squeal. "Tell me what Macie's like. Is all the dry humor real? Are they hotter in person? I feel like they would be hotter in person."

Sam laughed and was about to answer when she saw Sloan break away from Chad.

Then she saw Chad start walking toward her car.

No, *to* her car.

"Shit, Bex. I have to go. Text me when you're getting on a plane, any plane."

Sam hit the end button in the middle of Bex's "Okay," just as Chad gestured for her to put down her window.

"Hi there, Chad. What can I do for you?"

"Why are you sitting out here?" His eyes darted around the lot. There was nothing to see. She and Chad and Sloan were the only people on the roof of this parking garage, which no one could access but credentialed actors and studio employees. "Are you waiting for someone?"

"I'm listening to a podcast." The *Craven's Daughter* reunion special had involved Sam and Bex hosting what had become a notorious podcast, so Sam got asked about podcasts a lot by people who assumed she was an expert.

She was not. But Chad didn't know that.

The breeze lifted up the waves of his expensive hair, and he furrowed his eyebrows at her. There were tens of thousands of pictures of Chad Bevington making that same furrow between his brows, looking pained, yet artistic, yet hot.

"Did you see me talking to Sloan?" He said this offhandedly, glancing up at a seagull as though its screech had distracted him from his entirely trivial question.

Sam had spent enough time with Chad in front of a camera to know what he sounded like when he felt a situation had moved too far beyond his control for his comfort.

But why control this situation?

"I did spot you with Sloan," Sam decided to say. "I love to see a man find a style and stick to it. The fedora and sunglasses still work for him."

"Yeah. Whatever. I just mean we were having a private conversation."

He *was* trying to manage this. "And I was listening to a podcast." She raised her eyebrows as if to ask, *And why exactly are you making a giant deal out of this?*

Chad furtively scanned the lot one more time. Sloan stood fifteen feet away, both hands shoved in his pockets, looking like a cardboard cutout of himself.

"Yeah. Okay. I guess you can know. Obviously, I can trust you not to say anything."

Had that been a threat? Chad was still making an effort to sound casual, but he was also staring right at her, and one of his neck tendons was more prominent than usual. This was how he looked when he brought up his legal team. Sam raised her eyebrows again.

He sighed heavily. "Sloan and I did an episode of *The Howling* together."

It took Sam a few seconds to understand how this statement connected up to Chad's cloak-and-dagger paranoia. *The Howling* was a streamer-original horror series that had become an unexpected phenomenon in its first season due to the wry, winsome appeal of Ramona Watts, also formerly of the Ice Crew. Now filming its second season at StudioHonor with the full resources of Howell Motion Pictures behind it, *The Howling* was generating a lot of speculation regarding whether its star would fall apart under the pressure of her own success.

It was a pattern that had played out more than once for Ramona over the years.

Everyone knew *The Howling* kept a tight lid on its production secrets, but only Chad Bevington would treat a pre-airing nondisclosure agreement like a list of nuclear launch codes. "*The Howling*! Oh, wow. With Ramona?"

"Yeah, but shut up about it, right?" He scowled.

Sam mimed zipping her lips.

He looked at the sky again and then smacked the top of her car a couple of times. "Catch you at our pre-press."

When he walked away, Sam put up her window.

So strange.

People *were* strange with Sam, in part because she'd been an out lesbian in Hollywood for a very long time, in part because she was extremely tall, blond, and famous, and most recently because she was associated with solving a crime. While trying for a second chance on the *Craven's Daughter* reunion special, she and Bex had also used their TV detective skills to close the cold case of what had happened to their friend Jen, the show's makeup artist. On live television before a breathless audience of millions, they'd coaxed a confession from the man who killed Jen, setting off a firestorm of publicity and endless speculation.

The sleuthing adventure was a one-off, brought to their door by circumstances and old secrets Sam and Bex were particularly well-suited to investigate, given that the crime had happened on their show. But Sam couldn't say she had entirely put down a certain kind of *awareness* of undercurrents, obfuscation, and mysteries ever since.

It was fun to see how people in her professional life checked themselves a little harder and were less . . . *Hollywood* in her presence. Being a TV-detective-turned-detective made people assume Sam's bullshit meter was finely tuned. It warded off a lot of bullshit.

However, Sam thought, flipping through the stealth pictures she'd taken of Chad and Sloan, it would be disingenuous to claim she hadn't fantasized, since, of heading into a mystery again. It had been a good time to process through the clues with Bex and her sisters and to talk to people she might normally have never met. Interesting to set a bait in a trap and see what happened. Fascinating to track the aftermath as the case against Jen's killer wound its way through various pretrial motions on a slow path toward justice. All of it exercised Sam's mind and put her invisible youngest-of-five-siblings-and-only-girl powers to use.

Aaaaaand . . . she was distracting herself from the cocktail of feelings that had hit her system while talking to Bex, with Bex's arrival on the literal horizon. There were so many of these feelings. Sam was never sure which one was going to hit her at any given time.

If there was such a thing as love at first sight, then how Sam had felt about Bex the first time she met her was an argument in its favor. But Bex was right. Sam was being weird.

She was worried.

They were kidding themselves to count on getting six weeks together when six months apart was much more the norm for a Hollywood couple. Something always came up in this business—callbacks, reshoots, "amazing opportunities" that had to be seized before they were gone in a flash. Even now, there were half a dozen emails from Bradley's people sitting on Sam's phone, flagging up all kinds of details to review before she was supposed to be on his plane seven days from now, on her way to his rustic mountain retreat to talk about his agenda in front of his people.

It was how the game was played with someone like Bradley Wilhite. He would monopolize her time and make her come to him because he *could*. How else could Sam appreciate how big his dick was?

Men in this town could be exhausting.

Not to mention that Sam's brother Fergus was hogging her guest room, which meant she and Bex had no guarantee of privacy at Sam's, and Bex had her sister Vic living at home, with Frankie road-tripping her way west from her New York internship and arriving in a handful of days.

She and Bex were busy people with busy lives.

Six months ago, Sam would've said she liked it that way.

With a sigh, she pulled out of her spot to head home and execute Bex's plan. She trusted Bex's plans. Bex's plans had gotten them this far, and Sam had no reason not to believe that if they stayed the course, everything would get good, and easy, and they could just be Bex and Sam, always.

All they had to do was make it to the part where they were in the same room at the same time. After that, there would be nothing to worry about.

She was sure of it.

Visit our website at
KensingtonBooks.com
to sign up for our newsletters, read
more from your favorite authors, see
books by series, view reading group
guides, and more!

Become a Part of Our
Between the Chapters Book Club
Community and Join the Conversation

Betweenthechapters.net

Submit your book review for a chance to win exclusive
Between the Chapters swag you can't get anywhere else!
https://www.kensingtonbooks.com/pages/review/